What rea

FIVE STARS! "Loved this book!!! Another page-turner by talented Burgess and Neuman, my new favorite authors!!! I loved reading this book. It was very heartwarming in so many ways!!! Ready to read the next book from this writing duo!!!"

FIVE STARS! "I love these authors. I love the real feelings, thoughts, words, actions, etc., that they give to their characters. I love that it feels like a memoir instead of fiction. I love that it depressed me. I want to say so much more about what I loved, but I don't want to give too much away. A classic story that draws your emotions out of you to make you root for it to go one way, then in the next chapter, make a U-turn; just like the main character. It makes you reflect on your own life and happiness. It makes you check your husband's e-mails and credit card statements. I simply love your writing, ladies. Can't wait for the next one."

FIVE STARS! "I couldn't put it down! Great book! Maybe I could relate with the main character too much, but I felt as though she was my friend. When I wasn't reading the book, the main character was constantly on my mind! The ending was unpredictable in a great way! I think the authors need to keep on writing! I'm a huge fan!"

FIVE STARS! "Delightful! I so enjoyed my time with Jessie. I laughed with her, and ached for her. I knew her so well so quickly. I'll remember her story with a smile. I hope these authors keep it coming. What a fun read!"

FIVE STARS! "Love these writers!! So refreshing to have writers who really create such characters you truly understand and relate to. Looking forward to the next one. Definitely my favorites!"

FIVE STARS! "This book is about a woman's life torn apart . . . A lot of detail as to how she would feel . . . very well-written. I have to agree with the other readers, 5 stars."

FIVE STARS! "What a fun read *Dressing Myself* was! . . . I didn't expect the ending . . . It was hard to put this book down."

FIVE STARS! "Great, easy, captivating read!! The characters seem so real! I don't read a lot, but I was really into this one! Read it for sure!"

FIVE STARS! "Wonderful book! A fast read because once you start, you just cannot put it down; the characters become like your family! Definitely a worthwhile read!"

FIVE STARS! "Loved it! Read this in one day. Enjoyed every page and had a real feeling for all of the characters. I was rooting for Jessie all the way. . . . Hope there's another story like this down the road."

FIVE STARS! "*Dressing Myself* deals with an all-too-common problem of today in a realistic manner that is sometimes sad, sometimes hopeful, as befits the subject. My expectation of the ending seesawed back and forth as the book progressed. I found it an interesting, engaging read with fully developed characters."

FIVE STARS! "It has been a long time since I have read a book cover to cover in one day . . . fantastic read . . . real page-turner that was hard to put down . . . Thanks, Ladies!"

Dressing Myself

Rosalind Burgess
and
Patricia Obermeier Neuman

Cover by

Laura Eshelman Neuman

Copyright © 2014
Rosalind Burgess
and
Patricia Obermeier Neuman
All rights reserved.
ISBN-13: 978-0692328972
ISBN-10: 0692328971
www.roz-patty.com

Blake Oliver Publishing
BlakeOliverPublishing@gmail.com
This is a work of fiction.

Also by
Rosalind Burgess
and
Patricia Obermeier Neuman

The Val & Kit Mystery Series

The Disappearance of Mavis Woodstock

The Murder of Susan Reed

Death in Door County

Lethal Property

Palm Desert Killing

Foreign Relations

Acknowledgments

Thanks to our beta readers for their careful reading—and for convincing us they enjoyed it so much they had to reread just to look for errors. And thanks for finding those errors so our future readers don't have to. We really appreciate you, Betty Obermeier, Sarah Paschall, Kerri Neuman Hunt, Melissa Neuman Tracy, and Laura Eshelman Neuman.

To everyone who's been there, done that,
bought the T-shirt,
and then cut it into a million pieces . . .

Dressing Myself

CHAPTER ONE

I drove to the airport wearing a trench coat. Underneath, I was naked. I felt like a thousand-dollar-a-night hooker, and I was ready to do to my husband whatever a thousand bucks bought these days.

My plan had something to do with being married to the same man for twenty-eight years. Kevin had been in New York on business for a week, and my idea was to inject a little excitement into our marriage. It was already working for me. The silky lining of the coat caressing my naked skin felt very naughty. I couldn't wait to see my husband's reaction.

He wasn't expecting me to pick him up; he'd told me on the phone the night before that he'd catch a ride home with one of his sales reps. My excitement mounted as I pictured the surprise on his face when he saw me there.

Even though our relationship was loving, the years had taken a toll, and it had been a long time since we'd been enthralled by one another. In the early years of our marriage, we'd always surprised each other on holidays or birthdays or sometimes for no reason at all. We didn't have a lot of money back then, so what we came up with was fun and, most important, cheap.

The first Halloween we were married, Kevin strung tiny baby ghosts made from toilet tissue all over our apartment. And one Valentine's Day when money was still tight, I sneaked out of the house early in the morning, before Kevin woke up, and drew red-lipstick heart shapes all over the windows of his old Buick. He'd kill me now if I tried that on his Porsche.

As Kevin's career in chemical sales spiraled upward, leaving money shortages behind us, our gifts to each other grew more expensive and a lot less inventive. In fact, since my birthday was coming up, I was willing to bet Kevin had ordered something from Tiffany's. It would no doubt be fabulous and grossly expensive, and when it arrived, I would swoon over the small blue box wrapped in white ribbon. But no way would it be as exciting as the little surprise I had planned for him.

Just getting ready for my little escapade had been fun. The house rang with Van Morrison singing "Have I Told You Lately That I Love You" while I bathed in Dior's J'adore Body Milk and sprayed myself with the same fragrance.

This was my new favorite scent. I loved the way the model in the commercial, dressed in gold, strutted toward the camera, stripping as she moved forward. In fact, after much hinting on my part, Kevin might have bought this for me last Valentine's Day, but in the end he gave me a gift card from Macy's and told me to buy myself something I wanted. I told him I'd get the fancy new coffee maker I'd been eyeing, but at the last minute I stopped at the perfume counter and picked up the J'adore. He didn't notice my new sensual smell, or the old coffee maker still in use.

Carefully applying my makeup before heading to the airport, I recalled all the times Kevin had proclaimed it such an unnecessary ritual. "You don't need makeup," he'd say. Yeah, right. Maybe twenty years ago. But I noticed the only times he ever said I looked tired, or even sick, were when I gave Mother Nature no assistance.

After spraying a little additional perfume on my neck, I gave a quick spritz across my stomach and slipped into my coat. My final touch was a pair of four-inch black pumps. My daughter had insisted I buy them a few months ago, assuring me they were sexy and Dad would love them. So far, Dad had never seen me in them.

I made my way down the winding staircase of our spacious two-story. Treading gingerly through the kitchen, which was awash in the white dust of renovation and strewn with boxes holding the contents of 1990s-era cupboards that had been stripped from the walls, I made my way out to the garage and my white Jeep Grand Cherokee.

As I headed out of Carmel for the freeway that would lead me to the Indianapolis International Airport and the rendezvous with my unsuspecting husband, I reached in my purse for my phone to call Merritt. I talked to my daughter almost every day and my harder-to-reach son only slightly less often, usually from my cell phone. Even though my hectic life had all but halted the past few years, it remained my nature to accomplish at least two tasks at a time.

Just as I was changing my mind about calling Merritt now, thinking how terrible it would be to have even a minor fender bender, half-naked as I was, the phone in my hand began to ring.

"Are you doing it?" It was Ellen, my neighbor, my confidante, my best friend.

"Yes," I said proudly. Then "*Yes*," again, like I was doing something for women everywhere.

"Good for you."

"Gotta go."

"Call me later."

"I'll call you tomorrow. Not before."

"Tramp." I heard her laugh.

"Thank you," I answered, as I shut off my phone.

I returned my thoughts to Kevin, imagining his reaction when I told him I had nothing on underneath my new Burberry coat. He was going to love it.

Kevin had always had a higher sex drive than I, and a greater penchant for anything different. Although he'd never actually come out and said it, I knew my lack of initiative disappointed him. He'd be astounded but thrilled at my newfound sexual aggression.

And just thinking about the intense arousal that would create in him aroused feelings in me, feelings that at first I thought I'd *never* had. *Why had I waited so long to be daring?* I wondered. It felt so good.

But as I drove through the gentle rain, the wipers swishing as if in time to the music from my favorite radio station, I recalled the days before we were married. In those days I had indeed ached for the time Kevin and I could share a bed and each other's bodies as often and as freely as we wanted.

Before I could replay in my mind how we'd gotten from then to now, I reached the airport exit. A glance at the clock told me I was right on schedule. Kevin's plane had landed five minutes ago. I pulled into an empty parking spot and made my way toward the terminal, my stomach aflutter and my legs feeling as weak as a newborn baby's.

It was unusually crowded. The passengers spilled from the terminal, and at last my husband was one of them. I saw him before he saw me. He carried his confident aura of success with him as consistently as he carried his classically featured face and lean six-foot frame. I felt a thrill lift my stomach toward my heart. It was partly my attire—or lack thereof—and partly the sight of him. His thick, graying blond hair contrasted with his deep golfer's tan, offsetting icy blue eyes that demanded appreciative attention even from a distance.

Chatting amiably with two of his sales reps and the young woman I slowly remembered as a company attorney,

Kevin didn't notice me at first. I watched as his lips parted in laughter, displaying his even, white teeth and accentuating the cleft in his chin.

I stood taller to capture his attention, the ridiculous heels making me feel like an Amazon, though what I suddenly wanted to do was slink down before any of them spotted me. It hadn't occurred to me I might see anyone else I knew, however slightly. At first this made my nakedness seem more brazen than brave, more sleazy than sexy.

But as I moved into their path, Kevin's eyes met mine, and my lips formed a sultry smile. I dug my hands deep into the pockets of my coat as I approached him, leaning in with upturned face for a kiss.

And suddenly, knowing I had an audience, I felt more desirable than ever.

"Jessie! Jessie, what are you doing here? You know everyone—Jim, Rick, Taylor." My normally unflappable husband was nonplussed, and I hadn't even told him of my nakedness yet or hinted at the night that lay before him.

"Yes, hi," I said, nodding my head in greeting to each in turn. Then I took Kevin's free hand and laced my fingers through his. "I just wanted to surprise you," I said softly, looking up into his puzzled eyes and insinuating my body against his seductively.

By now I was oblivious to the other three. I stood on tiptoe and whispered into my husband's ear. "I'm not wearing anything underneath this trench coat. Welcome home."

But it was I, not Kevin, who was shocked. I failed to predict his reaction as surely as the weatherman had failed to forecast this unseasonably cool June weather we were having.

"Jessie." He withdrew his hand from mine as abruptly as if I'd just said I had infectious hepatitis. His eyes glanced furtively in the direction of his coworkers, who remained intent on their own discussion. "What are you doing? What are you thinking?" It was the same tone he used with Teddy whenever the subject of our son's bartending job came up. Then, as if sensing my discomfort, Kevin said, "It's just . . . it's just that . . . I need to talk to you. Seriously."

It didn't even occur to me to wonder what serious subject he had to discuss with me. My cheeks and ears burned in embarrassment as I felt a breeze blow up my bare legs. I watched as he bid a hurried farewell to the sales reps and attorney. I pretended not to notice as they waved halfheartedly in my direction and headed toward the shuttle-bus stop, leaving Kevin and me alone.

Slinging his three-suiter over one shoulder and his briefcase over the other, he took my elbow in one of the large, capable hands that had always represented security and safety for me and began to guide me in a no-nonsense way toward the parking lot.

Wresting control of my elbow—and the situation, I hoped—I moved ahead of him, hoping he'd notice my slightly swaying backside and my tan, bare legs as I led the way. I climbed into the passenger side of the Jeep, playing those legs for all they were worth and hoping they looked sexy. Recollections of Kevin's past remarks—*you've got great legs* and *I love your ass*—ran through my mind, and I defied him not to appreciate the view.

But I also recalled how I'd taken such comments for granted through the years. As if to make amends for that, I reached for him as he climbed in the driver's side. "Do I get a hello kiss?" I asked, putting my arms around his neck and pulling his face toward mine. I was reminded of the times I had tried to check a loose tooth in Merritt's or Teddy's mouth. That's how cooperative my husband was.

"Okay." I released him before our lips touched. "What is it?"

"We need to talk."

"So talk."

"Not here," he said. *You imbecile*, he didn't say, but once again his tone did. I wondered how long he might have been talking to me like that without my even noticing. Minutes? Weeks? Years?

Still stunned by the contrast between reality and the daydream I'd harbored all week, I watched him start the engine. This was not at all how I'd imagined it would play out.

By now Kevin was supposed to be drooling all over me.

He pulled away from the curb in silence. That deafening silence you read about all the time. When he started to pull into the Holiday Inn parking lot by the airport, I found my voice—and my backbone. "Why are you stopping here?"

"We need to talk. I thought we could go in here and have a drink."

As much as I dreaded the half-hour drive home before hearing what he had to say, there was no way I was going to sit in a public place in nakedness that my husband could, to my chagrin, so easily resist. "Kevin, if you think I'm going in there . . . like this . . . you're crazy. You can tell me whatever it is you have to tell me right now, right here."

I steeled myself for the pronouncement that we would be moving. I'd been through that before, and this is how it went. "We have to be in Timbuktu in six weeks," he'd say, and in just that short a time I would find myself far from the life I'd grown comfortable with.

It had been a long time—twenty years—since our last transfer, which had brought us from our roots in Minnesota via stints in Chicago and Michigan. Since that time, we had agreed to turn down two promotions but had both known we would face the company's request again. Only now, kids grown and settled—at least one of them, the other showing no signs of *ever* settling—we'd run out of excuses.

Nevertheless, even as Kevin parked the Jeep and tried to coax me into the Holiday Inn, I was already thinking of some new reasons we couldn't move. "Just tell me now," I repeated.

He heaved a sigh, drumming his fingers on the steering wheel and looking at the dashboard as if at cue cards. "I want a divorce, Jessie."

I couldn't have been any more shocked than if my husband of decades, my high school sweetheart, the father of our two children, my soul mate, had told me he wanted a sex change. "Is there someone else?" I asked, after what seemed an eternity, but what I really meant was, *who is she?*

"No. There's no one else. It's not that at all. It's just that . . ."

"What, then?" I asked, like a child not understanding something an adult was telling me.

"Jessie, it's not working anymore. You know it isn't. If you're honest."

"Honest? I don't understand," I said, incredulous.

"Okay." He sounded firm, ready to convince me. "Are you happy? Come on, admit it; you're not happy, are you? Neither one of us is happy."

"I'm happy," I said in a small voice that grew louder as I repeated, "I'm *happy!*" This wasn't happening. Why was I having to convince my own husband I was happy? Feeling sick, I watched him stare at the dashboard. "Tell me what it is, Kevin. Are you depressed about something? Is it your job? I know the pressure is unbearable sometimes, but—"

"It's not my job, dammit, it's . . ."

I silently finished his sentence, acutely aware, all of a sudden, of the hundreds of evenings we'd spent in the same house alone since Teddy had left for college, physically together but worlds apart, he at the television or mired in paperwork, me on the phone or at the computer working on my latest assignment. Was it just too boring for him? Was *I* too boring?

"Let's go away together," I suggested brightly, trying to stifle the desperation I felt. "Let's go somewhere really fun. Europe, or the Caribbean. You can play golf and—"

He interrupted me with a sardonic laugh. His face looked angry, and I suddenly wanted to smash it. "Golf," he said. "The last time we were in California, you bitched every time you looked at my golf clubs."

"Okay, you can play golf every fucking day, for all I care."

"I just need some space, Jess." His voice was softer and kinder now.

I found myself remembering my words to Merritt when her first boyfriend broke her heart with the age-old male whine of needing more space: "When someone says they need more space, tell them to move to Montana," I'd urged, all but forbidding her to wheedle or cry. I tried to take my own advice now, but instead I said, "You can do better than that, Kevin." And I truly hoped he could.

"I'm sorry, Jess, but that's what it comes down to."

"You disappoint me."

"Yeah, well, you should be used to that by now. I think I've disappointed you a lot."

"Really? Why do you think that?"

"Come on, admit it. You know that's how you feel."

"Stop telling me how I feel. You have no idea how I feel!" I was yelling now, aware that what I felt was fear at the prospect of being alone for the first time in my life. Gone was the feeling of lust I'd worn to the airport in lieu of clothes. The mere thought of that seemed sordid and disgusting. "Take me home," I said.

"Jessie, I don't want to hurt you." Kevin put a hand on my shoulder, and I roughly shrugged it away. He made it sound so simple. The cereal box is empty, so let's toss it out. The TV's too small; let's buy a bigger one. Did you just throw out a life and start over when the old one didn't suit you anymore?

I felt raw with humiliation, as naked as if I were not wearing even the trench coat. "Take me home," I repeated through clenched teeth. Then, more loudly, I said, "No, just get out. Get out right now, right here. I don't need you to take me home. I don't want you to take me home. I don't want you, period." My tears belied my tough talk, but I couldn't stop myself.

I'd never seen Kevin look so helpless. "I'll call you tomorrow." He scrambled to get out of the car. I could feel my fear threatening to overwhelm me, but I refused to give in to it just then. Retrieving his things from the back, he spoke once more. "I'll be staying here tonight, at the Holiday Inn."

Still feeling responsible to me, needing to apprise me of his whereabouts, I thought, as he slammed the door shut. How would we ever break such timeworn habits? And why did we have to? Numb, yet smarting at the same time, I climbed awkwardly over the steering column and into the driver's seat. I wasn't about to get out of my vehicle again until I reached the safety of my own garage.

So that's how it goes. A million years of marriage, and then it's all over in a five-minute conversation.

It was a long drive home. The seemingly interminable half hour gave me too much time to realize all that was wrong in our marriage.

Still, I wondered how he could so easily dismiss our history and forego our plans for the future—the motor home we were going to buy upon his retirement, for example, so he could satisfy his wanderlust while I wrote my way across the country on my laptop.

Guess he couldn't wait until retirement to start satisfying that wanderlust, to forge a new life, I mused, anger returning to supplant my humiliation. But better that than another woman, I consoled myself. Wanderlust I could maybe compete against or join forces with. Another woman would leave no hope, because even if Kevin would later want to reconcile, I wouldn't.

By the time I pulled into our driveway, however, I felt certain there had to be another woman. Why else would he be doing this? It had been only a year—on Merritt's wedding day—since he'd sent me those yellow roses, with the note that her wedding was reminding him how special *our* marriage was. How could he go from that to this—unless some other woman had come along?

I could hear Kevin himself say, of other breakups, that there *had* to be someone else, that people didn't just want a divorce. I hadn't agreed with him then, and I fought against it now. He'd done the hard part, presumably, asking for a divorce; why would he need to lie?

And why, I wondered as I entered the house through the back door and made my way through the kitchen, *would he get us involved in this renovation mess if he was just going to divorce me?* The new island looked as alone and strange as I felt, with its gaping hole awaiting the installation of the granite sink Kevin and I had so painstakingly chosen just six months ago.

But then my empty feeling filled again with rage. A Jessie I never knew existed picked up the new light fixture the electrician had left in the corner on the floor and hurled it across the room. It landed on the other side, and I heard the glass shatter when it hit the floor.

Climbing the stairs to our bedroom, I determined there couldn't possibly be another woman. I couldn't bear it. Besides, if there was, Kevin would have gone to her tonight; he wouldn't have stayed at the Holiday Inn.

I tore off my trench coat, pulling the sleeves inside out as I ripped it from my body. It was a revolting thing that I had to get away from as quickly as possible.

As I watched it land in a heap on the carpet, I felt humiliated all over again about my stupid attempt to seduce my husband.

I slipped into my paint-stained navy-blue sweats and a T-shirt, by now feeling as if I would go crazy if I didn't talk to Kevin, if I didn't try again to find out what was going on. Torn between the desire to scream at him and the urge to beg him to forget his crazy notion of a divorce and come home, I decided to call him. I didn't know what I'd say, but I sure as hell wasn't going to sleep tonight with all that had been left *un*said.

When I got no answer from his cell phone, I looked up the number of the hotel, desperation clawing at my insides as I continued to ignore everything I'd ever told Merritt about giving anyone space. To hell with space. Kevin was my *husband*, after all, not some passing teenage fancy.

As I dialed the number, I recalled the thousands of times over the years I had called Kevin while he was on the road. *Merritt fell off her bike; Teddy brought home a new friend last night; my dad just went into the hospital—come home.* He was always there, always at the other end. No matter what city he was in, we were always connected. Now Kevin had cut that cord without asking my permission. He'd just gone ahead and done it, and I'd never felt so alone in my entire life.

"Kevin Harleman's room, please," I said to the hotel operator, with a sureness I was trying my hardest to feel. *I shouldn't have told him to get out of the car*, I thought in panic. *I should have gone in at the Holiday Inn and had a drink. Maybe there was some problem I didn't give him a chance to mention. We could have at least talked it over.*

After a pause the friendly voice asked me to spell that, please. Then, after an even longer pause, I heard the words I most dreaded. "I'm sorry, but we have no Kevin Harleman here. Maybe he hasn't checked in yet?"

CHAPTER TWO

"Who are you?" I peered out at the man standing on my front doorstep. A complete stranger.

"Hector Dennehey." He tipped his baseball cap, an old-fashioned gesture that showed a courtesy I hadn't experienced for a long time. For some reason, it made me think of my father, who had been dead for nearly ten years. "Mrs. Harleman?" he said.

"Yes."

"The cabinets? I'm here about your kitchen cabinets."

"Oh." I opened the door wider to give him full access to my house, my body, my life. Never mind all I'd read about not letting ax murderers into your home.

"I thought Jeff was doing the work," I muttered. And even then, I still didn't have the slightest suspicion that this stranger had perhaps already murdered Jeff and was now planning the same for me.

"Jeff quit."

"Really?" I asked, this being all the information I needed to let a total stranger into my home. "Then you'd better come in. You work with Jeff, do you?"

"Used to." He laughed. His face was nice, I decided. But didn't all serial killers have nice faces?

I let this guy's pleasant face pass me into the hallway, but finally getting smart, I kept the front door open. Across the street, Ellen's husband was washing his car, and I waved frantically at him. "Steve! Good morning!" I yelled. At least now there would be someone who could identify the murderer.

"I doubt he can hear you." Hector Dennehey now stood behind me.

"What do you mean?"

"Your neighbor." His muscular arm reached past me. A callused hand pointed across the street. "See? He's wearing earbuds."

Indeed, I saw the telltale wires flowing down from his ears. "Oh well, at least he saw you . . . I mean me. Us."

"You know, Mrs. Harleman, you should be more careful about who you let into your house." He began fishing in the pocket of his T-shirt and handed me a business card.

"Ah," I said, reading carefully. *Dennehey Custom Cabinets*. "Says here you're the owner."

"That's right. Jeff worked more *for* me than *with* me."

"Well, he was very good. Are you as good?"

He laughed again. "I better be. I taught him everything he knows."

"Why'd he quit?"

"Personal stuff. I didn't pry. Look, Mrs. Harleman, would you like me to come back when your husband's home?"

I stared hard at him in silence, and I know my mouth dropped open. But I couldn't think of an answer. Except that maybe that might be a very long time. Kevin had been gone for more than two weeks now. On the other hand, he might be home tonight. Or tomorrow. "I . . ."

"Are you okay?"

"Yes . . . I'm fine. Why would you ask me that?"

"It's just . . . I don't know. Look, if this isn't convenient . . . I mean, if you'd rather do this another time, you've got my number; just call me." He was already backing out the door, tentatively, as if *I* were a murderer.

"Yes, perhaps that would be better. I'm . . . it's just that today . . ."

"Hey." He raised his hands, showing me his palms. "No problem. I'm in no rush. You just call."

"Thank you. I will."

As he stepped back out into the bright sunshine, I noticed his beard. Close-cropped and tidy, it was mostly gray and made him look older than he probably was. Like a false beard with loops that went around his ears.

"Hey, Jessie, how ya doin'?"

We both turned toward Steve, who had taken out his earbuds and put his green hose down on the driveway.

"Oh hell," I said to Hector Dennehey. "He's coming over. I have to go."

"No problem." He turned toward his black Ford truck.

"You and Kevin see that game last night?" Steve called. He was definitely on his way over.

"No. Kevin is out of town. Can't talk; gotta run."

Hector Dennehey caught my eye from behind the steering wheel of his monster vehicle. *Oh great, so now he knows I'm here alone.* But as he started to back down the driveway, he winked at me. Once again I was reminded of my father and his twinkling eyes when he was teasing my sister or me. I suddenly missed him more than anything else in the world. Even more than Kevin.

After closing the door, shutting out both the cabinetmaker and my friend—Kevin's friend?—Steve, my hand lingered on the doorknob as I fought the urge to open it back up and yell to Steve for help. Maybe he could talk to

Kevin, bring him back to his senses, bring him back home to me. Or maybe I could just cry on Steve's shoulder. Two weeks was a long time to be in agony, with no one to comfort me.

I knew I was probably being foolish, but I just hadn't been able to tell anyone that Kevin had left me. I almost did, of course, the very next morning when Ellen had called. After all, I told Ellen everything.

But this was something too horrible, and besides, I felt certain it was temporary. It had to be. So when she asked how my romantic tryst with my husband had gone, her voice full of envy and admiration, I'd started the lies.

It was as if saying the truth aloud would make it irrevocably true. Not to mention it was too embarrassing; and if Kevin did come back, I would have shared my humiliation needlessly. For the rest of our lives, people would think of us as the couple who almost split. They would be watching us, expecting us to break up again any minute. My pride couldn't bear that.

"Kevin didn't come home, after all," I told my friend the truth. And then, because I knew she'd ask why, I offered up my first lie. "His work in New York's taking longer than expected." My fabrication sounded totally transparent to my own ears, but Ellen had no reason to doubt me.

"Bummer. Well, you can just consider last night a dress rehearsal. Or should we say *un*dress rehearsal?" She laughed at her own joke, usually one of my favorite qualities about Ellen. She had a good sense of humor, and no one appreciated it more than she did. She also had an infectious laugh that could always lift my spirits and draw me in. But not that morning.

So over the next two weeks I avoided her. And when she called to schedule their turn to host gourmet club, our group of six couples—none of them divorced—who met once a month for dinner, I told her Kevin had a work function we had to attend.

"Then we'll just pick another weekend," she said.

"No. Don't do that. I mean, we have such a hectic summer. Don't wait for us." I quickly made some excuse to get off the phone, just as I made excuses to avoid talking to her the other times she'd called these past two weeks. And I never went out the front door, for fear I'd run into her.

I went back to my computer now, where my screen saver had produced a never-ending series of bubbles, each floating across the screen and inevitably bursting when it hit the side, only to be replaced by another.

I hit the space bar, and my article magically appeared. It wasn't much of an article, though. In fact, it wasn't an article at all. I'd been working on it for three days now, but all I really had was the title. And even that didn't feel right. "What's New in Skin Care?" *What the hell did it matter?*

I must have stared at the screen for exactly five minutes, because the bubbles reappeared. This was my cue to shut off my computer and go downstairs.

The worst part was trying to figure out what I was supposed to do with myself. I had racked my brain trying to remember what it was I actually did before. By now my life had cleverly rearranged itself into halves: before Kevin left and after.

I had always been busy. But what was all that stuff that never quite got finished because I just didn't have time? I glanced at my Gucci watch, an anniversary present from Kevin, then unfastened its black leather strap and threw it onto the coffee table. It was only eleven o'clock.

So far today I had drunk five thousand cups of coffee, overplucked my eyebrows, stared for a long time at the half-renovated kitchen, polished all my black shoes, read every word of *People* magazine (the British Royal family was eagerly awaiting a new baby), cleaned out my purse, removed Kevin's picture from my wallet, and then put it back in again. What *was* I going to do for the rest of the day? And this weekend? And the rest of my life?

No, no, no, I thought. *He'll be back. If not for the weekend, at least for the rest of my life. He wouldn't want to miss that.* Now I was crying again. Large, blobby tears that I knew made my face look ugly and red.

I began wandering around the house, a pattern I'd formed in the last two weeks. Past the coffee table that I had picked and Kevin didn't like much. Past the ugly ceramic figurine his mother had given us nearly ten years ago that didn't match anything in our home but had some sentimental value to him. And past our beautiful dove-white sofa that Teddy had spilled beer on the first time he sat on it. (Kevin had gotten mad at Ted's carelessness, while I felt secretly happy for the chance to test the Scotchgard we'd paid extra for. Especially since it did indeed work.)

Then, upstairs. Past Merritt's room—now my office—all pink and soft and feminine, just like her, and except for the addition of my desk, hardly changed from when she lived at home. I wiped the tears away from my face, closing the door behind me before traveling on down the hall toward our bedroom. Kevin's and mine. There was his exercise bike, with two shirts still hanging over the handlebars.

On my side of the dresser stood a photograph of the two of us taken last year at Merritt's wedding. We looked great, if I did say so myself. Kevin wore a black tux and resembled, as everyone always told him, Matthew McConaughey. I wore a black sequined Ann Taylor dress that was elegant and made me look slim and young.

I tried hard to remember what I was thinking when that picture was taken. Was I happy? Was he happy? We certainly looked the part. And he'd sent me those flowers that morning. Yes, we were happy. Then. I laid the silver frame facedown on the dresser, not wanting to get rid of the picture but not wanting to look at it, either.

On his side of the dresser stood various bottles of cologne. All where they should be, except for his Hugo Boss. It was his favorite men's cologne, and mine too. He'd taken that with him when he'd come back, briefly, four days ago.

That had been a ghastly experience. Frustrated that I'd missed him when he finally came for his car the previous week, I spent a good part of the day thinking up some reason to call him. Finally, I settled on a fictitious rattling sound in my Jeep—Kevin prided himself on knowing a lot about cars. He reluctantly agreed to stop by on his way home. (Where *was* home these days? I didn't have the courage to ask him.)

He breezed into our house, looking like an irritated stranger. He went straight out to the garage, listened to the car for about two seconds, and even though I knew there was nothing whatsoever wrong with it, diagnosed a muffler problem that I should get fixed. I felt worse than I had when he'd told me he wanted a divorce. For the first time in twenty-eight years he had suggested I take my car to an outsider, without even bothering to first rebuild the engine himself.

Then he dashed upstairs to "collect a few things," and I noticed he had actually brought a leather Tumi bag with him. I'd never seen the bag before, and I was consumed with where it came from. I was frightened to see him with something I knew nothing about. If he could have an expensive leather bag that was so foreign to me, he could have a whole life I knew nothing about.

I realized later that my weak excuse for getting him to come over had actually saved him the awkwardness of having to ask permission to come. I shouldn't have made it so easy for him. And what had hurt the most was that he couldn't wait to leave. That and the fact that we had nothing to say to each other. We'd spent decades together, raised our kids, buried our parents, slow-danced at our daughter's wedding, and now we had nothing, absolutely nothing, to say.

I was expecting so much more. Expecting him to realize the minute he saw me, or the house, or *something*, that he'd made a stupid mistake, and then beg me to forget all about it. But he had just stuffed that damn bag with who-knows-what and run out the door no more than five minutes later.

Most of his clothes (but not his really good ones, I noticed) still hung in his closet. I could cut all the sleeves off his suits and shirts. Or I could bundle everything up and give it to The Salvation Army. But then what would I do when he did come back, and he had nothing to wear? If I started to destroy things, then any hope I had would be destroyed too.

I looked up now at my face in the mirror and immediately wished I hadn't. I looked awful. Red, swollen eyes. Puffy skin. My hair pulled back in a greasy ponytail. *That's it*, I told myself; *get it together*.

Suddenly I felt I had a mission.

Almost chirpy, with something I really wanted to *do* for the first time in two weeks, I hurried to the bathroom and started the water running in the oversize tub. I needed to be fixed up. The way I normally was. That person in the mirror wasn't me; I had to get rid of her.

I bathed, washed my long brown hair so its reddish highlights would reappear, and put on a pair of J.Crew shorts and a chambray shirt. I applied my makeup and went from chirpy to practically breezy by the time I descended the stairs.

Yes, I felt better. I retrieved my watch from the coffee table. Even if Kevin had given it to me, I still loved it. I was almost whistling by the time I went back to the kitchen, but then felt immediately depressed again at the sight of its unfinished state. And the fact that it was now only noon. What *do* people do all day?

I was back at my computer counting bubbles when the phone rang. *It's Kevin*, I whispered to one of the bubbles before it burst. *I know it is*. I reached for the receiver, bravely not checking caller ID.

"Mom?"

"Who is this?"

"Mom! How many daughters do you have?"

"Merritt, honey, I'm sorry. I'm so engrossed in this article, I can't even think straight."

"I don't want to disturb you if you're working, but I need to talk to you." My sweet Merritt. She was so much from my side of the family.

"No, honey, I need a break. What's up?" I actually raised my arms and stretched, as if I really had been working.

"Well," Merritt said coyly. "Alec and I have news. Pretty exciting news."

I said nothing, waiting for her to continue. My mind was racing ahead, making me dizzy. If only Kevin would come back soon, immediately, Merritt and Ted need never know there had been any trouble between their parents. But one of the kids was bound to ask any time now where their father was. It was another reason for me to be furious with Kevin, for putting me in this situation.

"Mom, did you hear what I said?"

"Sorry, honey, my printer is buzzing. I didn't catch it."

"Mom, we're going to have a baby!"

Again, I said nothing. But this time my mind had stopped working entirely. Hundreds of bubbles had been born on my screen and died seconds later.

"Are you there, Mom?"

"Yes, darling," I said. "Merritt, I—"

"I know Dad's probably at work, and Alec wanted to wait until we could tell you together; but oh, Mom, I couldn't wait. I just did the pregnancy test—twice—and there are definitely two lines. I'm so excited! I told Alec I was going to call you first—"

"Honey, that's wonderful. Wonderful news."

"Do you want to call Dad, or should I? Or should we just come over this evening and surprise him? Or do you both want to come here, or—"

"Dad's out of town."

"Oh." I could hear the disappointment in her voice. "When will he be home?"

"I'm not sure. I think this trip will be longer than usual."

"Okay, then let's call him. You come over for dinner tonight, and we'll call him—"

"No. Why don't you let me tell him? I'm not sure where he's staying, but he'll call."

"Well, come over for dinner, anyway."

"No, darling. I've got so much to do. How about we get together this weekend? Don't worry about Dad. I'll get in touch with him somehow and let him know the wonderful news."

"Mom, you sound as though he's run off." She laughed her tinkling laugh, so like her grandfather, and I wanted more than anything to take her in my arms and hold her close. I wanted to save her from being hurt by anything, ever.

"Don't be silly. He's just moving around. You have a romantic dinner with Alec, and I'll call you tomorrow."

"Okay, Mom. Are you pleased? Really?"

"Oh, Merritt, I'm thrilled. I couldn't be more thrilled. And Daddy will be too."

"I hope so."

"Merritt!" I was flabbergasted. "Of course he will be."

"Well, you know how he is."

"What do you mean?"

"You know. About getting old. He hates the idea. And being a grandfather—well, he might not like that."

"Merritt, you think he hates getting old?" I was as shocked as if she'd said he hated playing golf.

"Mom, you know he does. He's not like you. It drives him crazy."

I had to think about that. Certainly, age had never bothered me, but I'd never noticed it bothering Kevin, either. "Merritt, you're being silly. Daddy will be as thrilled as I am."

"If you say so. You know him best."

"Precisely," I lied. I knew nothing about the man. He was sporting strange luggage, and I couldn't even hold a five-minute conversation with him.

"Okay," Merritt said in a singsong. "Gotta go. I love you."

"I love you too."

CHAPTER THREE

In the four days since I had spoken to Kevin, the hurt I felt had taken on a life of its own, threatening to swallow me whole. To keep myself from going insane, I think, I clung irrationally to the idea that if I could just see and talk to him again, everything would go back to the way it was, the way it was supposed to be. I felt more desperate than ever to accomplish this after talking to Merritt.

And now I had the perfect reason to go to his office and see him. I had to tell him Merritt was pregnant. I changed clothes, into something less casual, and drove slowly to his office, trying to get a grip on my nerves.

When I got there, his secretary of at least a dozen years greeted me warmly. "Oh, Jessie, Kevin didn't say you were coming."

"He didn't know, Lois. Is he here?" I hated the way I sounded, so anxious. Surely she'd guess something was wrong, and I couldn't bear the humiliation of that.

"Something came up; I'm not sure what. But he had me cancel his afternoon appointments."

I forced a stiff smile, which I intended to be nonchalant. Instead, it felt as if it would crack the flesh of my face. "Mind if I just sit at his desk to make a couple of calls?" I asked, not really knowing who I'd call or what I'd do next, but definitely not wanting to leave just yet.

"Of course not; go right in. Can I get you some coffee?"

Just the word made my stomach queasy. I'd drunk enough coffee this morning to pay Brazil's national debt. "No. No, thank you." I walked past her desk and into Kevin's office, an idea forming as I did so. Maybe his desk or computer would yield a clue. Maybe I could read his e-mails. Maybe he'd have a phone number scribbled somewhere. Or maybe there'd be a Post-it note with a heart doodled on it, my name tucked inside, and I would know he still loved me.

But what I saw was a computer turned off and an immaculate desk. Not a speck of dust to mar its surface nor a single scrap of paper to sully the tidy appearance created by his carefully arranged keyboard, phone, and calendar.

Kevin had not left here in a hurry. Anal as he was, even he wouldn't leave his desk *this* tidy if he were called away suddenly. No, this was the desk of someone who had *planned* to take the afternoon off.

And it wasn't likely he'd take the afternoon off to be by himself.

Then, like a message from a muse, an idea came to me. Chances were, he'd called whomever he had plans with before he left. I picked up his phone and pushed the redial button, feeling a rush of adrenaline.

I tapped my fingers impatiently on the desk. Then I heard a voice announce, "Hello, you've reached Taylor Stockton. I'm not in right now, but—"

In spite of my shaking hands, I managed to end the call. *Okay, okay,* I told myself, taking a deep breath. *Relax.* Taylor Stockton was one of the company's attorneys. No reason at all Kevin shouldn't call her on a business matter.

But if it was business, why didn't he call her on her office extension? And then I remembered seeing her at the airport that night. My eyes started to sting, an all-too-familiar warning of late that I was about to lose it.

"I'm just going down to the cafeteria," Lois said, popping her head around the door. "Sure I can't get you anything?"

"No, thanks, Lois. I'm leaving now."

"Okay, dear. I'll tell Kevin you were here. Although, of course, you'll probably see him before I do," she called, as she closed the outer office door behind her.

"Don't bet on it," I muttered to the closed door.

I walked as calmly as I could back to the parking garage and my car. Then I drove ten miles over the legal speed limit back to my house—not because I really wanted to go there, but because I had nowhere else to go. And I didn't really care if I arrived there safely or not.

***

Ellen was sitting on my doorstep, reading *People* magazine. *My* magazine, it turned out. She had the rest of my mail beside her on the doorstep. Obviously, I wasn't going to be able to avoid her, so I didn't bother pulling in the garage.

Emerging from the Jeep, I greeted my best friend. "El!" I said, as breezily as I could manage.

"Hey." She stood. "Where have you been? I haven't seen you in a coon's age."

"How long is a coon's age, anyway?"

"How do I know? Just one of those expressions we all use down South." Ellen was from El Paso, and she made sure we never forgot her Texas origins.

I unlocked the door, wishing she would leave and desperate at the same time that she stay.

"Wanna make me some coffee?" she asked, standing behind me now, my mail clutched in her hands.

"You know, El, I'm really so busy. Got a deadline. Can I call you later?"

I heard her laugh. "No way. I need some coffee now. Anyway, I want to know what you're fixin' to serve."

"What?" I pushed the front door open. "What do you mean?"

"The neighborhood dinner. It's your turn, remember? I'll bring a side dish, but I need to know what the main course is. You were supposed to call me, or at least return one of my calls. But you never write, you never call . . ."

For once Ellen couldn't make me laugh. "Kevin left me," I said. There, it was out. Like a cancer cut from my body. The relief was enormous. I had finally told someone. I could breathe normally again, for the first time in weeks.

But before I had time to enjoy my newfound lungs, Ellen's arms were around me.

"Oh, honey," I heard her say into my left ear, a long, drawn-out honeee, the way they probably do in Texas. "C'mon, let's sit."

She walked me over to the couch, pushed me down, and took my hand.

The great thing about Ellen is that there is never a who, why, where, or tell me all the sordid details. She just stared into my face, her own looking earnest. Concerned.

"So," I said. "I can't have the damn neighbors over for dinner. You understand?"

"Of course. I'll cancel. Are you okay?"

I took a deep breath. "Yes." Then, "No. No, I'm not okay. Merritt's going to have a baby. Kevin has a new piece of expensive luggage. I have no idea what's new in skin care."

"Merritt's pregnant? Oh, Jessie, that's just wonderful. Congratulations." She squeezed my hand. "You wanna talk about the other?"

"I don't know where he is or what the hell he's doing. He just left me, El. After all these years. I don't really know why, or at least he didn't give a reason. And that's it."

"I meant the skin care," she said, and then we both laughed, and I cried a little bit too. And then she took my hand and led me to the kitchen, where she produced double-chocolate-chip ice cream from my freezer, and I told her everything.

***

The ringing phone beside the bed greeted me the next morning. I'd had another fitful night of little sleep capped off by a drug-like stupor starting about the time I usually arose in what I'd come to think of as my former life. *It's Kevin*, I told myself, as I fumbled for the phone. *It has to be.*

It was.

"Lois said you were in the office yesterday," he said, not even returning the "H'lo" I'd managed, with great effort and a thick tongue, to mumble. "What's up?"

Suddenly I was as awake as if I'd downed a dozen cups of coffee. Sitting up in bed and clearing my throat, I answered him. "I wanted to tell you about Merritt. She's pregnant."

"I know. She told me."

I was speechless. He sounded about as thrilled as if he'd just found out our daughter was having her braces tightened. What was worse, our daughter told him we were going to be grandparents, and he didn't even want to discuss it with me. But then why would I expect anything else from a man I'd spent decades with who hadn't even acknowledged my birthday last week?

In spite of the warm day that loomed ahead, apparent from the hot, humid air seeping in through my screen, I pulled my down comforter up around my neck.

Just the memory of my birthday made me feel vulnerable and battered: the bitter disappointment every time the phone rang and it *wasn't* Kevin; the hurt I felt as I glanced at each envelope the mail lady delivered, only to find out it *wasn't* from him; the ache in my chest every time I heard a vehicle come down the street and it *wasn't* the florist with a bouquet from Kevin.

"When? When did Merritt tell you she's pregnant?" I asked at last. "I told her yesterday you were out of town—"

"I know. What was that all about? When I called her this morning, she was surprised to find out I'm here."

"Why did you call her?" I asked, as if Merritt were the other woman I now felt convinced he had.

"She's my daughter, Jessie. I'm leaving you, not her." As gentle as his tone was, the words still slashed through my heart.

"You didn't tell her about us, did you? You promised I could do that."

"I know, Jess, and so I didn't. But if you don't tell the kids soon, they'll figure things out. I'm not going to lie to them—or anyone else."

What about me? I thought. *Would you lie to me?*

"Kevin, are you having an affair with anyone?" I asked aloud. It wasn't a planned question; it just popped out of my mouth.

"Jessie, we've been through this. No. The answer is no. How many times do I have to say it? There isn't anyone else."

"What about Taylor Stockton?"

He laughed; he actually laughed, as if I'd just told a good joke. "Jessie, Taylor Stockton is practically the same age as Merritt."

I believed him, but regardless, I kept pushing. "You called her from your office. I hit the redial button and got her recording." Geez, I was pitiful. What was I doing?

"Jessie!" he exploded. "What the hell is this? Taylor was working at home, and I needed to speak to her. I didn't know I had to check with you every time I made a call. And besides, what *difference* does it make? We're divorcing."

Now I was crying, and neither one of us spoke for a while.

Then his soft voice returned. "Jessie, please don't cry. I can't stand it when you cry."

"Really?" I said through muffled sobs. "You can't stand it when I cry? Well, guess what? I can't stand it when you want to divorce me. I can't stand to think you'd rather be living who-knows-where than with me. And just where the hell *are* you living, anyway?"

"With a guy from the office. You don't know him. He's out of town. I'm looking after his place while he's gone. If you need me, you can get me at the office or on my cell."

How convenient. I reached for a tissue from the holder on the bedside table, and the entire contents spilled out. "Why are you doing this, Kevin?" I blew my nose loudly. "We got married *forever*, remember, for better or worse and all that? And what's been so bad about us? And how could you wait until I'm almost fifty?"

I was sobbing now, but I continued to rant through my sobs. "You're a bastard. I gave up my own education to put you through college and then stayed home all those years because that's the way you wanted it. I never even looked at another man. And you wait to leave me when I'm wrinkled, no kids left at home to be my family, too old to start a career—"

"You have your writing, Jess."

But even as I responded, I was acutely aware that he hadn't disputed my wrinkles or my getting older. "Oh, right. A few days of work a month, a few hundred bucks here and there—that's quite a career, Kevin. That'll really keep me busy and happy. Being a grandmother would have made me happy. Before this." I hated myself for sounding and feeling so frantic, but I was out of control now, beyond any ability to reason.

"Jessie, Jessie, I'm so sorry. I don't want to hurt you. You're such a good person, and I do love you. But it's just not—"

"Your kids will hate you. You'll never see your grandchildren. What would your mother have said?" I was really pulling out the big guns in my frenzy, and I knew I sounded demented. Besides, his mother had never really liked me, and probably would have thought it was about time.

"Look, why don't we talk later? I could meet you tonight if you want."

"Oh, how kind you are to try and fit me into your busy schedule. Well, don't bother."

"Please, Jessie, don't be like this."

"Fuck off." I threw the phone down without even bothering to disconnect.

***

Hours later I was still berating myself. I decided to call Ellen, but then it occurred to me again, as it had off and on, that I really should call my sister. Now that I was outed, it was time Nina knew as well. And she would console me too; she would never judge me as pathetic.

"Nina?" I was on the phone in my office. The pink walls still held Merritt's posters—one advertising Gap jeans, from her high school days working there, and one announcing a Lilith Fair concert—as well as various awards she'd won at cheerleading camps and debate contests. "Can you talk?" I asked, as I stroked the smooth mahogany surface of the desk Kevin and I had found at an estate sale one Friday night about five years ago. We'd been passing time newly bestowed upon us by Teddy's departure for college and had already seen the latest movies.

There was a pause, and then Nina spoke. "Jessie, is that you? Is everything okay?"

I burst into tears and cried all the harder as I thought of the role reversal that was undoubtedly about to occur. For forty-five years Nina had been my baby sister, and I'd always been the comforter. When she hadn't made cheerleading, when she didn't make grades to get in a sorority the first time around, even when Dad died and I was heartbroken myself. I took a deep breath and forced a calm in my voice I did not feel.

I hated to do this to Nina, to disillusion her so. I knew how she'd always looked up to me, right on into adulthood. I knew how my own marriage and two little kids had made her want that for herself. And indeed, she did live the same charmed life I'd thought *I* was living: a spacious, well-appointed home, hers in a Houston suburb; two children growing rapidly toward the independent adulthood mine had already attained (well, in Ted's case, *almost* attained); and a loving husband who worked hard and left her wanting for nothing. Yes, that's how anyone, including me not that long ago, would have described Kevin too. But I'd been left sorely wanting.

"Nina, are you sitting down?" I asked in a level voice, preparing her and at the same time putting off my announcement as long as I could. I breathed in deeply. "Kevin has moved out."

"What? *Moved out?* I don't understand."

A flash of impatience made me sigh. What didn't she understand? It took every ounce of courage to say the words out loud, twice in a twenty-four-hour period, no less. I couldn't bear to have to *explain* the words as well.

"You had a fight?" she asked next, and my heart broke at how hopeful that sounded. We just had a fight. We'd had a million fights. Doesn't every married couple?

"No," I said calmly. "No, we didn't have a fight. He just doesn't want to live with me right now."

"Oh, Jessie, what did he say? Where is he now? Why wouldn't he want to live with you? That's ridiculous."

"Nina, he wants a divorce."

"He said that? He actually said he wants a divorce? When did all this happen? You never told me you were having problems."

"I didn't realize we were. I went to pick him up at the airport one night, and he got in the car and said he wants a divorce. Now you know as much as I do."

"You had no clue?" she probed.

"No!" I yelled. Then I immediately regretted it. "No," I said again, softly. "I am, as the kids say, clueless."

"Oh, Jess, I'm so sorry. Is there another woman? Well, of course there's another woman. There always is. Men like Kevin don't just leave. He loves you, loves his kids. There's another woman, Jessie; there has to be. Did you ask him?"

"Did I ask him? Let's see. I asked him if he remembered to put the milk back in the refrigerator, and I asked him if he closed the garage door. And yes, Nina, yes, amazingly, I remembered to ask him if there was another woman, and guess what he said? He said no, there was no one else. It's me; it's me, Nina. I'm to blame here, not some other woman."

"Okay, steady, Jess. I'm sorry." I heard an exasperated sigh, as if she wondered what she was going to do with me. "Do you believe him?"

"Oh, Nina, I don't know what to believe. He told me he was staying at the Holiday Inn that first night; but when I called him there, he wasn't even registered."

"See, Jessie?" she said, as if I'd given her proof positive that Kevin had a lover.

"When I called him at his office the next day, he said he'd changed his mind and gone to the Sheraton at Keystone Crossing instead," I offered meekly.

"Jessie, there's another woman," she stated, closing her case. I wondered vaguely how my little sister had gotten so worldly and tough. That was supposed to be my job.

"How can you be so sure?" But I'd already had the same thought myself, since the Sheraton was farther from his office.

"Jessie, do you really believe there's no one else? You think he'd just up and leave because . . . what, he was bored?"

"Well, wait until you hear the other news, Nina." I sighed. "Merritt is pregnant."

"Oh, Jessie, how awful for you. This should be one of your high points in life, shared with Kevin. That son of a bitch. Does he know yet?"

I told her of my trip to his office the day before and my phone call from him this morning. "I sounded so pathetic, I could just kill myself."

"Don't worry; you're allowed to sound any way you want."

"I did turn down his suggestion that we get together to talk," I added, as if to make myself look less pathetic.

"Good. Just let him sit with that for a while. In the meantime, you have to find out for sure if there *is* someone else—rather, *who* she is."

CHAPTER FOUR

"How am I going to find out who she is?" I asked, realizing I'd agreed to her *who* and no longer wondering *if*, and also conjuring up recollections of more than one instance that should have alerted me.

While Nina remained quiet, no doubt forming a plan for me, I thought of Kevin's late nights at work and the growing frequency of his out-of-town trips, uncharacteristic for him. He used to fiercely protect his family time, even driving halfway across the state at night just to spend the time at home, although it meant returning early the next morning to complete business. But that had changed gradually, so gradually that I hadn't felt alarmed until now.

"Something happened, just last month," I said, thinking aloud. "We were driving to Teddy's house, and I told Kevin to stop and let me look in the trunk to see if we still had an old blanket in there. I'd told Teddy I'd bring him one. But Kevin wouldn't stop until I'd asked him several times. And then he hurried around to the trunk to check; that's just not like him, Nina. I remember how weird I thought he was acting. I didn't *suspect* anything, but now I wonder if he had something hidden in the trunk."

"Like what?"

"*I* don't know."

"Well, you've got to find out."

"How?"

"Go look in his trunk, for Pete's sake. You've got a key, don't you? You know where he parks, don't you? Do it." I wondered again when my little sister had grown so strong. I never before even thought of her as having her own opinion; she'd always echoed mine. Never before had I been so grateful for a sister.

"I will; I'll go right now." I sounded far braver than I felt.

"Good, and call me as soon as you find something."

I hung up, telling her I loved her, but I was a little perturbed that she was so sure I *would* find something.

After a quick shower, dressed in what I hoped was an unobtrusive black running suit, I was ready to go. And even though I felt like an aging Nancy Drew, I was amazed at myself for feeling so excited over what I was about to do.

I checked to make sure I still had a set of Kevin's car keys on my key ring—a foolish, compulsive gesture. For almost thirty years I'd carried a set of Kevin's car keys; but then for almost thirty years I'd also had Kevin, and *he'd* vanished, hadn't he?

Clasping the keys that would unlock his trunk—and his secrets?—I made my way through the maze of boxes in the kitchen toward the back door. Fury diminished my perverse sense of excitement as I stumbled around the mess. It was all Kevin's fault that everything was in ruins, my kitchen as well as my life.

It was in such a mood that I backed out of the garage—screeching to a halt just short of slamming into a Ford pickup parked in my driveway, the pickup that belonged to Victor or Hector or whatever the hell that cabinetmaker's name was. I put my Jeep in park and climbed out as he came down from my front doorsteps and walked toward me, removing a Cubs baseball cap as he approached.

"What in the hell are you doing here?" I fairly screamed, frightened by my near accident.

"Sorry, ma'am. I know I should have called first, but I was in your neighborhood. I thought if I could just take some measurements . . . but maybe this isn't a good time for you."

"Ya think?" I felt bad, knowing I was yelling at this poor man because he was there and Kevin wasn't. But I couldn't help myself. "*I'll* call *you* when it is. Now could you please move your truck?"

He was within arm's reach of me by then and had stopped to look at me long enough for me to notice what nice eyes he had. They were as brown and friendly as a cocker spaniel's; but as I ranted, I could see them fill with a look of hurt and then concern. He furrowed his brow, creating deep lines between the two strips of bushy, brownish-gray hair above those warm, expressive eyes, and I felt sorry for being such a bitch—for being such a bitch to the wrong man, anyway.

"Hey, I'm sorry, Mr. Dennehey."

"Heck. My name's Hector, but people call me Heck."

"Well heck, Heck." I smiled feebly and reached to give his upper arm a pat. "I'm sorry. I'm having a bad day and just took it out on you. But I thought I was going to hit your truck."

I was still shaken from that near encounter and still antsy to get on with my sleuthing. "Look, I'll call you; we'll set up a time for you to come back." I turned away from him and got back into the Jeep, feeling impatient at seeing him still standing there.

Then, after staring at me for a few seconds, he gave a wave and a shrug and went to his own vehicle.

I drove cautiously to the parking garage attached to Kevin's building. It was six stories high, and of course I had no idea where Kevin would park, if in fact he was even in the office then.

Entering on the ground level, I began my search, my eyes scanning the parked cars as my Jeep crawled past them. I rolled down the window and stuck my left arm out. I pressed on Kevin's remote key fob, listening for a response. Twice I had to sharply turn my steering wheel as another car approached, driving too fast.

Then, on the third floor, a loud beep responded to my beckoning, and I headed in the direction of Kevin's red Porsche convertible.

He'd parked it at an angle, taking up two spots to keep other cars from parking too close. It was an arrogant habit of his that I'd often criticized. I resisted the urge to run the key in a straight line across his door, something I was sure the other drivers would have thanked me for.

Instead, parking my Jeep across from Kevin's car, I checked to make sure there was no one around. Then I jumped out of my vehicle and ran over to his. My fingers fumbled with the remote, and my heart pounded as the trunk slowly opened.

At first glance, I was struck by the orderliness of its contents, although it was what I would have expected. The man might be a two-timing bastard, but he was neat. I saw two golf clubs, a KLM flight bag he'd gotten on a business trip to Amsterdam years ago, and a stack of greeting cards held together by a rubber band.

Picking up the cards and removing the band, I looked at the top card and its stick-figure drawing of a blond woman holding pencil and paper. Underneath the drawing it read *Here's a list of what I love about you* . . . With shaky hands, I opened it to read: *1. Everything.* It was signed with a drawing of a tiny heart.

Looking nervously behind and around me and noticing no one, I hurriedly rifled through the remaining cards in search of a real signature, but all were signed with the same sickening heart.

I replaced the rubber band and stuck the pile under one arm while slamming the trunk shut with the other. I'd return the cards later—or not. First, I had to get home and read them.

I drove like a madwoman, going through two red lights. Knowing how sick it was, I nevertheless felt proud of myself for the booty I'd captured. As I drove, several other ideas came to me for catching Kevin in what I desperately hadn't wanted to catch him. But it was too late now; I was on a roll.

I flew into the house, slamming the front door behind me, and went straight up to my office and the filing cabinet. I pulled out his cell phone bills for the past year. Even just skimming them, it wasn't difficult to spot a recurring Indianapolis number he'd called over the past six months. With a yellow marker, I highlighted all the calls to this number, noting that some were from when he was out of town. And those were more than two hours long. Two hours!

The calls Kevin had made to me while on the road were embarrassingly short by comparison—measurable in minutes, not hours. But instead of being saddened by this fact, I focused on the thrill of catching him at something.

When I'd finished marking up the bills, I reached for the phone and dialed the highlighted number. I got Taylor Stockton's voice mail. *I should have known*, I thought. Then I tried to calm myself. It could be business, after all. There was often litigation involved in Kevin's work, a number of reasons he might confer with legal counsel. He'd probably even told me about it. I had to admit that occasionally—okay, often—I did tune him out when he discussed his job. But oh, how he could go on and on.

Next, I went through the American Express bills. I stopped highlighting at some point, growing tired of the whole exercise. There were so many charges on there I hadn't questioned, or noticed. At least three to a florist for flowers that certainly never came to me. Yes, they could be business expenses, but then they should be on his company account and not our personal one. When I got to a Victoria's Secret charge for two hundred bucks, I stopped. There was no point in going on. It wasn't fun anymore.

Wearily, I shoved all the bills back into the filing cabinet and pushed it shut. I was exhausted. I needed a nap, but I had to call Nina first. I knew she was waiting, and besides, this kind of knowledge had to be shared.

"So?" she said, answering on the first ring. "Tell me."

"Cards, telephone calls, flowers, Victoria's Secret. What more do you want?"

"Oh, Jessie."

"You know the funny part? Not only did he not even bother to cover his tracks, I am the one who pays the bills. Can you believe how stupid he was? Can you believe how stupid *I* am?"

"No, he's the only stupid one. Oh, Jessie, I'm so sorry. But at least now you know."

"Yep, at least now I know. Ah hell, Nina, now I really do know."

***

I don't know how long I sat there, or how many times the doorbell rang. But when I went downstairs and answered it, I saw Ellen leaning against the doorjamb, her arms folded.

"Do you ever check your messages?" she asked. "I called you a million times this morning."

"Come in." I stood back to let her pass into the foyer.

"I'm taking you to dinner."

"Okay. But first, follow me; I want to show you something."

I ran upstairs, Ellen following behind me. "What am I gonna find up here?" she asked. "You haven't killed Kevin and cut his body into pieces, have you?"

"Not yet," I said, noticing how excited I suddenly felt at having some real evidence to show her. "But I did find some things in his trunk that you'll love."

Ellen had no visible reaction to my raiding Kevin's trunk; she just nodded her head like it was the logical place to start looking for proof.

I laid the cards and the bills across the desk, and she slowly picked up a couple of the cards and studied them. A thin smile crossed her lips. "I'd sure cut Steve into little pieces if I found these in his trunk," she said.

"Well, it would be a lot easier if Kevin *were* dead."

"No kidding. I think any woman would rather have a husband die than be unfaithful. You'd get all that sympathy and support."

"Yeah, that'd beat pity and nosy questions any day, which is what I have to look forward to. Oh man, what do I do, El?"

"What do you want to do, honey?" She looked at me, her earnest blue eyes penetrating mine.

"I don't know. I still keep thinking we can work it out. Is that dumb? After all this?"

"No, of course not."

"Well, how about we start with that dinner?" I asked.

"I'm right behind you."

And she was. And it felt good.

***

"Teddy!" I said, opening the door to my son. "What are you doing here?" It was eight thirty on a Monday morning. I'd been up since six, but awake since four. Ted looked like I felt.

"Can I wash this stuff? It's not much," he said, standing in the doorway. He was six feet tall and looked so much like his father, it almost made me swoon. I was really glad to see him.

"Sure, honey." I made a sweeping gesture, like a maître d' at a fancy restaurant. *Please walk this way.* "You remember where the laundry room is."

He bent down to kiss my cheek as he passed me, dragging behind him two black garbage bags bursting with clothes, and I was touched by his show of affection. It was all the incentive I needed to rescue the bulging bags and relieve him of his laundry.

When Ted had moved out, I promised myself I wouldn't cater to him, resolute in my attempt to make him a responsible adult. Likewise, his father had insisted we do nothing to prolong his adolescence, I think Kevin called it, that made him satisfied tending bar even though he'd earned, at last, his college degree.

But I was always secretly pleased when Teddy showed up looking for a decent meal or, like now, when he still needed his mommy to do his laundry. As I sorted his clothes, he joined me in the laundry room, already eating a bagel.

"So," I said, spraying prewash over the knees of a disgusting-looking pair of jeans, "what's going on?"

"Not much." He eased himself up on top of the dryer and leaned back against the wall.

"Ted, don't sit on that; you're too heavy."

He ignored my order. "Where's Dad? I called his office yesterday, and he wasn't there."

I stopped spraying. "Why'd you call Dad?"

"I thought he might get me some Indians tickets."

I resumed spraying.

"Besides, I haven't spoken to the old guy in a while." He popped the last of the bagel into his mouth. "I think I'm overdue for a lecture." He grinned as he said it, and there was great affection in that grin. He sounded as though he missed his father, and I was consumed with jealousy.

I was jealous of that bitch, whoever she was, who didn't even have the guts to sign her cards but who was keeping my family apart. Sure, Ted and Kevin had a tumultuous relationship at times, and I'd served as the buffer between them. But although I'd always hated that position, I longed for it now; oh, how I longed for it. I roughly shoved as many dark clothes as I could into the washing machine and slammed the lid shut.

"Come have some coffee," I said, stuffing my negative feelings deep down inside, determined to enjoy this time alone with my son.

He slid off the dryer and followed me into the kitchen.

"When are you gonna start on these things?" He waved at the bare walls waiting for cabinets. "This place is a mess."

"It's in the works." I poured water into the top of the coffee maker. "Sit. I want to talk to you." I really didn't, of course, but I knew I had to tell him something. And at least now I was fortified by my talks with Ellen and Nina.

"Whoa. Sounds serious." He pulled back a kitchen chair and sprawled onto it, his long legs reaching under the table.

When did my son get so tall? I could remember clearly when he was small enough to hide under this very table. I would pretend I didn't know where he was, and he would spring from beneath in his childish attempt to scare me. Where was that little boy?

I placed two empty coffee mugs on the table. Normally, I would have had something decent in the house to eat; but since I'd been living mainly on frozen entrées lately, I had hardly anything. I pulled out the chair across from him and sat down.

"Mom," Ted said, before I could even collect my thoughts, "if Dad told you to talk to me about—"

"About what?" I welcomed the interruption.

He sighed. "About how I'm wasting my college degree by tending bar and how I'm—"

"No, honey, it's much more serious than that." I reached across the table and patted his hand, feeling the same sorrow as when I'd had to tell him a grandparent was dead.

I knew I was about to hurt my son and that he'd never fully recover.

CHAPTER FIVE

Teddy sighed, obviously relieved I wasn't about to deliver another what-are-you-doing-with-your-life lecture. "Okay. Is it about Merritt's baby?"

"Why would I want to discuss Merritt's baby?"

"I don't know. You're acting weird, Mom."

At first I was offended. And then, well, then I was crying. Ted jumped up and pulled a sheet of paper towel off the holder by the sink. He looked terrified, which only made me cry harder.

"Mom, what is it?" He stood behind me now, his big hands on my shoulders. I remembered how much I hated it when I saw either of my parents cry, no matter how old I was, and the memory helped me compose myself.

"Sit." I blew my nose hard. "Sit down, for heaven's sake. I can't talk to you when you're standing behind me."

"Okay, okay." He pulled out the chair next to me. "Come on; tell me." His face was close, and I could see he hadn't shaved. I reached out to touch his cheek. When had my son started shaving? Okay, so he was twenty-three, and obviously he hadn't started shaving that morning; but where had the time gone?

"Dad left me." Amazingly, I didn't cry as I said it, but the words flew out of my mouth and filled the kitchen. I wanted to reach out and grab them so we could just go back to how we'd been before.

Through my scrunched eyes, I peered across at my son, expecting some reaction. He left the table and stood in front of the refrigerator, opening the door wide. I could feel a blast of icy air.

He stayed silent for a long time, and I turned to watch his back. It was so broad and manly, I wondered when—I stopped myself. *Face it: your son is a man.*

"Ted, did you hear me?"

"Did you stop buying groceries, or what?"

"There might be something in the freezer."

He opened the freezer door, peered in, and then slammed it shut. "Nothing but those stale bagels." He turned and leaned against the refrigerator, his arms folded across his chest.

"Let's go out to breakfast." I sniffed hard and blew my nose on the paper towel. It felt soggy.

"I don't want to go out," he said, and there, finally, was my little eight-year-old Teddy. *I don't want to take this medicine. I don't want to go to school. I don't want to be nice to Merritt.*

"Fine. Just have some coffee. Look, it's ready."

"I don't drink coffee; you know I don't."

"Then what do you want? Chocolate milk? A Coke? Did you just drop by so I could do your damn laundry? Is that all I am to you?" *Stop, stop, stop. This is not his fault.* I didn't want to be saying any of this. I was standing now, sloshing coffee into one of the cups, roughly spooning Coffee-mate into the steaming liquid. "Why don't you just leave?" I raised the mug to my lips and burned my tongue.

"Hey, hold on. Don't get mad at me because he left. Where the fuck did—"

"Teddy!" I couldn't stop myself. I had to wonder: when did my son start saying words he'd been forbidden to use? Probably long before he left home, I realized, feeling more defeated than ever.

"Where did he go, anyway? To some bimbo?"

"It doesn't matter *where* he went; the point is, he's not living here anymore."

Teddy ran a hand through his already-disheveled hair, and I felt so sorry for him I thought my heart would break.

"Okay, so let him go." He began to pace in front of the refrigerator, an earnest look on his face, as if in the past ten seconds he'd come up with a solution to the problem. "Who needs him?"

I do. I desperately do. Can't you see that? Can't you see anything? "Well, not me, that's for sure," I said, pulling out the kitchen chair and motioning for him to sit down. "Oh, Teddy, I'm so sorry." *For what? For not keeping it together? For not keeping Kevin in love with me? Why was I sorry?*

"What the hell are you sorry for?" my brilliant child asked. "Forget him. Let him go. Get a good attorney."

"Attorney?" I asked, as if he'd suggested I hire a hit man. Sure, I had used the word in one of my screaming sessions with Kevin; but the truth was, I felt far from the attorney stage. It scared me to hear Ted say it now, and before I could stop myself, I was crying again.

"Mom." Ted rose, looking uncomfortable. "Maybe I should leave. You need to be by yourself."

Unbelievable. Unfuckingbelievable. The last thing I needed was to be by myself. I'd been by myself for more than a month. I'd go insane if I spent another second alone. "You're right, honey. You run along. I'll finish your laundry. You can pick it up later."

"Okay." Already he was jingling his car keys in front of me like a prisoner who'd just picked the pocket of his jailer. "I'll come back later."

"Fine, honey." I ushered him out the front door.

"Does Merritt know?"

"Not yet." But now I had no choice but to ruin her life too. Sure, she had Alec and the baby, but this was at the very least going to put a big damper on her joy. I felt like I did when I had to postpone her fifth birthday party because Teddy had chicken pox. It wasn't my fault, but I had to give her bad news that would spoil her good time. "The only ones I've told, besides you, are Ellen and Aunt Nina."

"Good; that's good. They'll know what you should do."

But why? I wanted to scream. *How would they know? They have husbands who still love them.* "Yes, Aunt Nina gave me good advice."

"Great," Ted said, relief written on his face but not a speck of curiosity about his aunt's advice. He reached down and kissed my cheek. And then he was gone.

I stood listening to his old Mustang roar out of the driveway. "Well," I said aloud, "that went well." And then I couldn't breathe.

***

After I'd finished the entire pot of coffee, my sense of fairness (heightened, no doubt, by all that caffeine) prompted me to call Merritt. It stemmed from my need to make sure my kids got equal treatment. Equal amounts of money spent on presents, equal time spent at their various activities as they were growing up, and now an equal right to know their father had left.

I listened to Alec's voice-mail greeting promise that if I left my name and number, he or Merritt would call me back. Like a woman condemned to die by lethal injection, I found his recorded voice as welcome as a governor's reprieve.

But as soon as I replaced the receiver, the phone rang, sending my jangling nerves dancing throughout my body. Maybe Merritt *was* home, screening calls.

"Mrs. Harleman?"

"Yes?"

"Heck Dennehey."

"Who?"

I heard a tired sigh on the other end. "Cabinets?" He sounded irritated.

"Oh, Heck," I said, remembering who he was and hoping he realized I meant *oh, Heck*, as in his name, and not *oh hell*. "I'm sorry. I know I said I'd call you—"

"Look, I have another job starting. If you want me to finish yours, it has to be now. If you'd rather hire someone else, that's fine. Just say the word."

"Heck, no! I mean, no, Heck!" I felt like a character in a bad sitcom. "Whenever you're ready, just—"

"I've been ready for over a month. You said you'd call—"

"Okay, okay. I'm ready now. I'll be home all day. All week, in fact. Just come over whenever you want."

"Fine. Expect me later this morning."

"Good. I'm expecting." I hung up and was reminded by my words to try Merritt again. Still no answer.

I showered, put on some makeup, and tidied the house a bit in case this Heck person was close by. Then, forcing myself to do so, I sat down at the computer and turned it on.

The notes for my article were in a neat stack next to the keyboard, and I listlessly read through them for the hundredth time, not gleaning anything worthwhile that I could turn into positive information for the skin-care consumer, yet feeling my deadline bearing down. The stack of cards I'd retrieved (stolen?) from Kevin's trunk glared at me from the corner of my desk. I put down my notes and reached for them.

By now I knew every word on every card, all nine of them. At first they'd made me cry, and then I grew enraged. And then a tiny part of me felt thrilled by the sheer covertness of the situation. But with each line now committed to memory, they just made me sad.

Who was this person sending cards to my husband? *My* husband. I tried to visualize a strange woman browsing the

Hallmark stores as I myself had done so many times. Only I'd never been searching for the perfect card for someone else's husband.

And why had Kevin kept these cards? I asked myself, but I knew the answer. He *couldn't* throw them away. They meant too much to him. He undoubtedly wanted to savor them, probably taking them out and rereading them, finding solace or excitement in them when he couldn't be with her. When he had to be with me instead.

The phone rang again. Jolted out of my misery, I reached for it.

"Jessie?"

I caught my breath at the sound of Kevin's voice. *Okay*, I warned myself silently. *Keep it together. Don't get mad, don't cry, and most important, don't sound desperate this time.* "Yes?"

"How are you?" he asked.

"Fine. And you?"

"Okay. We need to talk."

My heart leapt. I knew I shouldn't have told Ted. It was all for nothing. And now I'd ruined that poor child's faith in his father. He need never have known. And Nina and Ellen. I shouldn't have told them, either.

"Do you want to come over?" I asked. I bit my tongue as punishment for doing exactly what I'd promised myself I wouldn't do.

"Okay . . . maybe that would be best. I'll be there in twenty minutes." He hung up before I could analyze his tone of voice, but I was still convinced his coming over was a precursor to his moving back home. He'd certainly had enough time to see how wrong he was.

I flew into action. First, I changed my clothes, donning a favorite striped knit dress from Banana Republic that Merritt had insisted I get because it was so flattering. I slapped on more makeup and doused myself with J'adore, which I immediately regretted. The fragrance was a humiliating reminder of the trench-coat debacle. When the doorbell rang, I added a sweet smile, wanting to look happy.

But it was Heck Dennehey. He was actually fastening a tool belt around his waist as I opened the door, and he looked up and grinned at me after he checked his hip pouches. Sort of like a gunslinger checking his weapons.

"You look nice." He strode into the hallway and staked his claim, as if he were afraid I would change my mind again and order him gone.

"Heck!" I said.

"Yes," he said. Not a question, a statement. He was going to begin those damn cabinets, and no one was going to stop him. Before I could protest, he was already in the kitchen, his Stanley measuring tape out and ready for business.

"I have someone coming over," I feebly addressed his back.

"Nooooo problem." He stretched the aluminum measure across the empty wall space.

"I may need some privacy."

The measuring tape sprang back into its case like a bullet from a gun, only in reverse. He turned to face me, his brown eyes boring into mine. "Do you want these damn cabinets built or not?"

"Yes. Yes, of course. I'm sorry for all the . . . inconvenience."

He turned to face the wall again. "You should be," I heard him mutter.

"Wait just a minute. Who's the customer here?"

"Damn good question." He spun around again. "You know, your husband signed a contract. This job should be finished by now. I've put other customers on hold because of you."

"Right. You're right. I'm sorry. I'll leave you to it."

"Oh, don't do that. I was counting on your help. Here, you can borrow this." He reached into one of the back pouches of his belt and produced an ominous-looking tool. He looked serious as he handed it to me. But then, after a few seconds of watching me stare dumbly at the thing in my hand, his face broke into a wide grin, and we both started to laugh.

"Look, I'll be upstairs in my office." I handed back whatever it was I was holding. "If the doorbell rings, I'll get it."

He turned toward the wall again. "Damn right you will. I'm not a friggin' butler."

Duly chastised, I went upstairs and sat down at my computer, but this time I didn't bother to turn it on. I sat there waiting for Kevin and listening to Heck downstairs making building noises.

For the first time in a long while, I felt almost happy. My kitchen was being transformed, and by the end of the day, I felt certain, Kevin would have moved back home. Together, we'd enjoy the new kitchen he'd arranged for my Christmas present last year.

***

Kevin showed up an hour and a half later. He used his key, and I didn't even hear him come in. I just felt his presence behind me as I sat staring at the black screen.

"Hi," he said softly, leaning over my shoulder to kiss my cheek.

It was a good sign. I didn't let myself wonder why it had taken him so long to get there.

"I see that guy is working on the cabinets," he whispered into my right ear.

"Yes." I twirled around gaily on my ergonomic chair to face him. I couldn't believe how casually dressed he was for a weekday. He had on a pink golf shirt and Dockers. I was struck immediately by how handsome he looked. "*Finally*," I said, in a manner indicating some universal problem with all cabinetmakers.

"That's good." He removed a pile of papers from a white wicker chair in the corner of the room and sat down. As he crossed his legs, my eyes were drawn to his socks.

They were new. Gray and covered with little pink pigs. I felt revulsion at their cuteness, then cold fear at the thought of who had bought them. Certainly not him. They were definitely purchased by someone from the same school of adorableness as the sender of the cards.

"We need to talk, Jess." He rested his elbows on the arms of the chair and brought his hands together in front of him, his fingers touching at the tips. He looked like a minister about to impart a sermon.

"Want some coffee?"

"No."

"A drink?"

"No," he said, with even more feeling, as if I'd asked him if he wanted some illegal drugs.

"Ted was here. He wants Indians tickets."

"Fine. I'll call him."

"Steve and Ellen got a new car. Did you notice it—"

"Jessie, stop. We've got to talk."

I shut up. This wasn't going to be what I wanted to hear. "Okay, talk."

"Well, first, I think you should get a security system installed."

"Why?" I asked, alarmed that he'd said *you* and not *we*.

"I just think it would be best. Now that you're living here alone, and—"

"I'm not afraid," I lied. Me, who was suddenly afraid of everything, though admittedly the least of which was intruders.

"I know. But I'd feel better knowing you had a security system."

"Ah, well, then perhaps I should. I certainly want *you* to feel better, Kevin." This was good; at least I didn't sound desperate.

"And we've got to get some money things sorted out."

"Is there someone else?"

"Hmm?" he said, but we both knew he was stalling.

"You heard me."

"Jessie, there is no one else."

His supercilious manner so enraged me that I rose, grabbed the stack of cards from my desk, and threw them at him. "Then what do you call these?"

They landed on his lap. He didn't move, and they stayed there in a heap until he uncrossed his legs. Then they tumbled to the carpet. "Where did you get these?"

"What's the difference? Just tell me who she is, Kevin. Let's not pretend."

I was pacing the room now, my arms folded across my chest, while Kevin remained in the chair. I could hear an electric something or other start up downstairs in the kitchen. When I finally turned to look at Kevin, I saw two fat tears roll down his cheeks before he wiped them away.

"No!" I yelled. "Don't you *dare* cry." But he only hung his head, and before I knew what I was doing, I'd walked over and slapped him hard across the face.

His head nodded slightly in an I-deserved-that gesture, and when he looked up to face me, his eyes were wet. "Jessie, I'm so sorry. I love you. I didn't mean for—"

"Who is she?"

"She's no one."

"She's *someone*. Who is she?"

"Jessie, I wouldn't have had it turn out this way for the world."

"Who the *fuck* is she?" I screamed into Kevin's face at the precise moment that Hector Dennehey turned off his electric whatever-the-hell-it-was he was using.

The house, the street, the entire world was silent. We were all waiting for Kevin's answer. "Taylor Stockton," he mumbled, his head bent to his chest again.

"Taylor Stockton?"

Okay, let's review this. Company attorney. Bright. Pretty (but not beautiful, definitely not beautiful). Slim. Young. Perky. Girl-next-door type. Company attorney (I already said that).

Kevin had introduced me to Taylor Stockton at the Christmas party. I remembered that she was wearing an exquisitely cut suit and had beautiful legs. Long and slim. Well-defined legs that belonged to someone who worked out. She was obviously smart, but unassuming. I had admired her down-to-earthness, her obviously successful career. I think I'd even thought how great it would be if Ted could meet such a woman. It seemed we'd had a conversation about Hillary Clinton over the Brie. I believe I'd left the party actually liking Taylor Stockton.

Fine. So it was Taylor Fucking Stockton. Next question. "Do you love her?"

He looked up, now wearing a don't-ask-me-that look.

"Do you love her?"

"Don't ask me that," he actually said, and I had to clasp my hands behind my back to stop myself from slapping him again.

"You don't think I have the right to ask you that? You don't think that's appropriate? You waltz out of this house, then waltz back in to discuss security systems, and you don't think I should ask if you're in love with the person who's sent you all these fucking cards?" I didn't know what I was saying, but I was on a roll and couldn't stop because if I did, it would hurt so much I just might explode and die.

"Jessie." He put a hand up to stop me, like a traffic cop directing cars.

"Just answer the question. Do you love her?"

His head was bowed to his chest again. And then, like one of those slow-motion scenes from an action movie, he silently nodded *yes*. Yes!

CHAPTER SIX

I wanted to take Kevin's head in my hands and rip it from his body. But I was paralyzed. Immobile. Whatever you want to call it. I couldn't move because the soft, gray carpet beneath my feet held me like Velcro, when what I wanted was for it to open up and let me fall to the center of the earth.

From the moment Kevin confirmed my worst fears, from the moment he put a name and face to my agony, I felt an excruciating pain. Now, instead of suspecting there might be someone else and dreading that my life might never return to normal, I *knew* my husband was in love with someone else.

And I knew I could never compete with her. It didn't matter that everyone had always told me how young *I* looked. When I thought of Taylor's fresh-faced youth, it was hard to ignore the lines around my eyes and mouth. And my long hair I'd once considered so feminine (even though I had to color it each month to keep it more auburn than gray-brown) suddenly seemed drab compared to her shoulder-length blond tresses. I tortured myself with thoughts of Kevin and Taylor talking, laughing, kissing—and worse, making love.

I took to having a glass of wine—or two—every night in a futile attempt to help me sleep. But still, I did little more than doze off and on. Always, a bad dream awakened me, and my thoughts started anew.

How had Taylor and Kevin gone from coworkers to lovers? What bantering, what flirtations, had taken place? Where did they meet? What did they talk about? What Hallmark cards had Kevin given her? What did they do in bed? And what the hell was I going to do with the rest of my life?

Oddly enough, the only lightness in my life, the only time I felt my dour expression give way to the hint of a smile—and occasionally even a laugh—was when Heck Dennehey came over or called. From the moment Kevin had left the house that day he'd told me about Taylor, the reclaimed cards in one hand as he tried vainly to give me a hug of comfort with the other, Heck had injected some indefinable emotion into me that saved me somehow from utter despair—at least for a few seconds now and then.

"Was that your husband I heard here?" Heck had asked, long after Kevin left through the front door that day and revved away in the convertible I'd once laughingly referred to as his midlife crisis. Now I despised that car, recognizing it as the first symptom of this new Kevin.

I had finally mustered up my courage to come down to the kitchen for a cup of coffee. I felt humiliated anew at Kevin's leaving me, especially knowing what this guy must have heard, even if he was just a cabinetmaker. "He used to be my husband," I answered Heck.

"Oh? You're divorced?"

"Gonna be." I wiped at my eyes, not caring about smeared mascara, not caring about anything, really.

"Sorry."

"I'll be fine." I didn't want anyone's pity.

"No, I meant for him. He's losing a beautiful woman—and some damn fine cabinets, if I do say so myself."

He had a way of talking—of positively twinkling—that made it impossible for him to offend. He paused, and I could feel him studying me. I could feel my self-control slipping away.

"Are you okay, Mrs. Harleman? Your face looks so sad."

"If you think my face looks sad, you should see my heart," I said, and then burst into tears. I stood in my strange-looking kitchen with a strange man, wondering what had happened to my marriage. Even now that I knew *who*, I still didn't understand *why*.

But Merritt would soon shed some light on that.

I pulled back from Hector Dennehey's tender touch almost as soon as he reached out with it in comfort. "I'm sorry to do this to you," I said. "Don't mind me. I'll be fine. Can you let yourself out? I have to leave."

I had to talk to Merritt. Here I was, telling a carpenter I was getting a divorce, when I hadn't even told my own daughter yet.

"Yeah, sure. I'm about done for today. Uh . . . we need to do some finalizing of the plans, but I'll call you to—"

"Whatever you do is fine. I don't care about the plans. You do whatever you think best."

He stood silently, and I wondered if I'd offended him. I hadn't meant to diminish the importance of his craft. I just couldn't give a damn right now what I had for kitchen cupboards or if I even *had* kitchen cupboards. I wasn't likely to be staying here, anyway. At that realization, I felt fresh tears forming.

"Ma'am." He reached toward me again.

I backed away. "Don't. Please don't."

"I'll call you later in the week," I heard him say to my back, as I hurried out of the kitchen and up the stairs to my bedroom. I went straight to the phone on my side of the bed, sickly aware that now both sides of the bed were mine.

Then, instead of calling Merritt, I grabbed my purse. I had to get out of the house, whether she was home or not.

I went the long way to my Jeep in the garage: out the front door, around back, and through the side garage door. As much as I inexplicably wanted to, I couldn't bear to see Heck and the pity in his kind eyes.

I thought of calling Merritt from the car, to let her know I was coming. I hadn't left a message when I'd called earlier, so she didn't have even the warning my strained voice would have conveyed. And I knew she was going to be devastated for me as well as utterly dismayed that her baby wouldn't have two happy grandparents doting together over their new progeny. But the short drive from my suburb north of Indianapolis to Merritt's didn't give me time to clear my head enough to call her.

As I made my way through the winding streets of her Fishers subdivision to her gray stone starter house, I could almost feel the soothing effects of the sympathy I knew she would feel for me. If she was home.

Indeed, she was, but she'd been asleep until my insistent ringing of the doorbell. She was a registered nurse at St. Vincent Hospital, and she'd probably told me she was on the night shift that week. But I was too self-centered of late to remember or consider anyone else's schedule. Even Merritt's.

"Mom, what are you doing here?" She rubbed sleepy eyes and opened the door wider for me to enter.

Her house was freezing, the air conditioner running full blast, full-time. She still didn't look pregnant, but she was always hot now, a victim of her changing hormones. I could relate, although mine were menopause induced.

I shivered as I apologized for waking her up, almost wishing for a hot flash to warm *me*. "I need to tell you something," I said, as I followed her into the kitchen and sat down at the table.

"What is it?" She handed me a sweater and then removed a carton of orange juice from the refrigerator. I thought how like me she looked. Same small stature, same shiny brown hair laced through with reddish highlights and hanging like a thick, silky scarf to her shoulders. And when she turned to look at me again, I saw the same large, wide-set green eyes. "Want some?" She held the carton toward me.

I shook my head and willed my voice to come out even and strong. "Your dad and I are getting a divorce." Proud of myself for not laying the blame on him, not asking her to take sides and causing her even more anguish in her delicate state, I felt stunned at her reaction.

She nodded her head, pursing her lips slightly as she pulled a chair out from the table and sat down across from me.

"You don't seem surprised," I said, knowing that as a mother, I should be grateful for the absence of the hysterics I'd envisioned.

"I was afraid of something like this, Mom, with the baby and all."

"Oh, honey, why would you say that? This has nothing to do with you *or* the baby."

"I told you being a grandfather wouldn't appeal to Dad, that it would make him feel old."

"That doesn't have anything to do with why he's deserting me." So much for not laying blame.

"No, but I suppose his feeling old is just the last straw."

"Last straw? And what might the other straws be?"

"Well, Mom, it's not as if you exactly make him feel—"

"What? Feel what?"

"I don't know. It's not all your fault—"

"*All* my fault? What's my fault?"

"Oh, Mom, this isn't any of my business. You and Dad should see a counselor."

I didn't blame her for wanting to extricate herself from her parents' problems—at least, I *shouldn't* have blamed her. But my shock at her reaction obliterated all rational thinking on my part. "Dad's too busy with his love life to see a counselor. You tell me what's my fault, Merritt." I knew I sounded like the me of yesteryear, like the mother who'd demanded the six-year-old Merritt tell her who spilled the Hi-C on the new carpet.

"Well, you can be pretty hard on Dad sometimes, Mom. I mean, when someone works all day, they want to come home and . . . and just *be*."

"I don't understand. I don't see what I've done to make you think it's all right for Dad to leave me for Taylor Stockton."

"For who?"

I felt a sick sense of satisfaction that at last I'd shocked my daughter. I didn't know what she was talking about, this business of my being at fault. Not to worry, though, she was about to tell me.

"Never mind; it doesn't matter who she is. And I don't want to kick you when you're down, Mom, but I'm sure it isn't hopeless. I'm sure you and Dad can work things out. I just think you need to face the facts. He's not perfect, and he has no right to do what he's apparently done. But if you don't recognize that your nagging and your putting him down and not listening to him, well—like you always told us, you can't improve if you don't first admit you need to."

"When have I put him down? When did I not listen to him? And if I nag, it's because he *makes* me nag." I could see Merritt roll her eyes, even as she tried not to.

It reminded me of the many times through the years that I'd defended my nagging to the kids as well as to Kevin. And whereas I still felt I had a valid point, I also knew I had an irritating way of lecturing instead of requesting, of noting the things my family *didn't* do and forgetting to show appreciation for what they *did* do.

"Just the last time we were with you guys, Alec asked Dad about one of his new products, and you interrupted him, telling him he was boring us all. You said *no one wants to hear all that, Kevin*." My daughter did a frighteningly accurate imitation of me and the pompous tone I could take.

"But Merritt, when he gets started talking about all that scientific stuff, I mean, that's not what Alec wanted to hear—"

"*You* don't know that, Mom. And it's embarrassing for everyone, not just Dad, when you do that."

"But isn't that what mates are supposed to do, point out to each other where they can improve or—"

"In front of others? No, Mom. And you always make Dad the butt of your jokes."

"He's never complained about my jokes." I was starting to get mad now, starting to feel Merritt was overstepping her bounds.

"Dad's easygoing, Mom, but it doesn't mean he doesn't have feelings. And it doesn't mean if someone else comes along who listens to his talk about chemicals and who makes him feel respected and appreciated—"

"Did you know about Taylor?"

"I have no idea who Taylor is. But she's probably no more than a symptom of what I've just been trying to tell you, Mom. It doesn't take a psychiatrist or a marriage counselor to see why Dad would want a Taylor in his life. I'm just saying I think you've taken Dad for granted—and I'm sure he's taken you for granted too," she said, her voice softening and a glimmer of the sympathy I'd expected showing in the eyes she'd inherited from me. She reached across the table and patted my shoulder.

I knew she was right about this: I had taken Kevin for granted. And in the last few weeks I'd come to long for Kevin's arms around me—arms I'd as often as not shrugged off as the years had slipped by. Lately I'd come to crave his lips on mine, and I couldn't even remember the last time I'd allowed, let alone enjoyed, a passionate kiss. I yearned for the sound of his voice, the sound of his footsteps on the stairs, sounds that had grown irritating to me through the years.

Things that once grated on my nerves now danced through my thoughts like a kid's Christmas wish list: the crunching sound of Kevin chewing ice or the stacks of literature on chemicals that threatened to overtake the den because he wouldn't throw anything away. Even his snoring would be music to my ears now, I thought, glad Merritt didn't know the way I'd always jabbed her father in the ribs whenever his snoring awakened me. She'd really blame me then.

But she'd be wrong, I thought.

What about the night at the airport? Wasn't I trying then? I could hardly tell Merritt about that, though, tempted as I was. Besides, I could imagine her reply: *too little too late*. She just didn't understand me or my needs. And I still felt almost as astounded at her reaction as I felt at her father's actions.

At last I took my self-pity and went home. Merritt tried to send me off with reassuring clucking about this being temporary on her father's part and my being okay even if it wasn't. But I felt utterly depressed at the knowledge that my daughter felt I had brought my devastating circumstances on myself, even in part.

I tried not to be mad at her, but I was.

CHAPTER SEVEN

"Why don't you come Saturday?" Ellen asked me.

"Because I can't bear the thought of seeing everyone. Not yet. Everything is just . . . so awful."

We were in my mess of a kitchen. I was heating bran muffins in the microwave, and she was making coffee.

"I know it is, but you've got to get back on that horse."

"Why? Why do I have to get back on the horse?"

"Because those people love you."

I stopped buttering the steaming muffins. "Ellen."

"Okay, okay. Maybe they don't love you, but they like you. And besides, *I* love you. And I miss you. Just come to the Webbs' Saturday. Steve and I will take you. We have fun with them."

"You'll have more fun if I don't come. You can all talk about me."

"Oh, come on. Just come for a drink. I'll take you home anytime you want."

"Ellen, I'm not a paraplegic. I can walk home. It's five houses away."

"Then you'll come?"

"No. I don't want to. Please, let's not argue about this. I don't want to spend Saturday night with four couples. I'd feel ridiculous."

"Okay. I understand."

"Boy, you give up easily."

She grabbed a muffin off the plate.

"But thanks," I added. "Thanks for including me. I'm just not ready. I may never be ready for the gang again. But thanks for—"

"You're welcome."

We took our muffins and coffee into the living room.

"Can I ask you something, El? And will you be really honest?" I sat down on the couch.

"Sure." She arranged herself across from me on the floor, her legs stretched out under the coffee table.

"Merritt seems to think I brought all this on myself. Somehow she has it in her head that I'm an incredible nag. Am I?"

"You? A nag? No way."

I felt a load lift from my shoulders. "Then why would Merritt say that?"

"Hormones. Youth. Newlywed. Looking for someone to blame. Daddy's girl. Plain old pissed off."

"Really?" I wanted to hug her for being on my side.

She put her mug down on the table. "Look, honey. My parents divorced when I was eighteen. I never got over it. I blamed my mother at first. Then my dad. I even blamed myself for a while. Divorce sucks. For everyone in the family. I don't expect Kevin's enjoying this too much himself, even though you might think he's having a good ol' time right now. Don't put too much stock in what Merritt says. She's hurting, just like the rest of y'all. She'll come around. She's a smart girl. But don't go getting any ideas that you did anything wrong. It's just like our new car."

"Okay. Your new car. Explain that one to me."

"Well, Steve went out and bought a brand-new car. We don't need it. There was nothing wrong with his old one. He was just tired of it. Probably drove by the dealership and saw himself in a fancy new ride. See what I mean? This Taylor Stockton comes sashaying around Kevin. She's new; she's shiny. She let it be known she could be taken out for a spin. And before you know it, ol' Kevin's trading in his old wife for a new one. It stinks. It sucks. But that's the way it is."

"Somehow this doesn't make me feel better."

She looked up and grinned at me. "Think how *he's* gonna feel when the new-car smell wears off."

I stood up. "Ellen, your analogy is atrocious."

"Honey, you need to think about getting yourself a fancy new ride. How about that guy you got fixin' your cabinets?"

"Okay, enough. Let's go to the mall."

"Can't hurt," she said.

***

Somehow, the days passed. Both kids kept their distance, I noticed. When I called them, or even the few times they called me, there was a coldness that chilled me. I'd never felt so separated from my children, and I resolved to put that right.

I'd begun calling Nina every night when I knew her kids were in bed and it was late enough for me to pour myself a glass of wine in the hope that it would make me sleep. The calls had become a ritual I looked forward to, and I sensed she did too.

"You need to get some cheer into your life, Jessie," she said one night. "What do you do for fun these days? Just call me?" She laughed, but when I didn't join her, she continued probing. "Don't you ever see any of your friends besides Ellen? Didn't you and Kevin spend a lot of time with a group from your neighborhood?"

"Oh yeah, just what I need. To hang out with a bunch of couples. Besides, I don't feel close to any of them except Ellen and Steve. In fact, apart from you and her, the only one I enjoy talking to is Heck." I laughed in spite of myself at the craziness of that.

"Your contractor?"

"My cabinetmaker. He's really a nice guy," I said, realizing for the first time just how much I looked forward to his coming over. "And he's kind of cute," I added. "And very funny. He always manages to say something to make me laugh. And let me tell you, that's not easy nowadays." I took a sip of the wine that I assured myself was only for sleeping purposes.

"Are you falling for this guy?"

"Don't be ridiculous, Nina. I could count on one hand the number of minutes I've spent with him. It's just that when he's here . . . well, I don't know. He just kind of lifts my spirits."

I couldn't admit even to myself what an understatement that was.

And the next morning, knowing he was coming to double-check the fit of the lazy Susan, I dressed for the first time in three days. I tried to tell myself it was the simple act of wearing clothes and a touch of makeup that lifted my spirits, but I knew I couldn't discount the way Heck acted genuinely glad to see me when I opened the door.

"How are you, Mrs. Harleman?" He thrust forward a hand that, in spite of its calluses, seemed too gentle, too delicate almost, to be in the world of construction, even cabinetry. Actually, it was, I would later learn, the hand of an artist.

"Jessie. Call me Jessie," I said, not for the first time. "I'm okay, Heck."

"Are you?" I could feel his penetrating gaze on me, even though I refused to look him in the eye. I remained uncomfortably aware that he knew my personal life matched the shambles of my kitchen. Soon he would have my kitchen back to normal—better than ever, in fact. I wished someone could fix my life that easily.

"I'm fine. But I was wondering about this one area." I led the way down the hall and into the kitchen, where I asked him if he could build a special cabinet to house my small kitchen appliances.

"Sure can. They call it an appliance garage. Actually, I've built what I think you're looking for in my shop. Maybe you should come take a look?"

I knew he worked out of Brown County, almost two hours away, but a trip to Southern Indiana, to a hilly country full of parks and trees, suddenly appealed to me. And maybe, just a little, the thought of spending extra time with Heck appealed to me too.

***

Late one warm August morning I went to Marsh Supermarket and asked for six sturdy boxes.

"You moving?" a young male employee of the store asked, as I led him out to my Jeep and watched him stash the boxes in the back of the vehicle.

"Yes." I nodded, not wanting to go into any detail. "Something like that."

"Good luck." He slammed the tailgate too hard.

His casualness offended me. What the hell did he know? I was in one of the black moods I'd been experiencing lately.

When I got home, I carried the empty boxes up to our (my) bedroom and began filling them with Kevin's belongings. He had not returned to collect any more of his stuff, and the whole house seemed full of his things.

First, clothes. I emptied his three dresser drawers, tossing his underwear, socks, and T-shirts into the first box. In one swoop of my hand, I cleared the junk off his side of the dresser, watching it all land on the heap of clothes. I threw shoes into a second box, followed by four suits still on their hangers. I watched with inordinate pleasure as they formed a pile, happy with the knowledge that they would be wrinkled and unwearable.

By midafternoon I'd carted two full, heavy boxes down to the front hall. And then I heard the phone ring.

I was still imagining, and hoping, that every call would yield Kevin on the other end. But even though I heard a man's voice, it wasn't my husband. Disappointment brought a lump to my throat.

"Jessie?"

"Yes?"

"Heck."

I'd forgotten about him. "Heck, how are you?" I walked into the kitchen, cradling the phone under my chin, and poured myself a glass of wine, glad he'd called and suddenly wanting a drink.

"I was just wondering," he said, in that offhand manner of his, as if nothing were really very important, "if you gave any thought to coming down to my shop. We talked about that appliance garage last week, and I'd like you to see mine."

"Heck . . . I'm not sure if I can get away." I returned to the living room and curled up on the end of the couch, phone in one hand, wineglass in the other.

"Ah, you're busy, are you?" he said, and I was suddenly twelve years old, with my father asking me if I was too busy to do the dishes when it was clearly my turn.

"Well, you know how it is."

"What? Being busy? Yes, I certainly do."

"Look, maybe on Sunday I could drive down there," I said, wondering *why*. But Sunday was several days away. Plenty of time to think about it.

"No need for that; I'll come get you. I have to be in your neck of the woods on Sunday. I'm bidding on a job up there. I'll swing by and get you. Maybe we could stop and have lunch somewhere. I know some great places in Brown County; we could—"

"Hold on."

He stopped talking, and I grew silent too, imagining Heck picking me up in his enormous truck and us eating a meal together. I was feeling something, but I wasn't sure what it was.

"Is there anything wrong with that?" he finally asked.

"Well . . ." I took a big swig of wine. "I guess there's nothing wrong with that. It might be fun."

"Don't do me any favors." He sounded almost surly, and I immediately regretted my own tone.

"I'm sorry, Heck; I would love to have lunch with you. Pick me up about eleven thirty."

"I'll be there."

I went back to filling boxes with a much lighter heart. I flung a tennis racket into an empty box and carried it to the living room, where I started on the CDs. I hurled all of Kevin's jazz collection into its new home. Billie Holiday fell on top of Ella Fitzgerald. Miles Davis landed on Billie. After that came his books. Good-bye, good riddance.

Then my hand stopped at a leather-bound copy of *Anna Karenina*. No. This was mine. I sat down slowly on the floor by the bookcase and opened its worn cover carefully. On the first page I read the words Kevin had written nearly thirty years ago. "*To my darling Jessica, my rose amongst the thorns. Love always, Kevin.*" I ripped out the page and then tossed the book in the box with the others. He could pass it on to Taylor.

No. For a few seconds, I rethought my action. It was *our* book. We both loved Tolstoy when we were young. Or at least I did. Did I force it on Kevin? Forget it; she could have the damn book. Crumpling up the torn page in my fist, I headed into the kitchen and tossed the ball of paper into the garbage.

Later, when all six boxes were full to the brim with Kevin's belongings and lined up by the front door, I called his office and waited impatiently while I listened to his voice mail inform me he wasn't there.

"Kevin, this is Jessie. All of your things are packed and ready to go. You can come get them anytime, but call before you do, so I can make arrangements to be gone."

As soon as I said it, I regretted every word. I was like a drowning victim tossing away my life raft. Giving him his things only took him further from me. No need for him to *ever* come home after that.

I settled back on the couch with my glass of wine and dialed Nina's number.

"Hi," she answered on the first ring, as if she'd been sitting by the phone waiting for me to call.

"Hi, Nina, what's up?"

"What's up with you?"

"Well, I packed up all of Kevin's stuff."

"Good girl!" she said, as if I'd just won first place in a competition.

"Yep, it's all ready to go." It wasn't true. I had saved several things I knew Kevin would want at some point in his life. Like the photo collection of vintage Porsches he was so proud of and the plaque some country club had given him when he'd scored a hole in one. "Wait." I reached across the coffee table and grabbed an ugly ceramic figurine. "I forgot something." I walked to the hall and tossed the figurine into a box.

"What? What is it?"

"Remember that awful-looking thing from his mother that we had on the coffee table? You know, those two Edwardian figures playing the piano?"

"Yes; I thought that was lovely."

"It sucks."

"Whatever you say, Jess. So have you spoken to the carpenter lately?"

"Well, funny you should ask. We're having lunch on Sunday."

"That's great, Jess. I'm so glad." I imagined her jumping up and down, pigtails flying, just like when she was a little kid.

"Yep, I guess I'm not quite the hideous old hag Kevin seems to think I am. At least someone wants to eat with me."

"Jessica, listen to me. You're not a hideous old hag. And you're not to blame. I don't care what Merritt said. She's pregnant, and she's upset about her parents and looking for someone to blame."

"Thanks, Nina—"

"No, no," she interrupted, and I could see the Nina of our childhood, explaining to me, the older sister, why I should apologize to our parents for some ghastly thing I'd done.

I felt a swell of love for her that almost choked me, and I had to swallow hard so she wouldn't know I was beginning to cry.

"You're a beautiful woman, Jessie. A lovely, intelligent, caring woman. Don't ever believe anything less about yourself."

"When did you get so smart?" I was crying openly now.

"Honey, don't cry. Not when I'm not there to hold you."

"Oh, Nina. How did it all go so wrong? What did I—"

"Jessie, don't start with that again. You did nothing wrong. Now get up, get dressed, and go to the mall and buy yourself something fabulous. Hey, you didn't give up Kevin's credit cards, did you?"

"Not yet." I sniffed. "We haven't had our *money* discussion yet."

"Good. So until you do, go out and run up the bill."

"Good idea, sis. But not right this minute. It's too close to my bedtime, and besides, I've been drinking wine. But I'll go first thing tomorrow," I said, wishing she were here with me. "I'll do just that."

***

As soon as the stores opened the next morning, Ellen and I were in babyGap, where I spent more than six hundred dollars of Kevin's money on our new grandbaby. I realized, as I signed the charge slip, that I'd already begun to think of it as *his* money, and the realization scared me.

Next, we stopped at Starbucks, and then, fortified by our cappuccinos, we went to Ann Taylor, where Ellen insisted I had to buy a to-die-for tangerine-colored dress.

"It's simple but elegant," she said. "But honey, you're so thin. You gotta quit losing weight. We're going to The Cheese Factory right now." And we did, right after I paid more than five hundred dollars for the dress and some gold earrings for both Ellen and me. In spite of her protests—maybe because of her protests—such extravagance made me feel even better than the cappuccino had.

My light mood continued while we made our way to the restaurant and talked about my upcoming lunch with Heck on Sunday.

"Your new dress will be just perfect," Ellen said, as she took a menu from the waiter. "A Diet Coke with lemon, please," she said, before he even asked for our drink order.

"The same," I said, but as he walked away, I assured Ellen I wasn't going to be getting that dressed up for my lunch date with Heck. "I don't think he's the type, nor is Brown County the place." Heck, I felt certain, was more the jeans-and-T-shirt or billowing-sundress-and-barefoot type.

"Oh hell, wear it anyway. You'll look marvelous in it. That's all that matters."

"Marvelous, huh? No wonder I love you, El." I smiled and thought *yeah, maybe I will wear it.*

CHAPTER EIGHT

On Saturday morning Merritt called to see how I was. Our conversation was strained, like all the conversations we'd had ever since I first told her about Kevin's leaving. But I made an effort to be cheerful. I couldn't bear the thought of us losing our closeness.

"You sound good, Mom," she said, her own voice sounding warmer and more natural than it had since our conversation a month ago about my shortcomings.

"I am. Oh, honey, I bought some wonderful things for the baby. I can't wait to show you."

"Come over for lunch tomorrow. Alec has to work—on Sunday, can you believe it? But he has a project he's finishing. It'll be just the two of us."

"Okay." Then I remembered Heck. "No, wait; I can't. I have plans for lunch."

"Plans?" Merritt asked, as if I'd told her I was interviewing for a job at Hooters.

"Yes, plans. Your old mother can have plans, can't she?"

"Of course. Who with?"

"No one you know."

A frostiness returned to her tone as she said good-bye, and I ached to be with her. I'd lost my husband; I didn't want to lose my daughter too. "Merritt—"

It was too late; she'd already hung up.

I called Nina right away, to hear her remind me that Merritt was wrong and I was right. When I got no answer, I made a beeline to Ellen's house, wondering what I would ever do without these two women in my life.

I pushed her back door open after giving our customary two-knock warning. "Got a minute?"

Ellen was sitting at the table, one hand wrapped around her coffee cup, the other tapping her iPad with a stylus, no doubt playing one of the games she loved. "Sure—everything okay?"

"Not really." I went to her cupboard and selected my favorite cup, her Kappa Kappa Gamma Mom's Weekend mug.

Ellen and Steve still had kids in college, and I envied her that stage in life. Freedom from the daily grind yet still such close bonds, such dependence on each other.

After she'd reassured me Merritt was wrong, stopping short, in her tactful way, of insulting my daughter, she moved on to another troublesome topic.

"Kick me while I'm down, why don't you?" I said, only half joking, after Ellen informed me—again stepping lightly but still bruising me—that "everyone" felt I was rejecting them.

"Oh, honey, I just thought you'd want to know."

"No, not really."

"Well, I thought you *ought* to know."

"Why?"

"Why?" She looked dumbfounded. "Because they've been your friends for more than two decades."

"They've been Kevin's friends too. Isn't *he* rejecting them?"

"As a matter of fact, he is. Joe said it was as if Kevin had fallen off the face of the earth. At least they know you're still alive because they see you drive in the neighborhood or cross the street to my house once in a while. But they don't know why you don't return their phone calls. That's why I really hope you're going to the shower for Krissi."

"Oh hell. I forgot about that. I suppose Merritt will be wanting to go, anyway. Hell." I knew it really was a must-show. Krissi and Merritt had grown up together, and I really did feel close to her parents, Joe and Leah Devine, having shared so much through our daughters. "Well, that's not until Labor Day weekend; I've got a couple of weeks." Then, hating to humble myself, even to Ellen, I asked, "What else are they saying about Kevin?"

"Same old, same old. That he's a stupid bastard to give up you and the family. That he's acting like a foolish teenager. That he's selfish."

"Tell me something I don't know. What about me? What are they saying about me?"

"That they feel sorry—"

"Yeah, well, now you know why I don't want to be around them."

"You don't mind *my* sympathy, or Nina's, do you?"

"No, no. But that's enough. That and the pity I have for myself. I could use a little more from my kids, but otherwise I'm wallowing in it. I couldn't bear to see everyone's faces. And besides, I'd feel so out of place being with all couples. Maybe the shower will be a good thing. Just us women."

"That would have been a good start, but . . ." Ellen looked as regretful and sympathetic as a doctor about to report a bad biopsy.

"Hell." That seemed to be my favorite word all of a sudden, and certainly the most descriptive word for my life.

"It's a couple's shower, isn't it? Whatever happened to the old-fashioned way of doing things?"

"I'm sorry," Ellen said, and I knew she truly was.

"Yeah, well, I'll deal with it." I took my cup to the sink and rinsed it out. I gave her a big hug before I returned home, hating that I'd brought her down too.

I tried to cheer myself with thoughts of my lunch date with Heck the next day, but as Saturday morning turned into afternoon, and then evening, I became filled with dread at the thought of it.

What had I been thinking? I didn't want to have lunch with a total stranger. I didn't want to have lunch with anyone but my own family. I wanted to help Merritt plan the baby's room. I wanted to do Teddy's laundry. And most of all, I wanted Kevin to come home and spend the evening with me, the way we had hundreds of times. Just the two of us. No Taylor Stockton or Heck Dennehey messing things up.

At nine o'clock I called Heck's number and left a message saying I couldn't make it tomorrow, that I was sorry, but maybe I could take a rain check. I had counted on his not being in his place of work on a Saturday night, and I was right.

Feeling both relieved and despondent that I no longer had a lunch date to look forward to, I thought of calling Nina. But I lacked the energy, and the fact that she didn't call me, either, reminded me that she was happily married and undoubtedly doing something with her husband on a Saturday night. As happy as I was for her, I felt a pang of envy that hurt only slightly less than my feeling of guilt that followed. Nina was too good to me. I had no right to begrudge her a happy marriage.

Knowing it might not be the best means of escape, I nevertheless turned on the DVD player and watched *An Affair to Remember*. Finally, at eleven thirty, doubting my own possibility for a happy ending, I took a sleeping pill washed down with a large glass of chardonnay. It wasn't so much to make me sleep as it was to make me stop thinking.

***

When I awoke the next morning, the message light was blinking on my phone. Convinced, as I always was, that it was Kevin, I eagerly pushed *play*.

"Jessie, this is Heck Dennehey. I got your message. No problem. I'll take a rain check, as you call it, on lunch. I'll be up on Monday afternoon to work on the cabinets. If that doesn't suit you, let me know."

I was disturbed that he *wasn't* disturbed. But I was also relieved that I didn't have to see him today.

Eagerly, I called my daughter. "Merritt," I said, as soon as she answered the phone. "Is your lunch offer still on?"

"Of course," she answered, sounding genuinely pleased to hear my voice.

"Good. Let's go out. Pick a place; I'll take you anywhere you want. Let's have some fun."

"Oh, Mom, I'm glad to hear you sounding so happy. I've been really worried about you. Dad said you—"

"You've spoken to Dad?"

"He called. We had a long talk. Mom, he's really hurting."

I wanted to fling the phone across the room. *He's* really hurting? A black rage consumed me. Again, I was mad at Merritt. And now renewed anger at Kevin surfaced, threatening to suffocate me. How dare he be calling our daughter? How dare he still be her father, when he couldn't be my husband?

"Honey, I'll be there at noon," I somehow managed to say, before hanging up and breaking down into racking sobs.

It all seemed so hopeless. Images of Kevin and Taylor danced in my head. Then, even worse, images of Merritt and Taylor played a frightening scene. The two of them laughing, becoming close. Doing all the things together that Merritt and I should be doing. *She already has my husband; she can't have my daughter too*, I thought in panic.

A black tunnel that had no end stretched before me, and I just knew it would go on forever. I didn't know how I could ever get through it.

Finally, with Merritt's sympathy for her father still reverberating in my ear, I slogged through a shower, where shaving my legs felt as arduous as mowing the lawn with a push mower.

I began to feel better as I blow-dried my hair and put on makeup. And my new dress lifted me out of my depression—at least for a while. I had to admit, I knew I looked good. The tangerine color set off my tawny skin and green eyes, while the cut of the dress accentuated my slim curves and showed off those legs I'd just found so hard to shave.

I desperately wished Kevin could see me. I even toyed with the idea of trying to find him and delivering his boxes myself.

But I knew Merritt was at least partially right: this wasn't about whether I was attractive.

At least my daughter appreciated the way I looked. "Wow," Merritt said, as she opened her front door to me. "When did you get that dress? What a great color for you."

"Like it? I got it when Ellen and I went shopping. But more important, I got these." I held my babyGap shopping bag out with one hand and closed her front door behind us with the other.

"Oh, Mom, you shouldn't have." She reached into the bag, looking like the Merritt of years gone by as she dug into the Christmas stocking I'd knitted when I was pregnant with her. I remembered adding her name in duplicate stitch while Kevin set up the Christmas tree and strung the lights that first Christmas we were a real family.

Tears sprang to my eyes now, as I watched my little girl's excitement at the prospect of having her own baby. And I found myself hoping with every fiber of my being that Alec would never hurt her. At the same time, I grew faintly aware of how self-absorbed I was becoming. Anymore, it seemed as if everything related to me and my pain. I needed to snap out of it.

And I did. For about an hour.

By then Merritt had finished oohing and aahing over the tiny unisex outfits in their pastel colors and driven us to Café Patachou. There, over turkey chili, Greek salad, and also a BLT for Merritt (she was always famished these days), I steered the conversation toward her father and *their* conversation.

"So you talked to your dad?" I tried to sound nonchalant but felt as nervous as a junior high girl asking a friend *did you tell him I like him, what did he say?*

I squeezed the wedge of lemon into my Diet Coke and took a sip, my eyes never leaving Merritt's, which looked pained. I fought back the urge to demand who she felt more sorry *for*, me or her father.

Her response surprised me. "I really owe you an apology, Mom." She poked at her salad with a fork.

A waitress appeared, and I forced myself to remain silent until she quit fussing over us and left. "An apology for . . . ?"

"You know, all the things I said that day, the things I said you did wrong. You were a great wife, and a perfect mother. I'm just so sorry . . . and Dad feels so awful."

I realized then that I'd been harboring a hope, however tiny and far-fetched, that her comment about her father "really hurting" somehow meant he missed me. She was about to disavow any such implication. "Just what did your father say to you, in this long talk?"

"He said what's happened has nothing to do with you, that he still loves you and wouldn't hurt you for the world."

"But?"

"But?" she repeated, looking puzzled.

"Well, I hear a *but* coming, don't I?" I abhorred the snotty, superior tone my voice had taken, but I had no more control over what was coming out of my mouth than a month-old baby spitting up.

"He just spent time with this Taylor, through work, and then that trip to New York, and, well, Mom . . . oh, it isn't right, of course; it isn't right. That's why he feels so bad." Then, as an afterthought, which told me she didn't believe a word of it, she added, "Maybe it will run its course. Maybe this is just a midlife aberration on his part."

"But you don't think so, do you? Merritt, tell me the truth. Don't encourage me to hang on to a life if it's never going to really be there for me." I reached across the table for her hand, and as I put pressure on it, her eyes lifted to meet mine. They were full of tears.

"Mom, it's so unfair, I know, but I think he's really in love with . . . with her. He wants to marry her."

I pulled my hand back as if I'd touched an electric wire with wet fingers. "He told you that? What else did he tell you?"

"Mom, I've already talked out of turn. Dad was confiding in me. You need to talk to him. He says you won't—"

"Why should I talk to him? What does he have to say that I want to hear?" My strident voice was rising, but I didn't care who could hear me. I felt out of control.

"Mom." She was using *my* voice again, the voice I'd saved for the times my kids needed to be threatened into behaving. And the look in Merritt's eyes was mine too. It said, *Stop that. Stop that right now. Or else.*

But whether it was because I knew she couldn't *or else* me—I was, after all, the mother, not the ten-year-old wayward daughter—I continued loudly. "Besides, I left him a message several days ago. Why hasn't he called me back to come for his things, if he's so damn eager to talk to me?"

"He's out of town right now, Mom. He'll be back tomorrow, I think."

"Coming back on a Monday, I see. I'm sure it was business that took him out of town, then. Monkey business." I hated how silly I sounded.

"What difference does it make?"

What difference does it make? Her comment depleted any energy I had left, and I lowered my voice. "Are you ready to go?"

"Yes, Mom, but I just want to say . . . please don't let this make you do something stupid."

I'd already tossed four twenties on the table—making it undoubtedly the best tip that waitress had ever received, but I wasn't about to wait around for change—and was heading toward the door.

But as I went, Merritt's words sank in. Once in the car, I forced myself to sound calm as I asked her, "What did you mean by *don't do something stupid*?"

"I mean, don't you go get involved with the first Tom, Dick, or Harry who comes along, just to get revenge."

I wanted to say *his name is not Tom, Dick, or Harry; it's Heck*, just to spite her, just to show her. She'd hurt my feelings, made me feel dumb, made me feel I was inferior to her and her judgment. She'd also made me wonder just how "involved" my feelings about Heck were, and if they *were* just about revenge. I remained quiet.

When she finally spoke into the silence, she sounded less stern but still firm. "I don't know who you'd made plans with today, but I do know it's awfully soon for it to be a man."

There was nothing I could offer her but continued silence. I certainly didn't feel like sharing anything positive with her, and enough negative words had been thrown out by both of us to last quite a while.

I continued to fume, however, even as she softened. After a few minutes and a quick, "I'm sorry; let's just drop the whole thing," she began to make pleasant small talk.

What made her soften, I don't know. Maybe it was just knowing she was wrong, or that I'd had enough abuse heaped on me.

For my part, that's how I felt—abused—and so I stayed mad through her chatter about possibly getting her hair cut and finding comfortable shoes.

When we reached her house, I stopped in front but didn't pull in the driveway. "Come on in, Mom; let's talk. I'm worried about you."

And then, striving to be the good mother I knew I was, I worried that this was too stressful for my pregnant daughter. Besides, she was the victim of her raging pregnancy hormones right now. She wasn't herself. "Oh, honey, don't. I'll be fine. I gotta go now, really. I promised Ellen I'd come for dinner," I lied.

As I headed back to Carmel, I felt sick to my stomach at how Merritt had become enmeshed in Kevin's and my troubles. It went against every belief I had about a kid's involvement in the parents' breakup, no matter how old the kid was. It was the ultimate in selfishness, I knew, to unload on a child. It was, in fact, abuse. But hadn't Kevin done it first?

Then again, what difference did that make?

***

My Sunday evening didn't go any better. I called Teddy to see how he was doing—or was it more to tell him how *I* was doing? Not that it mattered. I got his answering machine. "Dude. We're not in."

Duh. No kidding. And *dude*? Apparently, neither he nor his roommates held out any hope that a female would call. Or did modern women think that sounded cute? And what about prospective employers? Oh, what the hell did I know?

I grew so depressed, I didn't even pick up the phone when Ellen and then Nina called that night to ask how my lunch had gone. Ellen didn't leave a message, but caller ID told me it was my best friend.

Nina did leave a message, and I listened to my sister talk to my answering machine. "Jessie, are you there? If you are, pick it up. It's Nina. How was your lunch date? I guess you're not back yet. Hope that means you enjoyed your . . . uh . . . lunch." Nina giggled, and then I heard the click as she hung up.

I didn't have the heart to tell her my lunch date had been with Merritt, not Heck, let alone describe the disastrous conversation I'd had with my daughter.

I took a sleeping pill and my usual glass of wine, and still I had a sleepless night. How could I even doze off, when my head filled again with dozens of versions of how Kevin and Taylor might have started their affair and what they did when they were together now? Was I never going to run out of possibilities to explore?

CHAPTER NINE

Even though I felt as if I hadn't slept a wink all night, I must have. How else could Heck have awakened me that Monday morning?

In fact, it was from a sound sleep that the chiming of the doorbell pulled me. Disoriented, I reached to turn the alarm clock off before I realized it wasn't the source of the sound penetrating my sleeping-pill-induced fog.

I flung the sheet back, thinking how convenient that I'd fallen asleep in track shorts and a T-shirt—both remnants of Teddy's middle-school basketball practices. I stumbled downstairs and opened the front door just as Heck Dennehey was climbing back into his pickup.

"What are you doing here?" I called.

He stepped back down and peered around the door. "Good to see you too." He smirked.

"You said you'd be by this afternoon."

"Yeah, well, actually I'm going to have to put in that section of your cabinets later this week, if that's okay with you. But I was working up here and have to go back to the shop for something, and it just occurred to me maybe you'd like to ride along and look at that setup I was telling you about, see if it's what—"

"I just got up." Then I remembered Merritt's pointing out how I too frequently cut her father off, so I quickly added, "I'm sorry. I didn't mean to interrupt."

"No problem. You didn't interrupt anything worthwhile." He chuckled. "You look fine to me, but I'll wait if you want to change. No need to get fancy, though; it's just a shop full of sawdust and—"

"I'll hurry." I told myself I might as well get this over with or I'd have neither peace from Heck *nor* the cabinet I wanted for my small appliances. *Then again*, I asked myself, *how long will I even be living here?* On top of everything else, I detested this limbo my life was in.

"Come in and have a cup of coffee." I swung the door open wide and squinted into the sunny day as he made his way toward me.

Maybe I'd just been too long without a man, I mused, and Merritt would kill me, but I couldn't help but admire his lithe body in its worn blue jeans and faded navy-blue golf shirt. His tanned, muscular arms made him appear physically fit in spite of the slight potbelly he carried.

He wasn't quite as tall as Kevin, I started to note, but stopped myself as soon as I realized what I was doing. There would never be a good reason to compare anyone to Kevin. I pointed to the coffee maker as I pulled a small bag of French vanilla coffee grounds from the freezer. "Do you mind making the coffee? I just got up."

"So you said. What's this?" He wrinkled his nose in distaste as he read the label on the flavored coffee.

I left him to figure that out for himself as I hurried up the stairs and changed into a pair of dark jeans, white T-shirt, and deck shoes.

***

"This isn't half-bad." Heck sipped the coffee he'd made. He was behind the wheel of his truck now, and I sat by the other door, window down and wind blowing my hair as he drove us south on I-465. This was a route I'd taken many times, visiting the kids when they were at Indiana University in Bloomington.

I glanced over at Heck, who immediately returned my gaze and smiled warmly at me for no reason. I noted the way he smiled more with his dark-brown eyes than with his mouth. He was ruggedly handsome, and it felt good to be sitting near him.

***

"The food here is pretty good." Heck handed me a menu.

I looked around the truck-stop restaurant at the other diners. The women all looked overweight and frumpy. Most of the men were dressed like Heck—in jeans and baseball caps—but they were missing his aura of . . . what was it that lifted him above the ordinary? I decided it was the look of intelligence in his eyes, coupled with the kindness that made him a true gentleman, jeans or no jeans.

"Good." I took the menu and opened it. I was famished. That's why I'd agreed to stop, even though I'd declined his earlier invitation to dine at one of the quaint eateries in the picturesque town of Nashville, Indiana. "What do you recommend?"

"The pork chops are excellent." He smiled and kissed the tips of his fingers as if he were recommending chateaubriand.

"Okay, that's what I'll have."

"Good."

We closed our menus and placed them on the table. Then we sat looking out the window, watching an eighteen-wheeler try to maneuver into a parking space.

"That cabinet will be perfect for my stuff. I'm glad I saw it." I didn't know what else to say. I'd never sat down to a meal with a man I hardly knew. "It's really pretty down here. Have you always lived in Brown County? Did you go to school in Indiana—"

"Whoa." He put a hand out to stop my chatter. "Jessie, I wish you didn't feel so uncomfortable."

"I don't," I lied.

"Tell me what's on your mind."

"What? What kind of question is that?"

"It's an honest one. Tell me what's on your mind. If you want to, that is. If not, then I guess I can whip out my résumé, and we can go over it."

We both laughed, as a plump waitress approached our table. She was wearing a frilly pink apron and those white lace-up shoes that nurses wear. She filled our coffee cups and then took our order.

"You're a nice man, Heck," I said.

"Thank you. And you're a nice lady."

"I've never been out to lunch with a man who wasn't my husband—for no reason, that is."

"Then I guess I should feel honored."

"I wouldn't say that, exactly. It's been pretty rough lately. I haven't been myself." I knew I sounded so corny. So Joan-Crawford-on-the-verge-of-a-nervous-breakdown in a forties melodrama.

"Yeah." He sighed and reached for the sugar. "Divorce is shit. No getting around it."

"You sound as if you've been there, done that."

"Yeah." He stirred two spoonfuls of sugar into his coffee. "About ten years ago. And I was married for ten. One day, came home, and my wife tells me she's had enough. Wants out. So I helped her pack, took her name off my insurance policy, buried my wedding ring in the backyard, and me and Bo took off around the country for a while."

"Bo?"

"Black Lab. Best damn dog you ever saw. I buried him a few years later. Sad thing is, I cried like a baby when Bo went. Never even shed a tear over my wife."

"Really?"

"No, not really." He shrugged. "I cried over her too, only I never told anyone about that. Until now."

"I'm sorry, Heck." I sipped my coffee.

"Oh well. I figured I could replace the wife. But I could never replace Bo."

"And did you? Replace your wife, I mean."

"Not really." He leaned back in his chair as the waitress put two plates of food in front of us. "I've had a few female friends. Nothing serious. I've really put all my energy into my work."

"You make nice cabinets."

He laughed. "Not that. My real work. Painting."

"Oh, you paint too? We have some rooms—"

He laughed again. "Not walls. Canvases."

I felt foolish, as I unwrapped my knife and fork from the red paper napkin. "I didn't know. What kind of things do you paint?"

"Anything that strikes my fancy. I started out with landscapes. Then I moved to portraits. Dabbled a bit in contemporary stuff. You ever been to the Met in New York?"

"Yes. Kevin and I used to . . . I love that place. Do you get to New York very often?"

"About three times a year. Spend most of my time there at the museum. You find that hard to believe?"

"No, not at all," I lied again, trying to picture this man's man wandering around an art museum.

"It's okay. I guess I don't fit the profile. But it's my real love. Actually, Pre-Raphaelite stuff is what I've been studying lately. Are you familiar with it?"

I shook my head. I felt ashamed that I'd misjudged him. Then, wondering just how much, I asked, "Do you read?"

"Was that a *do*-you-read or *can*-you-read kind of question?"

"You're being unkind now."

"Yes, I am. I'm sorry. Yes, I love to read. History, contemporary literature; oh, and spy novels."

"Good for you." I smiled, the pork chops melting in my mouth, as I realized how comfortable I felt. Somewhere between the coffee and the pork chops, we had slipped into a cozy zone, and I was having a good time. "You were right; these pork chops are delicious."

"Yeah, nearly as good as mine."

"Don't tell me. You cook too?"

"You live alone as long as I have, you better learn to cook."

"I had no idea you were such a Renaissance man."

"There's a lot you don't know about me."

The waitress came back and refilled our coffee cups.

"So, what about you?" Heck asked, as soon as she left.

I cradled my cup in both hands, my elbows on the table. "What do you want to know?"

"Anything you want to tell me."

"Frankly, I'm a mess right now. I used to be so together. I don't know what happened, and I sure as hell don't know why."

"Is he giving you a bad time?"

"Kevin? Well . . . he's found someone else. Younger, prettier, smarter. It's such a cliché, I feel embarrassed even talking about it. He says he wants a divorce. I've been sort of hoping he'd change his mind. But I'm slowly coming to the realization that that's not going to happen. I just feel so . . . lost. I don't know where to turn. I want to talk to Kevin, and yet at the same time, I don't ever want to see him again."

"How about her?"

"Her? You mean the woman he's leaving me for?"

"What's she have to say for herself?"

"Well, I've hardly had a conversation with her."

"Why not?"

I put the coffee cup down. I couldn't believe he thought I'd spoken to her. "Surely you don't think I should talk to her."

"Don't see why not. Seems like she and you have some business to talk over."

"That's insane. I'm not going to talk to her. Why should I?"

"If you're not curious, then don't. I guess I just thought it'd be natural for you two to have a little chat."

"Oh, Heck. That's a really bad idea. I have nothing to say to her."

"Fine. Then have some of this apple pie instead. It's great."

"Excuse me. I have to use the restroom." I took the napkin off my lap and put it on the table. As I stood, Heck stood too, in a wonderful gesture that made me feel as though we were eating at a five-star restaurant in New York instead of a greasy spoon in the middle of Indiana.

As I wended my way around the tables, I realized how much class Hector Dennehey had, and I was filled with happiness that I was there with him.

Later, when he drove me home, he made me laugh all the way, telling me stories about difficult customers. I hoped he didn't consider me one of them.

When we got to my driveway, he jumped out of his truck and came around to open my door for me. Then he walked me up the sidewalk to the house.

"Thanks for having lunch with me, Jessie. I really enjoyed it. Maybe we can do it again soon."

"I'd like that very much."

He watched me unlock the door, then waved good-bye and was gone. I was suddenly sixteen again.

CHAPTER TEN

"Hello, Lois," I said, looking down at Kevin's secretary. She was sitting at her desk, writing something in an appointment book.

As she lifted her head, her kind eyes stared right into my own; there was no getting away from that stare. She stood, raising herself to all of her five feet eleven inches, and came around the desk. Then she took my arm, steering me by the elbow to a chair by the door.

"Jessie, it's good to see you." When she had planted me in the chair, she reached over and pushed the door shut. "Let me get us some coffee."

"No, no," I protested. I was still too full from my lunch with Heck to even entertain the thought of eating or drinking more. "I just needed to see Kevin. Is he here?"

"No, dear," she said. "Sales meeting."

"Ah," I replied, as if to indicate that I should have known. Actually, I *did* know. Or at least I *assumed* he still met with his sales staff late Monday afternoons. "Well, I was just in the area; I was so close, I thought I'd just—"

"Jessie, how are you?" Lois sat in the chair next to me.

"Well . . ." I wasn't sure what to say next, not sure what Kevin's secretary of the past twelve years knew. I was the outsider here, not belonging in my husband's place of business.

She stared at me intently, her small brown eyes, covered by out-of-date glasses, urging me to go on.

"Kevin has left . . . Kevin has . . ." I couldn't bring myself to say it. It was too humiliating.

She reached across and patted my hand. "I think I know what you're trying to say."

"He's left me for another woman, Lois," I blurted out, finding courage from somewhere. "And I need to talk to her." In fact, in the few hours since Heck had planted that seed, I'd had a growing need that now felt like an obsession.

She nodded her gray head up and down, a look of concern clouding her face. "Are you okay, dear?"

It was my turn to nod. Only I wasn't okay. I was an imbecile. What was I doing here?

She patted my hand and gave me a *buck up* look. "Men are such fools. Kevin in particular. You know, I look on him as more of a son than a boss. We've been together a long time."

"Has he said anything?"

"Oh no, dear. Not to me. He knows too well the response he'd get. But he didn't have to. I'm not blind."

"Lois," I said, in a voice so small I could hardly believe it was me speaking. "I'm not sure if I know what I'm doing, but—"

"Oh, you know exactly what you're doing. I have every confidence in you." She rose and went behind her desk, picking up the phone and punching three buttons. "Taylor?" I heard her say, as she winked at me. "This is Lois. I have some files Kevin needs you to go through. I wonder if you'd mind coming down here. Yes, that would be fine; right now is fine."

She hung up and hurried around the desk. "I'll leave you to it. Seems I have to go powder my nose. Oh dear, do women still powder their noses?" She gave a little laugh, patted me on the shoulder, and opened the door that led to the hall.

I sat there like a statue, too numb to wonder just how many other people here knew about Taylor and Kevin. Later, I would realize bitterly how humiliating it was that I'd probably been the last to learn. I reached for my purse, not really knowing why. Maybe I should be powdering my own nose, I thought inanely. But I didn't even carry powder with me.

After a few more minutes of garbled thoughts, I heard the door open and watched as a young woman stepped in. I knew it was Taylor, of course, but I didn't recognize her.

She had her blond hair pulled back in a careless but chic knot, and she was wearing one of those beautifully cut suits that look like they cost a fortune. Again, I was mesmerized by her long legs, which were emphasized by her short skirt and high heels. She stood in the doorway, as if considering whether or not to run.

Then, obviously deciding not to, she closed the door behind her and leaned against it, her hands behind her back. "Hello," she said, not afraid to look at me. If we hadn't been on the twenty-seventh floor, I might have tried to escape by the window. Even so, I didn't rule out the possibility.

"Hello." I was hypnotized by her youth. She didn't look as if she'd reached her thirtieth birthday yet. She was tall, and I noticed her excellent posture as she leaned against the door.

Still sitting, I felt at a disadvantage, so I stood up. But then, feeling so short compared to her, I sat down again.

"So." I picked an imaginary piece of lint off the hem of my skirt. Even though I'd changed into *my* best suit before coming here, I felt old and frumpy. Beneath my skirt my thighs felt like two lumps of cottage cheese, albeit smaller lumps than when Kevin had started all this.

Just don't start babbling, I silently warned myself. It was a terrible habit of mine: babbling to fill any awkward silence; and they didn't come any more awkward than this one. "So," I said again, as if commanding her to begin speaking.

She moved closer to me, and I could smell her perfume. Something I didn't recognize, but something distinctive and no doubt expensive. Had Kevin bought it for her?

"This is very difficult. I didn't know Lois could be so devious," she said, sounding almost friendly, like we'd both been caught up in some harmless prank. Her voice had a throaty quality to it that even I found sexy.

I raised my eyes to face hers. "Yes, I guess it is difficult." That wasn't at all what I wanted to say.

"Look." She leaned on the edge of Lois's desk. "I don't know what I'm supposed to say here."

"Kevin says he's in love with you." It was me talking; I know it was. But where had that come from?

She said nothing, and I was forced to continue. "He wants to divorce me. For you, I presume."

"Yes." That's all she said.

I desperately wanted Lois to come bustling back into the room and do some filing or something. But just thinking of Lois gave me the impetus to carry on. And Heck—what would he expect me to say?

"He's been my husband for twenty-eight years. We're going to be grandparents." *Stop, stop, for heaven's sake, stop. You sound pitiful. She knows all this. You don't have to explain your life.*

I looked up at her again, not afraid to meet her eyes now, and I was glad to see something there. Shame, maybe. Embarrassment, at the very least.

"I'm sorry," she said, not unkindly, returning my gaze. Then her chin came up, and a defiant look replaced whatever I'd seen before. "I'm sorry you're upset. But I don't think there's anything for us to talk about." She turned quickly and was gone.

I sat there for a long time, in shock. Then the door opened again, and Lois came in.

She walked over to me and knelt down in front of my chair. "Let me buy you a drink, Jessie. You can tell me all about it."

"No, thank you, Lois. Thank you, but really, I have a million things to do."

"Don't you want to wait for Kevin to come out of his meeting?" she asked, concern for me stamped on her face along with her curiosity.

"No, but tell him I was here, will you?" As if he wouldn't hear it from Taylor first.

"Of course, dear. Anything you want." Lois stood, raising me up with her. She handed me my purse. "Just let me know if you need anything. I'm always here."

Driving in my Jeep a few minutes later, I wasn't sure what I had accomplished. Other than the fact that I could see Taylor Stockton was a very attractive woman who dressed well and smelled nice and probably never had a single hair out of place. The best I could hope for was that I had at least ruined her day. But I wasn't even convinced of that.

I needed to talk to someone. Mortified, I realized I was experiencing that feeling again of perverse delight at what I'd done. As bad as it was, it somehow felt good too.

Just as I reached for my cell phone, it rang. "Okay," Ellen greeted me. "Steve will be home in five minutes. Tell me everything. Or are you still there?"

"Oh, Ellen. It was bad. It was stupid. I don't know what I was thinking. What *was* I thinking? I just did it. Lois must think I'm insane. No, I take that back. She set it up. But still, I just showed up there and—"

"Slow down. What the hell are you talking about? I'm talking about your day with that Heck fella yesterday. You did go, didn't you? Jessica Harleman, don't dare tell me you didn't go."

"Oh, that. Yes, yes, I went. But not yesterday. Today. It was lovely. He's very nice. But afterward, after he dropped me off at home, I went to Kevin's office."

She was silent, and I was aware of the brief time we had before Steve returned. She couldn't waste it thinking or being confused.

"So guess what?" I hurried on with my revelation. "I saw the famous Taylor Stockton. Lois set us up. It all sort of fell into place."

She was still silent.

"Ellen? Are you there?"

"Yes. Just trying to digest this. So. You went to his office. And this chick appeared. How was it?"

"Weird. She's beautiful, but I already knew that. And so composed. She didn't seem flustered, or even sorry. Well, maybe a little sorry."

"You sound as though you enjoyed it. Did you?"

"Is that wrong?"

"No. Nothing is wrong. You feel the way you feel; that's all there is to it. I'm more interested in Heck."

"I told you. He was nice. We had a great time."

"Did that inspire your little face-to-face with Taylor?"

"Kind of. He suggested it . . . acted like it was no big deal if I spoke to her. That I might feel better."

"And do you?"

Suddenly I felt exhausted. Drained, tired, downright sleepy. "I don't know how I feel. Except like taking a nap."

"Then do it, honey. Go home and take a long one. I'll call you later."

"Ellen, did I do the wrong thing?"

"Ain't no right or wrong. You just do what feels right. There are no rules for you, Jessie."

"And when will I feel sane again? How long will that take?"

"It will take as long as it takes. No more, no less."

"Thank you," I mumbled, and I shut off my phone.

***

As it turned out, Taylor had ruined *my* day. Of course that was only natural, since she'd also ruined my life.

I hadn't been home an hour when Kevin called to ask why I'd attacked Taylor.

I'd been unable to nap, of course. I tried, but just as I started to doze, I immediately felt wired, reliving every humiliating and spellbinding second of my short time with Taylor. I couldn't take a sleeping pill this early, so I decided to pour myself a glass of wine, hoping to still my hands that wouldn't quit shaking. But when the phone rang, my hand jerked away from the crystal glass that was my target, and wine spilled onto the cartons that doubled as a makeshift counter next to the refrigerator. I reached for the dishcloth with one hand while I scooped up the phone with the other.

"What was that all about, Jessica?" Kevin's deep voice demanded, not even bothering with a perfunctory hello-how-are-you.

"What?"

"You know what. Going to the office and attacking Taylor."

Attacking Taylor! I was speechless. On the drive home, I'd daydreamed that Taylor would tattle to Kevin, all right, but that he'd come to *my* defense and show up that night, jarred, finally, to his senses.

When would I come to my senses? I now wondered. Despair started to set in, but my anger shoved it out.

Before I could begin to shower that anger on him, however, he made me even madder. "I also wanted to talk to you about Ted," he continued. "What have you been telling him? He never returns my calls. I suppose you've told him how evil I am."

"Don't be so immature. Is that what dating a kid does to you? I haven't said anything to Ted." And it was true.

Because I didn't hear from Ted, either. But for some reason, I didn't want to tell Kevin that.

"Look, I got your earlier message, and I'll be over soon to collect the rest of my things. If not tonight, then sometime this week. And please, do us all a favor and don't bother Taylor again." And then he hung up.

***

I glanced at my watch and decided Kevin would never come this late to pick up his things. Besides, he'd said "sometime this week," not necessarily tonight. I knew that until he showed, I'd be as nervous as a teenage girl wondering if her ex-boyfriend might stop by any minute.

I went to my bedroom—noting how easily I now thought of it as *my* bedroom—and changed into a nightshirt with a hole under the arm. I'd learned in high school that if you wanted a guy to stop by and see you, look bad. They never dropped in when you looked good. So I guess I hadn't given up all hope that Kevin might come tonight.

I scrubbed the makeup off my face and eyes and put on more night cream than usual. After patting some ridiculously expensive eye cream around each eye, I searched for the phone and finally located it under a towel on the bathroom counter. (Why didn't I return it to its base lately? Why did I carry it around like someone waiting for a lifesaving organ donation?) Then I called Nina.

Just a few minutes into my maudlin conversation with her, she cut me off.

"Jessie, will you stop? Face it; Kevin did what a million other guys do every day. He met a younger woman, and he's willing to shuck everything and hurt whomever he has to hurt to have what he wants. Will you stop blaming yourself?"

"But Nina, I wasn't always—"

"Always what? Did he ever make a complaint to you, let you know he was unhappy with anything about your marriage, give you a chance to change anything he didn't like?"

"No . . . no, not really."

"And did you ever even look at another man, let alone do anything unfaithful? Did you not raise his kids and keep his home, like he wanted you to? Did you not keep your figure and your looks and start an interesting career, and travel with him whenever he wanted?"

I was touched that my sister didn't even pause for an answer between questions, so sure was she that I'd done all the things she apparently thought added up to being a good wife.

"You even took up golf," she continued, "and we both know you're as athletic as a ballpoint pen."

Okay, so my little sister didn't think I was perfect. But she managed to convince me I *didn't* deserve what Kevin had dumped on me, and I was ready again to do battle. I was ready to resolve something.

I couldn't wait for him to come for his things.

CHAPTER ELEVEN

I was feeling pretty good, putting some finishing touches on an article for the *Indianapolis Monthly*. I wouldn't get rich—or even self-supporting—on the pay, but it was the best in the city. Besides, I found my in-depth report on three local playwrights satisfying. I knew I'd done a good job.

Teddy called just as I was shutting down my computer. He asked if he could come by with his laundry and if I would fix him breakfast. Delighted, I agreed to both requests and was clearing the kitchen table so I could set it when he rang the doorbell.

"What are these things?" he asked, as I opened the door for him. He looked woefully at the boxes I'd packed with Kevin's belongings.

"Your Dad's stuff." I folded my arms across my chest.

He only nodded, looking sad, then stepped around them into the hallway.

"No hug?" I asked, as he walked past me into the kitchen, dumping his pillowcase of dirty clothes on the floor.

"You guys are really going through with this, huh?" He headed for the refrigerator. "Got any root beer?"

I watched in disbelief as he pulled open the tab on a can and then sat down at the table. He took a drink, leaned back in the seat, and stretched out his long legs.

"Ted." I moved some magazines from the seat across from him and sat down. "Why would you ask me that? Do you think this is a game?"

He took a long swig, and then, in the first tantrum I'd seen from him since he was a little boy, he threw the half-full can across the room. It landed in the sink, clattering against the granite.

"Ted! What's gotten into you?"

"Geez, that's a good one, coming from you. What's gotten into *me*? What the fuck has gotten into *you*?"

I was appalled and also a little afraid of him. I'd never known my son to display such physical or verbal anger, let alone both. "You can't talk to me like that." It was all I could think of to say, even though I could see his pain and instantly forgave him.

He was on his feet now, pacing around the messy kitchen, kicking at a box of tiles. Then he stopped and placed his hands on the back of the chair, and for a moment I thought he was going to pick it up and hurl it at me.

"You guys make me sick." He still held on to the back of the chair, but at least he didn't throw it.

He leaned forward at the waist, his irate face close to mine. "Why do you have to do this? Now? Now that Merritt's having a baby, and I'm getting it together? Why now? Why'd you have to go and ruin everything for the rest of us? You are both so selfish I can't stand to be in the same room."

"Then leave." I stared him down, mad at him and yet sorry for him at the same time. "If it's so unbearable, just leave."

"That would suit you, wouldn't it? You get rid of me and Dad at the same time. You can start your new life, and you don't have to bother with us."

Now I was on my feet. I had to clasp my hands behind my back to stop from slapping him. "How can you say that to me? Give me one, just one, example of when I've made you feel you were a bother to me. And as for your father . . ."

The unfinished sentence hung in the air.

"What, Mom?"

"I suggest you ask him to finish that sentence. I have never, not once, stopped wanting my family back the way it was."

"So this is all Dad's fault?"

"Do you see him around here?" I was shouting now, my hands clasped even more tightly, but not because I was saving Teddy from a slap. It was more from the urge to take him in my arms and hold him tight. "Did I leave him, or was it the other way around?"

"Maybe you threw him out. Maybe he left because of the way you are."

"And what way is that? Tell me, really, because I would love to know. What way am I?"

He spun the chair around and let go of it.

"C'mon, answer the question," I said. "You started this. What way am I?"

"Hell, I don't know." He was sitting down again, his head clasped in his hands.

"Teddy." I went to him and placed my hands on his shoulders. Then I remembered Ellen's words about feeling guilty over her parents' divorce. "Honey, I hope you don't think this is your fault. Any of this. Because it isn't; it has nothing to do with you."

He looked up at me, his brown eyes large and quizzical.

"I mean, it has everything to do with you," I said. "It's your father and your family. But it's not your fault."

He stood up again, clenching his fists at his sides. He spoke slowly, enunciating each word as if I were incapable of understanding plain English. "Why the hell would I think it's my fault? You've lost it, Mom. You've really gone and lost it. You couldn't hold it together, but I'm supposed to feel okay because you tell me it's not my fault. No fucking kidding."

Leaving his laundry, he stormed out of the kitchen and past the boxes in the hall, and soon I heard his car screech out of the driveway.

I was numb.

At last I went back to my computer, determined to give my article one last go-through.

As I reread my interview with Benjamin Foster, a twenty-four-year-old who'd written a first play about his mother dying of cancer, I tried hard to push Kevin's accusation of my attacking Taylor out of my mind.

Three days later, and I was still obsessing about it.

I was punching the keyboard so hard, I almost didn't hear the doorbell. As I ran downstairs to answer it, I heard the key being inserted into the lock from the outside. When I got there, I found Kevin standing at the open door.

My first thought was how good he looked. His hair was a little longer than he usually wore it, and I liked it. He smiled at me, and taking that as a good sign, I smiled back. "Come in."

"Thanks." He stepped around the boxes. "I see you really did pack up my things."

"Yes. What did you expect me to do?"

He walked past me and stood in the center of the living room, surveying it like a prospective buyer checking out a house. Then he turned to face me. "About your talk with Taylor—"

"Wait just a minute. First of all, it was hardly a talk. She didn't have much to say for herself, and I think I had even less. And secondly, where the hell do you get off saying I attacked her? I don't know what that bitch said to you, but—"

"Okay, okay, Jess." He raised his hands in a gesture of surrender. "I was out of line. I probably would have done exactly the same thing in your place. Can we just forget about it?"

"Forget about it? No, we can't just forget about it." I plunked myself down on the couch, not at all sure where I was going with this.

"Look." He sat down next to me. "This is difficult for everyone. But Taylor isn't to blame. If you have to blame anyone, blame me. I deserve it. Hurting you is the last thing in the world I wanted. I want us to be friends."

"*Friends?*" I screamed. "I don't want to be your friend. You're supposed to be my husband, Kevin, not my fucking friend."

And then, before I could stop them, the tears started again. Just when I thought I'd cried every last one of them out of my system, here they came again. Streaming down my face. I felt sure that when Taylor Stockton cried, her face didn't screw up, and her eyes didn't get red. Then again, what the hell did she have to cry about?

"Please don't cry, Jess," Kevin said softly. He took my hand and held it for a while. Then, even though his touch made me almost tingle, I roughly shook his hand away.

I sniffed hard and wiped my cheeks with the palms of my hands. "Why don't you just get your stuff and go?"

"I want to make sure you're all right." He reached for my hand again, but I pulled it away.

"Well, I'm not all right. I'm in agony. I just don't think I can do this."

He looked at me and nodded, but it was painfully obvious he couldn't come up with anything I wanted to hear.

"Tell me," I said, trying to think of some way I could point him back in the direction of our marriage. "Is this really what you want?"

His silence told me more than any words he could utter, and I felt my heart taking nosedives inside my chest.

"Answer me," I said. Some strange being had taken over my body, insisting that Kevin actually hurt me some more.

"I don't know what I want," he said at last. It wasn't what I wanted to hear, of course, but it could have been worse.

"But you are in love with her, right?" I went on, plunging the knife deeper into my own chest. "Right?"

"I guess so. I don't know. I just know . . ."

"Yes, go on. You just know what?"

"I just know I'm not happy . . . here." He looked around the room again.

Aha. So it wasn't *me*. It was the *house*. It was the wallpaper, or the coffee table, or the way I'd arranged the furniture.

"Don't do this," I said in a tiny voice. "Please don't do this." I couldn't look at him as I said it, but some part of me knew I had to at least say something along these lines. Twenty years from now, I didn't want to regret that I hadn't at least asked him not to leave.

"I have to, Jessie. I hate myself for what I've done to you, to our family. But I have to."

When I looked up, he was crying too. Of course he'd obviously been taking crying lessons from Taylor Stockton. No loud noises, no runny nose. Just perfect tears slipping down his perfect face.

I cried harder then, and without realizing how it happened, I was suddenly cradled in his arms. The two of us rocked together on the couch. "I miss you," I said into the wet stain my tears had formed on his shirt.

"I miss you too, honey."

"Then why? Why, Kevin? I know you haven't stopped loving me."

He pulled away from me a little, but still held me in his arms. "Jessica, I'll never stop loving you."

"Then—"

But now he pulled completely away. "Let's not go through this anymore. Let's stop hurting each other." He stood, thrusting his hands deep into his pockets, as if it were the only way to control them. "I'm going to start loading the car."

"Fine." I sniffed. "Get your stuff out of here."

I stayed seated on the couch, listening as he made six trips to the car. Without even looking, I could feel the emptiness in the hall once the boxes were gone. Could feel the absence of Kevin, could feel my life disintegrating, unraveling, as I heard the car door slam.

"That's it, I think," he said when he returned.

"Good-bye." I waved, not turning to look at him.

"Jess, there are a few things we need to discuss."

"Such as?"

"Money, for one."

"Not today, please. Call me. You are still allowed to call me, aren't you?"

"I'm allowed to do anything I want," he said. Was there an implied *now* at the end of that sentence? Now that he was about to be divorced from me? When I looked up at his face, there was a new hardness there.

I felt so weary I thought I could fall into a deep sleep right then and there. I wanted to sleep forever. I closed my eyes and felt him gently kiss me on the cheek.

"If you need anything, anything at all, just call me."

"Yeah, right," I said.

"Do you have enough money?"

"Money? I have *your* money, Kevin. No, wait, I just wrote an article, so I also have another three hundred fifty dollars pouring in any day now."

"I'll take care of things. Give me a few days to work things out. And before I forget, I went to see Bill Rizzo."

"Bill Rizzo?" I asked incredulously. He was one of our friends—*our* friends. And an attorney. A guy Kevin played golf with, married to a woman I played bridge with. I cooked dinner for him and his wife a couple of times a year, and they returned the social favor. "Not him! He doesn't handle . . . he's a tax attorney, for heaven's sake."

"Doesn't make any difference. He can take care of things discreetly."

I rose, feeling sick. "You better go now, Kevin. I have work to do."

"Okay. But I mean it; call me . . . if you need anything."

"There's nothing I need that you can give me."

***

"Ellen, I don't think I can do it. Really."

"It's no big deal. Just Joe and Leah and Mike and Marty. We'll just have a drink, and you don't even have to stay for dinner. Think of it as a rehearsal for Krissi and Ben's shower," she said.

"Oh crap. That's coming up, isn't it?"

"Not for another week. And I just remembered—Carol will be there without Dan tonight. He's out of town, so you won't be the only single woman."

"Right; I'll be the only one who'll soon be a divorcée."

"Wow. You make it sound so glamorous."

"Shut up."

The group was going to Perry's, a local eatery that had a piano bar where we'd spent many happy Friday nights over the years. About once a month we met, just a group of neighbors, and I'd always enjoyed it.

Kevin wasn't always with me; sometimes he was out of town. And a few times some of the other women had shown up without husbands, so going without him this time should have been no big deal. But it was. This time everyone knew he wasn't out of town or nursing a sprained ankle. This time they knew I was pitiful and pathetic and, even worse, alone. For good.

"If I go, will you stop badgering me?"

"No. But go anyway."

I hung up and began to get ready.

I insisted on driving my own car, even though I knew I would then have to forego the comfort alcohol could provide. More important, I wanted to be able to make a hasty exit if needed.

I was twenty minutes late, not on purpose but because I changed my mind about a hundred times before I actually picked up my car keys and headed out the door. And I had to drop by the grocery store for some Diet Coke and coffee, two of my writing staples.

I was dismayed to find out that even a stop at the grocery store turned into ruminations about Kevin: I found myself obsessed with the contents of other shoppers' grocery carts, trying to determine who was feeding a family and who was eating alone, like me. The other losers.

If the grocery store can plunge me into divorce despair, what is Perry's going to do? I wondered, as I pulled my car into the lot and parked next to Ellen and Steve's new Mercedes. I was suddenly reminded of Ellen's comparison between Taylor and a new car. With a slight giggle that threatened to turn into a sob, I headed toward the bar.

There were more of our friends there than Ellen had predicted. Probably because they knew I'd be coming without Kevin. And Carol, I noticed, wasn't alone, as Ellen had said she'd be. Her husband, Dan, sat right beside her.

Steve hopped up as I stood in the doorway, and rushed over to encircle me in a hug, as if he hadn't seen me in twenty years. "Ellen was ready to organize a posse." He released me and turned to the group, the only patrons in the joint. "Look who's decided to join us."

A few of the guys stood up, and everyone had big grins on their faces. "Jessie," Leah Devine said, rising as well. "Come sit next to me. We're just talking about plans for a trip to Las Vegas. Joe, get Jess a drink."

"How's Merritt?" Carol asked. "You must be thrilled about the baby."

"How's the kitchen coming along?" Marty Shields asked.

I eased into the empty seat between Leah and Joe and listened in awe at the millions of questions thrown my way.

I'd known these people for twenty years. We'd all raised our kids together. Sometimes along the way we'd had arguments, but only little ones. We still managed to get together once a month or so. And we always spent New Year's Eve together, and sometimes Halloween.

We'd been there for each other when Dan had a mild heart attack and when Lisa Rizzo had her breast-cancer scare. I knew them as well as I knew my own family. But it made no difference; I still felt like I'd forgotten to wear clothes or I had toilet paper stuck to my shoe and no one had told me.

"Should we get a table for dinner?" Steve asked.

"Yes, I'm starving. Get some menus," Dan said.

"Menus? Like you haven't memorized the menu after all these years?" Steve laughed.

I looked over the rim of my glass of Diet Coke and caught Ellen's eye across the table from me. She winked. It was an *atta girl* wink. At that precise moment Leah squeezed my knee under the table. It was a *glad you made it* squeeze.

And then, for no reason, I put my glass down and stood up, grabbing my purse from under the table. "Look, guys, I love you all, but I'm not staying. I have work to do, and I have to get up early in the morning."

Steve and Dan both stood at the same time. "C'mon Jess," Steve said. "Don't go. We'll do some singing after dinner 'round the old piano."

"Hell, if you're gonna do that, then *I'm* leaving too," his wife said.

"No, really, I must go. You've been kind, but—"

"Wait." Leah stood too. "We're not being kind here. You're not a charity case. We want to have dinner with you, our friend. You don't get to break up our little group, just because . . ."

"Because Kevin left me?" I asked.

Suddenly it was quiet, for the first time all evening, and Leah sat back down.

I sank back into my seat, but I kept my purse on my lap, ready to flee. "Look, I think we're all too busy not saying it, but I want to talk about it, a little, anyway. Kevin has left me. He has another woman. She's young and gorgeous and smart."

"Big whoop," Ellen said. "You're gorgeous and smart. Okay, you're not so young, but neither is Kevin. Neither are we." She waved her hand around, encompassing our whole group. Not everyone looked like they appreciated her remark, but I did. "The cat's out of the bag now," she continued, "so let's eat; and Jessie, don't even think of going anywhere."

"I feel like a fool," I said to my purse. "You're all so kind, but I feel like a freakin' fool."

"*You* feel like a fool? You should have seen Devine on the golf course this afternoon." With that remark from Steve, they all started laughing, and my little problem became just that. For that night, anyway. Just a little problem.

I wanted to hug them all, and in fact I did, several hours later, after dinner and more drinks for most. And after Ellen had given her famous rendition of *The Yellow Rose of Texas* back in the piano bar, while the men all howled like coyotes, the same thing they'd done for the past twenty years. We all laughed like we were hearing it for the first time, and I left feeling a little sorry for Kevin.

Somehow I couldn't envision Taylor Stockton being so silly.

Steve buckled me into the Jeep, while the others all noisily found their respective vehicles. "You can't get away from this group, Jess."

"Seems that way." I put my key into the ignition. "Thanks. Thanks for everything." I kissed him on the cheek.

And then I drove home happy. Until I got to my garage.

That's when it hit me: for the first time after such an evening, I was going home alone. I leaned down on the steering wheel and had a good cry.

CHAPTER TWELVE

The hallway seemed desolate without Kevin's boxes. It mirrored my life. I found myself constantly fighting a rising panic, which reached a peak by the next Friday night.

I was wandering around the house, wanting to talk to someone, anyone, but not having the energy to pick up the phone. Thank God, it rang, saving me and my carpet from any more of the pacing that threatened to wear us both down.

It was Heck, and on hearing his voice, I said a silent prayer of thanks that he'd called at precisely the right moment.

"Jessie, I'm just finishing up here in Zionsville. There's a movie I've been wanting to see..." He paused long enough for me to feel my hopes lift. "If you're not busy, I could come pick you up, and we could go together?"

"Oh, Heck, that's the best offer I've had all week. In fact, it's the *only* offer I've had all week. Unless you count my son and his laundry," I joked. But the thought of my visit from Teddy stuck in my heart, and I had to force myself not to think about it. "I'd love to go with you," I fairly babbled.

"Are you sure? It's a French film, subtitled. *Belle de Jour*. Catherine Deneuve."

"Just what I need. Two hours of watching a gorgeous French woman." I laughed, making my way up to the bathroom and turning on the shower.

"You haven't seen it?"

"Yes, of course, hasn't everyone? But it's been a long time." The truth was, I *loved* old movies, French *or* American.

"Okay, then, I'll pick you up in an hour."

"I'll be ready."

I can't say my thoughts of Kevin disappeared, but the idea of a movie, and a good old-fashioned French one at that, sounded so comfortable and normal. And I really looked forward to seeing Heck again.

After I blow-dried my hair, I dressed in skinny jeans—that looked better on me now than when I'd bought them—and a plaid cotton shirt over a gray Gap T-shirt.

We both laughed when I opened the door—he was wearing practically the same outfit. "This is scary," I said, automatically offering him my cheek to kiss.

"You have great style, Mrs. Harleman." He pecked my cheek and touched my shirt sleeve. "Nice-looking duds."

We had a wonderful evening, even though I had to push Kevin out of my mind about once every fifteen minutes. So many things in the course of an ordinary day sparked pain-inducing memories. But Heck was more talkative than usual, perhaps sensing my troubled state, and I felt so grateful to this nice man.

After the movie, we went to Bazbeaux in Broad Ripple and sat outside at a table for two, eating pizza and drinking wine.

"She certainly was a beautiful woman," Heck said of Catherine Deneuve.

"Was? She still is. A woman can still be beautiful in her . . . whatever she is, sixties, seventies."

"Hey," he protested, pouring me some wine. "I didn't say women couldn't be beautiful in their sixties and seventies—and beyond."

"Oh, right. And how many women that old look like Catherine Deneuve?"

"Jessie." He stopped pouring the wine. "Are you looking for a fight?"

"Heck, I'm sorry." I felt busted. The truth was, Kevin had loved this place, and I was filled with a memory of when we'd first discovered it. "I was thinking of something else."

"Your husband?"

"Yes. He came to collect his things last week. I guess it hit me harder than I thought."

"No problem. I understand. Just don't take it out on me, please." His brown eyes bore into mine, kindly. "But if you want to talk about it, I'm all ears." When I just stared back at him in silence, tears welling, he continued, "I know this is hard for you. And I want to be a good friend to you."

I reached across the table, meaning to pat his hand, but he grabbed mine instead, holding it firmly. It felt so good. I didn't want him to ever let go. Then he returned to the subject of the movie, and we finished off the bottle of wine. Or more accurately, *I* finished it off.

By the time he drove me home, I was feeling lightheaded, happy, and so very, very grateful that this man had brought something sweet and special to this otherwise dreadful period in my life.

***

"Mom!" Merritt chastised me, and I felt tears begin to burn my eyes. *Please don't let me start crying.* I wasn't sure what she was berating me for, my choice of words or the concept I was conveying.

"Men are such assholes," I'd just interjected into my conversation with my friends, women I'd felt comfortable enough with to be honest. I just hadn't realized I'd also been loud enough for my words to reach Merritt—and presumably her friends, with whom she'd seemed immersed in a conversation about maternity clothes.

But so what? Wasn't I old enough to swear if I wanted? Wasn't I wise enough to know if men were assholes or not?

The baby shower had been a disaster, from the time Merritt had called that morning and said she and Alec would pick me up.

"Alec's going too?" I'd asked—pointedly, I hoped.

"Well, yeah. It's a couple's shower."

"So it is." I took a deep breath. "Okay, I'll be ready by seven fifteen. Try not to be late," I'd said, in the same snippy tone she was now so embarrassingly using on me. But the last thing I'd wanted was to make an entrance into a crowd of couples. "You know what?" I'd suddenly changed my mind. "I'm just going to walk over." And I hung up, wondering if I'd made the right decision.

Well, I wasn't about to call my daughter back to change the plan. So on the dot of seven thirty, I was the first to arrive at Jerry and Tina Webb's.

"Oh, Jessie," Jerry said, as he opened the door and proceeded to just look at me.

"Hi, Jerry." When he made no move, just stood with his mouth and the door wide open, I continued. "Am I too early? For the shower?"

"No, no, no. I'm just . . . I was just . . . just come in."

Jerry was obviously at a disadvantage tonight, without the buffer of alcohol that had no doubt smoothed his way at the piano bar the previous week. He immediately grabbed a beer from the full tub of cans and bottles smothered in ice, and only then did he think to ask me what I wanted to drink.

"The usual." I reminded myself that this was Jerry, my friend, so I shouldn't add that I was still myself, that just because Kevin had left me, I hadn't turned into the three-headed monster I felt like. I still drank chardonnay, as had all the women in our group for decades. Except, of course, for Ellen. Everyone knew Ellen was *the* Bud Light woman.

For a second, Jerry looked blank, as if he'd never seen me before, let alone had any idea what I drank. "Yeah. Sure," he finally said, going to the sideboard and pouring me a glass of wine.

No sooner had he handed it to me than he embarrassed us both again. "Here, come fill out these baby bottles for our game . . ." His voice trailed off just as we both noticed that the construction-paper bottles on the card table in the corner came in pairs. I saw his and Tina's already filled out: Jerry's name written in black marker on the blue bottle, Tina's familiar calligraphy letters spelling out her name on the pink.

I grabbed a pair of attached bottles, scrawled my name on the pink half, and put it on top of Tina and Jerry's, promising myself I'd make my getaway before this stupid game started.

"Can I help you with anything?" I asked Tina, after making my way around Jerry and into the kitchen. I set my glass down on the counter, so I could do whatever task she wanted to assign me.

"No, but thanks. Everything's under control, I guess— no thanks to *him*, of course." Tina laughed, that you-know-how-useless-husbands-are laugh that wives love to laugh.

"Of course." I plucked my wineglass from the counter when I heard the doorbell ring and made my way to the living room, straining to hear the voices that filled the foyer. But my hope that it would be Merritt and Alec was in vain.

It was Joe and Leah arriving with the guests of honor, their daughter Krissi and son-in-law Ben.

"Look at this happy group," Jerry greeted them. "Wow, I don't know who I envy more: the grandparents-to-be or the parents-to-be!"

"I think we're the lucky ones, aren't we, hon?" Joe said. "We just get to play with the little one—no braces or college education to pay for." He laughed, as he encircled Leah's thick waist with his arm. She leaned her face up and brushed his lips with a kiss and then pinched his cheek, flirting as if he were her date instead of her spouse of decades.

"I think you ought to envy *us*, Mr. Webb," Krissi said. "We have the most eager babysitters in the world."

"Jerry. Call me Jerry, Krissi. How many times do I have to tell you?" But he took her bulk into his arms and gave her an affectionate hug. Then, patting her on the top of her blond head, he turned to her husband and said, "I suppose she calls you Mr. Paxon, eh?"

"Oh, she calls me a lot of things," Ben said, and there was merry laughter all around.

"Mom, I'm going to get a glass of water. Want one?" I heard Krissi ask her mother.

"Yes, please, sweetie. I'm so thirsty from those fajitas too. We ate at Don Pablo's," she explained to Jerry.

"Jess, hi, how're you?" Joe asked, as they all made their way toward me. He was as nonchalant as if it were perfectly natural for me to be there without Kevin.

"Hi, Jessie," Leah said, sounding as if she adapted to change as quickly as her husband.

"Fine," I answered, but they'd already moved on to Tina, who'd just joined us from the kitchen, making me literally the fifth person, if not the fifth wheel. "Tina, hi, how are you?" Joe asked. I'd never realized how irritating he was. Not to mention insincere.

And then Dan and Carol Fox arrived, and they were a little too lingering, too solicitous, in their hugs to suit me. "Hey, sweetheart," Dan said, showing his best feminine side as he hugged me and patted me on the back like someone consoling a crying baby. As Carol repeated her husband's little routine, they seemed cloying to me.

And things only went from bad to worse. When Steve and Ellen arrived, talk turned to the upcoming trip to Las Vegas. I could tell Ellen tried to change the subject, but everyone else was irrepressible.

"It's gonna be great," Carol said, sipping her chardonnay. "I'm sitting by the pool from sunup to sundown. It'll still be hot there, won't it?"

"Who cares about the weather in Vegas?" Joe asked. He went there half a dozen times a year, always claiming the trips paid for themselves. "It's never too cold or too hot for blackjack." He sounded positively giddy, and I felt positively sick.

Ellen followed me to the bathroom. "Honey, honey; I'm sorry everyone's talking about our trip," she said, slipping into the bathroom behind me and closing the door.

"Don't be silly. Why shouldn't they?" I sat down on the toilet.

"Because . . . well, because it must be boring to you." She sat down on the tub across from me.

"Ellen, I feel a lot of things lately, but boredom is certainly not one of them. Boredom might be peaceful."

"You know what I mean."

"Ellen, could you please . . ."

"Oh yeah. Sorry, honey; I forgot about your bashful bladder. I'll wait outside."

When I returned to the living room, I was glad to see that several young couples, including Merritt and Alec, had arrived. The conversation had obviously changed to include all of them. There was a buzz of catching up: who had bought their first home, who else was expecting their first child, who was working their way up the corporate ladder. I used to revel in the lives of these youngsters. But now I felt jealous of their happiness, even as I felt skeptical that they could retain it.

Alec, bless his heart, came over to me and asked if he could freshen my drink. "Thank you." I smiled at my son-in-law and thought how lucky Merritt was.

"No problem." He took my glass but paused before heading to the drinks. "I wish you would have let us pick you up. We'll definitely take you home."

"You're too kind. Actually, Alec, I wanted to get here early; I thought it would be less conspicuous."

"Why would you worry about being conspicuous?"

"I didn't mean conspicuous. Less awkward, maybe."

"You shouldn't feel conspicuous *or* awkward. You should feel lovely and loved. Because you are."

What a son-in-law. What a guy. I forgave Merritt on the spot for anything hurtful she'd ever done; she'd more than made up for it by giving me Alec.

By the time he returned with my drink, the men had managed to disappear to the pool table in the bonus room, while the women had gathered in the kitchen. We both made our way to our proper places, where I felt relief at being one of a homogeneous group.

The young women were sitting on stools around the breakfast bar, while my peers had arranged themselves nearby, around Tina's trestle table. There was the welcoming sound of ten women all talking at once, in various groups, with no one missing a thing.

I saw Merritt sitting next to Krissi, so deep in conversation I didn't want to interrupt, even though I hadn't had a chance to talk to my daughter since she'd arrived. I'd only waved across the room to her at one point. I made my way past her now, to the bench where Ellen was sitting. She scooted over to make room for me.

We covered a lot of topics in a short time, but inevitably, in spite of Ellen's best efforts, the topic became husbands. Leah had started by complaining that Joe liked Vegas just a little too much to suit her. And I was only trying to blend in, trying to put the others at ease—albeit with a newfound and fervent belief in what I was saying—when I'd assured my friends that all men were assholes.

I hated the way my daughter's rebuke made me feel so . . . so . . . uncouth? Unintelligent? Undone! If any of the other moms had said what I had, Merritt would either have pretended not to hear or giggled in agreement—depending, probably, on how she viewed Alec at the moment. But I, her mother, was apparently supposed to behave exactly as she felt appropriate, with no leeway for how *I* wanted to act. Talk about role reversal.

Tears continued to sting my eyes—and not just because of Merritt, but because of *everything*. When Tina left the table and called to Jerry to get ready for the baby-bottle game, I knew I'd had enough.

Telling only Ellen that I was leaving, I slipped out the back door while everyone else headed for the living room.

CHAPTER THIRTEEN

"So you like them?" Heck leaned against my kitchen island in that casual way of his that matched the way he dressed. On this September morning that held a hint of the fall crispness to come, he wore blue jeans, of course, and a tan cotton turtleneck sweater that made his brown eyes look almost black.

"They're beautiful, just beautiful. They're a work of art."

And they were, my new oak cabinets that now hung like luxurious draperies, encircling one end of my kitchen. And there were so many of them! I'd always wanted a lot of cupboard space, and now I had plenty. *How perfect, now that I'm the only one living here*, I thought.

I inhaled deeply to draw in the smell of new wood that I wished would never go away. Then I reached up and ran my fingertips across the door of my new appliance garage, reveling in its silkiness. It looked exactly like the one Heck had shown me down in his Brown County shop.

"I absolutely love them," I said. "I'll get in touch with Kevin today and make sure he sends you the rest of your money."

I hadn't spoken to Kevin since that night a month earlier when he'd come for his things. Since then, I'd refused to return several phone calls—feeble attempts on his part to "get things settled." *What possible difference does it make whether we ever settle things?* I thought, sapped of energy every time I heard his voice on my answering machine.

"I'm not worried about the money," Heck said with a grin. "I know where to find you."

"It won't do you any good to find me. I don't have the money to pay you."

"Still, I'd rather find you than that husband of yours—or anyone else." I suddenly realized maybe it wasn't the sweater that intensified the color of his eyes, as they stared at me now in anything but a casual way.

Over the past several weeks, I'd seen Heck almost every day—partly because he was there installing the cabinets and partly because he kept asking me to have lunch or dinner, see a movie, run to Menards with him to pick out something for the cabinets, or ride with him to his shop so I could see the splendor that was Brown County in the fall.

Whatever he suggested, I kept saying yes. But not because I felt desperate to get out of the house.

It had grown very comfortable at home, as a routine set in that included Heck showing up early each morning to begin work. We'd chat a few minutes (actually, more like an hour and sometimes two) over coffee, which I always had him make since I never woke up until I heard his truck in the driveway or the insistent ringing of the doorbell. (At night my thoughts returned to Kevin and Taylor and where my life was headed, and I still needed help getting to sleep—help that didn't usually work until three or four in the morning.)

Then I'd work up in my office, doing phone interviews and tapping away at my computer, happy now to take on any and all assignments. In fact, my newly content state made me put a job search on hold.

I'd started looking in the want ads almost as soon as Kevin left me. After he'd come for the six boxes that represented his life with me, I decided to get more aggressive in my search.

I needed more to fill my hours, and I didn't want to rely solely on whatever money Kevin had to give me. I didn't *want* to be entirely supported by him. I wanted only my fair share, to compensate for the sacrifice I'd made in staying home with our kids instead of finishing college and building a career.

But now it suddenly seemed so good to be freelancing, to be able to work from my home. Besides, I rationalized, I should be there when someone was working on the house.

I stopped to have a bite of lunch with Heck every day. In the beginning he brought his own—usually summer sausage and cheese on thick rolls. I warned him about such dietary dangers and scolded him when he told me he'd never had his cholesterol checked. I also convinced him, at last, to let me make his lunch since I was making my own anyway.

Soon I had him eating tuna fish—not tuna fish sandwiches, but plain tuna, packed in water—or cottage cheese with fresh vegetables and fruits.

"No wonder you're so skinny," he said when he ate the first lunch I served him. But soon he quit giving me a bad time about it and seemed to actually look forward to it.

"What are you fixing us today?" he'd ask, as I walked into the kitchen at about eleven thirty and began to remove things from the refrigerator to take into the dining room to prepare. I wanted to be out of his way and out of the reach of the sawdust and wood chips that flew as he worked.

"You'll just have to wait and see," I usually answered. And when I called him into the dining room, where I had fresh flowers in a vase and cloth napkins and the plates just so, he always kidded about my being hoity-toity. But I knew it pleased him.

Then we'd both work hard all afternoon, although every time I went to the kitchen to refresh my glass of ice water and lemon, we compared notes on what we'd accomplished in the last hour or so since my previous visit. At the end of each day, he invariably asked, "Want to do something tonight?"

And since I rarely had offers to do anything with my kids and little or no desire to see much of my friends, I almost always answered, "Sure. What did you have in mind?"

Our times together were simple. Sometimes he'd suggest an art exhibit or movie or some game he wanted to catch at a sports bar. Most times, he'd ask me what I wanted to do.

Once in a while there was a movie I wanted to see, but usually I made him decide. My favorite outing was the night after we'd gone to Editions Limited Gallery to see an exhibit, and I told him I wanted to see *his* artwork.

Admitting with a meaningful look that he'd been "newly inspired" and did indeed have some paintings he'd like me to see, he promised to show me "sometime." I pushed for the next night.

That's when I saw his cabin in Brown County. It was so Heck. I loved it. Set on thirty hilly acres of valuable land, it was a real log cabin. And he'd built it himself. Surrounded by trees exuding a pine scent that reminded me of my Minnesota roots, it stood as a testament to this man's creativity and self-reliance.

"When did you build this?"

"Right after my divorce. It gave me something to do." He opened his truck door and climbed out. I waited, knowing he would soon be at my door, as if he were a chauffeur helping me out of a stretch limousine.

The first thing I noticed when we entered the room he called, with a laugh, his *art studio,* was a photo of him. Practically buried on a bookshelf among tomes on art and various artists, it caught my eye. Maybe because it was in black and white, encased in a silver frame, among so many colorful book jackets. Or maybe because *he* was in the picture.

I went to it and picked it up, my fingers immediately feeling the dust that told me it had been placed in this spot a long time ago. "That's you standing in front of the art wing when it opened—you're *that* Dennehey?"

"My grandfather is . . . was."

"Wow."

He took the photo from me and placed it back on the shelf, face down. Then he showed me his paintings—the work of a gifted artist, even if the females he showed in two of them, with different outdoor settings, did bear a striking resemblance to me.

On the drive home, I returned to the subject of his divorce. "Were you sad?" I asked.

"Very."

I don't know why, but that still shocked me. "Want to talk about it?"

"There's not much to tell. And I think I already gave you the gist of it. Gail met someone else. Someone more her type."

"Oh, Heck. What type did she want, for heaven's sake?"

"Someone slicker, someone in a three-piece suit, someone debonair." He waved his hand haughtily in the air. "Someone like your husband."

I was amazed at first to realize that was how he saw Kevin. It wasn't how I saw Kevin. I started to rise to my husband's defense but then decided he didn't deserve it. Why should I defend someone like Kevin to someone like Heck?

"Why didn't you have kids?" I asked, surprised at my own question and sudden, intense curiosity.

"I can't. And she's not the type, anyway."

"What's the type?"

"I don't know. How would I know? But Gail had her hands full taking care of Gail. I'm not sure she'd really want to take care of anyone else."

"Did you see it coming, her going?"

He laughed. "You mean did I know if I was coming or going?" Then he grew serious again. "No, I really didn't. What about you? How are you doing?"

"I really don't want to talk about it." The words were out of my mouth before I had time to even think whether I wanted to tell him more about Kevin and me. I'd never filled him in on my visit with Taylor, even though he'd been the catalyst, and I liked that he respected my privacy, never prying. "Not now, anyway," I tried to soften my refusal.

"Hey, no problem. Only if you want to. Only if I can help."

And so Kevin's name never came up again—not until the cabinets were in and perfect and I had to tell him I'd have Kevin pay him.

I returned Heck's gaze now, feeling my cheeks blush at its intensity. Why, he was flirting with me, not just teasing as he'd always done—as seemed to be second nature for him—but actually coming on to me. I didn't know what to say or do, so of course I began to babble. I babbled about how I'd leave a message with Kevin's secretary, how I'd probably hear before the end of the week, how I had the checkbook and could always write out a check. Who knows what else I was going to say if Heck hadn't interrupted me.

"What do you say we go out and celebrate a job well done, if I do say so myself?"

"Oh, I don't know."

What was I going to do, suddenly turn him down for the first time in a month? But there was something different in his tone, as well as in his look. I felt like he was asking me out on a *real* date, not just a friendly outing or pseudo date. And it unnerved me. It also excited me.

That's why I said yes. "All right. Yes, that would be great."

"Yes, it will be great." He turned for the door, promising to be back at seven o'clock. "And dress up. I'm taking you someplace nice. Someplace hoity-toity." He stopped and looked back at me, grinning.

But I stood mute, my usual ready rejoinder not popping to my lips.

Something was different between us, I could tell. And I wasn't sure if I liked it or not.

But I thought I did.

***

Heck came back fifteen minutes earlier than he'd promised, but that was good. I'd been ready for a half hour before that. I'd had a glass of wine and called Nina to fill her in.

"He's here," I abruptly ended my call to her. "He's early, but he's here. I'll call you when I get home, if it's not too late."

"Call me no matter what time it is," she said, and I once again gave thanks for my sister.

I hung up and walked slowly to the door, opening it on Heck's second ring.

"Wow," he said. I had on a black jersey dress that came several flattering inches above my knees. "You look absolutely beautiful." I could feel his eyes rove appreciatively from my black pumps to the dress that clung to my body. But then Heck had grown used to seeing me in jeans and T-shirts, so he wasn't hard to impress. And even though I'd always worn makeup in front of him, I'd applied it more dramatically tonight.

"You look pretty dapper yourself," I said. "I didn't think you'd even own a suit."

"I didn't, until a couple of hours ago. See, it's taped." He lifted up his left foot and turned up his pant leg. "I need to take it back tomorrow to be hemmed. But otherwise, it fits perfectly." He stretched out both arms before wedging a thumb in his waistband to prove his point.

And then he led me to his vintage Lincoln Continental—one he said he rarely drove—and opened my door.

We dined in downtown Indianapolis at the revolving restaurant atop the Hyatt, and I felt for all the world like I had when Kevin and I had our first fancy dinner date after prom. We'd dined in a similar place, in fact, in St. Paul.

But now I was forty-eight, not seventeen, and so I had plenty of wine with my meal. At first I drank it to get over my nervousness, and then I drank because it felt good to feel so mellow, especially with Heck.

"I'd like to talk about it now," I said, halfway through dinner.

"About what?" His fork stopped in midair so suddenly that the more-than-bite-sized piece of baked potato it held fell off.

"About Kevin and me."

"Jessie, you don't have to—"

"I want to. I want you to know that I still love Kevin, but I'm sure I'll get over it. I've started to; I've started to go on. Look at me." I pointed both hands in toward myself and sat up straight. "I'm on my first date."

"I thought we had that already." He looked hurt.

"Whatever." I sounded like Teddy when he didn't want me to interrupt a story of his.

I told Heck about my talk with Taylor in Kevin's office as well as my last talk with Kevin, and he nodded sympathetically.

"I don't know what hurts most: losing a man I still loved, I think, or losing him to another—a younger—woman. I honestly have trouble telling the difference, you know? *Do* I really still love him that much after all these years, or do I just feel humiliated and possessive, like how dare she take what's mine?" I knew my words were slurring a bit, but it felt good to be sharing my feelings with him.

"I've thought about it a lot," I went on, "and I think I really do still love him. No, I know I do. Did. Whatever. But I also know it hurts like unbelievable hell, unfuckingbelievable hell, to think about them falling in love, of them working side by side in the office and starting to tease here and flirt there and then have lunch together and talk about their pasts and what their favorite everything is and share their hopes for the future. And then to be thrown together on business trips."

I stopped to take a breath, a deep one, like a woman in labor hoping futilely to somehow ease the pain. "And to picture them, the first night she slipped Kevin her spare room key, and he used it after their coworkers had all gone to their rooms and after arguing with himself for several hours."

"He told you all this?"

"No, but it's the way I most frequently imagine it—among a zillion other versions. I think it's really the not knowing for sure that is the worst, you know?"

"Yeah, I know."

"How long did it take you to get over your wife?"

"It's been ten years, and I don't think I got over it until just recently. Until I met you."

And when he looked me in the eye then, the *way* he looked me in the eye then, I knew we would kiss good night. And I could hardly wait.

But had I known what this evening held in store between that moment and the moment we would, at last, kiss, I would have wanted nothing more than to wait.

CHAPTER FOURTEEN

Heck ordered coffee and two brandies, and as soon as the waiter left our table, I stood up. "I have to use the ladies' room. Be right back." I clutched my tiny black purse.

He rose too, fumbling with his napkin and pushing his chair back awkwardly. I loved the way he did that. The only other men I'd ever known to stand when a woman left the table were my father and Kevin. I'd tried in vain to instill some old-fashioned manners in my son, but he insisted it was too lame for him. I always felt a little sorry for the girls Teddy dated.

I was feeling extremely happy on this first real date of mine: the romantic ambiance of the restaurant, the mouthwatering food, the expensive wine, and just being there with Heck. I wove my way past the other tables, all full of diners dressed in their Friday-night finery, and headed for the restroom.

The sky outside was black and dotted with lights from the other downtown buildings. It looked magical. In the ladies' room, I reapplied my lipstick and sprayed a little more perfume on my neck and wrists.

It was a good evening, indeed, and I was filled with a newfound sense that I was going to be all right. I could make it. I could do this. When I left the bright lights of the bathroom, the darkness of the restaurant engulfed me once again, and I had to adjust my eyes a little.

Where was Heck? Remembering that this was a revolving restaurant, one I'd eaten at a few times with Kevin, I stood by the restroom door for a few minutes to get my bearings. Then, stepping onto the wooden floor that moved almost imperceptibly, I walked in the direction that the moving floor took me. I figured I was on the other side of the restaurant, because none of the diners at the tables I passed looked familiar.

Then I saw Heck's back at our table for two against the window, and I hurried in that direction. Clutching my purse to my chest, I squeezed past a large table that seated a dozen or so people. I heard the diners all engaged in various conversations as I edged past them. Then I stopped in my tracks as a man rose from the table, putting a hand on my forearm to stall me.

"Jessie!" He dropped his napkin on the table in front of him.

It was Mark Sylvan, Kevin's boss.

"Mark," I said, at first afraid to let my gaze take in the entire table, but then unable to stop myself. There was Taylor Stockton. And the seat next to her was empty. I was glad to see she looked uncomfortable.

"You look great, Jessie," Mark said. "How are you?" He was clearly enjoying the moment. He'd been Kevin's boss for three years. He lived in New York but often visited Indianapolis. He'd never liked Kevin; we'd both known that from the beginning. It had caused Kevin great discomfort, and his self-esteem had taken a real beating. He wasn't used to being disliked, especially by a boss. I'd spent hours trying to convince my husband that Mark Sylvan was just jealous of him.

"How are you, Mark?" I extended my hand to shake his.

He ignored my hand and leaned forward to kiss me on the cheek, pausing long enough to check over my shoulder, no doubt hoping to see Kevin back at the table. "Fine. How are the kids?" He placed his hand back on my arm to stop me from leaving.

"Fine. I must go; I have someone waiting for me."

"I hear you're going to be a grandmother."

"Mmm." *Move on*, I commanded myself. *Get the hell away from here*. But at that moment, I felt Kevin's presence. I didn't see him immediately, but I knew he was there. He'd returned to the table, and instead of going around to the other side to join Taylor, he came up beside Mark.

"Jessie. You look lovely," Kevin said. He, too, kissed my cheek. I wanted the floor to go into a rapid spin. I wanted to run back to Heck. Kevin had no right to say I looked lovely. He had no right to kiss my cheek. It wasn't his to kiss.

I felt humiliated, and then livid, for the ten-millionth time. In a quick glance around the table, I saw Kevin's coworkers, all the gang I had known for so many years, had so many dinners with, just like this one. They all looked embarrassed, but not nearly as embarrassed as I felt.

I was also aware that Taylor was now standing. She pushed her chair back and came around the table to plant her arm firmly through Kevin's. It was such a possessive gesture, I thought she looked ridiculous, and I knew I should feel a little sorry for her. But I didn't.

What was supposed to happen now? Here was the soon-to-be-ex-wife caught on the revolving floor with her wayward husband and her replacement. My legs wouldn't move. Roots were growing out of my feet. *Get* out *of here*, I told myself again, but the fascination of seeing Taylor's slim arm entwined in Kevin's held me in a trance.

Mark was saying something, I don't know what, and Kevin's blue eyes bore into mine. *Don't make a scene*, he seemed to be silently urging. *Please don't make a scene*. I was aware of Taylor tugging him back to his seat, and Mark seemed to be telling a funny story—at least he was laughing at something—and I stood there through it all.

And then suddenly, like the cavalry arriving in the nick of time, Heck appeared. I felt his strong arm around my waist and looked up to see his smiling face. He said something too, but I didn't hear that, either. I just felt myself being eased along, away from Kevin and Mark and Taylor, back to the sanctuary of our own little table.

I drank my brandy in one gulp and felt it burn my throat.

"Thank you," I said, as Heck sat down across from me and raised his own brandy glass to his lips.

"I'm sorry." He signaled for the waiter and the check. "I had no idea."

"No, of course not; how could you?"

"I assume that was her."

"The one clutching my husband for dear life? Yes, that was her."

"Let's get out of here." He opened his wallet and laid some bills on the table.

"I'm fine. Really."

"I don't think so." He stood.

In the elevator on our way to the parking garage, I felt my face burning with humiliation. Mark had some nerve, using me to embarrass Kevin. Why did I allow it? Why hadn't I thought of something witty to say? Something clever and urbane? Why had I just stood there like a fool while Taylor staked her claim on my husband?

Heck was silent as we walked to the car, while I remained consumed in thought.

Taylor looked, I had to admit, stunning. Well, *hell!* She was young. Who wouldn't want a young woman like that hanging all over him? I was too outraged to even cry, thank God, and I remained mute as Heck opened the passenger door to the car and eased me in.

We were driving past the mansions on North Meridian Street before I came out of my coma.

"Heck, thanks. Thanks for coming to get me. I acted like an idiot. What must they have thought of me? What must *you* have thought?"

"Didn't think anything," he said, his eyes not leaving the road. "I just saw you there and thought you might need rescuing."

"Bless you."

***

I was glad to get to the safety only home can provide. Heck followed me inside, and I turned on the lamp by the couch in the living room.

"How about some coffee?" he asked, taking off his jacket and laying it over the back of the couch. "I didn't get to finish mine."

"Good idea." I was glad for something to do, as I busied myself in what seemed like an entirely new kitchen, grinding fresh coffee beans I'd bought the day before. Like a zombie, I stood there watching the perfect little beans turn to mush. Sort of like me. Then I felt two arms encircle my waist. I turned and was engulfed by Heck.

"This may not be the right time, but there's something I want to say." He kissed the top of my head.

"Go right ahead."

"I hate your husband."

"Why?" I asked, but stopped myself from leaping to Kevin's defense.

"Because he's hurt you so much."

I nodded against his chest.

Then he took my hand and led me into the living room. He sat me down on the couch, stuffing two pillows behind my back.

"You stay here; I'll finish the coffee." He gently pushed me back into the cushions.

As I heard him in the kitchen, I curled my legs up under me. I felt like I did when I was a kid staying home from school sick, with my mother fussing over me.

Heck came back into the living room with a tray bearing two cups of coffee. He'd used my best china, and as he handed me my coffee, the fragile cup and saucer looked wrong in his big hands. "Here, drink this."

"Thanks, Heck."

"It was still a wonderful evening for me." He sat down next to me.

"For me too," I answered, even if it wasn't totally true.

We drank our coffee in silence, and when he was done, he replaced his cup and saucer gently on the tray. "I think I better get going; it's late."

I didn't argue. But although I wanted to be alone, I also didn't want him to leave.

He rose from the couch and put his jacket back on. After I walked him to the door, he once again wrapped himself around me. I had a sudden urge to drag him back in. His body felt so good. I'd almost forgotten how good it felt to be held by a man.

We kissed, tenderly at first and then passionately, our lips parting and his tongue finding its way to mine. He pressed his body into mine, and now I really didn't want him to leave. I felt breathless, flattered and frightened at the same time. And I felt incredibly desirous of this man and the pleasures his body promised. It had been way too long. But he pulled himself away. "I'll call you tomorrow."

"Heck . . ." I didn't know what I wanted to say, but I had a sudden image of the two of us wrapped up together in my bed.

As if reading my thoughts, he took out his car keys and jangled them in his hand. "He's a damn fool, Jessie. I know I'd never let a woman like you go."

And then he left.

***

I lay in bed wide awake, luxuriating in thoughts of Heck and the warm, safe feeling that now surrounded me. But then something else, something stronger than thoughts of Heck, rose to the surface and engulfed me. My thoughts spun around in my head, like Teddy's laundry in my dryer.

I was picturing Kevin and Taylor, the way they had stood together tonight. No way was she going to give him up. He was ensnared like a rat in a cage. In my diminished mental state, all blame fell on Taylor. She was the bad guy, and Kevin was just a rodent caught in her trap. For the moment, I refused to look at it any other way.

Then, out of nowhere, a memory popped into my mind: an evening when Kevin and I were on our way to meet some business clients of his for dinner. He was driving, and I absently flipped on his car radio.

Kevin always had his dial set to either the university jazz station or the sports-talk station. I'd never known him to listen to anything else. But instead, a hard rock tune filled the interior of the car. It was the kind of music Teddy liked and not Kevin's type at all.

"What on earth have you been listening to?" I'd asked him, as taken aback as if I'd found him reading a book of hints by Heloise.

"Hmm. I didn't have it set to that station," he'd answered—sheepishly, I only now realized.

I pushed the buttons to change stations until at last one of the buttons returned me to the hard rock music. "Yes, it's set to this station." I was suspicious of nothing, only puzzled.

"Hmm. Just a fluke, I guess," he'd said, and quickly changed the subject. Now I wondered if that rock station had been Taylor's selection. Had she sat where I always sat and reset the Porsche's radio?

I bolted up in bed now, remembering other instances where I should have suspected something.

What about the time I asked Kevin to stop on his way home from work and pick up theater tickets I'd reserved earlier in the week? When he arrived home that night, he assured me he had them in his briefcase. Later in the evening, while Kevin was showering, I remembered the tickets and went to retrieve them. But the briefcase was locked.

I remembered how funny I thought that was at the time, a sweet example of Kevin's paranoia. I even teased him about it when he finished showering, accusing him of carrying state secrets around. Now I recalled how he'd waited until I left the room and then produced the tickets when I returned.

A feeling of regret came over me. Why hadn't I just found his keys and opened the case myself? Then again, there was nothing for me to be suspicious about. In hindsight, my naiveté embarrassed me.

If I lay there long enough, I realized, I could probably think of a million little oddities that should have been red flags, like the trunk that had yielded the cards. They suddenly seemed endless.

There was the time I strained my back and was confined to bed rest for a week. Normally, Kevin made a great nurse, but I remembered now with loathing the Friday night, after my having been in bed for four days, that Kevin told me he had to take clients out to dinner. He practically begged permission. "I'll be home late. Are you going to be okay?"

"Sure. Go have a good time."

He got home after three in the morning. There I was, waiting for him, groggy from painkillers but relieved he was home safe. I listened to his brief explanation about what a boring night it had been, and how he couldn't get away, blah, blah, blah. And I'd just accepted it all, not even asking where he'd been. Not even concerned when he suggested he sleep in the guest room so as not to disturb me. I just fell into my drugged sleep, while he slept in the room down the hall, no doubt dreaming of Taylor.

The phone ringing by my bed stopped my painful crawl down memory lane. Assuming it was Nina and remembering I'd promised to call her, I didn't check caller ID when I reached for the phone. But a glance at the clock told me it was nearly two thirty. What was she still doing up at this time?

"Hi," I said into the phone.

"Jessie?" It was Kevin. I felt like someone dumped a bucket of ice over my head. I could feel my heart pounding. "Jessie, it's me."

"Kevin, I—"

"Wait. Before you say anything, let me finish. I'm sorry about tonight. That was humiliating and uncalled for. You realize that Mark, being the asshole he is, loved every minute of the little spectacle."

"Yes, I realize that," I said, almost happy to be in cahoots with Kevin on at least one issue. All my earlier thoughts of his philandering flew out of my head.

"What am I saying?" Kevin asked. "Of course you do. You've always had Mark's number. I just wish it hadn't happened, that's all. It was so unfair to you."

"Forget about it. I have."

We were both silent for a moment. Kevin was probably as blown away as I was by the ludicrous statement I'd just made. We both knew I never forgot *anything*. I was still obsessing about a heated conversation I'd had with the dry cleaner when they lost a jacket of mine three years ago. I was hardly likely to just forget this evening.

"So how are you?" he asked. He was practically whispering, and I pictured him in a closet hiding behind

Taylor's Donna Karan suits with a hand cupped over the receiver. "You looked very pretty tonight," he said in a hushed tone.

"What the hell do you want?" I cut him short, suddenly, freshly, infuriated with the two of them.

"I just wanted to say I was sorry about what happened. You looked so . . . so lost standing there. Until Paul Bunyan rescued you, that is. By the way, isn't he the guy who's supposed to be putting the cabinets in the kitchen?"

"What of it?"

"He *is* the same guy, isn't he?"

"Yes, he's the same guy, and by the way, you owe him a lot of money. I faxed his invoice to your office; I assume you'll get it."

"Yeah, I'll get it. And your boyfriend will get paid; don't worry."

"He's not my boyfriend."

"Whatever the hell he is, he'll get his money."

"Fine."

"Great."

"Good-bye."

Before I could hang up, he beat me to it.

CHAPTER FIFTEEN

"Did you do it?" Nina's voice woke me. I didn't even realize I'd answered the phone, but I must have.

"Do what?" I asked my sister, feeling confused and then surprised as I looked at the clock. It was nine. The last time I'd looked at the clock, when I restlessly arose to use the bathroom, it had displayed three fours.

"You know, do *it*. I assume that's why you didn't call me last night. Because he was spending the night. Is he there now?"

"Nina!" What had my younger sister been up to all these years? "You mean did I sleep with him, on our first *date?*"

"Jessie, you're forty-eight."

"And there are STDs out there." I don't know why I said that. STDs had nothing to do with whether or not I'd sleep with Heck. He was hardly the type I'd worry about contracting any serious diseases from. If I worried about that, it would be because of my philandering husband. "Besides, he didn't ask me to," I said, growing more truthful as I grew more awake.

"Well, that's just as well. No sense rushing it. And of course you'll protect yourself when you do."

"Nina!"

"I'm serious, Jess. You do need to worry about diseases and stuff. But that doesn't mean you won't want to have sex again—sometime. If not with Heck, with someone. Be prepared."

"Nina, I'm really not in the mood for this conversation. For any conversation. I'll call you later."

"Don't hang up until you tell me what happened last night."

"Okay." I rose and headed to the kitchen. I felt awash with pleasure when I saw my new cabinets. I still wasn't used to them. As I opened the refrigerator to retrieve the remains of the coffee I'd ground last night, I began to tell Nina about the evening.

It was painful to describe the encounter with Kevin and Taylor, but when I got to the part about Heck's good-night kiss, I felt a thrill I hadn't felt in years. Finally, we hung up, and I dragged myself back upstairs to shower and dress.

As I was shutting off my blow-dryer, I heard the sound of someone in my house. Cabinets were opening, a door banged shut. I went to my bedroom door and opened it slightly.

"Hello!" I called, not loud enough for any intruder to hear. "*Hello!*" Louder this time. "Who's there?" For some reason, I wasn't in the least bit afraid.

"It's me, Mom." My son's voice floated up the stairs. "Sorry if I scared you."

I'd hardly spoken to Teddy since he'd dropped his laundry off a month ago and we'd had that painful scene. Several times I'd picked up the phone to call him but decided it was his behavior that had caused our rift, so he could damn well make the first move.

In fairness to him, he had called me twice, but both times he was sullen. When I'd suggested we get together, he grew cold, and I ended both calls before he could become insulting.

Still, as the parent, I felt it was my responsibility to patch things up. His clean and folded laundry, back in the pillowcase he'd brought it in, caused a tight pain in my chest every time I passed it.

"Wait a second. I'll be right down," I called. "Honey," I added, determined to make this a good visit.

He was sitting at the kitchen table in the same posture as the last time he'd been there. The long legs stretched out before him somehow added to his defiant appearance.

"So how have you been, honey?" I headed for the coffee maker.

"Okay. You?"

"I miss my son," I said, with my back to him as I spooned coffee into the filter.

"Kitchen looks nice."

"I'm glad you like it. I love it. You want me to fix you breakfast?"

"You seen Dad?"

"Yes. As a matter of fact, I saw him last night."

He stood up and came over to me. "That's great. I knew you two could work this out."

I started the coffee maker and then turned to face him. "Look, Teddy, you better get used to this. There is no working anything out. Your dad doesn't want to be married to me." I bent down to get the frying pan out of the cupboard. "And the sooner you face it, the better." I almost added that I would still be his mother, blah, blah, blah, but I could see by his face when I stood up that that wouldn't cut it.

"But you just said you saw him last night."

"Yes, I saw him. He was at the same restaurant as I was, with a group of people." I felt guilty that I didn't mention Heck. But then I didn't mention Taylor, either. It seemed like too much information.

He broke the silence by banging his fist on the counter. "Why the hell can't you two just grow up?"

I sat down. The empty frying pan in my hand felt like a tennis racket, and I felt as exhausted as if I'd just played an extra-long match. And lost.

"Darling boy, maybe it's time you grew up." I actually swung the pan in a tennis-like motion. "I know this sucks. I know you hate it; I hate it too. But the fact is, your dad doesn't want to be married anymore. Period. I have to accept that. And so do you."

"Do you still love him?" He spoke so softly I could barely hear.

"That's not the point."

"But do you?" His voice was louder now.

"Yes. Okay, I still love him."

"I don't understand. I don't get any of this shit." Now he was yelling.

"Teddy, please stop swearing. It doesn't help anything. Please just try to accept it."

I looked up at him and saw him wipe his large hand across his face. He wasn't crying, but he looked unbearably sad. "I hate coming home with him not here. Even if he can be a real prick . . . sorry . . . a real douche."

"Oh, much better." I smiled.

He came then and sat next to me, reaching for my free hand. "I hate the thought of you living here by yourself. Being all lonely and shit. Okay, sorry again. But who's gonna take care of you, Mom? How're we gonna deal with the holidays and Merritt's baby and all the other stuff we did as a family?"

"We'll just be a different family, son. And not so different, really. A lot of your friends have divorced parents."

"I don't care about my friends. I only care about you and Dad."

How many times had I used that argument on him, that I didn't care if his friends jumped off a bridge or drove a hundred miles an hour?

"I know. But I'll be fine, and honestly, I'm sick of talking about it. Can you and I be friends again? That's what I want right now, more than anything."

His hand grabbed mine. "Will you let me know when you get lonely?"

"I will; I promise. And will you continue to bring your stinky jeans over for me to wash and let me cook you a meal once in a while?"

"Only once in a while?"

I smiled and squeezed his hand. "Yeah, only once in a while should do it."

"Deal."

"Okay; good. Now, eggs? Bacon?"

"Three eggs and lots of bacon."

"You got it."

***

After a sated Teddy left with his clean laundry, I sat over more coffee and studied the course catalog from Butler University that I'd picked up a few days ago. I'd decided to go back to school and felt excited at the prospect.

Ellen told me that once my divorce was final, I might be eligible for financial aid, so I figured even if Kevin didn't have to help me, I could pay for it somehow. I was ready to move on with my life, especially now, after seeing Kevin and Taylor out together in public. As I anticipated this change in my life, I actually started to feel good. And then the phone rang, and I soon felt even better.

"Got any of that coffee left?" Heck asked.

"Absolutely."

"Good; I'm on my way."

He arrived, looking scrumptious, and we had coffee, never even mentioning the fiasco of the night before, or our new feelings for one another. I was disappointed when he left after an hour or so. But he'd invited me to dinner the next night, and that would have to do.

In the weeks that followed, we fell into a pattern of having dinner together every few nights. We were working our way through the *Indianapolis Monthly Menu Guide*, making a pact never to eat at the same restaurant twice. I cooked dinner for him at my place once, while another time I met him in Brown County and he did the honors.

He was always courteous, and every evening ended with a passionate kiss that held so much promise. But I was always left wanting more.

Heck suggested several times that we invite my kids to dinner, and once he wanted to invite them to a Colts game. He had extra tickets a customer had given him, but I refused to include my kids in this new life of mine. Something inside me felt determined to keep it to myself and not share it. Somehow, it seemed that if I "brought Heck home," I'd be crossing a line I'd come to think of as the point of no return in ending my life with Kevin.

And when I was alone, on those nights I didn't see Heck, my thoughts remained consumed by Kevin. I wasn't ready to give up on him entirely and still couldn't quite believe he'd given up on me.

***

One Saturday morning in October, Heck dropped by early. He'd told me of an estimate he had to do in my neighborhood, and I'd invited him to stop by for breakfast. He arrived with a bunch of lilies wrapped in green tissue.

"You look very pretty," he said, handing me the flowers and sitting down at the kitchen table.

"Thank you." It was so good to hear that. "One egg or two?"

"Let's go all the way."

I turned from the stove to look at him.

"Two," he said quickly, studying the front page of the newspaper, a sheepish grin spreading across his face.

Whistling to myself, I opened the refrigerator door. This was domestic harmony. A sexy man sitting in my beautiful new kitchen, me cooking breakfast for him. A glorious day outside, autumn at its best. And then the front doorbell rang.

I halted my whistling and froze. Who the hell could that be? I felt trapped, my domestic harmony suddenly silenced. I was caught. Someone was onto me.

Before I could move, Heck got up and strolled out of the room. "I'll get it," he said.

Wait! I wanted to yell after him. *Don't answer it. It could be anyone. It could be the secret police. Or worse, it could be one of my kids—or Kevin. We'll be found out.*

It was worse than any government crackdown. It was my son. And even though I still couldn't move, Heck and Teddy appeared in my kitchen, taking up all the space. When had this room shrunk?

"Hi, Mom." Teddy didn't look pleased. My son, who had apparently misplaced his poker face, approached me quickly and not only kissed my cheek but put his arm around me protectively.

"Ted." I felt a guilty grin form on my face. *But what the hell was I guilty of?* "Ted, this is Heck Dennehey. Heck, this is my son, Ted."

Both men eyed each other across the kitchen like boxers in a prizefight.

"Heck is my cabinetmaker," I added.

There was complete silence, unless you counted the coffee maker or the whirring of the ice maker in the refrigerator. Ted looked as shocked as if I'd introduced Heck as my drug dealer.

Heck smiled and stretched out a hand to shake, but Ted only tightened his grip around my waist. I felt sad as I watched Heck take back his offer of a handshake and shove both hands into the pockets of his jeans.

"So, Teddy, what are you doing here? I was just fixing breakfast for Heck. He's got a few things left to do around here. You want me to fix you something too?"

"Looks like the kitchen is finished to me, Mom."

"Well, yes, honey, of course it is. As you can see. Heck was just . . . er . . . giving me a bid on some other stuff I might have done."

As I babbled, Heck took a seat back at the kitchen table. He crossed his arms over his chest, and his eyes bore into mine, as if challenging me to come clean.

"If you need anything else done, I can do it," Ted said, finally releasing his grip.

"Oh, you." I gently nudged him in the ribs. "What can you do?"

"I can do anything you need done. Or Dad can."

"Your father is otherwise occupied these days, Ted. Now, do you want breakfast or not?" I didn't want to get into it with Ted again, especially in front of Heck. In fact, I wanted my son to leave. He was making me uncomfortable, and I didn't want Heck to see me like this.

I also didn't want Ted to think there was anything between Heck and me. That seemed so important. Like I'd lose ground if Ted thought I'd moved on. Like there would be no hope for either of us. Ted or me.

"Nah," he said, "I'm going."

"Okay, fine." I almost pushed him out of the kitchen and to the front door.

"What's going on, Mom?" he asked when we were out of Heck's earshot.

"Nothing; what do you mean?"

"What's he doing here, having breakfast with you? Did he spend the night?"

"Oh, Teddy, how could you ask such a thing? He certainly did not spend the night."

"Well . . . good." He still didn't look pleased.

"But even if he did—"

"I know; it's none of my business."

Smart kid. It was none of his business. Oh, but I wasn't ready for my life to be none of his business anymore.

He left without giving me his customary kiss good-bye, and I felt shattered as I watched out the long sliver of window next to the closed door while his car pulled out of the driveway. He hadn't even said good-bye to Heck. Of course he hadn't said hello, either.

When I returned to the kitchen, Heck was standing by the sink, looking out into the backyard. "Sorry about that," I said, returning to the refrigerator for his eggs and trying to sound normal. Truthfully, I was embarrassed by Ted's behavior. But more so by my own. "So now you've met my son."

"Did you forget to teach him any manners?" Heck asked, his back to me.

"Look, Heck, he's—"

"Maybe you just never taught him to shake hands with a cabinetmaker."

"I'm sorry."

"About what?"

"About the whole thing."

"No need. If that's all I am to you."

"Of course that's not all."

"Then what am I?"

"You know what you are."

"No, Jess, I don't think I do. Maybe I'm just a convenient way for you to spend your time while you're waiting for your husband to come back." He turned to face me. "Only I don't think he's coming back any time soon, and you better get that through your head."

His words stung worse than if he'd thrown acid in my face. I slammed the refrigerator door shut, and the two eggs I was holding fell out of my hand, smashing on my beautiful new hardwood floor.

"Now look what you've made me do." Fighting back tears, I grabbed a sheet of paper towel and knelt down to the sticky mess.

"You may not think I'm good enough for you—"

I looked up at him. "I never said that, so get the chip off your shoulder."

"But I'm not good enough to be introduced to your snotty kid as anything other than your fucking cabinetmaker?"

"Please, I don't want to fight—"

"You could have at least introduced me as a friend. I kinda thought I was."

"I know, I know." I shook my head like a wet dog.

"Jessie, it's time for you to take a reality check."

"I know all too well what's real."

"Well then, lady, you better figure out exactly what the hell it is you want."

"I—"

"Forget it." He grabbed his keys from the counter and, stepping around me, left the room. I heard the front door slam and his truck engine begin to roar.

I was left alone, trying to remember the manufacturer's instructions for cleaning up sticky messes on hardwood floors.

CHAPTER SIXTEEN

"Damn him," I said to no one. "Damn Heck, damn Teddy, and damn, damn, damn Kevin." I looked down at the broken shells and remembered a time when Kevin had been helping me bring in groceries from the car and dropped a whole carton of eggs. I was irritated with him then, but I was *furious* with him now.

When the current mess was finally cleaned off my new floor, I called Nina and told her what had happened—every detail, every word. "What's wrong with me? How have I managed to drive *two* men away?"

"Nothing's wrong with you, Jess. You're just not ready to jump into another relationship yet, and that's okay."

That's what I loved about Nina. She wasn't about to judge me or my decision, no matter what I did. When she thought I'd spent the night with Heck, that was fine. When she thought I *didn't* want anything serious, that was fine too. Still, even Nina had only so much patience.

"But you do have to figure out just what it is you want," she said. "You've confused the poor guy because of your own confusion."

"Tell me what to do. I feel out of control here, like things are happening that I'm causing, only I don't know how to stop them. Or start them. Or whatever." I felt short of breath, like someone running from an assailant and suddenly realizing she couldn't keep going.

"Calm down, Jess. Just call him and tell him how you feel."

"Call who?" I asked without thinking, and so we both knew how much I still yearned to make a connection with Kevin, to try once more to get him to change his mind and pick *me*, not Taylor.

"Call Heck, Jessie. Surely you don't think you should call Kevin. Kevin is history. That's about the only thing you can count on. Now, you don't have to let this other man— Heck—rush you, but you do have to accept the fact that Kevin's not an option. If that's why you're pushing Heck—"

"No, that's not why I'm pushing Heck away. I know Kevin is history. You don't have to tell me that."

We said our good-byes, but I didn't feel we'd really resolved anything.

Maybe Ellen could help.

"Want some breakfast?" I asked, when my friend answered her phone.

"Just a sec. Get some milk, will ya?" I heard her yell, presumably to Steve, undoubtedly heading out for his husbandly Saturday morning errands. "Sorry about that," Ellen said to me.

"No problem."

"Do you want Steve to get you anything while he's out? Steve! Wait a sec!"

"No, no, Ellen. You don't have to—"

"Don't be silly. What are friends for?"

"I don't need anything, but thanks."

"Never mind, Steve."

"I suppose you and Steve have had breakfast? I was hoping I could entice you over for some eggs and bacon."

"Scrambled or sunny-side up?"

"Pick your poison."

"No, now they say eggs aren't bad for your cholesterol. Make mine sunny-side up. Here I come." And the phone went dead in my hand.

"I hope the offer included coffee too," I heard Ellen say, after she'd knocked twice and then made her way into my house and then the kitchen. "I was so busy getting Steve organized to leave, I didn't get my quota." She started to yawn, as if to prove her point, but instead she said, "Wow. I still can't get used to this beautiful kitchen."

"Here." I handed her a full cup of coffee and a clean spoon so she could stir the huge amounts of cream and sugar I knew she'd add.

The truth was, Ellen didn't worry about cholesterol or any other facet of her diet. She always said Texans thought all food was good.

As we dunked our toast in the runny yolks, I filled her in on my eventful morning. "Nina thinks I should call Heck and come clean with him about my feelings. As if I know what they are. I sure as hell don't want him to be my boyfriend. I don't see how I could ever use that term, divorced or not."

"Yeah, that's a pretty vile word for someone our age."

"But he's certainly become way more than a friend these past weeks. And he deserved to be called as much in front of Teddy."

"Well, Jess darlin', why don't you tell him just that? As for exactly what your feelings are, well, you don't need to know. When you know, you'll know. Tell him *that* too. That you don't know, but you don't want to lose whatever it is you two have. It doesn't *have* to have a name."

"You think?"

"Yes, I think. And as for Teddy, he just loves you, that's all. He's trying to protect you. Be patient with him.

He'll come around. Just let him be with Kevin and Taylor a few times; he'll be glad his mom has someone."

"Hmm. I hope." I stood up and gathered our plates. After putting them in the sink, I refilled our coffee cups.

We sat quietly for a while. I never felt I had to fill a silence with Ellen, just as I never had with Kevin. I'd always felt too comfortable with both of them, and I still did with Ellen. Finally, I said, "You know what? For the first time in my life, I'm going to call and ask a guy out for a date."

And that was my intention. But in reality, I got Heck's answering machine when I finally mustered up the courage the next day. I didn't leave a message. I didn't know what to say. So I dialed his pager. Again and again and again, but he didn't call back. It was possible, I supposed, that he had it turned off. But that would have been out of character for him, even on a Sunday. Maybe he just didn't *want* to dial my number back.

***

I didn't hear from Heck all week. On Friday, in between fresh attempts to reach him, I got cleaned up and drove down to campus for my appointment with an advisor about registering for spring semester.

I felt elated when I got back to my car in the parking lot. I was going to be a college student again, and I felt certain my academic future held both excitement and success. I tried both of Heck's numbers once more, and when I still got no response, I headed home. But on the way, I decided to stop by the last job site I knew him to be working at.

I saw his black pickup parked among other construction-site vehicles on the street in the new master-planned golf community, and I felt so nervous I almost hoped he wouldn't be there. Almost. What I really hoped was that he'd be in the house alone, hanging his cabinets.

He was.

He didn't hear me enter, so loud did he have his music blaring. I approached him, tapping him on the shoulder, as John Mellencamp sang about making it hurt so good.

The look he gave me in that first instant of surprise was the only positive thing about the encounter. At least I *thought* I saw a flash of welcoming delight in his eyes. But he quickly regained his composure and said, "Hello, Jessie." Then he resumed hammering.

"Heck, can we talk?"

"I can't right now. I have to finish this today." He reached for another nail and hammered some more.

"Well, how about tomorrow? Can I take you out to dinner tomorrow night?" My mind was already picking the place, that new spot in Broad Ripple I'd read nothing but good about, and so it took a second for his answer to sink in.

"Sorry; I can't. I have other plans."

The rejection sent me below the depths of despair that I'd already thought of as rock bottom. So, like a dog whose master has put away the tennis ball, refusing to play fetch any longer, I put my tail between my legs and slunk away.

I listened for Heck's voice over the strains of *R.O.C.K. in the U.S.A.*, but he didn't call for me to come back.

***

I'd just received two checks in the mail from different publications for articles appearing in the November issues, and I decided it was time to open my own checking account. It felt stranger than anything I'd done recently. I hadn't had my own checking account for decades.

I assured myself I was making a stab at complete independence, although it felt more like a pin prick. Independence was when Mother Teresa had opened an orphanage in India. But maybe even she had started with her own checking account.

To hell with Kevin and to hell with Heck (and his ridiculous name). Who needed either of them? I now had a total of six hundred dollars in the bank, in my own name. I was flying high.

When I got home, my answering machine showed two messages. The first outlined a new assignment for a start-up online magazine I had high hopes for. The second message was from Kevin.

My heart skipped a beat at the sound of his voice. I had to actually sit down. Then I experienced the usual mixture of elation and sorrow that the thought of him continued to bring. He wanted to come and talk—get some things straightened out, was how he put it. I played his message five times, listening for some clue as to his mood, but finally convinced myself there was none and erased his voice.

I returned the call to the online magazine first. They offered me a ridiculously low sum to write an article on the growing phenomenon of psychics in the Indianapolis area. Even though I knew it wasn't going to boost my new bank balance by much, the idea intrigued me. It sounded like fun.

After talking with the editor, who sounded about twelve years old, I stalled as long as I could. Then, realizing it was almost the end of Kevin's workday, I poured a glass of wine and steeled myself for my call to him.

I hadn't seen or heard from him for a couple of months, since the terrible night at the Hyatt. But I still thought of him every day. And obsessed about him every night. I kept wondering if I should call him, push him to get things moving along, or beg him to come back.

But I'd resisted contacting him and remained relieved that he hadn't contacted me, because as long as nothing was decided, I still had hope.

I got as comfortable as I could on the couch, took a sip of wine, and then dialed Kevin's office number. He answered on the first ring, which I wasn't expecting him to do. Nervousness enveloped me.

"Can I come over?" he asked. "We need to talk."

"Yes. Of course." I gulped my wine and felt it immediately rush to my head. I hung up, thinking I should at least put on some fresh lipstick.

But somehow, when the doorbell rang thirty minutes later, I was still sitting there.

The first thing he did was hug me. Or maybe I hugged him. One of us initiated it, and we clung to each other for a long time. Eventually, I let go first. He took my hand and led me over to the couch, where we both sat down. It was awkward, and he looked as uncomfortable as I felt. But I noticed he didn't let go of my hand. I felt a thrill just touching him.

"So how are you, Jess?" He stared hard into my face, as if he hadn't seen me for a long time. Which he hadn't.

"Fine; I'm fine."

"Really?" he countered, as if I weren't telling the truth. Which, of course, we both knew I wasn't.

My hand stayed in his until I rose to refill my wineglass. "Would you like a drink?" I asked.

"If you've got a beer, that would be great."

"Yes, I think so." I had the last bottle of a six-pack I'd bought for Heck in what seemed like another lifetime. I grabbed it from the bottom shelf of the refrigerator and returned to the living room. "Here." I handed him the bottle.

He looked at it suspiciously. "When did you start drinking German beer?" He raised the green bottle before him like a grenade about to go off.

"No good?" I sat back down next to him.

"It's fine, I guess." He took a drink and then leaned back on the couch. He looked tired, and I noticed tiny lines around the corners of his mouth and eyes that I was sure had never been there before.

"So," he said, after a second swig, "we need to talk—"

"Right." I felt desperate to sound in control.

"Jessie, we've got a lot ahead of us to get through. I'm sorry about the words we had, and I think it's time we be friends, so—"

"We've been through this already, Kevin. You know that's not possible."

"Why not?" He looked amazed.

"Why not? I'll tell you why not. To begin with, you're fucking someone else—" It was not what I wanted to say at all. It wasn't anything like I'd imagined, all those nights I'd lain awake imagining Kevin and I alone, about to reconcile. I didn't want to sound angry and bitter, but I just couldn't stop myself.

"Please—" he started to interrupt me.

"You've destroyed my life. You've ruined everything. I don't want to be your damn friend. I don't even *like* you anymore."

Again, not what I'd planned to say. I was supposed to be telling him I still loved him, wanted him back. Of course he was supposed to be saying he wanted to be my *husband*, not my friend. Who *were* these people who'd taken over our bodies?

"Jessie, please don't make this any more difficult than it already is. What about the kids? What about Merritt's baby?"

"What about them? You left our family, Kevin. You walked out on us."

"Not really. I just—"

"What? You just what?"

"I don't know." He slammed his beer down on the table and dropped his head into his hands. "Give me a break here, will you?"

"I'd like to break your neck."

"Jessie, Jessie, I'm so sorry."

"What the hell did you come here for? What do you want to discuss?"

"I don't know. Nothing that can't wait. I guess I just wanted to see you, that's all." He raised his face, and I could see his eyes were wet. "You look so thin. Are you eating?"

"Am I eating? What do you care?"

He looked like a whipped dog. In my moments when I hated him, I'd imagined him looking like this, had wished desperately to see this look on his face, but it wasn't giving me the pleasure I'd hoped for.

I reached over and took his hand from where it was cradling his head. "Kevin, is this what you really want?"

He reached over and hugged me. For a second, I thought I had him back, but then he let go. "Jessie, I'll always love you. I love your courage and strength. I wouldn't be the man I am today without you."

"Oh please. Save your speech. I think you better go." I was standing now, actually walking to the door. Slowly, he got up and followed me.

"Let's talk soon, Jess. We have to talk. And I do miss you." He lingered by the door.

I swung it open for him. "Yeah . . . well, you'll get over it."

And then he was gone, and I was alone. Alone and sad and lonely and furious, completely furious. Mostly with myself.

***

About seven o'clock that night the doorbell rang. I was upstairs working on my computer and not ready for any more company. Annoyed, I descended the stairs.

When I opened the door, I saw Heck standing there. The funny thing was, he also looked annoyed.

"Yes?" I said. My heart all but stopped, and I vaguely acknowledged my fickleness that allowed two men to have the same effect on me in one day. But the new me was irritated with all men, and I was not in the mood to be nice to any damn one of them.

So I just stood there, feeling surly and hoping I looked the same.

"Sorry to come by without calling first. But I left a couple of tools here, and I really need them. They're in your garage. Could I just get them?"

"Fine." I opened the door wide for him to come in.

Without a word, he walked past me and through the kitchen, and then I heard him out in the garage. I closed the front door and leaned against it, my arms folded across my chest. He returned a few minutes later, carrying an item I didn't recognize.

"Get what you came for?"

"Looks like it," he said. "Except my wrench. I had a small wrench that I'm sure I left here, but I don't see it out there."

"Ah yes, your wrench. Well, I sold it on the street."

"If you see it, just let me know. Okay?"

"Too late; it's in the hands of a Colombian drug lord."

"You're a real funny lady, you know that?" Only he wasn't laughing, and somehow I didn't think I was his favorite comedienne.

"Look, Heck. I don't want to argue with you. You were a real friend to me. Could we just keep it that way?"

"Friends? You wanna be just friends, huh?"

I noticed the way he moved to the living room. It was slow and easy. He sat down on the couch and toyed with the tool in his hand. "Look, Jessie, maybe I was too hard on you."

"Heck, I—"

"Wait; please let me finish. See, I never thought I'd meet someone like you. After my marriage fell apart . . . I just sort of gave up." He was still fondling the metal object in his hands, running his thumb across it like it was something fragile. "I never . . . hell, I might as well say it; I've come this far. I never thought I'd feel this way again."

He looked up at me then, his eyes big and brown. "I've missed you, Jessie. I've missed being with you. Escorting you around town. Hearing all your stories. You made me feel alive, Jess. I haven't felt that way for a long time. And besides, it's not often I get asked out on a date by a beautiful lady. Only a damn fool would turn her down."

"Oh, Heck." I joined him on the couch. "I missed you too." It was true; I had missed him this past month.

"Got any beer?" he asked with a sigh, visibly glad his prepared speech was over.

"No . . . I drank the last one."

"You? I didn't think you liked beer."

"I don't much. It was just there, so I drank it."

"Can we start over, Jessie?"

"Friends?"

"If that's all you want, then friends it is."

Somehow it seemed like I'd scored a major point. I steeled myself so as not to blow it a second time with this man. He was good for me; I had a nice feeling being around him. "What if I ask you out again?" I said. "Right now. Let me buy you dinner."

"You got a deal."

"Great; give me ten minutes to change."

He smiled his dear, sweet smile.

I wanted to take him in my arms, but knew that was a little more than I'd offered. I knew I had to go slowly.

"I'll give you nine."

"I'll be back in eight." I laughed as I ran up the stairs to my bedroom. My loneliness had evaporated, and as I changed into fresh jeans and a black sweater, a warm happiness washed over me.

But like an Indian summer day at dusk, that warm happiness cooled off fast.

CHAPTER SEVENTEEN

We had a cozy dinner at a new pub in Carmel, though Heck never once tried to hold my hand. There was a definite difference in our relationship. It seemed we were indeed starting over. Just friends.

It had been my request, yet it left me with mixed emotions. I missed his touch and the intimate glances he'd been sending my way those weeks that our relationship had held so much promise. We'd been headed for something, no doubt about it, and now we were back at the starting line—or was it the finish line?

Whatever, I suddenly felt lonely and empty. Yet I also felt safer in some ways. If I didn't give myself completely to Heck, he couldn't hurt me as Kevin had. Plus, I hadn't entirely given up on my marriage, even though everyone else—including Kevin—assured me it was over.

"Tired? Or do you feel like doing something?" Heck asked, as we left the pub.

Tired? I was exhausted. I was flat-out sleep-deprived from almost six months of restless nights. But the thought of yet another filled me with absolute dread, and I didn't care if I never went home. "Yeah, let's do something. What do you have in mind?"

"Want to bowl?"

I laughed, but then realized he was serious. Well, why not? "Sure."

It was fun, and it was torment. I'd bowled twice, maybe three times, in my whole life, so we had some good laughs at my expense.

But when it was Heck's turn to send the ball down the alley, I almost sighed as I watched his form—and I don't mean his method. His long body looked so graceful each time he took three steps toward the pins and then thrust one leg out behind him as he released the ball.

After I'd thrown three straight gutter balls, he tried to give me a lesson. But all I could concentrate on was my teacher.

I felt an ache of desire as he encircled me with his arms from behind, his muscles pressed against my shoulders and his jeans rubbing against my own. I'm sure I would have been his for the taking that night, only he didn't try. He didn't even kiss me good night.

Disappointed as I was at the time, I felt glad later, as I lay in bed—not sleeping, of course. Why, just hours before my date with Heck, I'd sat on the couch longing for sex with Kevin. *What the hell was going on with me?* I wondered again.

My clock told me it was just after eleven, although it seemed much later than that. When the phone beside my bed rang, I took a deep breath before reaching for it. It might be Heck, or then again Kevin, and it flitted through my mind that I wasn't sure which one I wanted it to be.

Not to worry. My caller ID told me it was Ellen.

"I saw your light on. And wasn't that Heck's truck I saw there earlier? Wanna talk?"

"So late?"

"It's not that late. Steve's out of town, and I'm watching a Lifetime movie. I'm sure your sordid life makes better entertainment. Can I come over?"

"Bring popcorn." I climbed out of bed and started to pull on my robe. "Meet you on the couch."

Ellen was also in her pajamas and robe, one of the great benefits of having your best friend live right across the street. We both took an end of the couch, stretching our legs out against each other; and even though she hadn't brought popcorn, we each held a bowl of chocolate-chip ice cream.

"Did you have a fun time with Heck?"

"I did. He's a nice guy."

"But?"

"But nothing. He's a nice guy. Ellen, can I ask you something very personal?"

"Sure."

"How often do you and Steve have sex?"

"A lot," she answered, without even thinking. "Didn't you and Kevin?"

"Not really. Well, wait; let me think about that. Once a week, at the most. Usually less, especially when he was out of town. Is that weird, after so many years?"

"Did he still turn you on?"

"Did. Does."

"And Heck? Hey, wait a minute; did you and Heck have sex?"

"No. Didn't even come close. But the thing is . . ." I stopped, not sure how I wanted to continue this, even though I could certainly tell Ellen anything.

"The thing is, you wanted to," she continued for me. "Right?"

"Well, there's more to it than that. I wanted to, but I'm not sure if it was just with Heck."

"With Kevin?" She spooned ice cream into her mouth. "So you wanted a threesome?"

"Ellen, be serious. I think I might be losing my mind here."

"Perhaps you just want to have sex. With anyone."

"I feel . . ."

"Rejected? Heck didn't try to get it on, and good ol' Kevin's banging Miss America. You feel left out?"

"More to it than that, Dr. Phil. Shut up and listen."

"Shoot; I'm all ears."

I took a moment to collect my thoughts. It was going to feel good putting them into words; I just wasn't sure what the right words were.

"Okay, first I'm obsessed with Kevin and Taylor. What they're doing. How they do it. I have graphic images of them traveling to exotic places, and cozy evenings before a fire in a downtown penthouse, all the time having exhilarating conversations over brandy and coffee. All *I* can do is call Kevin to tell him the furnace is on the blink."

She was still nodding slightly but not interrupting, which pleased me and annoyed me at the same time. Shouldn't she have stopped me to say my imaginings were out of whack?

But I hurried on, before she could offer any comment. "I mean, they're out there living this exciting and glamorous life, and I'm lucky to be pecking away on the keyboard, scratching out yet another article on the Indianapolis Dream Home tour for the whopping sum of about twenty bucks an hour. Do you understand?"

"Sure. I get it. Go on, honey."

Before continuing, I grabbed her bare foot, which was nestled up against my thigh. "You are the *best* friend anyone could have. Do you know that?"

"Now you're telling Roy about Trigger. Go on."

"Okay. The worst thing of all was that night at the airport, back when this disaster started. When I think about him coming out of the airport walking next to her, talking and laughing, I realize now that he looked happier than I'd seen him in years."

"Bastard."

"How dense was I not to know there was something between them? I'd been in her company before, with him; why didn't I see something? And I wonder just how long it did take for them to go from business acquaintances to lovers."

I stopped talking again, as images of Kevin and Taylor crept back into my mind, his entering her office as she bent over a filing cabinet, her long, lithe legs titillating him in a way I no longer could, after so many years.

"Maybe—even worse—it was her mind, her wit, her intellect, her *niceness*, that grabbed his heart," I said aloud. I could just picture them bantering across the desk from each other, Kevin laughing heartily as she animatedly described a court session she'd dominated, interjecting witty asides about the various parties involved.

"Oh, Ellen, I can't stand to think of him comparing her body to mine."

How many sleepless nights had I envisioned their first kiss and imagined how Kevin felt as he cupped Taylor's firm, full, *young* breasts in his strong hands. And I'd often wondered where they'd first made love. Was it in her office? Some hotel? His Porsche (not unlike our own cavorting decades ago in his 1970 Chevy Impala)? And who had initiated it?

I felt Ellen's hand on my knee. "Honey?" she said, as if I'd fallen asleep and she had to wake me. "Jessie, what are you thinking?"

"I just need to know. Is it really sick to want to know everything? How it happened? Why he fell for her? Okay, okay, I know *why* he fell for her; of course I do. A blind man would fall for her. But enough to chuck our whole way of life? How do I stop driving myself crazy with all these questions?"

"Only one way I know of. Ask him for answers."

"I can't do that; can I?"

"Jess, I've told you a million times. You can do anything you want. If that's what you need to know, then that's what you need to know. And the only way to find out is to ask him."

"You're right. That's exactly what I'm gonna do."

***

"Hey, Lois."

"Jessie! How *are* you?" Kevin's secretary looked startled to see me.

"Good. I'm good." And I *did* feel good, as if I were about to do something proactive in my situation that might make a difference, instead of just responding to what everyone else in my life might throw my way. "Is Kevin in?"

"Yes, let me tell him you're here." She punched a couple of buttons on her phone and then said, "Kevin, your wife . . . er . . . Jessie is here." Her cheeks were red as she told me he'd be right out.

"Don't worry about it, Lois. I'm getting used to not being his wife. I'm getting over it all." Surely that would soon be true.

Kevin appeared at his office door. "Jessie, come in." He closed the door behind us. "This is a surprise. But I'm glad to see you. Here, sit down." He motioned to one of the wingback chairs in front of his desk. "We really do need to talk. About money, among other things." He lowered himself into his black leather chair.

I hadn't humbled myself by coming here in order to talk about that loathsome subject, and I wasn't about to be diverted. "Yeah, we will," I said. "But first, Kevin, I need your help."

"Sure, Jess, any . . . what can I do?" He looked almost relieved, as if maybe I would give him a chance to alleviate his guilt by making life easier for me somehow.

"You have to listen to me and think about what I'm asking. Don't just tell me no, Kevin. This is important. This is *necessary* if I'm to survive."

His eyebrows rose again, one higher than the other, such a Kevin characteristic. My heart hurt, and I wondered if I was about to break it irreparably.

"Kevin, I'm not sleeping at night. I haven't been since . . . since that night I picked you up at the airport. I just don't think I can go on anymore—"

"Oh, Jess, I told you; I'm so sorry—"

"Don't interrupt me." He looked so pained that I believed he really did regret everything; he just couldn't help that he'd fallen in love with Taylor. "I'm not pleading to have you back, Kevin. But I've realized there's something you can do to help me put it all behind me."

"What?"

I took a deep breath, not at all sure I was doing the right thing. "The reason I can't sleep is because I can't stop thinking. I've imagined you and Taylor doing a million different things, getting together a million different ways, making love a million times—"

"Yeah, I can imagine—"

"No, *I* can imagine. And that's my problem; don't you see?" I'd scooted forward on my seat and was grasping the edge of his desk like it was a cliff I was about to fall from. "If I *knew* exactly what transpired, I'd lose a few nights—okay, a few weeks or months—of sleep, mulling it over, but then I could put it behind me." I didn't add that it would also probably kill any hope I had for a reconciliation, which in the long run would do me a favor.

Kevin just looked at me, puzzled. Finally he asked, "What are you suggesting, Jess? I'm not sure—"

"Don't you see? It's the not knowing—not knowing things I think I have a right to know—that's killing me. I want to know about you and Taylor; I want to hear how you fell in love with her—and out of love with me. I want—"

He groaned. "Oh, Jess, there's no point in—"

"If *I* think there's a point, there's a point. I'm telling you what would make things easier for me. *You* don't know what would make things easier for me. *Obviously.*" I forced myself to stop. I didn't want to get mad again. More accurately, I didn't want *him* to get mad at *me*. I had to have his sympathy if I wanted the information that now seemed crucial for my very survival.

He stared at me in silence, his face looking more like his father's than his own at that moment. This was becoming a strain on him too, no doubt about it. Maybe that's why he agreed to talk. Maybe he was willing to try anything to get this chapter of his life closed. "What is it you want to know, Jess?"

"Everything."

This time he was silent so long, I thought he'd changed his mind. And I thought I'd go crazy. Then, just as I opened my mouth to rail against him with newfound strength and fury, he spoke.

"I met Taylor when we hired her, of course. I didn't choose her; I just had to interview her and approve Jake Logan's choosing her. It was all perfunctory. I didn't give her a second thought, Jessie; I wasn't looking for this to happen. I loved you."

He looked so earnest, I felt better already, although a dozen sarcastic responses threatened from the tip of my tongue. But I didn't want to stem the flow of recollections I wanted.

"We worked together the first time on the Hefner account, here in Indy. Taylor didn't plan for this to happen, either, Jess. She even told me she was engaged the first time we talked about calling on Hefner. She told me later it was a defense she'd used more than once to keep a man she worked with from coming on to her. She said she took me for one of those good-looking men always trying to score."

Now it looked like he was about to smile, and I was ready to slap it off his face. But instead, he just continued. "When she decided I was nice, after we'd worked together that first day, she told me the truth. She was unattached. We had a good laugh over it, Jess, because we both knew I wasn't the type to come on to someone."

No, you wouldn't have to, I thought, *with someone coming on to you with such a ridiculous line. And you fell for it*, I wanted to scream. *How naive. How fucking naive. Or was he just starved for compliments?* I suddenly wondered. Then, hearing Nina's voice in the back of my head, I refused to let myself start accepting blame for this horror story he was about to relate.

"Anyway, I don't know, we just talked a lot, you know, over lunches while we worked on that account, and on the drives there and back. But, Jess, I wasn't looking at her as a female I could love, I swear. It's just that we had a lot in common. At some point, she no longer seemed younger than me. She just seemed like a good friend who liked to talk about golf, about work things, about black Labs, about . . ."

I didn't even hear the rest of his laundry list. I was smarting over the black Labs. Kevin had always wanted to replace Oscar, our black Lab who'd died three years ago. I'd loved Oscar too, but I hardly thought we needed a dog now that our nest was empty. We'd want to be traveling more, and I was the one who was home all day and would have to train a puppy and . . . well, I'd given him so many reasons, he'd finally dropped it.

And now he was leaving me for someone who liked dogs. *Guess that'll teach me*, I thought, my head reeling as if I might faint.

" . . . you all right? Are you all right, Jess?"

"Yes, yes, I'm sorry; go on. This is what I need to hear, Kevin," I said, although suddenly I wasn't so sure. "Then I can get over it and get on with my life. Be brutal." I tried to grin, but my lips wouldn't cooperate.

He looked unsure for a moment and then, almost imperceptibly, shrugged his shoulders and continued. His honesty seemed cathartic for him, as he finished telling his story.

He soon appeared to have forgotten my presence, talking as if to himself, sometimes even showing delight at a memory he was sharing. I kept my hands and mouth in check so as not to stifle this story I needed to hear. But I never for a moment thought he was coming completely clean. There were many gaps that I knew he'd never fill, for fear of hurting me too much.

"I guess we crossed the line the time I took her out to dinner for her birthday. It was our second week working together out of town, in South Bend, if you remember, last... well, about a year ago. I felt sorry for her, being alone in South Bend on her birthday."

You idiot, I wanted to scream. *She was hardly alone. She had my husband with her, the same husband who would half a year later forget his own wife's birthday.* I bit my tongue, literally—and hard, tasting blood.

"We had champagne, which never helps, I'm sure. But still, if I hadn't already been falling in love with her, I don't think it would have happened. Anyway, it was an unseasonably warm night, and she asked me if I wanted to go for a walk. But she wanted to go to her room to change clothes first, and..."

"And you went with her, and you never made it on the walk." Damn; why did I say that? Why didn't I wait for his description, which might have been much more detailed? Maybe that's why I interrupted, I realized. Maybe I just had to defend myself from more hurt than I could bear.

"Yeah, something like that. Now are you satisfied, Jess?" He sounded mad.

He sounded mad at *me*, when I was the one who should be demanding, *you* guess *that was crossing the line?*

But instead, I asked, "Did you know right then, a year ago, that you were going to leave me?" I wanted to ask why he let me grow a year older and more useless before letting me in on the plan.

"No, no, of course not. I kept thinking it was just an affair. Every time, Jess, every single time we spoke or spent time together, I swore I'd never do it again. I thought I was just being selfish, having a midlife fling."

As opposed to what was really happening, which was... ? For a moment I thought I'd asked him that out loud, the way he paused so long. As numb as I felt, I knew I might have spoken, without knowing it.

"It was when we were in New York together, when Taylor told me she just couldn't be *the other woman* . . . well, that's when it hit me that I didn't *want* her to be."

"You wanted her to be your wife?"

He looked so sheepish, as if caught with his hand in the cookie jar, that I *would* have slapped him if I hadn't felt so drained.

This was not as innocent as robbing from a cookie jar. He was robbing from my life. He should look ashamed, not sheepish.

"Yes, Jess, I love her, and I want to marry her," he said, more gently than I'd ever heard him say anything.

***

Kevin apparently figured I needed only hours to complete my recovery, now that he'd given me what I "wanted." He came over that night for the discussion *he* wanted.

"Kevin, what is it?" For a change, I didn't immediately think he'd come for a reconciliation. I was still too mad and hurt about everything he'd confessed that morning to take him back even if he had.

"Jessie, we have to talk about money." He made his way past me and sat down on the couch.

I didn't offer him a drink, and he didn't ask for one. I folded one arm across my waist, propped the other arm on top of it, and rested my chin in my hand. I wished I could cover up my entire face. Scrubbed, ready for bed, and looking not a day under fifty, I felt at a disadvantage.

"Jessie, I think we should put the house up for sale, for starters."

Both arms fell to my sides, and my hands balled up into fists. "You what?" It wasn't enough that he'd broken my home; he wanted to take my house as well. I had a sudden image of myself in a dumpy apartment and wondered how I'd pay for even that.

"I think we should sell this house. It's certainly more than you need. And I'm kinda strapped, to be honest, making payments on this place and also an apartment."

I just shook my head. In spite of my flannel pajamas, I felt shaky and cold—and scared. "Kevin, I can't believe you're doing this to me. What did I do to deserve this?"

He sat up taller and straightened his tie. All the better to be self-righteous, no doubt. "Jessie, I plan to be fair. I know you'll need help. But mostly, I want to help you help yourself. You're going back to college, right? Merritt told me—"

"Merritt told you what?" I stamped a foot. "Kevin, there's no way I can ever make up for my decades out of the work world. Do you think it's fair that I suddenly start living like a pauper so you and Taylor—"

"Jessica, this isn't about Taylor. It's about why should you live in a four-bedroom, thirty-two-hundred-square-foot house that was more than big enough for a family of four? You won't have to live like a pauper if we sell it and split the money. I plan to be fair—"

"Oh, you bet you're going to be fair, Kevin." Now I folded both arms across my chest, tucking my hands tightly by my breasts and resisting—barely—the urge to walk across the room and slap him. "I guess it's time for me to get an attorney."

"Yes, I think it is." He stood up. To leave? To try to comfort me?

I didn't wait to find out. I turned and went upstairs, flinging myself on the bed and crying myself to sleep, the best night's sleep I'd had in half a year.

CHAPTER EIGHTEEN

I was driving to Heck's house. It wasn't something I'd planned; I just found myself in my Jeep late Wednesday afternoon heading down to Brown County. I didn't feel particularly happy or sad. I felt empty.

Heck and I had spoken earlier but decided not to see each other that day. We both had a lot of paperwork to catch up on. But now going to Heck's seemed like the right thing to do. Somehow, with no forethought, I'd grabbed my purse and headed out the door.

During the drive to Brown County, I thought of nothing. I was training myself that way. Instead, I concentrated on just enjoying the rolling hills, beautiful in spite of the barren trees, and the homes dotting the landscape.

Sooner than it seemed possible, I was turning onto the long, curvy road that led to Heck's cabin. When it came into view, I slowed down and finally came to a stop thirty feet from the circular drive leading to the front door.

The cabin looked like it belonged on a Christmas card, nestled as it was among the trees, a curl of wispy gray smoke winding its way out of the chimney. A faint dusting of snow covered the road ahead of me and lay sprinkled over the roof and windows of the cabin, reminding me of a giant cookie dusted with powdered sugar.

I sat there for a long time and then eventually proceeded slowly up the driveway to the front door. Before I had a chance to beep my horn, Heck came out, pulling a sweater down over his slight paunch. He looked happy to see me, a warm smile spreading over his face as he hurried to my door.

"This is a nice surprise." He reached for my arm to help me out. "What brought this on?"

"My Jeep just drove me here. I had nothing to do with it." I smiled back.

"Glad it did. Come on inside; it's cold out here." He ushered me through the door, which opened directly into the large living room. "Excuse the mess; I wasn't expecting company." He led me to the oversize couch covered in brown corduroy.

There was no mess, but there *was* a well-tended fire going. It mingled cozily with the late-afternoon light illuminating the comfortable room. He settled me on the couch, fussing over the cushions to be sure I was comfy.

"You sit here and relax," he said. "I'll make some tea. How does that sound? Here, take your boots off." He knelt before me, undoing the laces of my suede boots. "You're in luck, lady. I've got some of my famous chili on the stove."

"Is that what I smell?" I leaned back and let him remove the boots. It felt good to be so pampered.

"Damn right. You hungry?"

I nodded. I felt famished, in fact. I hadn't eaten much all day, and the delicious aroma wafting from the kitchen smelled enticing.

His smile broadened. "Good; then wait here. I'll serve you."

I was about to offer my help but then thought better of it. "That would be wonderful, Heck."

He was still on his knees in front of me, and without thinking, I placed the palms of my hands on either side of his face. His smile, like a moonbeam, filled the whole room. I'd forgotten what it felt like to be so wanted somewhere. Anywhere.

Humming softly to himself, he rose and headed toward the kitchen. I swiveled around so I could see him through the large archway. He had his back to me as he stood over the stove, and I watched him stir the chili and gingerly bring the spoon to his lips to taste it. Then he moved to the sink, glancing out the window above it.

"Jessie, Jessie, come here, quickly," he whispered loudly, beckoning me with one hand.

I rose from the couch and tiptoed toward him, certain that his whisper demanded silence on my part. And then I saw why. Outside the window two deer stood staring back at us. My eyes met those of the larger deer, and we were locked in immobility.

"Aren't they beautiful?" Heck whispered softly into my ear.

I could only nod. Yes, yes, they were beautiful. Beautiful and fragile. A slow fear for their safety began to creep over me. I blinked, the deer blinked, and then suddenly they were gone. In a flash. They disappeared into the woods behind Heck's cabin.

"Wow," I said, although it seemed so inadequate. I turned to Heck, noting how pleased he looked with himself, as if he'd arranged the whole thing.

"I see them quite often, although they've never been this close to the house before." He resumed tasting his chili. "I guess they smelled this." Grinning widely, he indicated the bubbling pot on the stove.

"Must have." I smiled. He was such a strong man, so capable and so independent. The kind of man who looked after himself and didn't need a woman fussing over him. Yet in that moment he looked to me as fragile as the two deer. I had the feeling his safety was in my hands.

He dished up two steaming bowls and set them on the oak table in the dining area of the long room. Pulling out a chair, he motioned an invitation for me to sit. Then he rummaged around for crackers, produced a bowl of grated cheese, and set the table with two red-and-white-checked napkins.

The chili tasted delicious. I ate two bowlfuls, and then, at Heck's insistence, I retired to the couch to watch him clear the table and load the dishes in the dishwasher with the precision of an engineer.

When he was done, he put a few more logs on the fire and turned on the table lamp next to the couch before retreating to the kitchen.

He returned with coffee. "This is so great, Jessie. To have you here."

"For me too." I took the cup of steaming coffee he handed me. I lifted the cup to my lips, but before I could take a sip, he took it back and put it on the coffee table. Then he leaned over and gently kissed me. Softly and sweetly at first, and then I felt his passion. Or was it mine? I wanted more, as I always did when Heck kissed me.

But this time, I decided, I was going to get what I wanted. I pushed him away and stood up. "You know, I haven't seen your bedroom," I said.

He jumped up, and I reached for his hand so he could lead the way. But instead, I was scooped up in Heck's strong arms, and we headed toward a door on the opposite side of the room. He pushed it open with his foot, and striding into the room, he bent over as if to lay me down on his king-size bed. We both laughed as we landed on the firm mattress.

"How Rhett Butlerish of you," I said, not releasing my arms from around his neck.

"And how Scarlett O'Haraish of you to be so bold, my dear," he murmured into my ear, pulling my sweatshirt up and maneuvering my arms out of the sleeves. Then he stopped for a moment. "Jessie, are you sure this is what you want?"

"Yes. Yes, more than anything."

"Oh, Jessie." He unzipped my jeans. "I want you so much. I've wanted you from the first moment I set eyes on you."

His words thrilled me. No one had ever said they wanted me, not in that way. Then, momentarily, I was filled with fright. I had never had sex with anyone but Kevin. I had never even seen another man naked. But it wasn't Kevin I was thinking of.

Instead, I remembered that I was wearing an old and tattered bra that had been washed too many times. That my Jockey underpants had torn elastic around the waist. That I hadn't even shaved my legs that morning.

I felt unattractive, and old, and was grateful that the room was semidark. I hoped Heck wouldn't notice the stretch marks on my stomach, or the chipped nail polish on my toes.

But as he undressed, I forgot about myself, so distracted was I by his body, as hard and muscled as I knew it would be, with only the slightest of potbellies betraying his age.

We made love more than once that night, and in between, we lay wrapped together, arms and legs entwined around each other's body. There was an intimacy about it I hadn't experienced for many, many years. It was *newly married* sex, or *lovers'* sex, so different from the sex that comes with being married for too many years, where you make love and then each turn on a light by the side of the bed and go back to a favorite book.

Guiltily, I realized that's what had happened to Kevin and me. Did he experience this abandoned passion with Taylor that I was feeling now? Of course he did. This is what new lovers did. Stroll around in front of each other naked, brazenly showing off their bodies. Not just willing, but eager, to try different things in an effort to please a partner.

***

The honking geese flying over Heck's cabin woke me, but Heck was already gone from the bed. I sat up, pulling the comforter around me and tucking it neatly under my arms.

I felt like Scarlett O'Hara again, a wicked grin spreading across my face as I remembered the night before. I could hear him in the kitchen making coffee, and then he was back in the bedroom, carrying a tray with two mugs of coffee and a plate of croissants.

"Good morning, gorgeous," he said, and I almost wept at the words.

I knew I must look far from gorgeous. My makeup had been demolished, and my hair was tangled. But with the spell he'd cast over me, I actually began to feel gorgeous.

"Happy Thanksgiving." He set the tray on the table next to my side of the bed and sat down next to me.

"Oh no! It *is* Thanksgiving." *How could I have forgotten?* I cupped his chin in my hand and pulled his face close to kiss him.

"Heck," I then said with resolve. "Come with me to Merritt's. She's cooking dinner today. I want you to come with me."

He sat back, and I prepared myself for an argument. But he didn't offer any. His eyes were amused as he handed me a mug. "Are you sure?"

"Oh yes. I'm very sure. I want you to know my kids. It will be just Merritt and Alec, and Teddy. This is the first time Merritt's had Thanksgiving at her house. I want you to be there."

"Okay."

While Heck showered, I called Merritt and told her I was bringing someone to dinner. A good friend was how I described him. I could have gone on to say he was also now my lover and that she would have to excuse me if I couldn't keep my hands off him during dinner. But of course I didn't.

Merritt actually seemed pleased I was bringing someone, which pleased me too. Then I put down the phone and boldly joined Heck in the shower. Something I had never in my life done, but had seen in so many movies.

I felt sexy as I opened the door and stepped in behind him, wrapping my arms around his waist, not caring about stubble on my legs or my hair getting wet. Just wanting to be as close to Heck as I possibly could.

***

We took Heck's truck, stopping first at my house so I could change clothes and grab a bottle of wine. My happiness was tinged now with nervousness at the thought of how my kids would react to Heck joining us for Thanksgiving dinner. Especially Teddy, given his prior record.

Alec answered the door. He hesitated for a moment, looking first at me, then at Heck. He was smiling, at least, as he silently took our coats and motioned us toward the living room, planting a kiss on my cheek as we passed in front of him. The aroma of roasting turkey, which somehow seems different on that particular day, filled the house.

Standing in the middle of the living room, we waited a couple of seconds before Merritt appeared in the kitchen doorway, looking lovely and domestic with a white apron covering most of the navy-blue polka-dot dress that stretched over her growing bulge. But her face wore a puzzled expression.

For a second we all remained silent, and then she came toward us. I hugged her as tightly as I could, aware that she wasn't hugging back. When I finally released her, the puzzled look was still on her face.

"Welcome to our home," Alec finally said to Heck, his hand outstretched. "I'm Alec." He deserved an award for being the first to speak. I hadn't realized just how nervous I was.

Heck was watching Merritt closely, and I saw now that she was like a trapped animal, ready to spring. I knew she'd probably spoken to Ted, and he'd undoubtedly given her his appraisal of Heck, one I felt certain wasn't flattering.

The holidays had always been so important to me. Perhaps the reason I'd driven off to Heck's, forgetting it was already the day before Thanksgiving, was because I wanted to ignore them this year. But now I wanted nothing more than to revel in my family, and Heck.

But I was stupid to do it this way. To bring him to her house on such an important day without warning. What had I been thinking? It seemed that lately all I ever did was act first and pay the consequences later.

I introduced Heck and Merritt to each other and watched as they shook hands and uttered the appropriate words. Then I took Merritt's arm and led her to the kitchen, leaving Alec and Heck to get acquainted in the living room.

"The table looks lovely," I said, as we passed the dining room.

"Alec did it," Merritt said dully, like a bad actress in an even worse play. "He's become quite the little homemaker." Once in the privacy of the kitchen, she turned on me, the trapped animal released. "*Mom*, who the hell is he?"

"He's a good friend of mine."

"Is he the cabinetmaker?"

"Cabinetmaker. Indian chief. What the hell difference does it make? He's a good friend of mine. If you had a problem with me bringing someone, you should have said so."

"I didn't think you'd be bringing your *boyfriend*, for heaven's sake!"

There was that word I dreaded. "Do you want us to leave?" I whispered, hearing at the same time voices and laughter from the living room, Alec and Heck yukking it up.

In my worst nightmare, I never would have dreamed I'd hear what I heard next. I would have bet everything I had that Merritt, who was so like me, would pretend that everything was okay. Even if she didn't believe it for one second.

But instead, she said, "Yes, I think it would be best if you left."

"What?" was all I could say. I couldn't believe the words coming out of my daughter's mouth. "*Merritt.*" I reached for her arm, but she turned from me and began pulling on oven mitts.

"Mom, I know this is hard for you."

"Merritt, I—"

"Wait; let me finish." She held up a hand in protest, an oversize fish made of printed fabric covering her small hand. "I know the holidays are going to be hard for you. I mean, since this is the first time we've had Thanksgiving without Dad. But I just want to say this. It's hard for us too. For Teddy and me. This doesn't affect just you; it affects all of us."

"I know," I said softly. But it didn't stop me from wanting to scream that it wasn't *my* fault we weren't all together.

"Look," she went on, "Teddy will be here any minute. I think it might be best if you and . . . whatever his name is—"

"Heck," I reminded her. "His name is Heck."

"Okay, Heck. I don't want a scene. And Teddy's not going to handle this well at all."

"He can't do much worse than you."

She turned back toward the stove, and I noticed the strings of her apron were stretched to the maximum to accommodate her new girth.

"I called him after I spoke to you this morning," she said. "He seemed a little—"

"A little what?" I felt hot—from fury, not the oven.

"Look, Mom. I don't want to appear rude, but I think it would be much less awkward if you and Heck just had a drink and then made a quick exit. I don't want Teddy to feel uncomfortable."

"But it's okay if I do; is that it?"

She took off her fish mitt and came toward me, her arms outstretched as if to hug me. But I was ready for her, like a batter up against the league's best pitcher.

I turned and quickly found Heck. Alec had just opened a beer for him, but before he could put it to his lips, I took it from him and handed it to Alec.

"Heck," I said, "it seems Merritt's not in the mood for company. Why don't you and I find a restaurant open for dinner?"

He sighed audibly and turned toward Merritt, who was standing in the doorway fanning herself with the oven mitt.

"I'll go," he said to me, but looking at Merritt. "Jess, you stay with your family. It's no big deal."

"Oh, but it is. We go together."

I patted Alec's arm as I passed him on my way to the front door. "Have a happy Thanksgiving, Alec."

He gave me a lopsided grin and kissed my cheek. "Sorry about this," he whispered. "These days Merritt doesn't know what the hell she's doing."

"Oh, I think she does. But we'll all get over it. Eventually. Just take care of your wife."

CHAPTER NINETEEN

Heck and I didn't go to a restaurant. I didn't have the heart for it, nor the appetite for any kind of dinner, let alone a Thanksgiving one. I suddenly had trouble feeling thankful for anything.

"Jessie, I don't want you to be alone," Heck said, when I finally told him he might as well go home and get a good night's sleep. I wasn't going to be very good company.

We'd gone to my house from Merritt's, once I finally convinced Heck not to bother trying to find a restaurant that was open. I sat on my couch drinking wine, while Heck put together something that resembled a meal from the paltry contents of my new cupboards: tuna fish, macaroni and cheese, pineapple chunks, and brownies laced with caramel. I wouldn't have touched it even if it had been the turkey and all the trimmings that Merritt had refused to share with us. Heck, on the other hand, ate with abandon.

"You know, I expected that of Ted," I said, as Heck stabbed a hunk of pineapple from his plate. He was sitting next to me on the couch, but I was talking to myself more than to him. "I expect Ted to be immature, selfish. But I can't believe how unfair Merritt is being, how unkind and unloving. What kind of monsters did I raise?"

"No, Jess—"

"I'm serious, Heck. And if I—their own mother—think they're monsters, what must you think of them?"

I didn't really want an answer. If only Heck had kids of his own, this would be easier. But how could I expect him to understand that what my kids undoubtedly ached for was their mom and dad sitting together over Thanksgiving dinner, both eager to hear about their jobs and their lives, both eagerly awaiting the birth of their first grandchild, both continuing to put their kids above all else, forever.

"I might not have kids of my own," Heck said, as if he could read my thoughts. He shoved some tuna fish into his mouth and then speared another pineapple chunk. He held it in midair, like a college instructor's pointer, as he spoke. "But I'm a human being, Jess. It isn't a huge leap for me to understand how conflicted your kids must feel. I'm disappointed, sure. And I think they're acting pretty . . . slow to come around; I think they're pretty slow to adjust, when their dad—"

"Heck, I really don't want to talk about it." I didn't want him to say something for which I could not forgive him. My kids were selfish brats. But they were *my* selfish brats.

"Okay; I'd just like to shake them for what they're doing to you. And just let me say this one last thing."

I stirred on the couch, ready to leave the room if I had to in order to stop the course of our conversation.

"I just want to tell you that I think you need to make things right with your kids," he said. "They might be wrong, and you shouldn't pander to them. But you're not going to be happy—ever—if you break with them. Like it or not, you're the mom."

"What exactly do you mean?" I felt he was giving me good advice, loving advice, advice that proved how much he cared for me. There obviously wasn't anything in this for him; my kids had done nothing to make Heck want them in *his* life. I would have thought he'd tell me to write them off and get on with my life.

But he was too wise for that. "Maybe you should just agree to disagree," he said. "Then we'll give them all the time in the world. If they never want to be around me, that's fine too. We can have our time and space, and you'll still have plenty left for them. Just don't try to get us together again unless they do change, Jess." So he might expect me to swallow my own pride, as their mother. But he wasn't about to swallow his.

Fair enough, I thought, though I couldn't at the moment imagine myself ever initiating contact with Merritt again. I was still too angry, and with her brother, as well. Had he been there, he would have acted just as reprehensibly, I knew.

"They'll come around, Jessie. You'll see." Heck set his plate on the table in front of us and patted my knee.

"I notice my phone isn't ringing off the hook with apologetic calls from my sorry—pun intended—offspring."

"Give them time."

"Yeah, right." I sighed. "You really should head home, Heck." I patted his hand on top of my knee. "I think I just need to be alone a while."

"I think that's the last thing you need."

"So *you* know what I need too? Like my kids do?" I said it tenderly, though, grateful for his concern. "Really, Heck, I just want to put in a movie and climb into bed."

"Alone?"

"Yeah. Alone. You need to go home and get a good night's sleep. Someone might as well."

***

I purposely put *Titanic* in my DVD player, as if to remind myself that couples do *not* always end up together happily ever after. I was vaguely aware of Jack and Rose's plight, my troubled thoughts scattered and random and only occasionally on the movie, when I realized my doorbell was ringing. I sat up in bed and lifted the corner of the Roman shade covering my window.

Teddy's Mustang sat in the driveway. Surprised I hadn't heard it, I hurried out of bed and down the stairs.

"Oh, honey, Happy Thanksgiving. It's so good to see you." I hugged him and pulled him in. So much for being angry with him.

"You alone?"

"Yes. Yes, I'm alone." I didn't even resent his question, so glad was I to see him. It had been more than a month, long enough, I noted, for him to grow some kind of scraggly beard. *Obviously, he's not in the midst of a serious job search*, I thought, wondering if Kevin had seen him lately.

"I thought you probably were. I didn't see his truck."

He said *truck* the way he might say *old beater*. It couldn't have been a snobby thing, I knew; too many of his friends drove trucks. Heck just couldn't do anything right in Ted's eyes. And maybe no one would ever be good enough for his mother except his father. I wondered for the thousandth time what my son thought of Taylor.

"Why weren't you at Merritt's?" He sounded like my little Teddy asking his dad why he hadn't made it to his Little League game those rare times Kevin had to miss. But his dad had been *wanted* at the games.

"I was uninvited. Didn't Merritt tell you?"

"She told me *you* were invited; she just didn't want you bringing *him* along, not to such an intimate family gathering."

Obviously Merritt's words, exactly. Teddy wouldn't know *intimate* from *intimidate*. "Oh, and since when is Thanksgiving dinner intimate?" I asked. "We never had fewer than a half dozen extra people." It was true; we'd had their college friends who lived too far away from their hometowns to make it back for both Thanksgiving and Christmas, and before that there were always friends in the neighborhood who lived far from extended family, or Nina and her family coming from Houston.

He tried to reword his explanation. "Merritt didn't want someone we didn't know—"

"Yeah, so she said."

"We're disappointed in you, Mom, that you chose not to be with us on a holiday. How do you think that makes us feel? Do you care what we feel?"

It sounded like my son was sent over here with his sister's words in his mouth. All Teddy cared about in regard to Thanksgiving, I felt certain, was food and football. Bring on the banana cream pie and a touchdown or two, and he'd be happy.

"What about your dad? He left the state for Thanksgiving; what do you think about that?" I was starting to yell now.

"Don't you see, Mom? Losing dad isn't half as painful as losing you." Those were his own words, no doubt about it. And they came complete with a shaky, sad voice and a longing so obvious it pained me.

"Oh, Teddy, Teddy, Teddy. You will never lose me." I went to him and put my arms around his waist. Only a few years ago, it seemed, I would have cradled his head against my bosom. But he was way too tall for that, so I snuggled into *his* chest and held him tight. "Let's sit down." I pulled back and grabbed his hand.

After we were seated on the couch, I continued. "The bottom line, I gotta tell you, is that you and Merritt cannot do this to me."

He withdrew his hand from mine and sat up straighter, but I continued. "I'm an adult; I'm your mother, not your . . . your . . . I don't know what it is you and Merritt are treating me like, but I know it's not good. It's not fair. And it's not acceptable."

"I know, Mom. And I tell myself that. Merritt and I tell each other that. And then, well, then we just can't help how we feel sometimes. We're just trying to look out for you. We hurt so much for you, with Dad, and we don't want to see you hurt more. We just don't think you should be leaping in like this with someone who's so not your type."

I stood up. "Teddy, you guys have to give Heck a chance. If you can't trust in my own good judgment, then at least give him a chance."

"I don't know, Mom. Merritt and I just—"

"You and Merritt just better think about this."

He stood up too, realizing he was being dismissed. We didn't part in anger; I'm not sure what the overriding emotion was, of the many mixed ones we both felt. I just knew it didn't feel good.

I heard *his* old beater start up as I entered my bedroom. The final credits for *Titanic* rolled up the television screen as I grabbed the remote off the pillow.

Then I climbed into bed, ready to actually watch the movie this time.

***

Most people expect the holidays to be the worst time for someone in the throes of a divorce. Even Merritt had predicted that. And I did have my moments.

Like the day Ellen came over just as I was headed to the attic to dig out the tree stand (the first time in my life I'd ever gotten involved with a tree stand; that had always been Kevin's domain).

"Can I help?" she asked.

"That'd be great. I'm afraid I'm going to run into some creature up there."

"Uh, like what kind of creature?" Ellen looked prepared to withdraw her offer.

"Don't tell me some good ol' Texas girl is going to be afraid of a little mouse or squirrel."

"Is that all? I thought you meant Bigfoot or something." She feigned bravery and followed me to the door in the upstairs hall that led to the attic.

"Here, put this on." I handed her the sweater I'd grabbed from my bedroom doorknob on the way. No matter how long she lived in the North, it seemed, she continued to feel the cold more than we natives. "It'll be chilly up there."

As she stood watching me—or was she watching for something to scurry across the attic floor?—I came across the box of Teddy's Lionel trains and tracks.

"Oh, Ellen, look. Teddy got these for Christmas in . . . well, whenever it was, I remember as if it were yesterday. Kevin setting up the track and the cars under the tree, just so, on Christmas Eve."

I also remembered the glow in Teddy's eyes the next morning, making the Christmas-tree lights look dim by comparison. But I didn't share that out loud. I didn't want Ellen to think I was getting sad.

But we both knew I was when I opened the box of Christmas stockings, identified by red-yarn lettering across their tops as belonging to Dad, Mom, Merritt, and Teddy. We knew I was sad because I began crying. "Oh, Ellen, what happened to that family?"

Ellen came over to me and knelt down beside me, cradling my head on her shoulder.

After just a moment—I was getting better—I pulled my head back up and said firmly, "One marriage, one baby on the way, and one almost-divorce, that's what's happened to that family."

I placed the lid back on the box, grabbed the nearby tree stand, and hastily descended from the attic and the memories it held, Ellen close at my heels.

That's why I so appreciated Heck. Being with him—even just the thought of him—could obliterate all those negative feelings, could quell all those bittersweet memories, could make me forget Kevin.

Because it was Heck's slow time at work, he and I were together most of the time. We remained too discreet to stay all night at one another's place, lest my kids suspect just how far our relationship had progressed. That thought remained unbearable to me.

But nevertheless, Heck and I rarely separated for more than a few hours, and I grew increasingly amazed that I'd ever been able to live without him.

"Nina, do you think I could be in love with him, or is it just such a relief compared to the way Kevin and Taylor had me feeling?" I asked my sister a couple of weeks after Thanksgiving.

"Jess, Jess, Jess, why must you always analyze everything to death? Whether you love him or not, you're happy. Just go with it. *Run* with it."

"I am. It's just that . . . I don't know, maybe I feel guilty, feeling so happy with another man, having such good sex with another man, when just six months ago I was happily married—I thought—to Kevin. Can you blame me for being confused?"

"Not for being confused, I guess; I'll give you that. But you have no reason to feel guilty, Jess. It's just that your kids have made you feel guilty. I still say Aunt Nina should have a heart-to-heart with them."

"No, no. We have enough relationships grown shaky. We all need to count on a good one with you. Besides, maybe *guilty* isn't the right word. But there's just this tiny part of me, whenever I get away from Heck . . . a small twinge that this somehow isn't right. Not this soon."

"Oh, Jess." Her voice exuded disgust, albeit loving disgust.

I changed the subject, for her sake as well as mine. "You should have seen Heck, Nina. He insisted on going with me this morning to register for my classes. It's so computerized now. It was nothing like it was when he went to college."

"He went to college?"

"Yeah; what'd you think? Because he works with his hands, he's illiterate?" I laughed, remembering how I'd grossly underestimated his depth, his intelligence, and *certainly*, I knew now, his passion. "He has a degree in anthropology from IU. He studied it because he found it most interesting, he says, and he always knew he'd build and paint, anyway. He just got a degree to please his parents and to give himself four years in a fraternity, he says, and four years to closely follow his favorite college basketball team."

I laughed again. "I never know when to take him seriously or when he's just being modest. He probably graduated with the highest honors; he probably has a doctorate. I know there's an art wing that's named after his family."

I told Nina how Heck had driven up from Brown County to pick me up and then driven me the half hour back down to Butler University to register. I'd told him we should just meet there, but he insisted. And he'd gone to my counselor with me, adding his opinion to hers about what I should take and how I should set my schedule up. He made it obvious he thought I was brilliant and capable of handling anything tossed my way.

Unworthy as I felt of that assessment, I accepted it gratefully. As I heard him make such statements as "Jess won't have any trouble with algebra," in spite of the fact that it had been thirty years since my last exposure to math, I felt my self-esteem heal and thrive.

Just talking about Heck brought tender feelings and a yearning to be held by him once more. I wondered if I'd ever had such powerful feelings for Kevin. Had I just forgotten?

I said good-bye to my sister, knowing Heck would be coming any minute. He had some business to tend to and was going to come back and stay with me that night, at least until four in the morning. That's when I always insisted he leave, to ensure he wouldn't be there if any early-morning visitors showed up. Like my kids.

Or, I always had to consider, Kevin. I knew he wasn't going to quit pressing for a resolution to his so-called money woes, any more than he would wait much longer to get a divorce finalized. I did think he might wait until after the holidays, however. Then again, maybe not. Maybe the role of Scrooge fit him all too well.

Except for that first time I'd stayed in Brown County, I always left Heck's place at four in the morning too, so I'd be home by six. But in spite of such interrupted sleep, in spite of the fact that we spent a good share of each night talking and making love instead of sleeping, neither of us ever felt tired.

In fact, I felt a surge of energy at just the sound of the doorbell announcing Heck's arrival that snowy December night. I'd just started the fire in the family room fireplace and warmed the mulled wine, so his timing—like Heck himself—was perfect.

CHAPTER TWENTY

"Hey, babe," I greeted Heck, as I opened the front door and then removed one of the two bulging grocery bags from his arms. "What's all this? I told you it was my turn to feed *you* for a change."

"I had to stop by the store, anyway, and I wasn't sure you'd get out in this snow." He removed his gloves and then his suede jacket with the sheepskin collar. I liked the way he hung it in my hall closet without hesitation. It made it seem like he belonged here.

And I knew—because he always told me—that he liked the way I kept my navy-blue corduroy robe and matching slippers at his cabin. It reminded him, he said, that I'd be back.

"I have a Jeep, remember? You think a little thing like snow could keep me from getting food for my man?" I slid my arms around his waist as he was bent over picking up the other bag of groceries, which he'd set down to remove his jacket. I noticed a frozen cheesecake—my favorite—as well as sausages, eggs, and a jar of blackberry jam. "Hey, what's with the breakfast stuff?" I stood up. "You know you can't stay—"

"It's really coming down out there. I thought just in case . . . surely you won't send me out in a blizzard?" He carried the sack in one arm and pulled me along to the kitchen with the other.

He barely got the sack on the counter before I turned him to face me. Encircling his waist in my arms again, I lay my head on the soft flannel that covered his chest. "I don't ever want to send you out, Heck; you know that." I hugged him more tightly, and then I looked up into his brown eyes, feeling a pull from his lips, as if they were magnets attracting mine. "But unless it's a real blizzard—"

"I know, I know." He lifted my face and kissed me with such gentleness and then with such fervor that I knew I would let him stay forever if he would just keep doing that. I was breathless when at last he pulled himself away and retrieved mugs for our wine. "This smells good," he said.

But before he could pour the aromatic brew into our mugs, the doorbell rang. "Who else would venture out in this stuff?" I asked, and then answered myself. "Ted."

And Ted it was.

"Honey, what are you doing out in this snow?" I asked, as he made his way past me and removed his down-filled jacket.

"I just wanted to make sure you were okay, that you didn't need me to get you anything," he said. "But I see Heck beat me to it."

I was startled by the absence of rancor in his voice. Instead, I would have sworn he sounded almost grateful, or at least relieved for his mother. "Something smells good," Ted said, sniffing the air.

"It's mulled wine. Want a cup?" I asked.

"Nah; if you're okay, I'm going to head on home before this gets any worse. You better too, Heck." It couldn't be possible, I knew, but there wasn't a hint of a threat or even displeasure in his voice, only the seeming innocence of someone who cared.

I grew more astonished—so much so that I couldn't join in—as I heard idle chitchat form between them. Talk of snow tires and four-wheel drives and yes, even the Pacers. It stopped short of Ted agreeing they should take in a game together, or even Heck's offering such a thing. But still . . .

I kissed my son on the cheek after he'd put his jacket back on. And then I grabbed him and hugged him so tightly I'm sure his ribs hurt into the next week. I wanted to hug him again as I saw how he reached out to shake Heck's hand.

As the door closed behind him, Heck and I just looked at each other, stunned. "Go figure." I shook my head and followed Heck back to the kitchen, where I watched him fill our empty mugs.

"Maybe he's spent time with Kevin and Taylor," I said in a non sequitur to Heck, after we'd been chatting for a while in front of the crackling fire.

"What? Who?"

"Ted. Maybe that's why he's had a change of heart. Maybe he's seen them and figures I deserve a relationship too."

"Maybe he's just matured."

"Well, I don't care what inspired it. I just feel so much better. Maybe Merritt will come around too. Maybe that will be her Christmas present to me." I lay my head on his shoulder and pulled my legs up underneath me, reaching for the cream-colored afghan I'd knitted years earlier.

Heck helped me cover both of us, and then he stroked my hair with his free hand. He took a sip of his warm, spiced wine and then asked me, "What *do* you want for Christmas, Jess?"

"I have it."

"Oh, and what might that be?"

"You. As if you didn't know." I poked him in the ribs, and merely touching him made me excruciatingly aware of how much I wanted him, how much I couldn't bear not having him in my life. Not that I had to worry about that, he proceeded to assure me.

"You know what I want to give you?" He sounded as nervous as a high school freshman contemplating his first kiss.

"What?"

"I want to give you an engagement ring."

I was silent, struck dumb, and more than a little panicked.

He set his mug down on the end table and eased off the love seat, kneeling in front of me. He took my mug from me, setting it next to his, and then he took both my hands in his. "Will you marry me, Jessie? As soon as your divorce is final, will you marry me? Please?"

Now I felt nervous. On the one hand, as much as I cared for him, needed him, craved him, I felt this was too much too soon. After all, what was the hurry? I hadn't even thought that far ahead. I was too happy with the way things were right then.

But on the other hand, I experienced a fleeting memory of how stubborn Heck could be. I remembered our one and only fight, and I figured I'd seen only a hint of his deep-seated pride and strong will. This couldn't have been easy for him. I had to be careful not to humiliate him, not to hurt him as his wife had hurt him.

"Heck, I'm not saying I won't want to marry you someday," I answered. "But not now, not for a very long time." If *ever*, I wanted to add, but thought better of it.

To my great relief and amazement, he answered, "I'll settle for that." Then he leaned up and kissed me slowly, tenderly. "You can't blame a guy for trying. But I'll settle for that," he repeated, his lips covering mine and then working their way down my neck and into my olive-green silk blouse.

After we'd made love on the floor in front of the fireplace and dined on pasta and salad, we sipped coffee and talked well into the night. We talked about his childhood, my childhood, his marriage, my marriage. We barely touched on our future, except for me to reiterate that it was just too soon to take the next step.

Then, as four o'clock approached and I saw that the snow had subsided, I extracted a promise from him not to fall asleep at the wheel and pushed him out of the house like a mother robin pushing her baby out to find his own worms.

I doffed the robe I kept at home—a thick white chenille robe Kevin had given me for Christmas two years ago—and replaced it with my red plaid pajamas. Then I climbed into bed, under my down comforter, feeling more right with the world than I had for six months.

***

I'd always loved Christmas. I adored it. I reveled in it, making it an entire season of its own. It was my absolute favorite day of the year.

But this year, as it approached like an invading army, it filled me with nothing but dread. I wished I were going away or that Christmas could be cancelled.

Even making up with Merritt didn't help.

A week before Christmas, I finally resolved to call her and straighten out our differences, or at least come to a truce. It was obvious she wasn't going to call *me*, and with the holiday bearing down, I felt compelled.

But I was so filled with relief the first time I called her and Alec said she was out shopping that I almost did a fist pump.

"I'll have her call you when she gets home," Alec said. "It should be any minute now."

Two hours later, when she still hadn't called, I plucked up enough courage to place another call to her home. This time she answered.

"Mom, I was just about to call you."

"Really? That's awfully good of you, Merritt."

"Okay, Mom, before you say anything, let me say this: I want you and that guy to come here for Christmas dinner."

"That guy has a name. And before I agree to anything, I think I deserve an apology from you." I suddenly felt on a roll, determined not to let my daughter push me around. I had a newfound determination. Not even sure where it came from or where it was going, I kept pushing. "Frankly, I was so embarrassed by your attitude—"

"I'm sorry. I'm embarrassed too. Please forgive me." A long silence followed, until she finally said, "Mom, are you still there?"

"Yes, I'm here."

"Did you hear what I said? I'm sorry. Can we put it behind us?"

"Of course. That was all I wanted to hear. But you must be sure you really want Heck to be with us Christmas Day. If not, then I won't come. I mean it—"

"Mom, I told you. I'm sorry. I want you here. Both of you."

Relief flooded through me as I realized she meant it. "Okay."

"I'm so glad. I've missed you, Mom. I was a beast, I know. Alec told me I was. Even Dad told me to make up with you."

"Dad? You spoke to your dad?" I was on the alert again, immediately bitter that she'd discussed *anything*, much less me, with her dad.

"Well, he's still my father." I heard that edge creep into her voice. "It is okay if I talk to him, isn't it?" The edge was now laced with sarcasm.

"I guess so." I was desperate to know everything they'd discussed, and I was irate at the thought of Kevin advising Merritt about her behavior toward me. But it was all so tiring, I dropped the subject. "Let me get some paper and a pen, and tell me what I need to bring."

***

As Christmas grew closer, my mood grew more melancholy. Two days before Christmas Eve I spent a brutal afternoon at the mall with Merritt.

We'd finished the remains of our shopping and were both in the wrung-out mood that is inevitable when you have two women, one heavily pregnant and one with a splitting headache, trudging through a crowded mall filled with far too many Santa Clauses and way too much Christmas cheer.

I walked Merritt to her car and made sure she was buckled in and safely on her way home before I got into my own vehicle. As I backed out of the parking space, my phone rang.

"Hey." It was Ellen. "What're you doing?"

"I just left Merritt; we've been shopping all afternoon. What about you?"

"Same shit. Different mall. I feel rode hard and put away wet."

I laughed. No matter how many times I heard Ellen's down-home expressions, they always gave me a chuckle.

"Why don't you stop over and have a drink tonight?" she asked.

"Do you mind if I don't? I'm bushed. I just want to go home, curl up on the sofa, and fall asleep."

"No lover-boy tonight?"

"No. He's doing volunteer work at some retirement home. Building something for them."

"Geez, this guy is too good to be true."

"He is, isn't he? Gotta go; I'll call you tomorrow."

***

My evening started out perfectly. I changed into my favorite old pajamas, worn-out but soft as a cloud, and curled up on the sofa with a fire in the fireplace and a glass of chardonnay on the coffee table.

Heck called early to say he'd be busy all evening and he'd talk to me tomorrow. I snuggled into the couch, the remote in my hand, flipping around the channels for a good movie.

When the doorbell rang, I was a little irritated. When I saw Kevin standing in the snow at the front door, I was still a little irritated, and also a little nervous. And even a little happy.

"Come in, come in." I watched the wind whip his hair. He was wearing a classic cashmere coat, one I hadn't seen before, and soft, brown leather gloves.

"Sorry to barge in." He removed his gloves. "I was in the neighborhood."

We both thought about that for a moment and then laughed at the same time.

"Okay, I had to drive fifteen miles to get into the neighborhood, but once I was here, I thought, what the hell. Maybe I should come see you."

He was now removing his coat, and even though I hadn't suggested he do so, I found myself helping him off with it, like he was the Lord of the Manor returning from a fox hunt, and I was the serving girl.

As I draped his coat over my arm, he headed toward the couch and sat down, holding his hands out in front of the fire. "It's a little chilly in here, Jess."

"I'm perfectly warm."

His hands remained out in front of him as he turned sideways to face me with a look that said *back off*. "Sorreee; just making an observation."

"Do you want a drink?" I found myself asking, suddenly the perfect hostess.

"That would be nice. Maybe a glass of wine?"

I retrieved another glass from the kitchen and poured it half full with the opened chardonnay.

"Merry Christmas." He raised the glass in a toast.

"Merry Christmas." I sat down beside him. I had to bite my lip to stop myself from crying as I watched him look around the room, his eyes stopping now and then at various decorations, items we'd purchased together over the years.

"Room looks lovely, Jess. You always made a beautiful house at Christmas."

"What are you doing? I mean, where will you spend it? The holidays, Christmas Day."

"I know what you mean. Not sure."

I felt my heart flutter. Perhaps he and Taylor had broken up.

"Taylor might go to Arizona," he said. "Her folks winter there."

I hoped he didn't notice me visibly deflate. "*Might* go? It's two days away. When will she come to a decision?"

He swirled the pale-yellow liquid around in his glass, a little smile on his face. "She's very, er, spontaneous. Not like . . ."

"Like me?" I straightened up, ready to defend my lack of impulsive thinking to the death. "You know, Kevin, there's nothing wrong with planning a trip more than five minutes before you take off—"

"Whoa," he said, still smiling. "I was going to say like *me*, not you."

"Oh."

"I was always grateful for your planning. You did a great job keeping me organized. I miss it."

"Really?"

"Yes, really. So how—"

"Please, Kevin, please don't ask how I am. You can see how I am. I'm fine. But I think the roof might need to be replaced this spring. I have a leak in the attic. And guess what? I found out that crazy woman down the street . . . you know, the one who always wears a hat . . . I found out her name . . . it's Finnoula . . ."

He stared at me as I babbled.

But I didn't stop. "I heard a Starbucks is going in—"

He leaned over and kissed me. Just like that. The wine was sloshing around in my glass as I leaned backward unexpectedly, and I felt a few drops land on the flannel of my pajama bottoms.

And then, somehow, the glass slipped from my hand. My arms, with no help from me at all, were around his neck, and my lips, totally without warning, were kissing him back. My tongue had found its way, all by itself, into his mouth, and when he leaned me back on the couch, my body went limp.

I was suddenly aware of the scent emanating from him. It was overpowering. But it wasn't the way he used to smell. This was something, no doubt, that Taylor had picked for him.

It wasn't so much Kevin I drew back from; it was more from her. I placed my palms on his chest and pushed him away. "What was *that* about?" I whispered, bending over to retrieve my wineglass from the carpet. It had landed against a pile of magazines and miraculously hadn't spilled.

"Why are you whispering?" He smoothed down the front of his shirt.

"I don't know. Maybe we'll wake up my mom and dad."

He actually looked over to the staircase, as if my parents might appear and tell him it was past my bedtime, and then we both started laughing.

But the laughter went on just a little too long, like we were both afraid to stop and confront the silence and what had just happened.

"I think I better go," he said. And I nodded.

I didn't want him to, of course, but I didn't want him to stay, either. I felt thrilled and scared at the same time from his kiss, our kiss. But mainly, I felt desired. I felt elated that he had initiated it and that I had stopped it from going further. It had clearly been my move. *Take* that, *Taylor Stockton*, I thought. *Your man still has the hots for his ol' lady.*

At the front door he took me in his arms and hugged me, but we were both careful to keep our lips in different hemispheres. And once again, like the damn serving girl I seemed to have become, I helped him on with his coat, actually brushing his shoulders.

"Have a good Christmas, Jessie," he said. "Forgive me for trying to . . . you know . . . to kiss you."

"No need to be sorry," I answered, my elation returning.

"I didn't say I was sorry."

"Kevin, I—"

"I know; I was wrong, maybe. But just don't think too badly of me."

"I won't," I said. And then he was gone.

I was so nonplussed, I wasn't sure for a moment that he'd actually been there. But when I returned to the couch, I saw his half-empty wineglass and smelled his awful aftershave and remembered his mouth against mine. I crawled onto the end of the couch, pulling a cushion to my stomach and hugging it.

Oh, he'd been there, all right.

CHAPTER TWENTY-ONE

The ringing phone shook me out of my reverie. I wasn't sure how long I'd sat there, hugging a cushion to me like a sleeping baby.

I reached for the phone lying on the end table by the couch. It was Kevin, I knew, calling to tell me our kiss made him realize he wanted to move back home, that he'd been out of his mind, that everything was going to be back to normal. It felt like a victory was coming my way.

But as I looked at caller ID, I saw it was Ellen. I threw the pillow to the floor, sitting up straight. "Oh, Ellen. I thought you were Kevin."

"I saw his car leave. You okay? Did you guys fight?"

I was bursting to tell her. "No, we didn't fight. He just stopped by to see how I was; he was in the neighborhood, you know. We had a glass of wine, and he admired the Christmas decorations. Oh, and he kissed me. Nothing out of the ordinary. Well, that's not true. The kiss was out of the ordinary. For us, anyway—"

"Wait; slow down. Kevin kissed you?"

I picked up the discarded cushion again and hugged it. "That's what I'm saying. It was one of those unplanned moments. Very quick, but very good too."

Her silence bothered me, mainly because it was so unlike her to be silent. A feeling of foolishness, of regret, of anxiety, crept in from somewhere. Now I was really glad I'd stopped things from going further. "Ellen. Say something."

"Hot damn!" was all she could manage. And that seemed appropriate.

***

It was snowing perfectly on Christmas Eve, the kind of snow that normally only Hollywood can produce on such a special day. My decorated house completed the picture, from the full, symmetrical tree with presents piled beneath it to the stockings hung by the chimney with care. (I'd hung only Merritt's and Teddy's.) I had a wonderful dinner planned for Heck and Ted, Nat King Cole was singing his Christmas songs, and the eggnog was ready.

But it all felt wrong.

I tried to tell myself it had nothing to do with THE KISS, as I'd come to think of it, but it was there with me all the time.

I hadn't seen Ellen since our phone call, so immersed had we both been in last-minute holiday preparations. But now I found myself desperately wishing I could hash over all my confused feelings with her.

I tried not to focus on the fact that THE KISS obviously meant more to me than it did to Kevin. After all, he hadn't called me afterward, begging me to take him back. I tried to tell myself it was *only a kiss*, but I was confused and depressed—and more than a little excited when I remembered how it felt.

Concentrate on Christmas, I told myself a thousand times. Get this holiday behind us, and then see what happens.

Merritt and I had carefully planned just who should be where, and when. I had Ted for Christmas Eve (she was spending it with her in-laws). And Christmas Day Heck and Ted and I were to drive to Merritt and Alec's for brunch and to spend the afternoon. Then, at the appointed time, Heck and I were to leave so Kevin and Taylor could have the evening with the kids. When we arranged this, I didn't tell Merritt I'd learned Taylor might be in Arizona; it was a delicious secret to have.

But now it was Christmas Eve, my first without all my family gathered together, and my mood was glum as I poured myself a glass of eggnog. I desperately tried to shake my sadness, but it only intensified. And I couldn't get Kevin and THE KISS out of my mind.

Heck arrived early, his arms laden with gifts that I took from him and added to the pile under the tree. I hadn't seen him since Kevin and I'd had our impromptu kiss that now seemed like a dream. I'd put Heck off, telling him I wanted everything all set for Christmas Eve, just so, before he came over.

Now, just the sight of him made me instantly think of Kevin. As if I'd cheated on Heck. *Ridiculous*, I told myself. *Utterly ridiculous. Pull yourself together, and get over it.* I kissed Heck on the cheek and, relieved of the parcels, he rubbed his hands together, then took off his coat and hat.

"So what's the program here?" He took the cup of eggnog I handed him.

"Heck," I said, a little irritated that he'd forgotten all the intricate plans Merritt and I had labored over. "We've already been through this. Ted has dinner here tonight. Then tomorrow we all meet at Merritt's."

He took a seat on the couch and patted the empty cushion next to him. "C'mere; sit down."

I followed his suggestion, sinking in next to him.

"What's wrong?" he asked, a strong arm reaching behind me and pulling me close.

"Nothing. What could be wrong?"

"You tell me. You look upset."

I couldn't break it to him that this *all* felt wrong. That today, of all days, I missed my old family. It seemed cruel, considering the wonderful month we'd spent together. I couldn't tell him it suddenly felt as though he didn't belong here.

"The holidays are the hardest," he said knowingly, reading my thoughts as usual, at least in part. "Especially the first one. I understand."

"Do you?" I asked, trying hard not to cry.

"Yes, I do. My first Christmas without Gail was unbearable. Bo and I spent Christmas Day driving around, not going anywhere in particular. I just didn't want to be home."

"Oh, Heck, sometimes I think I'm the only one anything bad has ever happened to. I forget there are thousands of people who have been through this. I'm sorry."

"That's right," he agreed, a little too readily for my liking. "You know, this is going to be hard for your kids too."

"So what do I do?"

"Suck it up. It's the only way to get through it."

I leaned over and kissed him. "You're a remarkable man, Hector Dennehey."

"You know," he said, raising his feet and putting them on the coffee table, "I could leave if you wanted me to. If this isn't right for you."

I reached for his hand that rested on my arm. "No. I want you here. You belong here," I said, even though I didn't quite believe it. "Let's have some more of this stuff. It'll put me in the Christmas spirit."

I stood up to refill our glasses, knowing how lucky I was to have him. Without Heck, I probably would be driving around too, not wanting to be home. I was going to force myself to have a merry Christmas.

Still, the nagging sadness didn't quite disappear. I was filled with thoughts of what Kevin was doing, right that minute. Was he thinking about our last meeting the way I was?

Ted arrived about an hour later than planned, which was typical but okay. We had dinner, beef Wellington, which I'd spent most of the afternoon preparing, trying to forget that it was the traditional meal Kevin and I'd eaten on Christmas Eve ever since our budget first allowed.

Ted was in a jovial mood. It didn't seem forced, but I assumed he'd been celebrating earlier with his friends. The fact that one of them had dropped him off was a big clue. As irresponsible as they could be, my son and his friends always had a designated driver.

He brought in some gifts—all wrapped with too much paper, not enough tape, and no tags. One was for me and one for Heck, he pointed out, urging us to open them immediately. I felt touched that he'd included a present for Heck, but I insisted we wait and take them with the others to Merritt's the next day. It was our tradition to open gifts on Christmas morning.

After we'd eaten, I cleared the table and ushered both men into the living room, assuring them I didn't need help with the dishes. I relished the time alone, and I wanted the two of them to be by themselves.

Carefully, I rinsed my best china. The last time I'd used it was when Kevin brought home important customers for dinner early in the year.

I pushed the memories aside and instead filled the sink with soapy water to hand wash the silver, a wedding gift from my parents. I shuddered, almost glad they weren't alive to see this turn of events. They'd both adored Kevin and would be devastated.

I could hear Ted and Heck in the living room laughing at something, but instead of it making me glad, it just made me sadder. It'd been a long time since I'd heard Ted laughing with his father like that.

Suddenly I heard Ted's voice from right behind me. "Mom, come play poker."

"What?" I spun around. "On Christmas Eve?"

"Why not? This guy here claims he's pretty good. Let's show him the famous Harleman poker faces."

My son stood there before me, imploring me to enjoy myself. My heart felt heavy at how hard he was trying to have a good time. For me. For all of us.

But whoever heard of playing poker on Christmas Eve? It wasn't our tradition. Then again, maybe it was time to make some new traditions.

I dried the last knife and placed it on the towel next to the rest of the silverware. I'd put it away later, after I'd reassured my son—and myself—that Christmas Eve could still be good, even without Kevin. "Okay, honey," I said. "Let's show him how it's done."

***

Heck left around midnight, promising to come back early the next day, but Ted decided to spend the night. I was glad to have him in the house. I fussed unnecessarily, digging out some "comfy clothes," as he'd always called them, and making up his old bed with clean sheets.

When he joined me in his bedroom, dressed in the tattered T-shirt and sweatpants I'd found, I was sitting on the edge of the bed, ready to tuck him in as if he were ten years old again.

"Here, open this." He handed me a present.

"Ted," I said, "you know the tradition. We open—"

"Mom, just open it, will you?" He bounced down beside me on the mattress. "I don't want to wait. This is something special."

"Okay, if you insist. But this doesn't mean you can open anything—"

"Yeah, yeah, I know."

It was the shape and size of a magazine, but hard, and the wrapping paper looked as though it had been used several times. Regardless, I carefully unwrapped it.

Inside was an ornate silver frame that held an old black-and-white photograph that had obviously been enlarged and enhanced by the wonders of modern technology. There were my twentysomething parents, smiling happily, my mother dressed in a 1960s outfit, my father looking handsome beside her in a business suit with broad shoulders and notched lapels.

"Oh, Ted. It's wonderful. What made you think of such a thing? Where did you get the photo?"

"Aunt Nina helped me. She said it was your favorite picture of Grandma and Grandpa when they were young. I had her send it to me, and then I had it, you know, fixed up. Grandma looks pretty hot."

"Oh, darling." I encircled him in my arms. "It's wonderful. I remember this picture so well. Dad used to carry the original in his wallet." I also remembered that Nina had purloined it when we were clearing out my parents' home after our mother died.

He released himself from my grip and pulled the covers back from the bed, looking very pleased with himself as he climbed in. I tucked the blankets around his chest and then leaned over to kiss him on the cheek.

"Thanks for coming tonight, Ted."

"Hey, it was great. Heck's a good poker player."

"Yep." I reached over to turn off the light. "Who knew?"

I made my way to the bedroom door in the dark.

"Hey, Mom."

"Yes?"

"Heck's all right."

High praise, indeed. "Yes, he is, isn't he?"

I made my way to my own room. Things were better, but they still weren't as they should be.

***

"Oh, Mom, it's beautiful." Merritt removed the Lalique figurine from its box.

"Really?" I knew the delicate female shape was something Merritt and I had admired in a magazine earlier in the year.

"Yes, it's gorgeous. Alec, look. Oh, Mom, it's way too expensive. Really, what were you thinking?"

I was thinking, of course, that this was the last Christmas I would have the benefit of Kevin's bank account, and so I'd spared no expense in buying gifts for my family.

Ted had a plane ticket and accommodations to a ski lodge in Colorado where his friends were going. Alec had an outfit from L.L. Bean that Merritt helped me select. And lastly, I handed Heck two gifts.

These were bought with my own money. They'd almost cleaned out my meager bank account, but I was determined to give Heck something wonderful. We all watched as he opened the first, a coffee-table book of Pre-Raphaelite works of art.

He held the enormous book in his hands, as if it would break if he dropped it. "Jessie, it's wonderful."

"Open the second one," I said, pleased with myself for remembering his love of this particular school of art.

He ripped open the smaller package. A black-and-white photograph, in a simple silver frame. Two deer, staring into the camera as if they were models posing.

"Like the real thing," he said quietly.

We raised our glasses of champagne and silently toasted each other, oblivious to the others in the room. "And this is for you," Heck said, taking the last remaining package from under Merritt's tree and handing it to me.

It was tiny, and wrapped in gold paper. I undid the ribbon and opened the paper to reveal a gray velvet box. Inside was a small, solid-gold heart on a delicate chain. As I held it up, the lights from the tree danced off it.

"It's lovely, Heck. Just lovely. Please, help me put it on." I handed him the chain and then turned around so he could fasten the necklace. I felt him kiss my neck when he finished fumbling with the dainty clasp.

"Now you have two hearts," he whispered, so that only I could hear. "This one *and* mine." When I turned to face him, he lightly tapped his chest.

"Thank you," I whispered. "Thank you for everything."

But what I was really wondering was, *what is Kevin giving Taylor?*

***

Merritt and Alec insisted they needed no help, so we watched them set out their scrumptious feast. Even though it was supposed to be only brunch, Merritt had cooked a turkey with all the trimmings. We all, except Merritt, had more champagne and ate too much food.

Afterward, the men were given the chore of cleaning things up. Then Alec brought in a tray of coffee, and we all sat together in the living room.

Things were going well, even though I noticed Merritt glance at her watch a couple of times. I knew, of course, that Kevin and Taylor were coming this evening, and I was determined that Heck and I would leave early enough for Merritt to get herself reorganized for the next meal (leftovers, I assumed). Ted, sprawled on the floor in front of us, was in the middle of one of his stories about some particularly annoying customers he'd served that week, when the doorbell rang.

I didn't pay much attention as Alec rose to answer it, thinking it must be neighbors or friends. But my heart literally stopped beating—at least that's what it felt like—when he returned to the living room with Kevin and Taylor in tow.

We all looked at our watches. This wasn't supposed to happen. This was the *last* thing that was supposed to happen.

But there he stood. My husband. Father of my children. The man who kissed me three days ago. Standing in the living room doorway, his arms full of presents. At first I couldn't breathe. Then that awful sadness rose up in me, and I thought I might cry.

Taylor's face was flushed from the cold. She looked beautiful. I was instantly aware that I hadn't reapplied my lipstick after eating. That my hair hadn't done what I'd paid so much money for it to do. That I should have worn something else. Something more glamorous or flattering or, even more important, something younger.

"Dad!" Merritt raised herself with difficulty from the couch. I could see she was uncomfortable, and not just with her enormous belly, and then I grew incensed with Kevin for showing up earlier than planned.

"Hi, honey." He kissed her cheek. From the way Merritt greeted Taylor, I knew they'd spent plenty of time together, and I was consumed with jealousy. Ted got to his feet, shaking hands with his father and nodding to Taylor. He, too, looked uncomfortable.

And then Taylor spoke, in that throaty voice of hers. "Kevin, I told you we should have called first."

I wanted to smack her in the face. That beautiful face of hers that was only enhanced by being out in the cold.

"Give me your coats." Alec removed the packages from Kevin and helped Taylor with her coat. Fur! The bitch was wearing fur. Who wore fur anymore? Had Kevin bought it for her? Was that his Christmas gift to her?

My hand went to my throat, and the tiny heart hanging there on its spindly chain seemed suddenly so insignificant I wanted to hide it inside the edge of my sweater.

Kevin came into the room and over to the couch, holding out his hand to Heck. "Good to see you. Kevin Harleman."

"Yes, we've met. The cabinets?" Heck reminded him.

This was a nightmare. I wanted to scream as Heck stood and graciously shook hands with my husband. I didn't have the good sense to be thankful until much later that Heck hadn't also reminded Kevin that they'd seen one another that night at the Hyatt, when he'd had to rescue me from Kevin's boss. At the moment, all I could think of was THE KISS.

Kevin turned his attention to me. For an instant, we stared hard into each other's eyes, his penetrating gaze reflecting my own, as if we were reading each other's thoughts. The same, the exact same, look we shared when saying our wedding vows. The same look that involuntarily came upon us immediately after both our children were born healthy. And when my dad died, and I searched the hospital hall looking for safe refuge. There was that face, and those eyes, reassuring me as only Kevin could that he was there, that everything was okay. That we still had each other.

I rose from the couch on unsteady legs. Everyone else disappeared from focus. I could think of him only as I'd seen him last. His face close to mine as we kissed.

And then there was Taylor, her hand reaching for his arm, protectively pulling him back toward her. Forbidding him to get any closer to me. Had he told her about THE KISS?

Suddenly Heck's arms were around my shoulders, Ted was saying something, Alec was handing them drinks, and Merritt was holding her Lalique up for praise. And Christmas came to a screeching halt.

I'm not sure how we got out of there, but at some point I was putting on my coat, and Heck was beside me, gathering our gifts, and someone was saying thank you for something, and Alec was steering me by the elbow, and then we were at the door and we were leaving, and Heck and I were walking to his truck.

It reminded me of when I was a child, when our mother had taken Nina and me to New York City one year, the week before Christmas. On our last day there, we'd gone to Macy's, and I remembered vividly the cold hitting our faces as we left the warmth of the store behind us.

Determined not to lose the wonder of that Christmas, I let go of my mother's hand and ran back to one of the store windows and pressed my face up to it.

It was a Christmas scene, a mother and father and two children sitting around a glowing fireplace where stockings were hung. The two mannequin children were just like Nina and me, except they were wearing red velvet hooped skirts with lacy white bloomers peeking below the hemline. Their frozen molded-plastic faces had happy smiles and bright eyes. I was filled with joy just watching them sit there in anticipation of a visit from Santa Claus. I didn't want to leave the thrilling city just yet; I wanted to break through the window and be a part of the scene before me.

Now, sitting in Heck's car with Alec waving to us from the front door, I felt numb. This time it wasn't a make-believe family in Macy's store window. It was my *real* family. I belonged there, but I was being forced to leave. At the very least, I wanted to run back and press my face against the window and watch the scene.

CHAPTER TWENTY-TWO

I was having trouble recovering from what I described to Nina as the confrontation with my future.

"I know I've got to get used to being on the outside looking in when it comes to Kevin and the kids," I said.

"Yeah, but he does too. He's going to spend plenty of occasions alone, when you and the kids are celebrating something or, you know, vacationing, or just *being* together—without him."

I debated once again whether to tell Nina about THE KISS. *It was no big deal*, I was still trying to assure myself. And maybe that's why I hadn't told her—because it was, obviously, no big deal to Kevin. It had changed nothing. And with each talk I had with my sister that I didn't tell her, it grew more impossible. Now, a week after the fact, I opted out—or chickened out—again. *Whatever*, I said to myself.

Out loud, I reminded Nina, "He's never going to be alone; he'll have Taylor to occupy his time."

"You have Heck. You're going to be with him New Year's Eve, aren't you?"

"Yes." And yes, I did have Heck. I just wasn't sure how I felt about him. He was wonderful, I knew. I also knew gobs of divorced women would kill to have a Heck come into their lives so effortlessly. *Divorced women.* I suddenly realized I already considered myself divorced. Maybe I was accepting my fate better than I'd thought.

It had been partly an attempt to accept reality and partly revenge, I think, that had led me to allow Heck to spend his first night at my house. *In fact,* I thought, as we shared my bed that Christmas night, *I'm going to let him stay as long as he wants. Forever, maybe.* Besides, I didn't think I had to worry about any interlopers that night or even the next morning—they'd all be exhausted from celebrating the night away at Merritt's.

What's more, I suddenly felt like flaunting my sex life in their faces, at least in Kevin's. As much as I felt a thrill at THE KISS making me the *other woman* in Taylor's life—turnabout being fair play and all that—I also wondered what kind of snake my husband was.

Did he just have to get it on with someone else, no matter what? And surely that's what he'd been trying for, wasn't it? The old screw-the-ex routine? Was that the kind of man I *wanted* in my life?

Then again, what kind of woman was *I*, to be sleeping with Heck and yet feel the way I had when Kevin kissed me? Or maybe none of that mattered, when you'd been spouses for almost three decades.

Still, I knew I should be glad to be rid of Kevin, glad to move on to a life with Heck. Yes, it smarted that our kiss had obviously meant nothing to Kevin, but I knew I should just forget it too. A kiss, after all, *was* just a kiss.

"Are you okay?" I asked Heck, as we snuggled in bed Christmas night.

"I've never been better." He hugged me. "Why do you ask?" He continued to embrace me while I responded.

"Well, that couldn't have been fun for you, either, today."

"I had a wonderful day, Jess. Oh, you mean the part about Kevin showing up at Merritt's?"

I pulled out of his bear hug just enough so that I could poke him in the ribs with my index finger. "Well, I didn't mean the part about your opening presents or eating turkey or—"

"Okay, okay, dumb question." He chuckled and pulled me back to him, burying his lips in my hair and sending shivers up my legs, bare under the new flannel nightgown I'd gotten for Christmas from the baby-to-be. *To Grandma*, the tag read, *a flannel nightie to wear when you sit in your rocking chair holding me.* It was signed—in Merritt's neat, round lettering—*Lauren or Jacob*, followed by a question mark and a smiley face.

Now Heck stroked the flannel that covered my back and hips. "No," he said, "seeing Kevin didn't bother me, at least not much. I felt sorry for you. But I know it's just something we both have to get used to, and I'm sure the day will come when it won't seem any different than running into . . . the mailman."

"Mmmm," I said in apparent agreement, but what I really thought was, *I didn't skip class with the mailman and make out with him in the back seat of his car; I didn't hold the mailman in my arms and comfort him when his father died; and I didn't bear the mailman's children.* Most of all, I thought, *I didn't kiss the mailman three nights ago.*

Still, I hoped Heck was right. I longed for the day when I'd bump into Kevin because of the kids and not feel my heart break again.

And just a week later, on New Year's Eve, I thought I'd come a long way toward that goal.

***

As Heck and I prepared to kick off the new year together, my one and only resolution was to put my old life behind me.

We had plans with Heck's buddies from high school, a group that had gathered every New Year's Eve for more than thirty years. Scattered though they were—one was in real estate in California, another a banker from Colorado, and several were from various walks of life in the Bloomington and Indianapolis areas—they managed to pull at least three-fourths of them together each year. Heck had missed only once, he told me, the year he and Gail were honeymooning in Hawaii.

I wondered if that should make me feel jealous, thinking of Heck and Gail in Hawaii. It didn't, but then neither did running into Kevin and Taylor again. Well, at least not as much as it had just a week ago, on Christmas Day.

We'd stopped by Merritt's for a drink before meeting Heck's friends downtown. In her naiveté, Merritt had seen no need to warn me that her father had the same agenda: a celebratory drink with his daughter and son-in-law before heading off to a New Year's Eve party.

I'm sure she felt everything had gone so well when we'd stumbled upon one another Christmas Day that any discomfort was behind us. And I decided she was right when I saw Kevin's car parked in her driveway, so I didn't insist that Heck and I flee.

Instead, we made our way up the sidewalk, Heck holding on to my elbow as I minced along in my black strappy high heels over the freshly fallen snow. I felt cared for, the way he steadied me as if I were a one-year-old learning to walk (or an eighty-year-old he feared would break a hip, I realized ruefully).

But I didn't feel like an eighty-year-old as Merritt helped me remove my black wool coat, revealing the black sequined dress that flattered my figure and showcased my legs. It was the dress I'd worn to her wedding, the dress

Kevin—and tonight, Heck—had raved about. I could feel Kevin's appreciative gaze on me. I swear I could.

I looked him squarely in the eye, feeling a growing if inexplicable confidence. "Hello, Kevin." I sounded, to my own surprise no less than his, downright friendly. Then I nodded at Taylor. "Hello, Taylor," I said, before walking right past both of them, where they sat speechless on the couch. I made my way to the kitchen under the pretense of seeking Alec out. But I knew as my hips sashayed within a foot of Kevin's face why I was really passing through the room.

And Heck knew too. He followed me into the kitchen, where we both greeted Alec. Then, as soon as my son-in-law left the room and I started to follow, Heck took my arm. As always, his voice and his touch were gentle but firm. "Jess, *now* I'm bothered."

"What?" I asked blankly.

"That bothers me."

"What? Seeing Kevin and Taylor here? I thought you said—"

"I said I knew we'd bump into them from time to time, and that wouldn't bother me. But the way you wiggled by Kevin, the way he looked at you—"

"Heck, what are you talking about?" I demanded, but inside I was gloating. So Kevin *had* ogled me. Still, I knew that my only motivation was to inflict at least a little pain on him. I sure as hell didn't care about him anymore. I'd resolved not to.

"Nothing, Jess. Forget I said anything," Heck said, but his stare seemed to search my soul for the truth.

Well, good luck with that, I thought. *If you find it, please share that truth with me.*

I put my arms around his waist and pulled him close, breathing in the scent of him as if it were lifesaving oxygen. "Did you and Gail ever . . . get together again? You know, kiss or have sex, after she left?"

"Jessie! Have you and Kevin . . . are you—"

"No, no, no." *What was I doing?* I berated myself. "I just thought maybe that's why you were accusing—"

"Of course we didn't." He sounded relieved, making me squirm with guilt. "And forget I implied anything about you and Kevin."

He leaned his face down to mine and lifted my chin with one of his strong hands, kissing me. I ran my hands roughly through his hair and then slid them under his suit coat, rubbing his muscled back and then his firm derriere.

"Excuse me," a deep voice broke through my consciousness.

I opened my eyes to greet my son. Only it wasn't Teddy. It was the only other man in the world whose voice sounded exactly like that. It was Kevin.

"No, excuse *us*," Heck said, with a politeness that sounded uncharacteristically phony. "We just—"

"So I see." Kevin made his way to Merritt's refrigerator.

I grabbed Heck's hand and pulled him back out to the living room, where we found Merritt and Alec among a group of their neighbors who'd gathered while Heck and I were otherwise occupied in the kitchen.

I tapped my daughter on the shoulder. "You know what, Merritt? Heck and I didn't realize how late it was getting. We're supposed to be meeting the others—"

"Oh sure, Mom; I'll get your coats. I'm just so glad that you stopped by. And I'm so glad that you and Dad are all right with—"

"Yeah, Merritt, so am I." I felt Heck grab my hand, and I glanced up to see his eyes twinkling merrily, the eyes of a cohort in a well-executed practical joke. Kevin *deserved* that.

Troubled by the knowledge that Heck *didn't* deserve the fact that I'd enjoyed a kiss with Kevin a week and a half ago, I vowed to make it up to him. And indeed, we had a wonderful night. We drank a little, danced a lot, laughed even more, and then went home and made the wildest love I'd ever experienced.

I couldn't help but marvel at my mounting passion. Was this some menopausal fluke of fluctuating hormones? Or was it the titillation of being torn between two lovers? No, that was an exaggeration; and besides, I wasn't torn.

Heck and only Heck was my new focus.

***

On the third day of January I received a strange call from Kevin. "How are you, Jess?"

"I'm fine, Kevin. What's up?" I knew he wasn't calling to ask about my health.

"Nothing, really."

"Have you filed for the divorce yet?" I felt proud that I could now face the subject head-on. And having assumed Kevin was waiting for the new year for tax purposes, I figured he'd set things in motion by now.

"Uh, no. But I'm meeting with Bill Rizzo this week."

"Okay. Is there something I'm supposed to be doing?" *Why did I feel I had to guide this conversation? He had called me.*

But he seemed reluctant to speak. "No. Not yet."

I forced myself to keep quiet, to make him tell me why he'd called.

After a seemingly interminable silence, during which I kept a finger pressed to my tightly closed lips, he spoke. "So you and this Heck seem pretty serious."

"Yes." I couldn't believe how quickly and firmly I answered. "Yes, we're very serious."

"Jess, don't you think this happened a little fast?"

"What are you talking about?"

"Do you love this guy?"

"Why do you ask? Kevin, did you call just to ask me if I'm in love?"

"I guess so. It's just that I worry about you, Jess, about you being on the rebound. We've been separated such a short time, and the way you kissed me the other night—"

"*I* kissed *you*? *You* kissed *me*."

"Whatever, Jessie. That's not the point."

"And just what is the point, may I ask?"

"It doesn't seem like you should think you're in love so soon—"

"Oh, so you could fall in love with Taylor *before* we separated, but I need to wait. Tell me, Kevin, how long do I need to wait?" I didn't like the shriek I heard in my voice, but dammit, he drove me to it.

"I wouldn't think you'd fall in love with the first guy you meet."

"So Taylor wasn't *your* first?"

"My first what?"

"The first *other woman*."

"She's the only other woman there ever was, Jessie. You know that. Don't change the subject."

"I thought this was the subject, married people falling in love with others. Tell me, just what is the subject?"

"Never mind. Forgive me for still caring about you, for wanting to watch out for you, for not wanting some guy to hurt you."

"Oh, that's rich. You don't want some guy to hurt me. Well, why didn't you watch after yourself a little bit better, then? Why didn't you keep your pants zipped?" I recognized my words from the half-joking reminder Kevin used to give Teddy as he headed out on a date.

"Let me try this one more time. One *last* time," Kevin spoke calmly, enunciating his words as if I were a three-year-old he was explaining bedtime rules to. "I fell in love with Taylor. I didn't mean to; I didn't want to. But that doesn't mean you should screw the first guy who comes along, some carpenter, for Pete's sake. I want you to have a new life, Jess, a good life. I just want you to find the *right* man."

"The only wrong man I ever found was you, Kevin. I appreciate your concern, but *you'll* forgive *me* if I find it a bit unreliable. I'm sorry it disturbs you that the first man I happened to date turned out to be the one I want to spend the rest of my life with. You'll just have to trust me on this one. Not that trustworthiness is anything you're familiar with. I gotta go now."

I was shaking when I hung up. Not until that night, when I talked to Heck, did I begin to calm down.

"He's just jealous, Jess."

"He *should* be jealous of you. You're too good for him to even be mentioning your name."

"No, he's not jealous of *me*. He'd be jealous of anyone who won your heart, whether it's someone you meet before the divorce is final or someone you meet twenty years from now. It's a territorial thing, really, a possessive thing."

"Yeah, I suppose. I just wish he'd keep his caveman thoughts to himself."

"They'll wane, I'm sure. He'll get over it, or at least get used to it—probably sooner than we think, if he's as shallow as I think."

And Heck seemed to be right. I'd had no more phone calls from Kevin by the time Heck and I left for Lake Tahoe three days later. And I'd all but forgotten about *that* phone call.

***

The Tahoe trip was Heck's other Christmas gift to me, the one he'd presented to me that night when we returned to my house alone. He hadn't wanted to put me on the spot in front of my kids, he explained. He wasn't sure how they'd feel about us going away together. Of course I would tell them, but it was for another reason that I felt nervous when I first saw the itinerary.

I feared the timing was too close to when Merritt's baby was due. But as Heck described the breathtaking views, the scenic ski slopes, and the exciting night life, I didn't have the heart to put a damper on it. I'd just get the first flight home if Merritt had the baby early. And I wouldn't tell Heck I'd already skied Tahoe several times—with Kevin and the kids.

The fact that we'd vacationed there as a family also made me fearful that being back on skis at the Heavenly ski resort or looking out a condo window at snow-covered evergreens would bring memories too bittersweet to bear.

But I needn't have worried.

Tahoe with Heck was like a different world, different from the Tahoe I'd visited before and different from life in Indianapolis.

Our flight landed in Reno in the early evening, so by the time we got groceries and drove our rented Suburban to the California portion of Tahoe, it was the wee hours of the morning according to our body clocks. Heck built a fire while I poured wine, and then we snuggled and talked until our eyelids grew heavy and sleep overcame us.

I awoke to the aroma of coffee and followed it out from the massive bedroom to where I found Heck sitting at the oak table in front of the great room's heavy floor-to-ceiling draperies.

"Hey," he said, the look on his face radiating the same combination of love and lust that his voice held. He shoved his day-old newspaper aside, and in spite of myself, I couldn't help but picture Kevin reading his paper over coffee. Tearing him away from it had been as hard as getting the four-year-old Teddy to leave a McDonald's PlayPlace.

Heck, on the other hand, seemed as happy to rid himself of the paper as if it were an empty McDonald's sack.

"Good morning." I sat on his lap and encircled his head with my arms. After he nuzzled my neck for a few moments, he asked, "You ready to see the view? I wanted to wait and open the curtains with you."

"Let's do it." I rose from his lap and freed him to do the honors.

We both gasped as he pulled the cord that let in the splendor of snow-drenched Lake Tahoe. He pulled me back in his arms, and we stood silently, feeling a peace and communion such as we'd never known. At last he broke the spell. "You ready to hit the slopes?"

"I will be, as soon as I've had a cup of coffee. Mmm. It smells wonderful."

"Tastes that way too, if I do say so myself."

The next seven days found us up early, on the slopes all day, and too tired to take advantage of the area's nightlife. But we engineered a better one of our own, one consisting of hot tubs, hot toddies, tender talks, and a lot of lovemaking.

Those seven days really cemented our relationship, I told myself on the flight home.

But my happiness stopped—or at least wavered—almost as soon as the plane landed in Indianapolis.

Among the phone messages from Kevin, the latter ones demanding to know where I was and why I hadn't returned his calls, was one informing me he'd removed me from his health insurance.

"What the hell do you think you're doing?" I screeched into the phone before he even finished his *Kevin Harleman here* greeting. "What if I'd broken a leg skiing?"

"Skiing? What are you talking about, Jessie?"

"I'm talking about the fact that you had me taken off the health insurance."

"Jessie, it's time we separate our finances. You sounded pretty hell-bent yourself on getting things going the last time we talked. But why are you talking about skiing? Oh . . . is that where you've been? Skiing with the help?"

"Kevin, don't you change the subject. And don't do this to me."

"Do what? Bill just advised me . . ."

I cursed myself for not having gotten that attorney I'd threatened him with and vowed that would be my very next phone call, after the insurance agent, of course. But where would I start? Bill Rizzo was the only attorney I knew. And Taylor Stockton, of course. I could hardly ask either of them for a recommendation.

" . . . also sell the house," Kevin was saying.

"What?"

"Jessie, we're going to have to sell the house to split our assets. You might as well get started."

"Oh no, Kevin. I'm not getting started. I'm *finished*." I had no idea what I meant by that, but it seemed just the right thing to say before hanging up on him.

CHAPTER TWENTY-THREE

"Have you told Teddy?" Merritt asked. Only a month after we'd made up, I found myself in the middle of a quarrel with her.

"No. I haven't seen him since I've been back, and it's not the sort of thing I want to discuss on the phone." I spoke softly, hoping Merritt would realize I also didn't want to discuss it in front of the whole world, and she should lower her own voice a few decibels. I looked around Starbucks as I took a sip of my latte, checking to see if I knew any of the other patrons, the people I didn't want witnessing a mother/daughter disagreement.

I'd been busy the past week, moving onward toward divorce and examining—really examining—my options. Through a friend of a friend of Heck's, I'd obtained the name of Janice Barth, an attorney with a practice in Carmel—a lucrative practice, thanks to her reputation for convincing judges that her almost exclusively female clients deserved their fair share. She agreed to take my case, explaining my rights and how we would go about winning them.

I'd already phoned Kevin's human resources department for information on insurance I was entitled to—at no small cost, of course. I'd had to call Kevin back and have him give permission to deduct the cost from his paycheck, assuring him this would all even out in the divorce. Janice, in turn, assured me I would be reimbursing Kevin for absolutely nothing.

"He's the one who wants a life change. My job is to make sure *your* life changes as little as possible, at least financially." She gave a half smile that was fully sympathetic for my plight. "As for selling the house, the necessity of that is not a given. How do you feel about it?"

I'd been thinking about that, and even though I wouldn't concede it to Kevin, I'd begun to find the idea somewhat appealing. With more than the usual mixed emotions any move would spark, I nevertheless saw the exciting potential.

"Maybe it would be easier for me to move on with my new life if I weren't surrounded by all these memories," I'd said to Ellen, as we sipped coffee and I told her about Kevin's welcome-home phone call informing me I was uninsured.

"Jess, I could throw up at the thought of you not living across the street."

"Oh, Ellen, I know. Me too." I reached across my kitchen table and grabbed her hand. Squeezing it, I continued, "But we both have to admit, my lifestyle is now drastically different from yours."

"Jess, if you mean that bridge night—"

"No, no; I was fine with that. Or I *am* fine with that."

The Saturday night before we had left for Tahoe, Heck was busy with his work, tying up loose ends before leaving town in two days. I'd impulsively called Ellen to see if she wanted to see a movie, knowing the chances that she was doing nothing on a Saturday night were good. Like Kevin and I had done, she and Steve spent many a weekend night at home, each doing his or her own thing. "Oh, Jess, I'm so sorry, but I . . . we . . . uh . . . Steve . . . we . . ."

I'd never known Ellen to lie to me, or even keep anything from me, but it was obvious something was up now. "For Pete's sake, I don't need a charity date, Ellen. And you don't owe me any explanation."

Realizing I was irritated, she hemmed and hawed all the more. "No, Jess, I know you . . . I just want to . . ." She sighed heavily and then reverted to her usual frankness. "Jessie, we're having a couples' bridge night here. I just didn't want you to feel excluded, but you know—"

"I know how couples' bridge works, Ellen. Forget I asked." And I hung up. I couldn't believe I'd done that, and I was glad, when I called the next day to say good-bye, that Ellen and I could both act as if the conversation had never taken place.

And I didn't need her reassurance that day as we drank our coffee, either, although I was grateful for it nonetheless. I squeezed her hand again and stood up. I put my cup in the sink and glanced at my watch. "I gotta go."

Ellen and I walked to the garage together, and she waved good-bye as I climbed into my Jeep to drive to that first meeting with my attorney. "Good luck. Call me when you get home," she said, just before I closed the car door. As soon as I was sure she was safely out of the way, I pulled out of the garage.

That night I told Heck I was seriously considering a move. "I'm not sure I'll have a choice, anyway, of course; but I mean, I think I just might *want* to move. Maybe I'll make this part easy on Kevin. And myself."

"If you do, I've got just the place for you." He pulled me closer, as we sat in front of a raging fire in my living room.

"It wouldn't by any chance be in Brown County, would it?" I pulled away slightly, just enough to look him in the eye.

"How'd you guess?"

"I'll definitely be living alone, Heck, wherever I move." Then I added, not to appease him but because the idea had already occurred to me and held great appeal, "But I very well might move elsewhere in Brown County."

It offered so much more than just the proximity to Heck. Kevin and I had always referred to Brown County, with its tranquility and woodsy beauty, as the Northern Minnesota of Indiana.

But try telling that to Merritt. I realized now it wasn't something I should have attempted in public.

"I think that sounds pretty selfish, Mom." Before I could find the words to remind her that a move was her father's idea, she continued to place the blame on me. "I can't believe you'd think of moving out of that house and farther away, *ever*, let alone with your grandchild coming."

She sipped the last of her decaf latte and, obviously not buying into my description of the fun that Brown County held for my grandchild, she set the paper cup down with as much of a bang as she could manage.

Wanting to finish our conversation in the car, I rose and shoved my arms into my jacket, the Heavenly ski-lift ticket still attached to the zipper reminding me of a more carefree time—and relationship. *What a difference a week makes*, I thought ruefully, as I followed Merritt out of Starbucks and to her car.

"I'm going to take you home; I'm beat." She settled her bulk behind the steering wheel.

"Fine." I didn't feel any more in the mood for crib shopping than Merritt did.

We rode in silence until we pulled up in front of *my* house—not *her* house, I wanted to remind her.

I was glad for my restraint and silence, though, as I heard my daughter say, "You just have to realize, Mom, that this house holds a lot of wonderful memories for me." She took one hand off the steering wheel and motioned to the brick two-story where she'd turned from a little kid into a teen.

I felt tears spring to my eyes, and so I looked at the house and not her. "Me too," is all I said, because I could feel my voice begin to crack. As I turned to hug her goodbye, I closed my eyes, all the better to hide my conflicting feelings.

"Think about it, Mom. At least think about it."

***

I thought I was prepared for the phone call that I was sure would come any minute from Alec, or Merritt herself, telling me it was time. But I wasn't.

It was an unseasonably warm Groundhog Day, the temperature poking into the sixties, the sort of day that always made me glad we'd moved from Minnesota to Indiana. I'd actually been studying out on the deck all afternoon: doing some heavy reading for my Religions of the World course, which would fulfill a humanities requirement, and writing an essay about myself—in *German*, no less.

Heck was getting ready to barbecue steaks, and we were having a friendly argument about how long they should be marinated. He had his way of doing things, and I had mine. I'd just playfully punched his arm when the phone rang.

"Don't even think about taking them out of that dish yet. They haven't been in there long enough," I said on my way into the house through the screen door. As I picked up the phone, I noted that the caller ID said simply UNKNOWN NAME, so I was clueless as I answered. "Hello?"

It was Alec. "Jessie . . . Mom . . ." Poor Alec had never quite decided what he should call me, but either way, I always took it as a term of endearment.

"Yes, Alec?" I held the phone with my chin and threw my arms up in mock alarm as I watched Heck through the patio door. He was removing the porterhouse steaks from the Tupperware dish they'd been nesting in. He waved them at me menacingly, daring me to stop him from plopping them on the grill.

"I'm at the hospital. I had to bring Merritt in."

I immediately forgot the steaks. I could think only of Merritt and her tiny body bulging with a baby. My grandchild. It didn't seem possible.

"Is she okay? I'll come right away." I was glad I lived so close and wondered how I could have ever considered a move away from my children. "Is everything all right?"

"Yes, everything's fine." I could tell by his voice that it was. "She started having pains this morning, and she called me at the office—I was trying to get ahead on some stuff."

I smiled, wondering how my workaholic son-in-law was going to reconcile his career with fatherhood. Everything he did, he did well, so I was certain he'd find a way to manage both.

"The doctor's been here already and decided to keep her in," Alec continued, then hesitated for a moment. "He thinks this is it." I could hear the pride and excitement in his voice, and for the millionth time, I was grateful he was my daughter's husband.

"I'll be right there."

"No need, really; you can wait if you like. I could call you—"

"No, I want to come now." Then, remembering the day Merritt got engaged and my vow to be the perfect mother-in-law, or die trying, I added, "If that's okay."

"Yes, that would be great."

It sounded as though he meant it, and I was grateful for that too. "Heck!" I called out to the patio, where he was still busy tending the steaks, looking pleased with himself. "That was Alec. Merritt's in the hospital. I'm going down there."

"Everything okay?" He looked up, crinkling his face at the heat from the gas grill as he closed the lid.

"It's time," I said, with a smile that started in my heart and enveloped my entire face. "Merritt's going to have her baby." I could feel my forehead lifting as I spoke, and I didn't even care that it displayed the four deep furrows I'd earned from my expressive countenance.

"Want me to come with you?" He waved a spatula in his hand like a flag.

"No. That's okay. You stay here. I'll call you."

"Okay."

I was a little taken aback he didn't insist. But on the twenty-minute drive to the hospital, I felt relieved to be by myself. As dear as Heck was to me, this was one event I secretly didn't want to share with him.

As I made my way through light traffic to the hospital, my thoughts meandered to Kevin, and I wondered if Alec had called him too. I felt amazed at the tiny knot of excitement that stirred within me at the thought that I might see Kevin within the next few hours, if the baby came that night. Surely he wouldn't bring Taylor with him, if he did show up at the hospital.

I shook my head in dismay. My grandchild was about to be born, and I was once again consumed with thoughts of my own future. Feeling selfish, I nevertheless reapplied my lipstick as I pulled into the hospital parking lot. Just in case.

The nurse in the family-life center led me right to Merritt's room, where she was propped up, looking hot, angry, and in pain.

"Oh, Mom." She reached across her huge stomach for my hand. "I'm glad you're here. This is hell!" She stared hard at Alec, as if she wanted to kill him right there, and I had to stifle a grin.

"You're doing fine, baby." I patted her hand and smoothed back the hair from her sweating forehead. I saw her wince in pain, and all the love I felt for her welled up inside me at that moment. I wanted nothing more than to take the pain away. "Just remember to breathe," I said uselessly.

"That's what I'm doing," Merritt informed me hotly, and I glanced across the bed at Alec. He was holding her hand, but she shrugged him off and let out a piercing yell.

We sat together for a long time, it seemed, until finally a nurse came in and checked Merritt. Next, she informed us she was calling the doctor back in. It was time. Merritt grabbed Alec's hand in panic. He was planning to be present at the birth, but I could tell by his sickly pallor that he wasn't relishing the task before him.

I kissed Merritt's cheek and squeezed her hand.

"Don't go far, Mom," she said through clenched teeth.

"I wouldn't dream of it, honey. I'll be out in the waiting room. I promise." As I heard her moan, I felt certain she was unaware of my departure.

But she startled me as she called after me, "Mom, would you call Dad? And Alec's parents?"

I felt my mouth drop open as I looked back toward Alec, but he was busy. "Sure, I'll take care of it," I said, more agreeably than I felt. I might like the idea of *seeing* Kevin, but I sure as hell didn't want to call him.

I found the waiting room and prepared to make myself comfortable for the duration. Once I was seated on the red fake-leather couch, I extricated my phone from my purse and called my home number.

"Yeah?" Heck answered.

"Hi, it's me." I felt excited, but also a little worried something might go wrong.

"Are you a grandmother yet?" His laid-back demeanor irritated me. Of course I couldn't expect his feelings to match my exhilaration. That wouldn't be natural. It wasn't his flesh and blood we were talking about here. Still, his lack of enthusiasm disappointed me.

"She's having the baby right now, as we speak," I said breathlessly, still in awe of the whole process, in spite of my own two deliveries.

"How's Alec?" Heck asked.

"Alec? What does it matter how Alec is? He's not the one who has to give birth."

"Steady; I was just asking a question."

"Sorry." Why was I snapping at him? He knew how fond I was of Alec and was undoubtedly just humoring me to even ask about my son-in-law. "I guess I'm just a little nervous."

"Perfectly understandable. Anyone else there?"

"No, just me."

"Want me to come keep you company?"

"No." I said it a little too quickly, and I knew we both noticed.

"Fine; then just call if you need me. I'll be here."

"Thanks, love; I'll call you later, when there's some news."

Next, I scrolled through my contacts for the Nelsons' number and called Alec's parents. They were a nice couple, always generous with their affection for their daughter-in-law, for which I felt grateful. I told them not to rush, that probably nothing would happen for several hours. I urged them to take their time.

But Barbara said she was just waiting for Ed to get home from the store and then they'd leave for the hospital immediately. She sounded excited, and I felt a strong bond between us.

Then I called Kevin's cell. I still had his number programmed into my own. As I heard his phone begin to ring, I felt nervous. I was certain I wouldn't reach him and was trying to compose the message I would leave, but to my surprise, he answered on the second ring.

"Jess, what's up?" He sounded so casual, as if he were still my husband in more than name only and I was calling to ask how his day was going. Except, of course, that I'd never called just to ask how his day was going.

"I'm at the hospital; Merritt's having the baby."

"Now?" His voice showed a little more interest.

"Yes, now. Any minute. She wanted me to let you know."

"Should I come?" He sounded nervous. Why? Because of the baby? Because he'd have to admit he was old enough to be a grandfather? Or because he might have to tell Taylor he had to leave her side for a while?

"That's up to you. But if you want to greet your grandchild when he or she arrives, it'd be wise for you to hurry."

"Okay. I'm at the Convention Center, at a show. But we've got enough coverage, so I'll leave now. Randy?" I heard him call out to someone, and for the first time I realized there was a lot of noise in the background. "Think you can cover the booth the rest of the time?"

Then he was back to me. "Yeah, I'll be right up." He hesitated a moment. "Are you there alone?"

I hesitated too. "Yes," I said softly. "Quite alone."

"I'm on my way."

CHAPTER TWENTY-FOUR

I paced the floor, the way expectant fathers always did in old movies. Poor Alec; he'd probably be so much better at this than acting as Merritt's coach.

I was really excited now, mainly about the baby that I was sure would be born this very night, but also because Kevin was on his way. Maybe I could have him for a few minutes to myself, I thought, astounded that I'd want to.

I pushed guilty thoughts of Heck out of the way. *Let's face it*, I rationalized, *this is a special time that only Kevin can share with me.*

The door opened, and I took a deep breath. It was a nurse, blond and sort of fluffy, exactly the type of nurse I'd want in the delivery room with me.

"Are you Merritt's mother?" she asked kindly.

My hands flew to my cheeks. "Yes, yes. Did she—"

"Oh no, not yet. We don't have a baby yet. But I think it's going to be soon. I just wanted to let you know everything's okay. There's a coffee machine down the hall, if you want, or you can get a soda there too." She pointed through the glass double doors.

"Thank you. I'll wait for a bit. My husband's coming."

"Oh good." She smiled. "What about Merritt's father? Is he coming too?"

My own smile evaporated. "My husband *is* Merritt's father." I felt indignant.

"Oops; sorry." She looked down at her sensible white nurse's shoes. "Merritt said her parents were... not together. I assumed... I'm so sorry."

"That's okay." I took a seat.

"Don't worry; Merritt's doing fine. I'm a bit concerned about Alec, though; he seems in worse shape than your daughter." She giggled and then waved good-bye before leaving. I hoped Merritt didn't find her as annoying as I suddenly did.

Picking up a magazine from the coffee table, I leafed through it, determined not to let the dumb nurse upset me. This was a great day, a special day.

I jerked my head up as the door opened again, and the Nelsons appeared. "Oh, Jessie." Barbara came toward me with outstretched arms. "Isn't this thrilling? How's it going?"

I hugged her back and accepted a kiss on the cheek from Ed. "Fine; everything's fine. They said it probably won't be long now."

"Oh good." She nestled her plump body next to mine on the couch, and Ed took a seat on the other side of me. I felt trapped by them, by their niceness and their togetherness.

Where is Kevin? I wondered. *He should be here by now.* My mind wandered as Barbara began reminiscing about Alec's birth, and I only half listened, not taking my eyes from the door.

What was keeping Kevin? It was ridiculous; it had been an hour since I'd called him. I refused to entertain the possibility that he could have anything to do that was nearly as important—or exciting—as getting to the hospital.

The Nelsons chatted away like two birds; it was like being in a nest. I attempted to get up once, saying I would get coffee, but Barbara put a hand on my arm to detain me. "Ed can get it. Off you go, honey."

As I watched Ed dutifully rise and check his pockets for change, I wondered if I'd ever ordered Kevin to do such things. No, no, I hadn't. And yet Ed was still with Barbara. He hadn't run off with a glamorous blond.

I listened silently to Barbara, whose stories grew almost unbearably dull, and then Ed returned with lukewarm coffee. We drank the watery substance that no one would ever confuse with a Starbucks brew, but at least it silenced Barbara for a while.

When the fluffy nurse reappeared, obviously bearing an important message, we all three stared at her. "Okay," she said in her annoyingly pert way, "we have a baby." She announced it in a singsong fashion, sounding as if she were personally responsible.

"Oh my!" I heard Barbara gasp beside me, and when I looked at her, I saw she held a tissue to her eyes.

"Is Merritt okay?" I rose, breaking free from the Nelsons.

"She's fine. Just fine. A little tired. But mother and son are doing fine."

"Thank God," I heard myself say. And then I said, "A boy," with the same reverence I would use for saying "a miracle." Barbara must have handed me a tissue, too, because I found myself sniffling into it. A little boy!

"Wait just a bit, until we get Merritt fixed up, and then I'll take you down to see her," Fluffy said. I could picture her hastily setting Merritt's hair in curlers and doing a quick makeover. But soon she came back and held the door open for us. I let the Nelsons go ahead of me and then followed the tiny procession down the hall.

At the prospect of seeing first my daughter and then my new grandson, I forgot all about Kevin. And then I felt a hand on my shoulder. I knew it was him, even without looking. And when I turned, there he stood. He still wore his business suit, but his tie was loosened and he looked a little frazzled. He'd never looked better.

"Jessie. I'm sorry I didn't get here sooner. You wouldn't believe the accident I saw."

It didn't matter, as long as he wasn't in it. He'd arrived, and I slid so easily into his extended arms. Relishing the warmth of his body against mine, I momentarily forgot why we were even there. It just felt so good to be wrapped up in his strong arms, to feel his heart beating, to recall how the top of my head always reached to just under his chin.

And then I felt him kiss the top of my head, the way he'd done a million times, and I wanted to melt.

"It's a little boy," I said. "Jacob Kevin Nelson." I looked up into his face, and I saw his eyes growing wet. "Can you believe it? We have a grandson." I raised a hand to wipe his cheek.

He hugged me close again. Then, glancing down the corridor, he swung me around but still didn't let go. "Hey, the Nelsons are way ahead of us," he said. "We better get moving."

"Right. Let's go."

He released me, but his hand sought mine, and together we rushed to Merritt's room. Hand in hand, we entered. There she was, a tiny bundle in her arms and a husband standing beside her looking somewhat green.

"Daddy," she said, "come look. And Mom. Come meet Jacob." The Nelsons moved away from the bed. They'd had their first look, and now it was our turn. I started to let go of Kevin's hand, but he tugged me along with him, and together we approached the bed.

Jacob was perfect. A tiny little face, sleeping soundly. I was overcome with happiness and started to cry. And then there were those strong arms around me again, and my joy was complete.

***

When Kevin and I left the hospital together a half hour later, I followed his Porsche to a nearby cigar bar. Of course he'd want one of the occasional cigars I remembered him enjoying. He also wanted us to have a glass of champagne. We did, after all, have a new grandson to celebrate.

Just driving behind him and knowing we would at least have some time together, alone, was the perfect ending to this perfect day. It didn't matter one bit about all that had gone on in the past months; this was all I wanted.

We parked next to each other in the quiet lot, and then Kevin was there, opening the Jeep's door for me. Again, I felt his arm around me as he steered me into the bar. It was dark and not very crowded. It was like some famous movie director was orchestrating the whole scene.

I took a seat at a table in the corner and watched as Kevin went up to the bar, requesting a bottle of champagne. He looked so handsome. I saw him say something to the bartender, and then they both laughed. When he turned and headed to our table, I felt as nervous as I had on our first date.

He sat next to me—not across the table, as he might have—and once again took my hand. "I'd thought maybe the baby would come on Teddy's birthday," he said.

Why am I surprised he remembers when Teddy's birthday is? I wondered. "Well, if Jacob hadn't come until February 28, your daughter might have set a world record for length of gestation," I said. "That's four more weeks!"

"Oh, I guess I didn't realize exactly when she was due."

A feeling of anger started to form, but I couldn't sustain it. So instead of a snide remark about his obviously being otherwise occupied, I said, "Men! If you carried the babies, you'd keep track of the time." I smiled, and it wasn't a fake smile. I felt ecstatic.

Just then a curvy waitress appeared with a green champagne bottle and two glasses. "You guys celebrating something special?"

Dressing Myself

I looked at Kevin as he answered. "Very special," he said, and then smiled.

How I'd missed that smile. I felt eager for her to open the bottle and leave.

When she was gone, Kevin handed me a glass. My hand shook as I reached for it.

"Here's to the most beautiful grandmother in America." He stared at me.

Oh, those damn eyes. I took a sip to hide my trembling lips and then placed the champagne flute on the table, sloshing its bubbly contents onto the napkin as I did so.

"Aren't you going to have a cigar?" I asked, just for something to say. I felt nervous, being with him like this. I hated it, but at the same time I couldn't think of anyplace I'd rather be, or anyone I'd rather be with, at this moment.

He placed his drink down and reached into the inside pocket of his jacket, pulling out two cigars. I watched as he produced a gold clip and trimmed the edges of the cigars. "Will you join me?" he asked.

Again, memories overwhelmed me, this time of all the occasions I'd chastised Kevin for smoking the smelly things, usually after some business dinner or special occasion. I felt sure Taylor not only never harped about that, but probably smoked right along with him. "Of course." I took the cigar and delicately held it between two fingers. "Light me."

We both laughed at my Bette Davis imitation, and I put the cigar in my mouth. He picked up the book of matches from the ashtray, and I watched as he expertly lit the end of the cigar. He might just as easily have been single-handedly building the next shuttle to the moon, I was so impressed with him.

I took a tiny puff and then instantly blew the smoke out. It felt daring, and naughty, and like the most glamorous thing I'd ever done.

He puffed on his own cigar. Then, squinting through a cloud of smoke, he easily slid his arm behind me, letting out a sigh of satisfaction. We were like Bogie and Bacall sitting there. I was lost in the romance and the sophistication of the moment.

"You know," he said, placing his cigar in the ashtray and raising his glass toward his lips, "you look damn sexy smoking that thing."

"Oh, *you*," I said. But even if I didn't believe I looked it, I certainly felt it.

"Really, I mean it. But you already know that."

"I do *not*," I said coyly. I was eighteen again, sitting in the front seat of Kevin's car, wearing my brand-new push-up bra and pulling my shoulders back so that he couldn't miss the outline of my faux-full breasts.

"No, look at you. How do you stay so gorgeous?"

"Oh, *puh-leeze*!" I giggled. I was a teenage beauty, tantalizing the boyfriend I knew wanted nothing more than to feel me up.

He leaned over and kissed my cheek. Only it wasn't enough. I wanted him to kiss me on the mouth. I wanted to feel his tongue inside me. I wanted to be naked next to him, in a hotel room somewhere, where I could do all the things he loved, where I could drive him wild and go on and on feeling this sexy.

I watched him pour more champagne and then take off his jacket. The sleeves of his shirt still held the crispness of the dry cleaner's starch. This was a man who never wore flannel. A man who insisted on a freshly laundered white shirt every business day, never bowing to the business-casual trend.

"Here's to you." He raised his glass.

"And to you too." I sipped my champagne and enjoyed my cigar, relishing the moment and the camaraderie that was binding us together.

"Ha! To me. An idiot," he mumbled. I almost didn't hear him, so I asked him to repeat it.

"You heard me, Jess." He looked down into his glass. "A fucking idiot to let you go."

"Now, wait just a—"

He put a hand up to stop me. "I know, I know. I didn't let you go. I *left* you. But what was I thinking?"

I put my cigar in the ashtray next to his, and I watched the smoke from both of them curl up and join together. "Kevin, let's not ruin—"

"I'm pretty good at ruining things, Jess. Let me just say this. A day . . . an hour . . . hasn't gone by that I haven't thought of you."

Even with the champagne, my bubbly mood began to evaporate. I knew there was something I should say, but I couldn't think what it was.

"You know what I miss?" He took up his cigar again. "I miss sleeping with you," he answered his own question. "I don't mean the sex, necessarily, although I miss that too, of course. But I'm talking about waking up with you next to me. I even miss the way you hog the bed."

"I do *not* hog the bed."

"And the way you talk in your sleep," he continued, not letting me interrupt his thought process. "I always thought I would learn some deep, dark secret about you, but I never did. You were generally having a conversation with Abraham Lincoln or Madonna or someone." He laughed, and then I laughed too.

Our hands brushed against each other's as we reached to the ashtray at the same time. I felt a flutter fill my chest, as if I were in a car that had just zoomed over a steep hill. I didn't think I'd ever desired Kevin that much before in our lives.

"Oh, and the way you can watch the same old movie over and over and be just as bowled over by the ending as you were the first time you saw it." He sucked on his cigar, looking lost in thought.

"Kevin," I said, trying to stop him. This wasn't going the way it should. I didn't want him to talk about me; that was too much. "Remember when Teddy was born?"

"Of course. Like it was yesterday. You were so beautiful."

"I was *not*. I was a bear. I wanted to kill you."

He laughed again. "Yes, you did, didn't you? You wanted to kill me. And after I'd spent most of nine months frying chicken for you."

"Ah yes." I remembered my insatiable craving for fried chicken. Poor Kevin had fried a lot of chicken back then.

"Do you remember the last time we had champagne together?" he asked. "Like this, just the two of us?"

"No, not just the two of us. We drank a lot at Merritt's wedding, I remember, but we weren't alone."

"It was when you sold your first article."

"Yes, so it was." I think Kevin had been prouder than I was. It had been a wonderful evening. He arrived home from work with yellow roses and a bottle of champagne. We had drunk a little too much and then made love on the living room floor.

No, no, I silently urged myself, *don't—whatever you do, don't—even think about him making love with Taylor. Not now.*

The champagne glasses were empty. The cigars were all smoked. And the mood was getting a little too maudlin.

"I have to get going," I said. "It's very late." If he'd asked me to stay, or to go with him to a nearby hotel, I'm not sure what I would have done.

"Right; I'll walk you to your car. Are you okay to drive? I could take you home."

"No, no; I had only one glass. I'm fine."

We rose together, and Kevin called out to the bartender that he was just seeing the lady out and would be back for a nightcap.

"I bet they think we're having an affair," he said, as we stood by my Jeep.

It was chilly, and I wrapped my arms around his chest, still clad only in his oxford shirt. I wanted very much to take care of him. "I did not talk to Madonna in my sleep," I said, the top of my head nestled under his chin again.

"Madonna, Mother Teresa, Laura Bush—"

"Stop." I laughed. "You are so full of it."

I felt grateful for that moment. I'd thought I'd never be able to talk to Kevin this way again. That I'd never feel comfortable with him again, that we'd never laugh together again. I'd thought so many things. But I knew right then that deep down, I'd never stopped loving him and never would. We shared too much history. We were just too much a part of each other.

His fingers pulled my chin up so that my face was close to his. And then he kissed me. Suddenly we were young and in love, with our whole lives ahead of us, standing on my front porch saying good night, with my parents inside watching TV. Nina was probably peeking at us from her bedroom window. My heart raced, and sweat formed on my palms. I remembered how I thought back then that we would go on like this forever.

The sound of a car pulling out across the parking lot brought me back to reality. I pushed Kevin away, but gently. Turning, I pulled the keys out of my purse and opened the door to the Jeep. We just stared at each other, and then I scurried in and started the engine.

As I began to back out, I could see him in my rearview mirror, standing there, hands in his pockets, the wind blowing against the cotton of his shirt. He looked like the young Kevin I'd first fallen in love with all those years ago. My heart ached for him, for us.

How did we ever get to this point? Were we destined to go the rest of our lives sharing a stolen kiss every month or two? And nothing more?

It took two red lights for me to remember that tonight my grandson had been born, that I was now a grandmother, that our family had a new and wonderful member.

And that I hadn't even bothered to call Heck.

CHAPTER TWENTY-FIVE

The next three months were joyous, thanks to one guy and only one: the little guy named Jacob Kevin Nelson. I was stunned to find I could love yet another human being as much as any who had come before him.

It was my good fortune—though Merritt claimed it as hers—that when she returned to work part-time after six weeks, I watched Jacob when Alec couldn't. It fit in perfectly with my new status as a student because Merritt worked the evening shift at the hospital, and my classes ended at one thirty.

"Everyone at work says you're a saint, Mom, and they're right," she told me a thousand times. "I'm so lucky I can keep up my nursing and yet know that Jacob is either with Daddy or Grandma."

And a thousand times I responded, "No, *I'm* the lucky one. Do you know how many times through the years your dad and I would have given anything to relive a day when you and Teddy were little?"

"Yes, I do, Mom." She rolled her eyes but smiled. "I think I was in college when you'd still say, *Oh, Kevin, remember how Merritt used to say* gully, gully, gully *right before she fell asleep?* Really, *gully, gully, gully?* What was that about?"

"We didn't know what it was. You were only one; who knows why you were saying it? But it was so cute. And now it's like I do have you or Teddy as a baby all over again, to see those cute things."

"Well, Jacob's never going to say *gully, gully, gully*, I can assure you." But she hugged me and handed me a fistful of daisies she'd bought at the hospital gift shop.

"Merritt, I'm telling you. I should be buying *you* flowers." And even though she'd shrug off my gratitude as if I were just trying to make her feel better, it was true. Indeed, all the clichés about the glory of grandparenthood proved true.

The only damper on my euphoria came from my inability to share it with someone. Heck was okay—for an unofficial step-grandparent. But I felt he got less pleasure from Jacob than he would have from a black Lab puppy.

Heck seemed happy to join me with Jacob any time our plans meshed. But the truth was, I found I preferred being alone with my grandson to being with someone who didn't feel as passionately as I that Jacob was the greatest human being ever put on earth.

If Heck was with me when Jacob worked his little rosebud lips into a coo so seemingly heartfelt it brought tears to his baby eyes, I found myself wishing I were alone so I could really savor the moment, instead of wondering if Heck was bored or if he thought I'd gone completely daft to be cooing right back, with tears in my own eyes.

When I *was* alone, and Jacob would coo or lift his head up and peer around the room, so eager to see everything in his new world, I found myself wishing Kevin were there to see it. Just because he was the only other person alive who could know exactly how I felt about that baby, and who could love that baby in the same way I did. I knew Alec's parents felt the same way, of course. But it wasn't as if I could share my experience as a grandparent with them; not really. They had each other for that.

Surprisingly, given how much I heard Kevin stopped by to see our grandson, I didn't run into him again after the night Jacob was born, the night I'd gone home and lied to Heck.

I'd felt guilty as Heck listened attentively to the details of Merritt's labor and delivery. Never once did he ask if Kevin had been there, and never once did I mention there'd been the slightest connection between my husband and me, let alone that we went for a drink together—and kissed.

By the next day I'd rationalized that I was right to keep such details from Heck. My feelings had been an aberration, conjured up from the emotional experience of Jacob's birth, feelings that weren't real but rather based solely on memories of times past.

For my part, I knew with the dawning of the new day that even if grandparenthood weren't quite the perfection it could be if shared with the other grandparent, well, that loss was more than compensated for by the part of my life that *didn't* center around Jacob (which was still most of it). And that was the part of my life that Heck so enhanced, more so every day.

For Kevin's part—I soon realized when he made no move to call or see me again—he had made innuendos and implications (or had I just made inferences?) that stemmed from his own euphoria at having a grandson, not to mention too much champagne.

***

Mother's Day was a special treat. Well, once I cleaned and tidied the house to perfection, that is, so the Realtor could hold an open house.

I'd listed the house the middle of April, not knowing where I would live but knowing I had to move on. Teddy and Merritt hadn't stopped cajoling me to at least wait a while, but I'd grown adept at sidestepping their arguments and doing what I felt I had to do.

Merritt had invited Heck and me over for my first Mother's Day as a grandma, her first as a mother, and Teddy joined the family gathering. It felt blissful to have both my kids there, and of course our baby Jacob.

As soon as we arrived, Alec ushered Heck out to the garage to discuss a problem with his car, and I found myself at the kitchen table, Jacob on my lap, Teddy and Merritt sitting across from me. Something was up, and I figured it had to do with the open house. Here came their don't-sell-our-childhood-home spiel.

"Tell her," Teddy said, "before Heck and Alec come back."

"What's going on?" I asked, captivated by the way Jacob's tiny finger curled around my own.

Merritt leaned forward, elbows on the kitchen table, her eyes dancing. "Dad and Taylor broke up." She looked elated.

I stifled the joy I felt, trying hard to stay focused on Jacob. "No kidding?"

"Yeah, isn't that great?" Teddy added.

I looked over at my two children, their faces bursting with promise. Like we'd all just won the lottery. "Didn't you like Taylor?" I asked, daring them to say anything other than that she was the Wicked Witch of the West.

My smart kids dodged the question. "He called yesterday and just let it slip," Merritt went on. *"Hi, Merritt, blah, blah, blah, and by the way, I'm not seeing Taylor anymore."*

She was interrupted by Alec, whose head appeared at the kitchen door leading from the garage. "Merritt, didn't we have a whole case of oil out here?"

"How should I know? Just look, Alec." When he closed the door, she rolled her eyes. "Men. Anyway, what do you think, Mom? Isn't that good news?"

"For whom?" I was still concentrating on Jacob's chubby hand, resisting the urge to leap up and dance around the kitchen.

"Well, not for Heck, that's for sure," Teddy said.

"Oh really? Why not for him? You think I should kick Heck to the curb now and resume the happy family with Dad?"

"Something like that." Teddy looked flabbergasted that I would even question it.

"Don't you like Heck?" I asked my kids.

"Yes, we like him," Teddy said. "He's okay. But . . ."

"But what?"

"But he's not . . . you know . . . Dad," Merritt finished for her brother. And no doubt for herself.

"No. No, he's not. He's never cheated on me or run out on me. Or made me feel worthless. You're right. He's definitely not Dad."

Merritt rose with a sigh, a sigh that said I was possibly the stupidest woman on earth, one who just didn't get it. She took her baby from me and cradled him in her arms. "Sorry, Mom; I thought you might be pleased, that's all."

"Look, you two. I thought we had this discussion months ago. Your dad and I are over. I know you'd probably like nothing more than for us to all be together again, but it's not going to happen. Your dad has chosen his life, and I have mine. And that's the way it is."

I sounded so brave, so resolute. I just wished the fluttering in my stomach would settle down and I could believe at least some of what I was asserting. "Just because Taylor dumped your father, it doesn't mean—"

"Wrong." Teddy's eyes looked excited, as if he were about to offer irrefutable proof that I should pull the For Sale sign from my yard and welcome his father home. As if Kevin would want that, anyway. "Dad dumped her."

"Yes," Merritt said, sitting back down again. "*He* dumped *her*. Said he'd had a midlife crisis . . . temporary insanity."

I'd had enough of Kevin's midfuckinglife crisis to last me a lifetime. "Let's change the subject, please, and enjoy the day. Okay?"

Only because it was Mother's Day, I felt, they both nodded. But their expressions told me they were less than thrilled with my reaction.

As if on cue, Heck and Alec rejoined our group. Alec, wiping his hands with a rag, looked around the room. "So did you tell your mom?" he asked, turning on the faucet. "Pretty surprising, huh?"

"Tell her what?" Heck asked, standing behind me, his hands on my shoulders.

"My dad and Taylor broke up," Teddy said. But I didn't like the way he said it. Not one bit.

***

Heck reached across the front seat of his pickup and took my hand in his as we wound our way out of Merritt's subdivision.

"So, how do you feel, hearing Kevin and Taylor are no more?" He looked at me so intently, I grew nervous he'd forget to return his eyes to the road.

"What do you mean?"

Now he was staring straight ahead, but still I felt nervous. Nervous that he'd see—or hear—through the lies I was about to tell him.

"How does that make you feel?" he repeated. "Surely you have to feel something when you hear the man you were married to for twenty-some years is no longer with the woman he . . . left you for." His kind tone tempered the pain those words could still inflict.

And so I returned the favor by sparing his feelings. I didn't tell him that once my numbness from the news wore off, I felt overjoyed. I didn't even care who broke up with whom. I wished only that there were some way they both could be suffering the way I'd suffered at being broken up with—at being, more accurately, broken apart.

But I worried Heck would interpret any joy on my part as my still having feelings for Kevin. And I didn't. So it seemed only right I tell this white lie and put it all to rest.

"I don't feel anything, really." I was trying to give the answer of a sane person, not one still mentally shaky from what Kevin and Taylor had put me through. "I guess I'm having trouble believing it," I added in a truthful understatement. After a brief pause, I added another truth. "Then again, maybe this was predictable."

"What do you mean?"

"The age difference. And I'm sure it seems multiplied tenfold since the birth of Jacob, and Kevin's undoubted devotion to him." I didn't expect him to understand the devotion, but *I* did. "I can see how Kevin might suddenly seem like a doting old man to Taylor," I added, "or how *she* might suddenly seem trivial to him."

"Why trivial? You mean because they don't share the grandparent thing? What about us?" he asked so quickly that I knew this concern had been festering in him since Jacob's birth, like a splinter working its way up through the skin. He'd needed only this opening from me to push forth those questions.

"It's so different for us. At least we're of the same generation. Even though you don't have grandkids, it's not that great a leap for you to understand me. Is it?"

"Not at all." He squeezed my hand and sounded relieved. "Not at all."

I returned the squeeze, relieved myself to know that he did understand my priorities, that he didn't mind sharing my love with my kids and Jacob.

But I still wondered why I felt such satisfaction at the knowledge that Kevin and Taylor were over. I felt like I had won. But won what?

***

Later that night, when we were home alone, Heck fixed ribs, and I made a potato salad. I loved to watch him eat. He had such gusto, such an uninhibited way of savoring every morsel.

It reminded me of how he treated me in bed—like he just couldn't get enough of me. I felt a great sexual tenderness toward him as I watched him clean off a rib bone and then wipe the barbecue sauce from his chin with a paper napkin.

As if he felt my eyes on him, he looked up at me questioningly. "I want you to marry me, Jess. C'mon, make my day. Make my life. Marry me."

It came from nowhere, or had it come from our conversation earlier that day and the knowledge that Kevin was on the loose? It made no difference. The timing was all wrong.

"Who needs marriage?" I asked in my best seductive voice, rising from the floor where I'd sat across the coffee table from him, eating my own dinner. I pushed him down on the couch and ran my hands up underneath his yellow golf shirt, rubbing them sexily into the patch of curled hair on his chest, the hair that was turning gray and giving him an endearing quality of vulnerability.

"No, I'm serious, Jess," he said, pushing me up to a sitting position and grabbing both of my hands in his as he snuggled next to me. "I want us to get married. Now. Right now."

"But I'm not even divorced yet."

"Why not?" he shot back.

So this had been on his mind a long time too, I realized. Heck didn't say things casually; he didn't do anything without thinking through every angle, as if he were planning cabinetry for an architecturally unique kitchen or an oil painting of a treasured landscape.

"Because . . . well, I'm not sure why not. My attorney says the ball's in Kevin's court, whatever that means."

"So, can't you make him hit the damn ball? Can't you push him?"

"Yeah, she asked me if she should. But I don't know . . . I just figured since the house isn't sold yet, and he's still putting money in the bank for me—"

"You don't need his money, Jess."

"No, I know I don't. I don't need anyone's money." And it was true, I felt convinced. Janice Barth had assured me she would get me the money I was *entitled* to—*my* money. So I didn't need Kevin's—or Heck's. So I supposed Heck was right. Might as well get the show on the road. "I'll call Janice tomorrow."

"Promise?"

"I promise." I shoved him back down on the couch and silenced him with my lips.

CHAPTER TWENTY-SIX

"Kevin and Taylor broke up."

"Ah, so how do you feel about that?" Nina asked, in the same tone Heck had used. Even though she was many miles away in her kitchen, I felt like a mental patient being scrutinized for my reaction to a potentially triggering piece of news.

"Feel? I don't feel anything," I lied.

"Of course you do. You must. Was it him, or her?"

"Him, apparently. So Merritt and Teddy tell me."

"Hmm." There was a loud silence as my sister pondered this piece of information.

"Okay," I abruptly broke the quiet. "I feel . . . I feel . . . well, glad, in one way. Glad they don't have each other anymore. I hope they're both feeling miserable. But . . . I also feel sad."

"Why?"

It seemed so obvious why I should feel sad that I was almost insulted she felt the need to ask. "Because.

Because . . . well, look what Taylor put us all through. And for what? For nothing."

"Hold on there. Don't blame Taylor for this. *She* didn't put you through anything. It was Kevin. Let's face it. Taylor had no commitment to you. Kevin did. He's the one who broke everything."

I felt suddenly so tired of discussing it, weary at the thought of just saying their names. "Look, Nina, I've got to go. I'll call you tomorrow. Give my love to everyone there, okay?"

"Yeah, okay. But, Jess, one thing . . ." Here it was, that damn *one thing* that always hung at the end of every conversation lately. "Don't let their breakup affect you. Go ahead with your divorce. Don't let it stand in the way of your happiness with Heck."

My happiness with Heck! What about the happiness I'd had with Kevin? I felt pushed on all sides, by my family and, most of all, by Heck. "I am going ahead with the divorce."

"Good girl."

I hung up and, remembering my promise to Heck from the day before, dialed Janice Barth's number. Like all good attorneys, or members of any profession, she was usually too busy to be readily available. But I left a message asking her to push Kevin's attorney for the papers. "I want to put this behind me," I added.

And indeed, I knew it was time.

***

"Jessie, Janice Barth here." It was eight o'clock, almost my bedtime, and here she was, still working. I didn't know if I should feel sorry for her, or for myself. Maybe I'd go to law school, get a job where I could immerse myself in other people's problems. As always, as I grew tired, my situation took on a grimmer look. Most mornings I felt things would be okay, somehow.

"Hi, Janice. Thanks for returning my call."

"I wish I had more for you. The thing is, your husband's attorney tells me he's had the papers for Kevin to sign for months now. But it seems your husband isn't returning his calls."

I let that sink in a minute. I had no idea what was going through Kevin's mind, but it occurred to me this had something to do with his and Taylor's breakup. "Well, I suppose he's lost his sense of urgency," I told my attorney, and then explained to her that he was no longer engaged.

"So maybe he's had a change of heart?" she asked.

"No, I don't think it's anything like that, or I would have heard from him. Not that it matters, anyway. *I* want this divorce." I was surprised by my own firmness. "I'll get ahold of him and tell him to get to Bill's and sign those papers."

"Good. When he does, then you can sign them, we'll go to court, and it's a done deal."

"That simple?"

"That simple. And that hard."

I was so glad I had a female attorney. Somehow, dear as he was, I didn't think our friend Bill could comprehend the complexities even Kevin must be feeling. "Okay, then. I'll contact Kevin," I said.

With a heavy heart, I hung up the phone. I knew I should try to contact him immediately, just as I knew I should be studying for finals. But nothing was possible in my present mood. So instead, I went to sleep watching Cary Grant and Doris Day dance around one another until inevitably they landed in each other's arms.

***

I had no classes the next day because of finals. So even though I'd told Heck to stay away that week so I could study, I drove over to Merritt's to see Jacob. Merritt had some errands to run, so she gladly handed him over and left us alone for a couple of hours. I lost myself completely in the adorable little person he'd become. Not putting him down once, I managed to clean up most of the breakfast things on Merritt's counter and even start a load of wash for her.

Jacob and I were at the window, where I was prematurely intent on getting him to notice a robin that had landed on the fence in the backyard, when the phone rang.

"Oh, in another month or two, you'll be so excited to see a robin," I said to my grandson, as I switched him to my left hip and reached for the phone. I didn't even bother to check caller ID since I didn't have my reading glasses on. Cradling the phone under my chin, I answered.

"Jessie? Is that you?"

It was Kevin, and I felt like a thief who'd been caught robbing a house. "Yes. It's me. I'm watching Jacob. Merritt's out." As if I needed to explain why I was there.

"How are you?" he asked. I pictured him as I'd last seen him, standing in the parking lot, hands dug into the pockets of his pants, his body tightened against the cold wind.

I tried to erase that image from my mind's eye as I answered him. "I'm fine. I was going to call you. My attorney says Bill Rizzo—"

"Ah, Bill. Yes. I should call him, I guess."

"Why haven't you? He has the papers for you to sign." Jacob wriggled in my arms, and I moved back closer to the window, as if I could distract him with the bird he was too young to notice.

"I . . . I guess . . . I don't know, Jess. I just don't know."

We both remained silent for a minute, as I held Jacob's face right up to the window. He looked fascinated at *something*—maybe just the bright sunshine—and I wished Kevin were there with me, so he could see how cute Jacob was at this moment.

"Do you want me to?" he asked, after a while. "Is that what you want?"

A touch of the old anger flared up, and I nearly dropped the phone from between my ear and shoulder as I attempted to switch Jacob to my other hip. "Look, this is your deal. You started this whole mess. Since when do you care what I want?"

"Just tell me, Jessica; should I sign those papers?"

Tears of frustration stung my eyes. This was so unfair. "How could you do this? Why are you putting this on me?"

A million memories washed over me, of other times he'd asked me what he should do. Should he change jobs? Should he question his boss about a promotion? Should he let this or that employee go? Always I had been his sounding board, and more often than not, he'd taken my advice. Only this time *I* was the employee he'd let go.

"Look, you do whatever the hell you want to do," I said.

"But what do *you* want?"

"Kevin, I have to go; Jacob is fussing. This is too difficult. I can't talk now."

"This isn't like you, Jess."

"Meaning?"

"You haven't answered the question."

"Good-bye; I'm hanging up."

And I did hang up then. I just couldn't answer the question.

***

When Merritt returned, she quickly took Jacob from my arms, as if she'd been gone for two weeks instead of two hours. I knew exactly how she felt.

"Oh, Mom." She snuggled into her baby's cheek. "Is it normal to miss someone so much? Or is it just mothers with babies who feel this way?"

"Well, honey," I said, filling the tea kettle with water, "I missed you and Teddy when you went away to college. But what you feel for Jacob is special. He's so tiny and so helpless. With you and Teddy, even though you were still my babies, you weren't helpless. Well, *you* weren't. Teddy I'm not so sure about."

She laughed and then grew quiet. "What about Dad?"

As always, my skin tingled at just the mention of Kevin. "Yeah, Dad missed you as much as I did." I took two mugs from the cabinet.

"No, I mean do you miss Dad *now*?"

I spun around, caught off guard by her question. "Of course I miss him. Merritt, I love your father very much. Why wouldn't I miss him?" I was struck by my own honesty.

"Then what's going on with Heck? You act as though you're in love with him."

"I don't know." I dropped a tea bag into each mug.

"Mom, you said you *love*, not loved, Dad. You were talking in the present tense."

I was reminded of the teenage Merritt, who insisted upon arguing every little point until I wanted to reach out and shake her. "Oh, Merritt, let's not go there now. Your father and I are getting a divorce, and that's that."

"I'm not suggesting you don't. But . . . Mom, don't get mad when I say this, but sometimes you seem to me to be trying just a little too hard with Heck. Don't get me wrong. Alec and I both think Heck is a great guy. I just wonder, sometimes, if—"

"Merritt." I thought of Heck and his reminder that this was as hard on the kids as it was on me, and I softened my response. "Heck and I have discussed getting married. And maybe we will someday. But I'm still married to your father, and we have a little divorce to take care of first."

"You sound almost happy."

"Well, I am. I really am."

"Yeah, but Mom, what are you happy *about*? Happy that you might marry Heck? Or happy that you're still married to Daddy?"

For the second time that day I was confronted with a question I couldn't answer. And so instead, I took Jacob from her arms and let her finish making the tea. Together, my grandson and I went back to the window in search of a robin.

***

Two days later I received an envelope addressed to me in Kevin's handwriting. I knew it wasn't the divorce papers; it wasn't nearly thick enough. My heart started to beat fast as I held the envelope in my hands, but I wasn't even sure what I was hoping for.

I went upstairs to my office and took a letter opener from my desk and slit the envelope open. Inside was a page torn from a magazine. It was an ad for a company that delivered flowers all over the world, with a picture of a crystal vase filled with lush, velvety, yellow roses.

At the bottom of the page, Kevin had written in black marker: *The real ones will be delivered in person.*

I sank down on my desk chair. A quarter of a century ago, when Kevin and I were apart for two weeks while he attended a sales-training conference in California, he'd sent me a similar page torn from a magazine, with almost the same message.

It had been a difficult separation, our first. Even though we'd been married a few years, we were still in the heady stage of love where even the smallest amount of time apart was unbearable. A couple of days later he'd come home bearing three dozen of my favorite flowers.

I gazed at the picture, recalling the longing I'd felt for Kevin all those years ago. Was it really any different from the longing I felt now?

I heard a key in the front door. Racing to the top of the stairs, I leaned over the banister, certain it would be my husband, armed with yellow blooms.

But it was Heck, using the key I'd given him to let himself in. There he stood in the hallway, armed with an electric hedge trimmer.

"Hi." He looked up at me. "I thought I'd trim your hedges around the house."

At that moment I felt so sorry for Heck. No matter what he did, it would never be as good as Kevin. Not because he didn't measure up in any way. He was his own man, and he didn't have to measure up to anyone. But simply put, he just wasn't Kevin and never would be, and that wasn't his fault.

I was confused and sad, until I felt the magazine ad in my hand. And then the wonderful excitement, the thrill that only Kevin could inject in me, took over.

"What you got there?" Heck indicated the ad.

"This . . . oh, this is nothing. An article on . . . flowers. It's nothing."

"I guess I'll get started." He headed out to the backyard.

Later we ate a quiet dinner together, but all the while I was conscious of my secret message from Kevin, stored safely away in my desk drawer. Before I went to sleep, having apologized to Heck for being "too tired," I crept into my office and took it out of the drawer to study one more time. Then I held it close to my heart. *Oh, God, please help me*, I thought. *Tell me what to do. Tell me what I want.*

***

My next contact with Kevin came the following day. He phoned to ask if I could meet him. He said he'd spoken to Bill Rizzo and that we had some things to discuss. It was late afternoon, and even though I acted as though I had a million things to do and that this was the most inconvenient of them, I agreed to meet him at six at The Columbia Club's bar in downtown Indianapolis.

Forget Bill Rizzo, I wanted to say; what about my flowers? I'd taken my last final that morning, and I felt I deserved flowers more than ever.

Confused, I checked my watch and realized I had two hours to wash my hair, shave my legs, pluck my eyebrows, and try on a dozen different outfits. When I was satisfied that I looked as good as I possibly could, I called Heck and got his answering machine, as I knew I would.

Feeling guilty, I left him a lie about an interview I had in Kokomo and said I wouldn't be home until very late. *Don't come up tonight*, I told him. I said I'd call him later, and we'd celebrate the end of my semester the next night.

Feeling panicky, excited, and happier than I had for the last year, I drove slowly to The Columbia Club. Kevin was sitting at the bar when I got there.

I sidled up next to him, and he turned to face me. "Jessie," he said.

I perched on a bar stool and leaned toward the bartender. "Chardonnay, please," I said. Then I turned toward Kevin. "So, what is this about?"

"Hold that wine," Kevin said, as he quickly downed his scotch. "Jessie, I want you to trust me."

I should have laughed in his face, but something told me not to. Not then, at least.

"Just trust me, and follow me." He reached in his pocket for some dollar bills and tossed them on the bar. Then he took my hand and led me out to the lobby.

"Kevin, what are you doing?"

"Jessie, remember when you met me at the airport wearing just a raincoat? You were so brave and so wonderful. And remember when you asked me to the Sadie Hawkins dance in high school and later told me how scared you were that I'd say no? Will you be as brave again? Please don't *you* say no. Just follow me, and don't say a word."

Maybe because I felt touched that he shared the same high school memories I did, I let my husband take my hand and lead me. We went to the elevator and got in. I didn't say a word, and neither did he. But his expression was both sweet and excited, and I was getting excited along with him.

We got out on the fifth floor, and he led me along the corridor to the last room on the right. Before he opened the door, he said, "Remember, don't say a word."

"Have I said anything so far?" I asked, and we both laughed.

"Okay. Now." He threw the door open all the way. The room itself was resplendent in luxury. An oriental rug covered the floor. A mahogany four-poster bed, not quite queen-size, filled the middle of the room, and on every surface, on every table, on every ledge, were roses. Hundreds of beautiful yellow roses.

"Oh!" My hands flew to my face. "Kevin, how did you . . . when did you . . ."

He looked so much like Teddy at that moment. So young and innocent, so pleased that he'd pleased me. "I took the room last night, and I had the flowers delivered. I wanted it to be perfect for you."

On the bed was a tray with an ice bucket, a champagne bottle nestled in a bed of ice. Two chilled glasses waited nearby.

"Okay, okay, don't say a word. Let me speak." He raised his hands as if to silence me, but it wasn't necessary. I was speechless.

"I nearly went to see Bill," he continued, leading me to the edge of the bed and sitting me down. Then he was on his knees before me. "Jessie, I was all ready to sign the papers and bring them to you. But then I knew that's not what I want. I don't want a divorce. I love you. I want you to take me back. I know it won't be easy to forgive me for all I've put you through, but Jessie, honey, I want to come home."

I opened my mouth to speak, not sure what I'd say, but he silenced me.

"Wait; I'm not done yet. I don't know how you feel. I don't know if you even want me back. You may hate me; hell, you *should* hate me. But I have to try. I can't just let you go without trying. Without telling you how much I love you, and how stupid I've been. How you're the only thing that matters to me. I can't sign those papers without first showing you I'm fighting for you, Jessie. I'll do anything, anything at all."

He rose and was opening the champagne now, pouring two glasses and handing me one.

"Kevin, I—"

"To us. Please, Jess, drink to us. Please, please say I can come home. Please say you'll at least think about it?"

I took the glass he handed me. Slowly I took a sip.

CHAPTER TWENTY-SEVEN

I slipped my shoes off and sank down onto the bed, my back leaning against the headboard, my champagne glass in hand. I could hear myself laughing at something Kevin was saying, some funny memory he was recalling.

But I wasn't really listening.

Instead, I was soaking up the feeling of just being there with him. It was like slipping into a tub of luxurious bubbles. The feeling was exhilarating and yet comfortable at the same time.

I'd won him back. I sighed in relief; he was mine again. I felt sure of it. But oh, how easily I'd lost him. And although the months of pain had left their mark, it seemed I just as easily had him back again.

I watched as he refilled our glasses and sank down beside me. How easily he wrapped an arm around me, and how right it felt. I was like a cancer patient suddenly pronounced free of any bad cells. A mother whose child has been kidnapped, holding him safely in her arms again. A wife whose husband had wandered—and returned.

Yes, that's who I really was. The past year was over; Kevin was back. His madness had subsided. He was mine again.

I put my glass on the table beside the bed and reached for his glass, removing it from his hand. Then I snuggled into the crook of his arm and rested my head on his chest. I felt almost unbearable relief.

As he continued to talk, a voice (it was mine) broke his reverie. "What about Taylor?"

He was silent for a moment, and I could feel his body tense. "We broke up," he said softly. "I thought you knew; I assumed you would know."

"That's not what I mean, Kevin. What *about* her? What was she? *Why* was she?"

He uncurled his arm from around me and turned to face me, taking my hands in his.

"Jessie, I was a madman. I can't explain it any other way. Don't blame her. She was as innocent in this debacle as you were."

"Hardly innocent. She knew you had a wife."

"Okay, hardly innocent. I'll grant you that. But blame me, not her. I'm the one who vowed to be faithful to you." He moaned. "And I was out of my mind. I don't know what I was thinking. No, that's not true. Let me be truthful."

He paused, and I nearly fainted.

"She made me feel a certain way, something I hadn't felt for a long time. I felt . . . with her . . . the way I used to feel with you. Suddenly there she was; and there I was, aching for that feeling again."

"Do you know how *selfish* that is?" My voice dripped with repulsion. "Who wouldn't want those feelings? But married people don't do that. As you say, you made a vow." I released my hands from his as if they were on fire, but he caught them back in his grip.

269

"Jessie, I know I'm asking a lot of you, to forgive me, to trust me again, to love me again. But I'm asking you to at least try. Please muster up some of that courage of yours, and don't give up on me. I'll do anything. I'll go to counseling . . . whatever you say. Please just don't give up on us—on me—without even trying."

"It's not that easy, Kevin. How *can* I trust you?"

He let go of my hands and put his arms around me, holding me close. "I don't know. Just please say you'll try."

After a moment of quiet I pulled away from him, but our faces were only inches from each other, and then suddenly we were kissing. It was slow and passionate. It felt good, and sexy, but comfortable, like slipping into a silk peignoir. I felt a gnawing in the pit of my stomach, and our kiss became harder as I felt his tongue in my mouth.

But it was different from THE KISS that night on my couch. Wonderful as that was, that kiss had been pure lust. With this one, I felt that same glorious combination of lust and love I'd felt when we'd kissed good night in the parking lot after celebrating Jacob's birth.

"I love you, Jessie." His mouth was on my cheek, his breathing as rapid as mine. "I've always loved you and no one else. I was just—"

"Shh . . ." I didn't want him to break this fragile mood. I slid my hands over his strong back, and then I was unbuttoning his shirt, until he pulled away.

"Jessie, I didn't bring you here to have sex with you."

"What?" I asked, a little hurt.

"I mean it. Look, I want to make love to you more than anything else in the world. It's all I've thought about for the past few months. But not here. Not now. I didn't bring you here for that. I brought you here to tell you I love you and want to be your husband again. When you agree, then I'm going to ravish you from head to toe."

"*When* I agree?" I leaned back against the headboard.

"Okay, *if* you agree." He stood up. "Say yes, Jessie; say yes now."

"I told you; it's not that simple. I have a different life now." I was a little humiliated by his rejecting my sexual advance, but in a strange way also proud of him.

"Ah, the carpenter."

"Heck."

"You aren't really serious about him, are you?" He looked scared.

"Yes, I really am."

"Do you love him?"

I couldn't answer. I stared back at my husband, the face I adored, but I couldn't answer that question. Not for Kevin, nor for myself. I hurried off the bed, gathered my shoes, and looked around for my purse. "I better go."

"Stay a little longer, please? Let's have dinner. We can order room service. Or go out, if you want."

"No. I have to go." I found my purse and retrieved my jacket from the chair by the door.

Kevin reached out to help me on with it. "Okay," he said. "Go; I understand. But just promise me you'll think about everything I've said."

"Yes; yes, I will." As if I could think of anything else. But I felt suddenly anxious, desperate to get out and be alone.

He kissed my cheek and hugged me close to him. "I'll be waiting to hear."

"Good-bye, Kevin." I pulled myself out of his arms.

"Wait." He extracted a yellow rose from a vase on the nightstand. "Take this. And when you look at it, remember you're the love of my life."

Why didn't you remember that? part of me wanted to demand, but my soft, forgiving mood remained dominant.

As if reading my thoughts, he continued, "I did a deplorable thing, and I don't deserve a second chance. But I love you."

I yanked the door open and hurried down the hall to the elevator, too scared to look back.

***

After parking my car in the garage, I walked straight to Ellen's, glad to see their lights on and no strange cars in the driveway. I was afraid they'd be at Perry's, singing around the piano with the others.

But I should have known my best friend would be there when I needed her most.

I burst through her back door and called her name, forgetting to give even the perfunctory two knocks.

"Hey, Jess." She came into the kitchen from the living room. She was in her pajamas, scrubbed free of makeup, hair pulled back in a low ponytail. "I thought you'd be out celebrating the end of finals with Heck."

"No; tomorrow night." I sighed. "I think."

"Okay." She looked puzzled. "Let's you and I celebrate. I've sure missed you while you've had your nose in those dang books." She went to the refrigerator and returned with a bottle of wine. "You look like you need this. But why?"

In less than twenty minutes, I'd summed up my quandary. "This was my fantasy, Ellen. And it's actually happened: Kevin on his knees, begging me to take him back."

"But?"

"What do you think? Could it ever work? Could I take him back and forget about Taylor? Just go on as if it never happened?"

"People do," she said. "Maybe not like it never happened, but they do get back together and go on."

"So that's what you think I should do?"

"Whoa. I'm not saying that. Only you—"

"And what about my part in our breakup? I know I took Kevin for granted when I had him. And I know I was a nag and control freak."

"Oh, Jessie, you were not. You were a wife."

"Yes, but I always knew what tie he should wear, how we should celebrate his birthday . . . but if only we could have discussed it. If only he'd told me how unhappy he was. Had he? Had he told me, and I wasn't even listening?"

I was thinking of a phone call from Kevin, after Ted left for college, suggesting we take off for the weekend. Go anywhere, just get away. Things were bad at work, he said; he needed a break.

But I was too busy; I had a deadline to meet. Some stupid article that was so important at the time, and now I couldn't even remember the topic.

"Jessie, Jessie, what are you thinking? Don't be so hard on yourself. Besides, Kevin's come to his senses. He knows what he wants."

"Yes, Ellen, but I don't know what *I* want. He really opened Pandora's freakin' box." I shoved my untouched wineglass across the table to her. "Sorry, honey. I've got to talk to Heck."

"Jess, maybe you ought to sleep on this." She rose and followed me to the door, as if she might try to physically restrain me. But instead she gave me a big hug.

I went back to my garage and climbed in the Jeep. Then, off and on, my fingers stroked the yellow rose as I made the long drive to Heck's.

***

"Hey." Heck looked pleased to see me as he opened the door, even though I'd obviously awakened him from his night's sleep. "This is a treat."

I almost didn't have the courage to enter, but I'd come this far. So I stepped past him, pretending not to notice when he leaned down for a kiss. When I sat on the couch, he joined me.

"What's wrong?" he asked, but he didn't look concerned. He looked like he was trying to fully awaken, rubbing his eyes and then stretching his arms above his head.

"Heck . . . I . . ."

Even though I stopped talking, Heck said nothing, just continued looking at me with an almost jovial expression. He wasn't going to make this easy for me, but then why should he? Had I made it easy for Kevin when he first confessed about Taylor?

"I saw Kevin today," I said at last.

Again, he said nothing, although his expression did change. I could hear music coming from the bedroom for the first time. Classical music from the radio. Then an ad for a collector's edition of the entire works of Mozart.

I heard Heck sigh and watched him lean back on the couch. He now wore the same expression I'd seen when one of my kids was younger and knew verbatim the lecture I was about to impart.

"He wants me to take him back." I looked out the window at the thick stand of trees that sheltered his cabin.

Again, silence, as if he wanted me to continue. Indeed, when he spoke, all he said was, "And?"

"And I don't know what to do."

Now he stood up, stuffing his hands into the pockets of the jeans he'd no doubt thrown on before answering his door. It was a gesture I had come to recognize as exasperation on his part.

"So . . . you came here so I could tell you what to do. Is that it, Jessie?"

I nodded slowly, not daring to look at him. It wasn't fair; I knew that. I was behaving like a selfish child, but I couldn't stop myself.

"I'm sorry, but you're on your own for this one." He walked to the kitchen and then returned. When I looked up, he was sipping from a beer can. "You do whatever makes you happy," he said.

"I'm sorry, Heck. I'm just confused. I don't know what I want."

Then he was sitting beside me on the couch again. He put the beer on the floor between his feet and reached for my hand.

"Okay, Jessie," he said softly. "I'll make this real easy on you. Let me ask you one thing, though: do you love him?"

"I don't know," I mumbled.

"Oh, you know, all right."

"No, Heck, really; I don't. I thought I did. I thought I would love him forever, and then you came along, and then—"

"Jessie, I came along too soon. I was the proverbial transition guy. We never get the girl, no matter how much we want her and . . . love her."

"Oh, Heck." I took his hand. "I feel so . . . I don't know . . . so confused. I know this isn't fair."

"Yeah, well, life ain't fair. Look, as much as I love you, and want you, and can't think straight when you're not around . . . I guess I knew you and I'd be having this conversation one day."

"Heck, how could you know—"

"Because it's like this." He removed his hand from mine. "You either love someone or you don't. Hell, I knew you were still in love with Kevin when I first met you. It was too soon. I knew my chances were slim that you'd get over him and fall for me."

"But I did—"

"Shhh, let me finish. I've been on my own a long time. And I pretty much gave up on ever feeling this way about a woman again. For a while there, I thought it might work, but I'd have to be deaf, dumb, and blind not to see that you still had it pretty bad for your ex."

He paused and shook his head. "Okay, he's a bastard, a piece of shit, and if you take him back, then you're going to be looking over your shoulder for the rest of your life. But you know what?"

"What?" I asked, barely above a whisper.

"I'd rather have you looking over your shoulder than me looking over mine to see if Kevin's lurking anywhere near."

"So you think I should take him back?"

"I didn't say that. Only you can decide that. What I'm saying is that you're no good to me if you're in love with him."

He stood again and once more dug his hands into his pockets. "You should probably leave. I've got things to do around here, and this conversation's not going anywhere."

I stood, and he walked me to the door. As I turned to kiss him, he offered only his cheek.

"You're just letting me go?" I asked.

"You think you're worth fighting for?" The smirk on his face looked sad, not cruel.

"Kevin seems to think so."

"Then I guess that makes him a better man than I." I felt his light touch on my elbow as he steered me outside.

Next thing I knew, the door closed in my face.

CHAPTER TWENTY-EIGHT

By the time I was halfway home, I was sobbing so uncontrollably I was as dangerous as a drunk driver. I knew I should pull over and get control of myself, but I couldn't think straight.

When I got off I-465 and stopped at the traffic light on Meridian Street, my eyes fell on the wilting yellow rose lying on the passenger seat. I picked it up and breathed in the fragrance that could always take me back in time, back to proms, back to my wedding day, back to anniversaries, back to countless good times with Kevin.

But as the light turned green, I thought *forget you, Kevin* and crumpled the velvety yellow petals in my fist before tossing them on the floor of the passenger side and driving off.

My tears had stopped, but my renewed anger had just begun by the time I pulled into my garage. It felt spooky, and I felt lonely, as I entered the dark kitchen. Usually, I left lights on all over, but I hadn't planned on coming home this late. I hadn't planned on anything that had happened this day. I was, I realized, in shock.

I had to speak to Nina, whether I liked what she would say or not. As I dialed her number, I prepared myself for her bossiness. As my life had undergone changes, so had our roles. These days she was the one with all the answers and advice that usually I, as the older sister, felt was my duty to dish out to her.

And right now I needed all the answers and advice I could get.

"H'lo," she said in a sleepy voice, and only then did I glance at my watch.

"Oh, Nina, I'm sorry; I didn't realize it was so late. I'll call you tomorrow."

"Don't be silly. You know I'm always glad to hear from you."

Then my sobbing started anew.

"Jessie, what is it?" I could picture her bolting up in bed and then hurrying out of the bedroom with her phone so as not to disturb Dave.

It took me more than an hour to fill her in on all the details. Her periodic *mmm hmm* and clucks of empathy, as well as her refusal to be shocked by anything, calmed me like nothing else could.

"You know," I concluded, "I think I went to Heck's to get his permission to see Kevin. I think I had this vision of seeing both of them until I made up my mind. Man, what was I *thinking*?"

Nina was silent on the other end of the line, and I was afraid she might have fallen asleep. I knew *I* was exhausted after recalling all the events, so she certainly had a right to be nodding off.

"Nina, you go back to sleep; I'll call you later this week."

"No, no. I was just thinking. Is that what you want? To see both Heck and Kevin? Are you asking *me* for permission?"

"Don't be ridiculous." But once again I felt amazed at her perception as I realized she might be right.

"Listen, I'm calling the airlines in the morning. I'm coming to see you."

"No, no, you don't have time to come here."

"Jessie, I would love a break. It would do Dave good to take care of the kids for a few days. I want to see my new great-nephew, and more important, I want to see you."

It had been an eternity. "But Nina . . . you're so busy."

"Not so busy I can't come visit my sister. You go to sleep now; I'll call you in the morning with my flight details."

"Nina," I tried to protest again, although it was halfhearted. The thought of spending a few days alone with my little sister was too seductive. "Are you sure Dave won't mind? There's no need, really—"

"Jessie, I miss you. I need to see you."

That was just what I wanted to hear. I hung up smiling. A perfect end to a very weird day.

***

The next morning everything seemed so much better, as things always do the next morning. Nina called to let me know her flight from Houston would arrive the next day at eleven fifty, and I was thrilled at the prospect of seeing her.

I allowed myself just a few moments to think of the previous day. When I thought of Heck, I felt sad but had no regret at what I'd done or at what he'd said. And when I thought of Kevin, an excitement stirred inside me. I could have him back. It was what I'd desperately hoped for the past eleven months.

For a couple of hours I busied myself getting the house ready for Nina. I washed sheets and towels and cleaned the guest bathroom.

When I was dressed and ready to head out to the grocery store, I stopped in the kitchen to take a quick inventory of what I needed for her visit. It didn't take long. I basically needed everything. But to make sure I wouldn't forget anything, I jotted down a quick list of staples.

I had my car keys in my hand, ready to leave by the back entrance, when the doorbell rang. I went to answer it, and there stood Kevin.

At the sight of him, the familiar twinge of excitement fluttered through my body. But I wasn't ready to see him. Not yet. Not until I'd thought things through, not until I'd had a long talk with Nina.

He leaned against the door frame, an anxious look on his face. In one hand, he had a yellow rose wrapped in green tissue. "Hi," he said.

"Hi."

"Can I come in? I was hoping maybe I could take you to lunch. I was going to call first, but . . . I wasn't sure what you'd say, or if you'd answer the phone. So I just came over."

I opened the door wider to let him in, and suddenly I felt fifteen, opening the door to my date.

But Kevin broke the spell by asking, "Jessie, did you think about it? About us?"

The fluttering in my chest subsided, as I thought of Heck and how he'd been my savior, whereas Kevin had torn my world apart. "I've thought of nothing else." I closed the door behind him. "But it's not as simple as you make it sound."

He was standing in the middle of the living room, and I could tell he was ready to interrupt. I stopped him cold, pointing a finger at him like a stern teacher. "Please, let me finish," I said. "You hurt me. You hurt me a great deal. But the last thing I want to do right now is punish you for that."

I was as astounded at this revelation as he. There was a time not too long ago (as recently as yesterday?) that daydreams of punishing him had filled my empty hours and my heart.

Now, if anything, I was tempted to take him back to reassure him I held no more ill will. At the moment. But we both knew that whatever life was to bring us—separately or as a couple—I was condemned to have flashes of resentment and hurt for the rest of my life over what he'd done.

"I went to see Heck after I left you," I said, taking no pleasure in the pain and fear I saw cloud his face. It was quickly replaced with an I-deserved-that look, but I took no comfort in that, either.

He nodded his head and then sat down on the arm of the couch. "What did he say?"

"Well, he wanted no part of my waffling."

Kevin looked up quickly, a flicker of hope in his eyes. "You're waffling?"

"Kevin, it might be better if I don't see either of you for a while."

"How long?" He sounded like Teddy wanting to know how many more hours before we arrived at Grandma and Grandpa's. That made me think of my father and how he would never have put my mother through anything like this.

Feeling the scale tip in Heck's favor, I answered abruptly. "I don't know. Right now I have only one thought in mind. Nina's coming tomorrow, and I have to go to the grocery store. I can't have lunch with you today, and I think you better go now."

He stood up. "Okay, I'll go. But just remember this. I love you, and I'll wait forever if I have to."

"I guess you really have no choice. If that's how you feel," I heard myself say. I went back to the kitchen to count how many eggs I had.

***

I was filled with excitement as I drove to the airport to meet Nina. I'd planned so many things for us to do, but the part I was looking forward to the most was just being with her.

I parked the Jeep and made my way to the terminal. Checking the arrivals board, I saw I was about twenty minutes early, which only heightened my nervous excitement. But as I made my way through the throng of travelers toward the arrivals area, a depression descended upon me.

The last time I was at the airport, I was wearing my trench coat and was headed to meet Kevin. It was the beginning of the nightmare. It seemed like only yesterday, but oh, how much had happened since then. Determined to let nothing mar my happiness today, I shrugged away those nasty thoughts and proceeded at a quicker pace toward Nina.

A crowd of passengers began to approach, some looking for friends or relatives who would be meeting them, some just looking glad to be on the ground and determined to get out of the airport.

And then I saw Nina. My feet wanted to run to meet her, but my heart made me wait just a few seconds, so I could take in the sight of her. Her hair was longer than it had been the last time I'd seen her, and she'd lost a little weight. She looked about eighteen as I watched her crane her neck in search of me.

My feet finally won out, and I ran toward her with arms outstretched to swoop her up. We both screamed with delight at the same time. It was magical to have her here. We released each other and stood at arm's length, holding hands and squealing some more.

Then I put an arm around her shoulders, and she put one around my waist. Together—laughing, and crying just a little—we walked the long corridor to the luggage carousel. We were forced to let go of each other, but just long enough for Nina to retrieve her suitcase. And then, arms entwined around each other again while I pulled her rolling suitcase with my free hand, we headed toward the parking garage.

"How's Dave? How're the kids? How was the flight? Oh, Nina, it's so good to have you here."

"Fine; they're all fine. All send their love. And believe me, I'm so glad I came."

When we reached the Jeep, we disentangled from each other long enough for me to open the car door and put her bag on the back seat. Then, just once more, before she climbed in on the passenger side, we gave each other a bear hug, just because it felt so damn good.

We had lunch at a new Italian restaurant after we left the airport. We chatted and chatted, but never mentioned the real reason for her visit. We both wanted hours free from interruption for that talk.

I phoned Merritt from the restaurant to tell her I was bringing Aunt Nina by to see Jacob. I was terribly proud of my little grandson and wanted to share him with Nina, but a selfish part of me wanted to get that visit over with so I could have Nina alone and we could talk, really talk.

As I knew she would, Great-Aunt Nina oohed and aahed over little Jacob. She was only slightly less thrilled to see Jacob's mom and his Uncle Teddy, who'd come to see his favorite aunt (okay, his only aunt; but they both always said she'd be his favorite no matter how many he had).

The two hours at Merritt's passed quickly, as we all played catch-up on family news. The good news, that is. I felt glad when Jacob rubbed his eyes and grew fussy.

"Well, we'll leave and let you get him down for his nap," I said to Merritt, trying to hide my eagerness.

Nina and I drove back to my house, and within ten minutes of arriving, she'd exclaimed her delight at my renovated kitchen and unpacked her belongings, while I poured us each a large glass of chardonnay.

"How's Ellen?" she asked. "I'll get to see her, won't I?" Nina knew Ellen was my "other sister," and she'd expressed her gratitude more than once for that, comforted to know I had someone close at hand to administer sisterly duties.

"No; sorry. She and Steve are in Chicago. They had a family wedding, and then Steve had some work stuff."

"Bummer."

At last, both clad in yoga pants and T-shirts she'd brought all the way from Texas (the same ones my nearby Target carried), Nina and I got comfortable on the living room couch.

"Okay," she said. "Talk."

***

Later that night, when the pizza was long since finished and a second bottle of chardonnay was almost demolished, Nina sat down on the floor and attempted to paint her toenails Corvette Red. She'd squeezed a spongy blue divider between her toes, and we both giggled drunkenly as she attempted to stand and hobble across the room.

"This is how those Chinese women with bound feet must have walked." She retrieved a piece of paper and a pen from the kitchen and then plopped down on the floor again. "Okay," she said. "I have the solution to your problem. We'll rate them."

I watched her draw a line down the center of the paper and then write *Heck* on the top of one column and *Kevin* on the other.

"Good idea." I poured the last of the wine into our glasses. "Kevin's starting to get hairs growing out of his ears. Put that down." I pointed a finger at her, once again the older sister in charge.

"Wait a minute. You mean Heck doesn't have hair on hiz sears?" Nina slurred. "But he's older than Kevin, isn't he?"

"I think he does. But on him, it's cute; it matches his beard."

"Okay," Nina said. "That's a minus for old Kev."

"Triple minus."

"Now, who has the most money?"

"Dunno. Well, I know how much Kevin has. Or had. I've spent a hell of a lot of it lately."

This sent us both into gales of laughter that had us snorting as Nina drew a sloppy question mark in Heck's column and a crossed-out dollar sign in Kevin's.

Nina made an effort to compose her drunken self. "Okay, what about sex?"

"Well, let's see. Heck is good. He's *reeeally* good."

"Aha, now we're getting somewhere." Nina licked the end of the pencil and in an exaggerated manner, drew a smiley face in Heck's column. "And what about Kevin? Seems I recall you two were pretty hot in the early days."

I sat up straight. There was a pain in my chest, like I couldn't breathe. The game suddenly wasn't fun anymore. Suddenly I couldn't think about sex with Kevin without thinking about Kevin and Taylor. Sobering up, I reached over and took the paper from Nina's hand. "This is a dumb idea, Nina. Let's call it a night."

Dear Nina, who sensed everything, released the paper to my grip. "Okay, honey; you're right. We're drunk and tired, and my toes look like shit. How could you let me paint my toenails when I'm in this condition, for heaven's sake? What the hell kind of sister are you?"

It was all that was needed to stop the threatening storm. I helped her to her feet and kissed her on the cheek. Then we went to bed.

***

Nina left two days later, and we drove to the airport with a sad silence enveloping us both.

I pulled up to the terminal and put the Jeep in park. Turning toward my sister, I reached across and took her in my arms.

"Thanks for coming, Nina. Thanks for everything."

"It was good. Just the two of us. I wouldn't have missed it for the world. You do whatever you have to, and I'll be okay with it."

"Really? Still no advice?"

"You're on your own on this one. But I'll back you, whatever you decide."

"You're the best sister in the world. Now get out of this car, before I start blubbering."

She giggled, but her eyes were moist. I watched her as she pulled her suitcase toward the terminal doors. She turned once to wave and blow me a kiss. I blew one back.

Driving home, I felt more alone than I'd ever felt in my life. We hadn't resolved anything, of course, but I hadn't expected us to. I'd just wanted my sister to hear me out, maybe give me her opinion, and then let me do exactly as I wanted.

If only I could figure out what that was.

For now, I'd finally convinced myself and Nina, that meant seeing neither man. I desperately needed some time to get to know Jessie before I could decide which man—if either—she wanted.

***

I decided to throw myself into my work, my kids, and my grandson. I even signed up for a summer-school class—statistics, no less. That would keep me busy.

And for nearly a month I successfully avoided both men. That wasn't hard with Heck, since he made no effort to contact me; but it took a week to convince Kevin I wanted no part of his phone calls or even his messages, and certainly not his cute little cards that only reminded me of Taylor.

I needed time to be with just Jessica.

But by the end of my man-free month, I knew I had to do something about my dilemma. I started by calling Nina.

"This isn't working," I whimpered into the phone.

"What? You mean seeing neither of them?"

"Right. I thought all I needed was to get to know me."

"Yeah," Nina said, and then mimicked Sammy Davis Jr. "You gotta be you . . . ," she crooned.

I continued, ignoring her. "Well, I went from Mom and Dad to Kevin to Heck. I thought it would be good for me to be alone for once."

"And what have you discovered?"

"That I'm lonely. That this is a couple's world. That I don't want to live in this house by myself. That if it ever sells, I don't want to live anywhere by myself. That nothing is much good if you can't share it with someone."

"You've been reading Hallmark cards again, haven't you?"

"Nina, please be serious. I'm trying to tell you that I want to spend the rest of my life with someone I love."

"And that would be . . . ?"

"Kevin . . . or Heck." I knew I sounded pathetic.

"Okay," she said, as if soothing a mental patient, "which one will it be?"

"Nina, I miss Kevin every single second of every single day. But don't you see? I can't make a decision based on my *memories* of Kevin. Obviously, the man has changed. I need to know who Kevin is *now*. And the only way I can find out is by spending some time with the man," I said urgently, aware that this was at least the third plan I'd tried to sell her—and myself—on.

"That sounds reasonable," she said after a thoughtful pause. "But what about Heck? Don't you also need to be seeing him, to decide?"

"Well, that's not an option. He'd have no part of it. Not that I don't think I could convince him to come back. I have to believe we really had something. Er, *have* something. Whatever. But he'd never see me if I'm seeing Kevin at the same time. That's okay, though. I know exactly who Heck is. And if Kevin weren't an option, then I'd know how I felt about Heck."

I took a deep breath. "So it's very simple. I just need to get to know Kevin and find out how I feel about him now."

"You've got one hell of a plan there, Einstein." But her voice was soft, especially when she added, "Good luck."

Even before I'd finished uttering my thanks, I pressed the button on the phone to disconnect Nina, and then I dialed Kevin's number.

CHAPTER TWENTY-NINE

"I'm sorry; he's not in. Would you like his voice mail?"

Lois didn't even recognize my voice, I realized. But it had been a long time since I'd called Kevin's office. Since I'd called Kevin anywhere.

"Uh, yes, I guess so. Lois, this is Jessie." Now I half expected her to ask, "Jessie who?" But surely it hadn't been *that* long.

"Jessie! I'm sorry; I didn't recognize your voice. Actually, Kevin *is* here. I'm sure he'd want me to tell *you* the truth. He's just busy trying to finish some reports and didn't want to take any calls. But let me tell him you're on the phone."

Yes, I thought, Kevin would want Lois to tell me the truth. Too bad he hadn't always wanted to do that himself. Then again, I'd realized as I was dialing his number that in a strange way, I didn't regret *everything* that had gone on the past year.

The past year, after all, had held more excitement than the entire previous decade. There'd been Heck, for starters. And now this new feeling I had with Kevin, like we were fourteen and fifteen again. Or was I just trying to see the bright side of things?

Before I could delve any deeper—as if it made any difference—Kevin's voice interrupted my psychoanalysis. "Jessie! I'm so glad you called."

"Hello, Kevin." I hadn't heard from him the last three weeks, so I felt it was safe to assume he hadn't moved forward with the divorce.

"Jessie, are you there? Did you hear me?"

"I'm sorry, Kevin. No, I didn't. What did you say?"

"I said, does this mean I can see you now? Is that why you're calling, I hope?"

"Well, yes. I thought maybe we should talk."

"Great. How about lunch today? You didn't sell the house, did you?" He sounded worried. Kevin was as bad as our kids. No one wanted change now but me.

"No, I didn't sell the house—yet. Anyway, it's almost noon already, and you have reports, so why—"

"Reports will wait. I can't. Can I pick you up in an hour? Does that give you enough time?"

I found the eagerness in his voice touching. And I needed to start somewhere separating fact from fancy. Might as well start with lunch. "Yeah, I'll be ready in an hour."

And in only forty-five minutes my doorbell rang. I quickly brushed on some mascara and applied lipstick before going to the door.

"Hi," I said, breathless at the sight of my husband. His hair had grown gray at the temples just since I'd last seen him. It didn't make him look distinguished, I noted with alarm. It made him look vulnerable.

Had I done that to him? I wondered, feeling a new tenderness toward him. "Come in."

"Jessie, you look wonderful." He reached out his arms.

But I pulled back, running up the stairs as I called behind me, "I'll be ready in a sec. Have a seat. Or help yourself to a Coke or something."

I carefully applied my foundation and eyeliner so as not to smear the mascara I'd prematurely applied. Then I added another coat of mascara and redid my lips before grabbing the old Coach purse Kevin had given me for Christmas almost a decade ago.

When I walked into the kitchen, I saw his back as he perused the magnets on the refrigerator that held a lifetime of photographic family memories—minus him. He didn't notice me as I stood silently behind him. Finally, I tapped him lightly on the shoulder.

"Oh, Jess." He turned around and then motioned toward the side-by-side. "I see you've de-Kevined the refrigerator." He said it jokingly, a reference, I knew, to the time we'd teased Merritt about de-Todding her room after breaking up with her high school boyfriend. But I could hear the hurt in his voice as he asked, "What did you do with the pictures of me? Tear them up? Use them for dart practice?"

"Does it matter?"

He paused. "No. No, I suppose not. The point is, you saw fit to rid me from your life."

He looked sad, but I felt void of any pity now. Maybe it was his choice of words. "No. *You* saw fit to rid *me* from *your* life," I said.

"Touché." Now he really looked sad. "What's your pleasure?"

"For lunch?"

"What I really want to know is, what's your pleasure for the rest of your life, but I promised myself I wouldn't push. So yeah, where would you like to go for lunch?"

"Surprise me."

And that he did. We were in the car two hours before it even dawned on me that we *were* still in the car. We'd been talking about Merritt and Ted. We talked about them as kids, we talked about them as adults, we talked about their future.

And we talked, talked, talked about Jacob. We'd seen him together only twice, so we spent most of our time filling each other in, in great detail, about the times we'd seen him when the other hadn't.

"Gosh, Kevin, there's no one else on earth I can talk to this way. I mean, I always start to, whether it's Nina or Ellen or some friend I run into at the store." *Or Heck*, I carefully didn't add.

"I always start gushing about how Jacob rolled over or how he recognizes me or how he smiles all the time," I said. "And then I stop myself because I know no one can possibly understand or care like I do. But you do, don't you?"

"Of course I do."

I stared at him, in awe of this bond between us. And then my eyes fell on the clock in his Porsche. "Kevin, is that clock right?" But even as I asked the question, I looked at my watch and knew it was. "Where are we going? Where are we? It's been two hours!"

"You told me to surprise you."

Soon, I saw an I-65 North sign and figured he was taking me to that fish place in Northern Indiana he'd always tried to talk the kids and me into. To no avail, I recalled with more than a twinge of guilt.

But then we began talking about Teddy and how we'd seen such promising signs of his maturing lately, so the Chicago skyline loomed before I again took note of where we were. "Kevin, it's after four o'clock. What are you doing?"

"Right now, I'm standing still in the middle of Chicago rush-hour traffic." He grinned and grabbed my hand. "Would you mind having dinner with me instead of lunch?"

"Oh, Kevin. This is so typical of you. I give you an inch, and you take a mile."

But I didn't mind a bit.

***

Dressing Myself

For the next week I saw Kevin every day. He'd stop by for coffee before he went to work, or he'd bring me lunch from my favorite deli, or both. And every night we had dinner together.

He brought food and cooked for me twice and took me to a different restaurant four nights in a row. Twice, including the night we'd had dinner at Tuscany in Chicago, we'd stayed up all night talking—and nothing more.

"Are you sure?" Ellen had quizzed me, after popping over to complain that she couldn't get a visit in edgewise, what with Kevin's car always there, or me gone.

"I'm sure, Ellen. Kevin must think it's his best shot at winning me back for good. Or do I flatter myself? Maybe he just doesn't find me attractive anymore."

"Yeah, *right*. Don't be ridiculous."

"Well, I'm afraid *he* might be all that holds *me* back. I think I'd find him irresistible if his restraint ever fails him."

That had nothing to do with my insisting on making him dinner at the end of that week, I assured myself.

I was humming between sips of wine as I banged pots and pans in the kitchen, awaiting Kevin's arrival. I almost didn't hear the phone ring. Before I picked it up, I noted Merritt's number on caller ID.

"Mom, please say no if you have any other plans or if you just don't want to," she said.

I felt the excitement I experienced every time she uttered those words. I knew I was about to have a chance to see Jacob. Not that I didn't get to see him almost every day. And not that I didn't know that Merritt—as well as Alec, he assured me—welcomed my every visit. But because I was determined not to be a pesky mother or mother-in-law, I preferred it by far when they initiated the contact.

"What?" I asked innocently.

"Alec just got tickets to an Indians game, and I wondered—only if you have nothing else to do—if you'd want to come stay with Jacob. I mean, we can ask Beth or Jackie. They both owe us."

Two of Merritt's best friends from high school lived right in her neighborhood, but so far they'd never watched Jacob. I'd never given them the chance. I'd made Merritt promise to always ask me first, if Jacob's other grandparents couldn't help out, assuring her I'd say no if I ever wanted to.

"Merritt, I'd love to come over. But ... uh ... can I bring your father?" I started to put away the utensils and ingredients I'd been gathering to make Kevin's favorite pasta.

"Dad? Bring Dad? Mom, what are you talking about?"

I'd spared Merritt the details of my plan to see neither man. She knew only that I wasn't seeing Heck anymore, that I'd decided it was too soon for me to be making a new commitment. And she had *no* idea her father and I were seeing each other. I didn't think it would be fair to risk falsely raising her or Teddy's hopes.

But now I had no choice. I had a date with her dad, and I didn't want to break it. Yet I also didn't want to pass up the chance to be with Jacob. And the truth was, the thought of sharing him with Kevin sounded like one of my daydreams come true.

"Well, I was going to see your dad tonight. He'll be here any minute. Can we both come?"

"Of course, Mom."

The joy in her voice made me nervous. I said a quick good-bye and phoned for a pizza for us to pick up on the way to her house. I knew Kevin wouldn't mind, and I loved that about him. But most of all I loved him now because he was the grandfather of my grandson.

And that night, with the three of us together, intensified that feeling. We played and giggled over our chubby little Gerber Baby, and Kevin and I clapped our hands as Jacob laughed out loud right back at us.

"I remember the first time he smiled at me," Kevin said. "It just melted my heart."

No wonder, I thought. It melted my heart when Jacob smiled at me, too, but I'd never seen anything like his adoration for Kevin. I had no doubt my grandson recognized and even loved me, but the look on his face when he laid eyes on Kevin—not only when we'd first arrived, but every time he looked up at his grandpa—transcended anything I'd ever seen. And after spending the evening together, I figured out why.

Kevin took Jacob outside to feed the bunny rabbit that roamed the neighborhood. Kevin gave him forbidden licks from a spoonful of ice cream. And after I changed Jacob's diaper and put his pajamas on him, Kevin bounced him gently on his knees, singing "My Pony Boy" and eliciting baby giggles every time he sang *giddyup, giddyup, giddyup, whoa!* In other words, Kevin did all the things Jacob loved. Kevin was, I saw, the perfect grandfather.

But could he ever be the perfect husband?

***

For several more weeks, I soaked up all of Kevin that I could. Heck grew to be a distant memory—if I thought of him at all, that is.

But that changed the minute I saw him.

One morning he simply appeared at my door, two large cups of steaming coffee and a bag of Dunkin' Donuts in hand. My first thought was how typical this was: Kevin would appear with roses, Heck with coffee and donuts.

But it didn't make me like—or love?—him any less. "Heck! Come in!" I was genuinely glad to see him, only vaguely embarrassed by my disheveled hair and pajamas. I'd expected the ringing doorbell to be a signal from Kevin, and I realized that I'd given up worrying what I looked like for him.

"I was in the neighborhood," Heck said sheepishly. "I just thought I'd see how you were doing."

I remembered the time Kevin had claimed to be in the neighborhood. "I'm doing fine, Heck. Fine. How are you?" I took one of the coffees from him and sipped carefully before walking into the living room with it. "Come. Sit down."

"I can only stay a minute. Like I said, I was—"

"I know. You were just in the neighborhood. Heck, you don't have to have an excuse to come see me."

"Jessie, just let me say what I came to say. Before I chicken out. I know I said I was just your transition man—"

"Heck, you were way more than that." I couldn't believe the feeling that my voice held. I couldn't believe how good it was to see him.

He took a long drink from his coffee, obviously burning his mouth but trying not to show it. He reached for a glazed donut and then held the sack out for me.

I shook my head, my eagerness to hear what he had to say diminishing my usually hearty appetite for donuts.

"Never mind what I came to say. Just tell me. Are you and Kevin back together?" He looked around, as if realizing for the first time that Kevin might be in the house.

"No, we're not back together. But I am seeing him."

"Are you . . . did you . . . have you . . ."

"I'm just seeing him, spending time with him, talking to him, trying to figure out whether I should stay married to him . . ." As I saw his face fall, I just had to add, although I didn't know if for his sake or mine, " . . . or go through with the divorce."

"So I still have some hope?"

"I didn't know you still wanted hope."

"That's what I came to say. I *do* still want you, Jessie. I always will. Whenever you'll have me."

He started to reach for my hand and then seemed to think better of it. Instead, he rose. "I've got to get to my job site." He glanced at his watch. "I'm supposed to be there in fifteen minutes, and it's a half hour south of Bloomington."

"I thought you were in the neighborhood," I said, smiling as I walked him to the door.

"Oh, Jessie." He grabbed me then and held me tightly to him.

I felt a surge of conflicting emotions, but before I could even begin to sort them out, he was gone.

CHAPTER THIRTY

I agreed to have dinner with Heck. It worked out perfectly because Kevin had a two-day trip to New York. I felt, oddly, like I was cheating on Kevin by seeing Heck, although I'd made no promises whatsoever to Kevin.

Heck arrived on a Wednesday night wearing a suit and tie and smelling of expensive cologne.

"You smell delicious," I said, as he kissed my cheek.

"It's CC or CK or something."

I felt touched that Heck had bought cologne. It seemed so unlike him, and I assumed it was to impress me.

"It's a gift from a customer," he said. "Can you believe that?"

"Obviously a satisfied customer."

He looked pleased with himself, and it made me feel a little sad. Was this an attempt to make me jealous? It couldn't be, I knew; Heck just wasn't the type to play games.

When he said nothing about my appearance, I mumbled, "You said to dress up; I hope I look okay." I immediately regretted my remark. It sounded like I was fishing for a compliment, which I was. But I didn't catch one.

When he told me where he'd made reservations, I felt the delight of anticipation. It was the city's newest upscale restaurant. I'd covered the opening in a recent dining article for the *Monthly*.

"I know the owner there." I locked the door behind me as we stepped outside. "I did an article for—"

"Yeah, I know. I saw it. *French Cuisine at Its Finest*." He sounded almost irritated.

"Wow. You actually *read* it?"

"It was a slow day." His remark, so unlike him, stung. A memory flashed before me of Kevin, dutifully cutting out any article with my byline and putting it in a scrapbook.

We drove to the restaurant in an almost uncomfortable silence. But I couldn't think of anything to say that didn't sound trite. Finally, we reached the entrance to the restaurant, and the parking valet ushered me out of the car. Inside, we were invited to wait in the bar because our table wasn't ready.

"You should have put *this* in your article," Heck said, as we walked toward two empty bar stools.

"What?"

"You make a reservation, but the damn table isn't ready when you arrive."

His hands were spread on the bar, and I reached over and put my hand on top of one of his. "Heck, what is it? You sound mad. This isn't like you at all. Tell me what's wrong."

"Nothing. What do you want to drink?"

"The usual."

"Sorry, you'll have to fill me in. I forget what your usual is."

"Chardonnay." I removed my hand.

Our drinks were placed before us, and we both sipped. Neither of us bothered to make even a small toast.

I looked around. There was another couple at the end of the bar, managing to hold hands and drink at the same time. They looked lost in each other. "They must be having an affair," I joked, nodding in their direction.

"Why do you say that?"

"Because . . . well, look how they're talking to each other."

He turned on his stool and glanced in their direction, but said nothing.

Suddenly I wanted to be home, on my own, without having to make conversation or pretend to be having a good time. After another five minutes of silence, I was about to suggest we leave, but a waiter approached to tell us our table was ready.

"About damn time." Heck dropped some bills onto the bar. He got down from his stool and followed the waiter, not looking back to see if I was behind him.

A wave of loneliness hit me. What was I doing here? This was a huge mistake. I drained the remains of my glass and then saw Heck standing at the entrance to the restaurant, waving me over.

I picked up my purse and lowered myself off the stool. A glance at my watch told me it was only eight thirty. With any luck, we'd eat fast and be out of there in an hour.

Sure enough, by nine twenty we'd finished our meal, Heck had paid the check, and we were free to leave.

Driving home, he gripped the steering wheel tightly and stared ahead at the road in front of him. Eventually, he pulled into my driveway. He turned the engine off and leaned back in his seat.

"This was a mistake," he said. When I didn't respond, he added, "Wasn't it?"

"Heck, let's just call it a night. I'm tired. You're in a horrible mood. And you're probably right. It was a mistake."

"I'm sorry," he mumbled.

"What?" I asked, although I'd heard him.

"I said I'm sorry. Forgive me?"

"Like I said, I'm tired; I want to go to bed—"

"Can I just say this? Jessie, this has been really hard."

"What? What's been hard?"

"You and me. Not seeing you. Knowing you were seeing him. Jessie, I want to bundle you up and take care of you for the rest of your life. I don't want to compete with your fucking husband. I want it to be the way it was. When you needed me. Just a little. I can't stand it, knowing you live in the same state as me, that you wake up in the morning and I'm not there to fix your coffee. When you said you'd have dinner with me, I thought I could put it all back together, but you look so . . ."

"So what?"

"So . . . happy. So in control. Like you've got it all together. Which you have; I can see that. Only . . . now *I* don't have it together. I miss you. I miss you every day."

I opened my purse to search for my keys. Amid the debris that always formed in my purse, I located them. There was a picture of Jacob on the key ring, his bald head, round blue eyes, chubby cheeks, and toothless smile reduced to the size of a quarter. I ran my thumb over the plastic that covered his precious face.

"You're wrong, you know," I said, breaking the silence. "I'm not in control. I don't have it all together."

"Do you ever miss me?" he asked.

Jacob's sweet little face beamed up at me in the glow of the yard light that had come on automatically at dusk. Oh, how simple for a baby, never having to make a decision about anything. I said nothing. I didn't want to tell Heck that while seeing so much of Kevin the past month, I'd hardly even thought of him. Until he'd shown up at my door.

"I guess that answered my question," he said into the silence, looking sad. He opened the car door and came around to get me.

"Good-bye, Heck," I said, when we arrived at my front door.

I felt him kiss me on the cheek, and then he was gone. As I let myself in, I heard him backing out of the driveway. And then, unexpectedly, I did miss him.

There was a message on my answering machine from Kevin. "Hi, babe. Looks like this meeting is going to run a day longer than I thought. I hope you're having a good time, wherever you are. We're going out to dinner now, and it might run late, so I'll call you tomorrow. Have a good night's sleep. I love you."

I took off my shoes and poured myself a glass of wine. Did it matter that Kevin's meeting was running a day over? Was I jealous, or suspicious? Who was he having dinner with? Would he sit next to someone who was prettier or smarter or younger than me?

At one time such thoughts would never have occurred to me. The truth was, I'd generally felt content when Kevin was out of town; I enjoyed the time alone. Taylor, and Kevin too, had changed all that.

But as I finished my drink, a feeling of well-being poured over me as I realized another change had taken place: I didn't feel jealous these days. I could even sleep through the nights.

***

When Kevin called the next morning, I didn't answer. I just listened to his voice on the recorder. He sounded nervous that I wasn't there and said he'd call me later, that he loved me. I don't know why I didn't take the call. But it was comforting to lie in my bed and listen to him sound nervous.

When the phone rang again, it was Ted. I picked up as soon as I saw his number on the caller ID. "Hey, you. What's going on?"

"Mom, what are you doing tonight?"

"Nothing; why?"

"I want to stop by, about seven. Someone I want you to meet. Okay?"

"Sure. Anything I should know?"

"Hey, I should be asking *you* that. I hear you've been seeing Dad."

"Yes." I didn't offer an explanation, but I could tell by Teddy's tone that he was pleased.

"That's great, Mom."

"Really?"

"C'mon. You know you two were meant to be. So the guy fucked up—"

"Teddy!"

"Sorry. He made a mistake. But he's meant to be with you, Mom. You're the only one who could put up with his sorry ass." He laughed, and I could just picture him.

"Some mistake," I said, not in the mood to defend Teddy's father.

"Don't be pissed off, Mom. We'll be there about seven."

"Yeah, okay. I'll see you then. You want to have dinner?"

"No; no time. I'll see you later."

Feeling hungry, I meandered down to the refrigerator and stood in front of it with the door open, staring at the half-empty shelves. I stood there a long time, recalling how often I'd chastised Teddy through the years for doing the very same thing. *Just pick something and close the door*, I'd said a million times.

Halfheartedly, I reached for a tub of salmon spread and then grabbed a box of Triscuits from the pantry. Slowly, I spread the pink mixture over four crackers and then just as slowly took them to the sink and threw them down the garbage disposal.

I wasn't hungry, but suddenly my contentment had been replaced by a huge hole inside me. Food wouldn't fill it; of that I was sure. It was the only thing I felt certain of.

I lazed around all day, and at six thirty I panicked and ran upstairs to the shower. It was like I had just learned Teddy was bringing someone for me to meet.

A girl? It had to be. I quickly got ready and was back downstairs by five to seven, suddenly a little nervous as to who was coming with Ted.

When I opened the door, he stood with his arm around an angel. At least that's what she looked like. The sun cast a halo around her silvery-blond hair. Her face was that of a cherub, her smile celestial.

"Hi, Mom," Teddy said, not letting go of the angel's waist but reaching out to me with his free arm. I did him the favor of moving in close so that he could kiss my cheek without letting go of his friend.

"Mom, this is Jennifer." He smiled broadly, his own face lit up as if he too had just flown down from heaven.

"Hello," she said, her voice a delicate whisper. She was beautiful. A golden girl in an angelic body.

"Hello, Jennifer. Come in; please, come in." I stood back to let them enter and noticed how my son's arm never left her tiny waist.

"Mom," Teddy said, as if he were offering me the Holy Grail, "Jennifer is a graduate student at IU."

"What are you studying, Jennifer?" I asked, astonished, since I had never seen my son interested in academics of any kind.

"Art history," she said, her smile once again revealing perfect white teeth.

"Art history," Teddy repeated, in case I hadn't understood the first time. He didn't add *can you believe it*, but I could tell he was thinking it.

"Would you like a drink or something?" I asked, not really sure what I had to offer.

"No, we're on our way to eat. I just wanted to stop by so you two could meet." As he said it, his arms reached up to encircle both our shoulders, and he pulled us close. His girls.

"Are you from Indianapolis?" I asked Jennifer, through the scrunch of Teddy's embrace.

"I'm from Dallas," she said, and then I noticed her slight twang. It was, of course, charming. What else could it be?

"Texas," Teddy added, in case I didn't know where Dallas was. He gazed at Jennifer's perfect face, and I don't think I'd ever seen him look so happy.

"My best friend is from Texas. El Paso." It sounded dumb, like Jennifer should know Ellen because they were from the same state. Then, equally dumb, I added, "And my sister—Teddy's aunt—lives in Houston."

"Yeah, they're great too," Teddy said, still looking at Jennifer, not me. "So . . . Mom," he said, finally tearing his eyes away from her and removing his arms from around our shoulders. "We could get together this weekend, maybe? We'll be free on Sunday."

I giggled, despite Jennifer's divine presence. Such planning ahead was unlike my son. "That would be nice. Come here; I'll cook dinner."

"I would enjoy that, Mrs. Harleman," Jennifer said, and out of the corner of my eye I saw Teddy reach for her hand.

"Okay, we gotta go. See you Sunday." Teddy kissed me again on the cheek, and I walked them to the front door before watching them glide hand in hand to Teddy's car.

After he opened her door and made sure she was in safely, he turned to me and winked. It was a wink of promise, a wink of pride, a wink that said *look how well I've done*. I was happy for him.

***

I thought of Teddy and Jennifer off and on for the next few days. Their delight in each other was infectious, and I couldn't get them out of my mind. Especially after spending Sunday afternoon with them, watching them feed each other my summertime soup and Hawaiian pork chops, watching them hang on each other's every word, and watching them simply watch each other.

I told myself it was sick to be jealous of my son's newfound happiness and then decided it was envy, not jealousy. I wanted to feel that way too.

And then the biggest sense of relief, gratitude, and happiness consumed me. I *could* feel that way. In fact, I *did!*

I hadn't heard from Heck since our disastrous evening. And even though Kevin was back in town and had called me twice, I'd put him off so far, feigning illness and exaggerating deadlines.

But suddenly it was clear to me what I had to do. There wasn't the slightest indecision on my part. It was there waiting for me; I had only to reach out and grab it.

At five o'clock on Tuesday evening, after I was dressed and perfumed and looking as good as I possibly could, I made the call.

"Can you meet me at The Canterbury Hotel in an hour? In the bar. Oh, and get a room."

"I'm on my way," came the startled reply, and I put down the phone, grinning to myself.

I checked my appearance one more time in my bedroom mirror, and then I found myself ripping off my clothes. When I was naked, I searched for the trench coat. Holding it up to my face, I could faintly smell the J'adore I'd doused myself with the last time I'd worn it. Just for good measure, I resprayed myself before slipping into my black pumps. Even though this attire had failed me miserably before, I had confidence that because this time everything was so different (especially me), it would serve its purpose.

Driving downtown, I don't think I'd ever felt so happy. So sure of myself. So in love. It wasn't just Teddy and Jennifer. Okay, maybe they'd reawakened something in me, but it had been there all the time.

I let the valet park my Jeep, and I paused in the lobby of the old, elegant hotel for a moment before heading for the bar.

Dressing Myself

I saw him sitting there, his back to me. I stood and watched him for a while, and then, as if sensing my presence, he turned. He smiled and slightly nodded his head. It was okay; this was okay. Everything was okay.

I thrust my hands deep into the pockets of my coat and sauntered toward him. He was standing now, holding out his arms to me. It was home for me; it was the only place I ever wanted to be.

"Jessie," he said, but he looked unsure.

"I have rules, Kevin." I took the empty bar stool next to him.

He nodded, sitting beside me and taking my hand in his. "Let's hear 'em."

On the drive to the hotel, I'd made a mental list of things I expected from him; only now I couldn't recall even one. I looked into his eager face and squeezed his hand.

"I want my best friend back," I began hesitantly. "I want to trust you again. I want to be waiting at home for you when you leave town, and I want you to be waiting for me when I go to class or to the mall. I want us to be together with our kids on holidays, and I want you to buy me ridiculous presents that I don't really need and we can't really afford. And I want us to share everything, and I want you to adore me—"

"I *do* adore you." He no longer looked unsure.

"And I want us to hold hands in the movies, and plan summer vacations, and read the Sunday newspaper in bed, the way we used to."

"Jessie, we *never* read the Sunday paper in bed." He didn't add that I couldn't stand the mess, but surely he was thinking it. He was holding both my hands, and there was a merry twinkle in his eyes.

"Well, we *should* have," I said. "We should have, Kevin. And we should have made love in the car in the parking lot of Target, we should have gone to Italy, we should have put a hot tub in the backyard—"

"Like I wanted," he said, looking hopeful.

"Like you wanted. And we should definitely have a black Lab."

"Honey, it wouldn't have made any difference; you know that, don't you?" He looked sad for a moment, and I squeezed his hand again.

"I know, Kevin, but what the hell. Let's do it all anyway. I don't want to do it with anyone *but* you. Let's keep trying and make it all work out."

Hope. There was hope for both of us. It was all I needed.

"Jessie?" Kevin said, and as he spoke, I could hear the hope in *his* voice. "What do you have on, underneath that trench coat?"

Patty and Roz
www.roz-patty.com

About the authors ...

Now a proud and patriotic US citizen and Texan, Rosalind Burgess grew up in London and currently calls Houston home. She has also lived in Germany, Iowa, and Minnesota. Roz retired from the airline industry to devote all her working hours to writing (although it seems more like fun than work).

Patricia Obermeier Neuman spent her childhood and early adulthood moving around the Midwest (Minnesota, South Dakota, Nebraska, Iowa, Wisconsin, Illinois, and Indiana), as a trailing child and then as a trailing spouse (inspiring her first book, *Moving: The What, When, Where & How of It*). A former reporter and editor, Patty lives with her husband in Door County, Wisconsin. They have three children and twelve grandchildren.

The Val & Kit Mystery Series

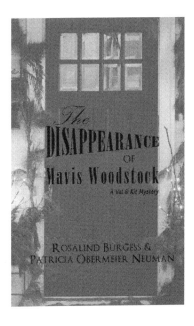

The Disappearance of Mavis Woodstock

Mavis Woodstock (a vaguely familiar name) calls Val and insists she has to sell her house as quickly as possible. Then she fails to keep her scheduled appointment. Kit remembers Mavis from their school days, an unattractive girl who was ignored when she was lucky, ridiculed when she was not. She also remembers Mavis being the only daughter in a large family that was as frugal as it was wealthy. When Val and Kit cannot locate Mavis, they begin an investigation, encountering along the way a little romance, a lot of deception, and more than one unsavory character.

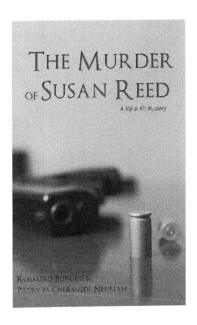

The Murder of Susan Reed

When Kit suspects Larry of having an affair with one of his employees, Susan Reed, she enlists Val's help in uncovering the truth. The morning after a little stalking expedition by the lifelong friends, Val reads in the newspaper that Susan Reed was found shot to death in her apartment the night before, right around the time Kit was so certain Larry and Susan were together. *Were* they having an affair? And did Larry murder her? The police, in the form of dishy Detective Dennis Culotta, conduct the investigation into Susan's murder, hampered at times by Val and Kit's insistent attempts to discover whether Larry is guilty of infidelity and/or murder. As the investigation heats up, so does Val's relationship with Detective Culotta.

Death in Door County

Val embarks on a Mother's Day visit to her mom in Door County, Wisconsin, a peninsula filled with artists, lighthouses, and natural beauty. Her daughter, Emily, has arrived from LA to accompany her, and at the last minute her best friend, Kit, invites herself along. Val and Kit have barely unpacked their suitcases when trouble and tension greet them, in the form of death and a disturbing secret they unwittingly brought with them. As they get to know the locals, things take a sinister turn. And when they suspect someone close to them might be involved in blackmail—or worse—Val and Kit do what they do best: they take matters into their own hands in their obsessive, often zany, quest to uncover the truth.

Lethal Property

In this fourth book of The Val & Kit Mystery Series (a stand-alone, like the others), our ladies are back home in Downers Grove. Val is busy selling real estate, eager to take a potential buyer to visit the home of a widow living alone. He turns out not to be all that he claimed, and a string of grisly events follows, culminating in a perilous situation for Val. Her lifelong BFF Kit is ready to do whatever necessary to ensure Val's safety and clear her name of any wrongdoing. The dishy Detective Dennis Culotta also returns to help, and with the added assistance of Val's boss, Tom Haskins, and a *Downton Abbey*–loving Rottweiler named Roscoe, the ladies become embroiled in a murder investigation extraordinaire. As always, we are introduced to a new cast of shady characters as we welcome back the old circle of friends.

Palm Desert Killing

When one of them receives a mysterious letter, BFFs Val and Kit begin to unravel a sordid story that spans a continent and reaches back decades. It also takes them to Palm Desert, California, a paradise of palm trees, mountains, blue skies... and now murder. The men in their lives—Val's favorite detective, Dennis Culotta; her boss, Tom Haskins; and Kit's husband, Larry—play their (un)usual parts in this adventure that introduces a fresh batch of suspicious characters, including Kit's New York–attorney sister, Nora, and their mother. Val faces an additional challenge when her daughter, Emily, reveals her own startling news. Val and Kit bring to this story their (a)typical humor, banter, and unorthodox detective skills.

Foreign Relations

After sightseeing in London, Val and Kit move on to a rented cottage in the bucolic village of Little Dipping, where Val's actress daughter, Emily, and son-in-law are temporarily living and where Emily has become involved in community theater. Val and Kit revel in the English countryside, despite Val's ex-husband showing up and some troubling news from home. The harmony of the village is soon broken, however, by the vicious murder of one of their new friends. The shocking events that follow are only slightly more horrific than one from the past that continues to confound authorities. The crimes threaten to involve Emily, so Val and Kit return to their roles as amateur sleuths, employing their own inimitable ways.

What readers are saying about . . .
The Val & Kit Mystery Series

FIVE STARS! "When meeting an old friend for coffee and a chat, do you think to yourself 'Wow, I really miss them. Why do we wait so long to catch up?' That is exactly how I feel every time I read a Val & Kit Mystery. Like I just sat down for a hilarious chat over coffee and cake followed by wine and chocolate. These girls are a hilarious mix of Laurel and Hardy with a dash of Evanovich sprinkled with Cagney & Lacey. Comedy, love and mystery: a brilliant combination."

FIVE STARS! "The authors always give us a big cast of suspects, and each is described so incredibly . . . It's like playing a game of Clue, but way more fun . . . the authors make the characters so memorable that you don't waste time trying to 'think back' to whom they are referring. In fact, it's hard to believe that there are only two authors writing such vivid casts for these books. So come on, ladies, confess . . . no, wait, don't. I don't want to know how you do it, just please keep it up."

FIVE STARS! "I love these stories and hope there will be more to come. I was reading in the car and laughing out loud. My husband looked over and just shook his head. Thanks again for another good one."

FIVE STARS! "Valerie and Kit are witty and entertaining characters constantly on the move."

FIVE STARS! "It's always fun to see where a book series story picks up and where it will take you! Getting to know the characters is half the fun."

FIVE STARS! "I've fallen in love with Val & Kit. Seriously. They're great gals, working their way toward middle age and dealing with all the hassles that life brings."

FIVE STARS! "I enjoy reading about Larry and Tom as much as I enjoy reading about Kit and Val's relationship. The stories are always very exciting." (This from a *guy!*)

FIVE STARS! "Val and Kit are hilarious! I love a good girlfriend silly caper. . . . I see a big fan base growing here."

FIVE STARS! "I love these Val and Kit books. Fun to read, and I feel like they are girls I can totally relate to."

FIVE STARS! "Fun, witty, believable dialogue between the characters."

FIVE STARS! ". . . Val and Kit . . . the combo is dynamic. What one doesn't research, the other imagines . . . they could have been the love children of Erin Brockovich and Columbo! . . . they mix their fun-loving, diverse personalities with a by-the-seat-of-your-pants investigation . . . Val and Kit are a couple of sometimes-serious, wise-cracking hometown gals . . ."

FIVE STARS! "As a fan of this genre . . . I just have to write a few words praising the incredible talent of Roz and Patty. One thing I specifically want to point out is the character development. You can completely visualize the supporting actors (suspects?) so precisely that you do not waste time trying to recall details about the character. . . . Roz and Patty practically create an imprint in your mind of each character's looks/voice/mannerisms, etc."

FIVE STARS! ". . . liked main characters, Val and Kit . . . well written . . . light romance, good suspense . . . I'm off to find another book by the authors."

FIVE STARS! "Fun series. . . . just finished reading all . . . and am already missing the stories. The characters were fun to follow as they solved the murders."

Made in the USA
Monee, IL
20 March 2023